Praise for *F*

Praise for the *Out of Uniform* series

Also available from Elle Kennedy

***

A full list of Elle's print titles is available on her website
www.ellekennedy.com

Hotter Than Ever

Out of Uniform

Elle Kennedy

Author's Note

I am SO excited to be re-releasing the *Out of Uniform* series! For those of you who haven't read it before, this was one of my earlier series. It also happens to be one of my favorites, probably because this is when I realized how much I love writing bromances!

Seriously. The boy banter in these books still cracks me up to this day. You see more and more of it as the series progresses, and by the later books there are entire chapters of crazy conversations between my sexy, silly SEALs.

For new readers, you should know that a) you don't have to read the stories in order, though characters from previous books do show up in every installment. And b) the first six stories are novellas (20-35,000 words), while the last four are full-length novels (80,000+ words).

I decided to release the novellas as two books featuring three stories each (*Hot & Bothered*, *Hot & Heavy*) making the total books in the series SIX rather than the original ten.

Hotter Than Ever is the third of the full-length novels.

***PLEASE NOTE: This book has NOT changed, except for some minor editing and proofreading. There are grammatical differences and some (minor) deleted/added lines here and there, but for the most part, there is *no new content*. If you've previously purchased and read *Feeling Hot*, then you won't be getting anything new, aside from a gorgeous new cover!

So, I hope you enjoy the new cover, the better grammar, and the hot, dirty-talking SEALs who to this day hold such a big place in my heart!

Love,

Elle

Prologue

"Your friend looked wrecked," Claire McKinley said as she followed her future brother-in-law into the darkened front hall of his townhouse. She bent down to unlace her sneakers, feeling Dylan Wade's green-eyed gaze boring into the top of her head.

She expected him to make a bitchy remark, inform her that his friend's state of mind was none of her beeswax, but he did none of the above.

"Sophie taking off like that really shook him up. Shook me up too," Dylan confessed.

"Yeah, me too. I keep thinking about what would've happened if we hadn't found her…" She shuddered. "Oh God. Imagine losing a child."

The silence that followed was surprisingly free of tension. Weird. Since the moment they'd met, she and Dylan could barely be in the same room without sniping at each other, but almost losing that little girl at the carnival had been so very sobering. Tonight, Claire had witnessed a different side to Dylan. He'd been focused, self-assured, calm under pressure. Which was double weird, because normally he was a cocky, antagonistic asshole.

He was still watching her, even as he kicked off his boots and shrugged out of his blue button-down shirt, which left him in a snug white T-shirt and cargo pants. Claire couldn't help herself—she swept her gaze over his handsome face and incredible body, so hard and muscular and annoyingly drool-worthy. Chris was in great shape too, but there was something thrilling to be had from the knowledge that Dylan's ripped six-pack came from bona-fide SEAL ass-kicking, and not the gym that Chris visited three times a week.

Your fiancé's brother…

The little reminder jolted her out of her thoughts. Oh for heaven's sake, she had no business admiring this man's chest, no matter how deliciously ripped it was.

She cleared her throat. "Anyway, I'm going to bed."

"At nine o'clock? Gee, *dear*, did all the excitement get to you?"

Claire frowned. Of course. She should have known he couldn't maintain the Nice Guy act for long. "Annnnnd he's back."

"You know you missed me."

His roguish grin succeeded in raising her hackles—and making her heart skip a beat. She ignored the latter response and took a step toward the doorway.

"Missed the smartass remarks and not-so-veiled jabs about my character? Sorry, can't say that I have. Good night, Dylan."

"'Night, honey."

Her back stiffened. She'd told him on more than one occasion how much she despised it when he called her *honey*. She was *not* this man's honey.

As she stalked down the darkened corridor, a flash of silver winked up at her, drawing her gaze to the two-carat princess-cut diamond on her fourth finger. The engagement ring Christopher James Wade had slipped onto her finger nearly five months ago. Usually the sight of the gorgeous, sparkling ring brought a smile to her lips. Tonight it just pissed her off. *Chris* had pissed her off. He'd convinced her to join him on this overnight visit to San Diego, promising they'd spend some time together after he wrapped up his meetings, but what had he done instead? Deposited her on his brother's doorstep and abandoned her to hang out at a country club with his colleagues.

Cut him some slack. He's got a lot on his plate.

Claire forced her muscles to relax. She entered the guest bedroom and sat on the edge of the double bed, releasing a weary breath. Chris *did* have a lot of headaches to deal with. For the past year and a half, he'd been working his butt off to fix the mess his mother had made.

The mess that Chris's brother couldn't be bothered to help clean up.

Anger rippled through her as she dwelled on the sheer selfishness of that. She understood that Dylan was serving their country, but he couldn't be bothered to offer *some* assistance? Maybe send some money home every now and then? Someone ought to give that jerk a real tongue-lashing.

What's stopping you?

Claire's brows dipped in angry contemplation. Why *shouldn't* she confront Dylan? After all, Chris refused to do it. He insisted that as the man of the house, it was his responsibility to take care of their mother, not Dylan's. But enough was enough. She'd promised Chris she wouldn't interfere, but her fiancé wouldn't be killing himself at work if his brother would just step up and carry some of the load.

Setting her jaw, she stood up and marched out of the guest room, but when she heard the murmur of male voices coming from the hall, she stopped in her tracks.

Crap. Chris must be back. She couldn't tell his brother off in front of him.

Especially when he'd explicitly ordered her to stay out of it.

She was about to turn around and abandon the plan when she heard a loud thump, as if something—or someone—had slammed into a wall. Fighting a flicker of fear, she crept forward.

All the lights were off, and the house's layout was still unfamiliar to her, making her feel disoriented as she tiptoed her way back to the main entrance. She rounded a corner, peered at the shadowy doorway—and froze.

Holy fucking shit.

Claire's jaw fell open. Eyes widened. Brain kicked into overdrive, trying to make sense of what she was seeing.

Clearly she was hallucinating.

Right. She had to be. Because no way was she witnessing Dylan kissing another man.

She blinked a few times, but the scene in front of her didn't disappear in a puff of hallucination smoke. There he was. Dylan Wade, her fiancé's infuriatingly sexy, self-absorbed brother.

Kissing another *man*.

Claire blinked again, focused on the dark-haired guy whose lips were glued to Dylan's. She couldn't see his face, but his body was equally hard and incredible, and the two men were going at it like they had one minute left to live and they planned on making every last second count.

The punch of lust that hit her was completely unexpected. But…oh sweet Lord, shock and confusion aside, this might actually be the *hottest* thing she'd ever seen in her life.

"You sleep with anyone else this summer?" The question came from Dylan's visitor. Or, Dylan's…lover?

Her thighs clenched at the thought.

"Yes." Dylan's raspy voice sent a shiver running through her and shot Claire up to a new level of arousal.

She shrank back into the shadows, ordering herself to walk away, to respect their privacy, to duck into her room and make herself come like *right now*, but she couldn't tear her gaze off the two men. Their voices lowered for several moments, making it difficult to hear, so she studied their body language instead. The stranger had one hand on Dylan's broad chest, the other behind Dylan's neck. Dylan's right palm rested on the other man's shoulder, his left one idly stroking the man's hip. And when they kissed again, the flash of tongue she glimpsed made her bite back a moan.

That moan damn near slipped out when the man spun Dylan around and pressed his groin against the SEAL's ass.

A second later, Claire's entire body went up in flames as she watched Dylan reverse positions so the dark-haired man was the one facing the wall now.

Her senses went on overload. She had no idea what to focus on. Their words? Their mouths? Their bodies?

She was so close to exploding she could barely think straight. She couldn't believe she was watching her fiancé's brother making out with another man, and suddenly a hundred questions started buzzing through her head.

Was Dylan gay?

Did Chris know?

Why was she so turned on?

The sound of a door clicking shut jarred her back to the present.

Dylan's friend—*lover?*—was gone. The blond SEAL flicked the deadbolt, then turned around with a grin on his face.

A grin that dissolved the second he spotted Claire.

Their gazes locked. She could see the wariness swimming in his eyes. She gulped. "I…"

Her gaze swiftly dropped to her feet. Oh man. What did one even say in a situation like this?

She opened her mouth and tried again. "I…" After a beat, she raised her head and met his gaze head-on. "I won't say anything to Chris."

Then she darted away before he could respond.

I won't say anything to Chris?

She wanted to kick herself as she hurried back to the guest room. *That* was the best she could come up with?

In her defense, she was still too stunned to hold any sort of coherent conversation at the moment. Her heart continued to beat in a frantic rhythm, her mouth was drier than the Sahara, and her clit was actually aching. Pulsing. One touch away from orgasm. If she brought her hand between her legs right now, she would literally self-combust.

The bad girl in her wanted to let it happen. To picture Dylan's tongue in that hottie's mouth, slide her hand inside her panties and enjoy the results, but she forced herself to derail that train of crazy.

This was Chris's brother. Chris's *gay* brother? The same questions flashed through her mind again, but there was one in particular she couldn't seem to let go of.

Why didn't she and Chris have that? The passion. The intensity. That need to consume each other.

Dylan and his dark-haired stranger craved each other on a primal level Claire had never experienced—or dreamed possible.

She sucked in a shaky breath, unable to erase those dirty images from her head. She wondered if she ought to go and talk to Dylan about it, *actually* talk instead of blurting out a random promise and sprinting away. But she couldn't force her legs to carry her to the door. She and Dylan might have called a brief cease-fire tonight at the carnival, but they weren't friends and she got the feeling he wouldn't appreciate her poking her nose in his business.

The best thing to do was pretend she hadn't seen what she'd seen. Never mention it to Dylan again. Never think about it.

And never, ever masturbate while thinking about it.

A shudder racked her body, and it took Claire a moment to realize that her hand, of its own volition, had slid beneath the waistband of her pants. And her fingers were already sneaking their way inside her panties…

After a beat of indecision, she decided to give her fingers permission to continue. One time wouldn't hurt, she assured herself.

Just one little indulgence.

And *then* she'd pretend tonight never happened.

Chapter One

"You have to tell her I can't marry her."

Dylan gaped at his older brother. Okay. Well. That was *not* what he'd expected to hear when Chris had summoned him to the elegant suite of the sprawling mansion that housed the Marin Hills Golf Club.

It took a second for him to snap out of his shock. "Yeah, right. Very funny, Chris." He managed a hasty laugh and clapped his brother on the arm. "Come on, pal, it's time to go. The ceremony starts in—"

"The ceremony isn't going to start," Chris interrupted with frazzled green eyes. He shoved Dylan's hand away and made a wild dash for the wet bar across the room.

Dylan watched in dismay as his brother picked up a glass, poured whiskey all the way to the rim, and slugged back half of it in one gulp.

"I can't marry her. I can't do it. You have to go tell her!"

Shit. Chris had crazy-person eyes. And crazy-person hands—he was gesturing wildly, even with the hand holding the glass, and his frenzied movements caused the liquid to slosh onto the rich burgundy carpet beneath Chris's black leather wingtips.

It was becoming painfully clear that Chris was not joking around.

"Put the whiskey down," Dylan said quietly.

His brother ignored the order and swallowed another mouthful.

With a sigh, he marched over and forcibly grabbed the glass from Chris's shaky fingers. The suite had a dressing area on one side of the room and a living area on the other, which offered a set of leather armchairs in front of an enormous stone fireplace. Dylan promptly dragged Chris over to one of the chairs and forced him to sit.

"What's going on? Why can't you marry Claire?" Rather than sit, he crossed his arms and loomed over his brother.

"Because she's not the right woman for me."

Are you fucking kidding me?

He tamped down the retort before it could pop out of his mouth. But come on, Chris was only reaching that conclusion *now?*

Dylan had known from day one that Claire McKinley wasn't right for his brother. He'd been hoping Chris would eventually see it too, but he hadn't expected it to happen ten minutes before the couple's frickin' *wedding.*

And it wasn't just a small, private gathering that could easily be disbanded if Chris was actually serious about all this. This was an expensive, showy affair that would unleash waves and waves of gossip if the ceremony were cancelled. The senior partner of Chris's law firm had graciously rented out the country club for the day so the couple could marry there. There were five hundred people waiting in the banquet hall, including Dylan's mother, Shanna, who was over the moon about welcoming a daughter into their family.

Shit. His mom was going to be crushed.

"I've been deluding myself for months," Chris was saying, his voice lined with so much misery that Dylan felt a pang of sympathy for the guy. "I kept telling myself that I'd made the right decision by asking her to marry me. Claire's smart, she's successful, she's beautiful. But she's got a lot of flaws too, and…I thought…"

Dylan sank into the other armchair. "You thought what?"

"That she would change." Chris shrugged helplessly. "I was hoping she'd eventually start acting like…I don't know, like the woman I wanted her to be."

"For fuck's sake, Chris, you were waiting around hoping your fiancée's entire personality would *change?*"

It also didn't escape him that his brother hadn't said a word about love. Not even once. But he decided not to point that out.

"I'm an idiot, okay?" Chris dragged a hand through his perfectly groomed blond hair. "Deep down I knew it wasn't right but I kept telling myself I had to go through with it. The invitations were already sent out, and Mom was so excited, and then Lowenstein booked us the

Lavender Ballroom at the frickin' Marin Hills Golf Club as a wedding gift—I couldn't exactly tell the senior partner of my firm, *hey, no thanks, the wedding is off*."

Chris's breathing grew labored. He was visibly trembling, and Dylan had never seen his brother's face so pale before.

"I should have listened to Maxwell," Chris muttered. "He told me she wasn't a good enough prospect, he—"

"Wait a minute, what?"

"Pres Maxwell—he's one of the associates at the firm. He and his wife are members here—they're the ones who nominated Claire and me for membership. Last weekend we had lunch with them, and I played a few rounds with Pres and the boys, and Claire spent some time with the other wives." Chris's lips tightened. "I don't know what was said exactly, but Pres pulled me aside on Monday morning and said that Claire told the women some personal details about her past. And they weren't *respectable* details, if you know what I mean."

Dylan resisted the urge to roll his eyes. He sometimes forgot what a prude his brother was.

"Okay, so she talked to the country club ladies about sex. Are you telling me *that's* why you're breaking it off?"

His brother's eyes flashed with annoyance. "I *told* you why I'm doing this, Dylan. That was just one example of how she's not a good match for me." Chris abruptly shot to his feet. "I can't marry her. I can't be with a woman who doesn't respect me."

"Who says she doesn't?"

"There's a lot more you don't know," Chris said darkly. "Unlike Claire, I'm not going to talk out of turn. Our personal shit and certain *indiscretions* aren't anybody's business but ours. Just trust me when I say that I need to end this."

Dylan narrowed his eyes. "Are you saying she fucked around on you?"

"I'm not saying anything." Now those green eyes were imploring him, shining with fear. "You've got to tell her the wedding is cancelled."

"I'm not breaking up with your bride for you."

"But you're the best man," Chris protested. "And you're my brother."

"As your best man, I'm in charge of holding on to the rings and standing next to you at the altar. As your brother, I'm responsible for supporting you and clapping politely when you kiss the bride. Neither of those roles requires me to call off your fucking wedding!"

"Please, Dyl. I can't do it. I don't want to hurt her."

His jaw fell open. "Dumping her five minutes before your wedding is going to hurt her. You realize that, right?"

"I know. But...goddammit! If that friend of hers was here, she could be the one to talk to Claire, but Dr. Dyke couldn't be bothered to fly in, so—"

"Whoa," Dylan interrupted, an edge to his voice. "Uncool, dude."

Chris's expression conveyed a flicker of remorse. "Shit. I'm sorry. That was rude. I'm just so irritated that her so-called best friend skipped the wedding."

Maybe she knew there'd never be a wedding.

Dylan bit back the snippy remark. "Well, Claire's BFF isn't here to do your dirty work, and I won't do it either. You have to talk to her, bro. You have to clean up your own mess."

The panic that erupted in Chris's eyes would have been comical if it weren't so infuriating. "Dylan—"

"I mean it. You can't dump this on anyone else, no matter how painful and uncomfortable it's going to be. You're a thirty-two-year-old man, Chris. You can't ask me to break up with Claire for you."

After a long moment of silence, Chris's shoulders slumped in defeat. "I know. You're right."

An enormous weight lifted off Dylan's chest. Finally, his brother was seeing reason.

"Talk to her," he said gently. "Tell her everything you're feeling, man. Maybe you two can work through it and the wedding will go on as scheduled."

"It won't." Chris drew a deep breath, then smoothed out the front of his black suit jacket. "The partners will understand, right?" he said, sounding desperate.

Disapproval stiffened Dylan's muscles. Was Chris seriously concerned about how his law firm's partners would react instead of worrying about how his *jilted bride* was going to feel? Wow. His brother had always been a bit self-absorbed and pretentious, but at the moment, Dylan didn't recognize the man in front of him.

"Forget about the partners," he ordered. "Focus on your fiancée. Go find Claire. Now."

With a quick nod, Chris turned around and left the room.

Battling his disbelief, Dylan took a moment to collect his composure. Shit. This was a complete clusterfuck. Should he find his mother and fill her in? Or should he wait until he knew for certain whether the wedding was off?

No, he needed to get his mom. If anything, she could at least be there to offer Claire some comfort after Chris dropped his bomb.

He was still stressed as hell as he marched out the door and down the pristine white-marble floor in the hallway. He'd just rounded the corner when he heard the click of high heels.

Speak of the devil—his mother was bounding toward him, her teal dress fluttering around her ankles with each quick step she took.

Dylan met her halfway, shaking his head in aggravation. "Thank God you're here. We've got a bit of a situation."

Shanna Wade's green eyes were the same pale shade as her sons' and swimming with the same shock Dylan was currently feeling.

"Dylan," she said in a grim voice, "can you please explain why your brother just asked me to tell all the guests to go home?"

His heart dropped to the pit of his stomach like a sinking rock. "He did what?"

"He told me to make an announcement that there won't be a wedding." She hesitated. "He said you were responsible for telling Claire."

Dylan's shoulders tensed. "What? Where is he now?"

His mom's voice trembled. "He left."

"Are you fucking kidding me?"

For once, Shanna didn't reprimand him for dropping an F-bomb. "He went out the back. I was too flustered and confused to stop him, and then when I finally snapped out of it and ran outside, he was already driving away."

Chris, you fucking asshole.

Fury whipped through him, along with a wad of disgust that knotted around his insides. He couldn't believe this. Chris had actually fled without telling Claire McKinley it was over. His brother had actually pulled an Elvis and *left the fucking building.*

"What do we do?"

His mom's frantic demand penetrated his enraged thoughts. Taking a calming breath, Dylan reached for her hand and found that it was icy cold. He squeezed her delicate fingers and met her confused expression.

"You're going to have to make the announcement," he said softly. "Tell everyone there won't be a wedding today."

She looked panicked. "And say what? That my son got cold feet?"

"No. Don't give any details. Just say the bride and groom had a change of heart, and the decision was mutual."

Tears filled Shanna's eyes. "Oh my God. How is this happening? Will you come with me?"

"I can't. I have something else to take care of."

"What are you doing?"

"What Chris was too much of a coward to do." Dylan's jaw tightened with anger. "I'm going to break up with his bride."

"Do I look okay?" Biting her lip, Claire stared at her reflection in the full-length mirror. The butterflies in her stomach were flying around in crazy circles, making it difficult to focus on the vision in white staring back at her.

"Okay? You look more than okay, sweetie. You look beautiful." Nora McKinley appeared in the mirror, her brown eyes gleaming with pride and sparkling with unshed tears.

A queasy feeling tickled Claire's belly. "Mom…"

"I mean it. You're beautiful, inside and out." Nora sniffled. "You're the most wonderful daughter a mother could ever ask for, and I'm so very proud of you."

Claire's teeth sank harder into her bottom lip.

"Oh, sweetie, don't cry. You'll ruin your makeup."

She hadn't even noticed the moisture welling up in her eyes, but that did explain why her reflection was blurry all of a sudden.

She blinked away the tears and turned to face her mother, who looked gorgeous and elegant in a peach-colored empire-cut dress that stopped just below her knees. Nora's auburn hair was pulled back in a neat chignon, and with her perfect complexion and naturally red lips, Claire's fifty-three-year-old mother didn't look a day over forty.

"What's going on, Claire? Are you nervous?"

"Yes." She gulped. "But that's normal, right? People get nervous before their wedding, don't they?"

"Of course. It's a perfectly normal response," Nora said in a gentle tone. "Lots of brides get jittery right before the ceremony."

"I wish Nat was here," Claire murmured.

Her mother let out a soft sigh. "I know you're upset that Natasha couldn't be here, but you can't dwell on that. Do you want me to get Michelle? Your maid of honor should really be here to help you get ready."

"No, it's all right. I just…I think I need a moment alone. Do you mind?"

A wrinkle appeared on Nora's forehead, but she didn't object to the request. "Of course not." She stepped closer and gently stroked Claire's cheek. "Michelle and I will come get you when it's time."

The second her mother was gone, Claire slid down to the carpeted floor in a pile of white lace.

Was this normal? The nerves, the shaky hands and damp palms? When she was a little girl, she'd constantly fantasized about her wedding, imagined how thrilled she'd be when the big day finally came. Cold feet had never been part of the fantasy.

And neither had a full-blown panic attack.

The bodice of her dress suddenly felt too tight, making it impossible to breathe, and her hands were shaking so hard she had to dig her fingers into her thighs to still the erratic trembling.

Oh boy, this was bad. Heart racing, forehead dotted with sweat, palms tingling. Her wild gaze darted around the beautiful room, taking in the wood-paneled walls and expensive carpeting, the commanding fireplace and elegant furniture, the scent of money and leather hanging in the air.

Nothing about this felt right. She shouldn't be getting ready in this fancy room. There shouldn't be five hundred strangers in that ballroom waiting to watch her get married. And her best friend in the whole world should be standing up at the altar with her, not some random coworker Claire had been forced to ask because her groom refused to accommodate Natasha's schedule. Since Nat went overseas for three months out of every year as part of a foreign-aid program run by the hospital where she worked as an ER resident, there'd been no way for her to fly back to San Francisco for the wedding. Which meant that Claire's best friend of twenty-three years—hell, her *only* friend—couldn't be her maid of honor.

Claire had been more than willing to push the date to the spring if it meant having Nat by her side, but Chris's boss had sprung the Lavender Ballroom gift on them out of nowhere and Chris insisted it would be rude to turn him down.

He's changed.

The thought slunk into Claire's head like a stray animal, but she forced herself to shoo it away.

Chris hadn't changed. He was just under a ton of pressure. His position at Lowenstein and Tate was stressful, and it didn't help matters that half his paycheck went to help his mother. Stress like that took its toll on a man.

Does stress also turn men into pretentious, inflexible, judgmental strangers?

She pushed aside the mocking thought. Enough. She had to snap out of this. She'd fallen in love with Chris for so many reasons—his work ethic, his passion to help others, his dry humor.

He might be acting…*different* lately, but once his mother's finances were in order and his workload eased slightly, he'd go back to being the man she'd fallen for.

Right?

A knock on the door derailed her internal train of panic and confusion. God, if that was Michelle coming to pretend they were best buds and that Claire hadn't asked her to be maid of honor out of sheer pathetic desperation, then she was literally going to scream.

There was another sharp knock. "Claire, it's Dylan. Can I come in?"

Crap.

Dylan Wade was the last person she wanted to see right now. Actually, he was the last person she wanted to see *anytime*, but as his knocking became more persistent, she reluctantly walked over to the door and flung it open.

"What do you want, Dylan?"

"Listen," he began, "I need to—holy fuck."

The awe and embarrassment that tinged his voice caught her by complete surprise. "What?" she said warily.

Dylan stepped into the suite. His green eyes were glued to her, and the reverent expression on his handsome face was completely unexpected.

"Wow," he breathed. "Claire, you look...*wow*...you look so beautiful."

It took a few dumbfounded seconds for her to fathom that he wasn't being sarcastic. Since he'd never looked at her with anything other than annoyance or scorn, his visible appreciation compelled her to glance at the mirror again and really study her reflection this time.

A different woman was looking back at her, a woman in a gorgeous satin-and-lace gown with a sweetheart neckline, full skirt and short train. Her auburn hair was arranged in long, flowing waves, slightly pulled back with tiny white flowers threaded through it. Her minimal, shimmery makeup gave her skin a radiant glow, and the heirloom diamond bracelet around her wrist caught the light and sparkled whenever she moved.

God, she *did* look beautiful.

The realization dimmed some of her panic. If Dylan, a man who disliked her, could appreciate the way she looked right now, then clearly she was about to knock her groom's socks off.

"Thanks," she said, keeping her gaze on her reflection.

"Um..." He cleared his throat. "Anyway, I came by because I needed to tell you...uh..."

The agitation in his normally confident tone had her turning to face him. Okay, weird. Dylan was shifting around as if he couldn't get comfortable. His hands slid into the pockets of his black trousers, then back out. His black dress shoes tapped the carpet a couple of times, and then he edged backward toward the door, his expression downright pained.

For the first time in three months, Claire was able to look at Dylan without blushing or visualizing the intensely erotic scene she'd witnessed between him and—*nope, not going there.*

She shoved the memory right out of her head and focused on the odd tension thickening the space between them.

"What's going on, Dylan?" Fear darted through her. "Is everything okay? Is Chris all right?"

"He's fine," Dylan said quickly.

"Then what is it?"

He shuffled awkwardly, raking a hand through his short blond hair.

"Look," he started, his voice a tad hoarse, "Chris is...um...aw shit, there's no easy way to say this, okay? So I'm just going to do it, and I want you to know that doing this brings me no pleasure. You and me...we don't really get along, and then there was that whole visit thing and...you know, what you saw at my place...which you never brought up again, and I'm really grateful for that, by the way—"

"Oh for the love of God," she interrupted. "Quit babbling and say what you came here to say."

"Chris left."

Claire blinked. "What?"

"He left." Misery flashed across Dylan's face. "He couldn't go through with the wedding. He...uh, he doesn't think you two are right for each other."

Shock slammed into her, so powerful she nearly keeled over.

Chris was calling off the wedding?

A rush of humiliation joined the unwavering shock. Oh God. The groom backing out at the last minute was *definitely* not part of her childhood fantasy.

As tears filled her eyes again, she looked at Dylan with dismay. "I can't believe this."

He looked upset. "I'm so sorry. I shouldn't be the one telling you this. My brother is a bastard for running away, and I promise you, I tried to get him to do the right thing. I told him it was his responsibility to talk to you, but I guess he thought it would be too painful or something."

"Wait a minute," she burst out, as something suddenly registered. "What do you mean, he *left*?"

Dylan's throat jumped as he gulped. "He left. As in, no longer here."

"You mean he left the country club?" Her mouth dropped open. "He just drove away?"

There was a quick nod.

Her pulse careened into cardiac-arrest territory, her throat tightening with horror when she realized what that meant. "He's going to make me face all those guests by myself?" Her breathing went shallow. "I'm the one who has to tell everyone there won't be a wedding?"

Shock flitted through Dylan's eyes. "What? No, of course not. Don't worry, my mom will make the announcement."

Agony and embarrassment heated her cheeks as she pictured Dylan's sweet mother getting up there in front of hundreds of strangers and telling them they'd wasted their time in coming here.

"You can't put that on Shanna," she moaned. "Oh God. This is so humiliating!"

"Claire. Hey, calm down, honey. Take a deep breath."

She ignored him, her brain continuing to run over all the mortifying implications of Chris's cowardice.

"I have to tell my parents," she mumbled between unsteady breaths. "And Father Thomas. Oh gosh, do you think Frank Lowenstein will expect us to reimburse him for renting out the Lavender Ballroom?"

Her hands started shaking again. More and more thoughts flew into her head. "My boss is out there, and all my colleagues. I can't go out there and have everyone feeling sorry for me." Her gaze darted toward the mirror again. "Oh shit, I can't be wearing this gown when they see me."

The next few minutes were a blur of irrationality, a heart-pounding, panic-induced daze that somehow ended with Claire's wedding dress turning into a pool of fabric at her feet. She had no recollection of getting undressed—and apparently no sense of modesty, either—but suddenly she was wearing nothing but a strapless white bra and matching thong, completely on display for her runaway groom's brother.

And yet when it finally dawned on her that she'd just stripped down to her underwear, she couldn't even dwell on the fresh round of embarrassment because a new realization had swooped into her head.

"Where am I supposed to go?" she said miserably. "Is Chris at our apartment?"

Dylan looked utterly disoriented, his green eyes moving from her nearly naked body, to the discarded wedding gown, then up to her face. "I don't know," he sputtered. "Look. Claire. You're freaking out and you need to dial it down, okay?"

"Where am I supposed to go?" she repeated, raising her voice over the loud drumming of her heart. "I don't even have a car! My parents drove. Oh shit, my parents. They'll want to take me home. I can't go home with them, Dylan! They'll hover over me and my mom will stuff me with cookies because she thinks cookies are the solution for all of life's troubles, and—"

A sharp sting on her cheek made her head jerk up.

She blinked in shock and reached up to rub away the pain. "Did you just slap me?"

Dylan's perfectly sculpted jaw tensed. "No, I flicked you."

"You *flicked* me?"

"Yes." He moved closer and gripped both her shoulders. "Get it together, McKinley. My brother is the asshole in this equation, okay? My mom is handling the guests, so there's no reason for you to go out there at all. You don't need to face your boss or coworkers, and if you're not ready to talk to your parents, then you don't have to. And fuck all those country club jerks from Chris's firm. You don't owe them any explanations. Understand?"

She nodded, feeling numb.

"But you're right," Dylan went on. "Chris is probably at the apartment, so maybe going back there isn't a good idea at the moment. Unless you're ready to get the big talk over with?"

She shook her head. Talking to Chris was definitely on her agenda, but not now. As furious as she was that he'd taken off instead of handling the situation like an adult, she couldn't deal with him right now. Not until she got far, far away from this stupid country club and made sense of her muddled thoughts.

"I guess I can go to a hotel," she said in a tired voice. "Can you drop me off?"

Without waiting for his response, she hurried toward the suitcase and carry-on she'd left beside the door. She and Chris had been scheduled to leave for their honeymoon immediately following the reception, so her bags were already packed and waiting.

She kept her back to Dylan, rooting around in her suitcase and pulling out the first item of clothing she found, which happened to be a bright blue sundress. She yanked the dress over her head and smoothed it down her body, not caring that you could see the white band of her bra, thanks to the dress's backless halter style, or that the skirt was indecently short. This dress had been meant for Aruba, the first stop on their three-week honeymoon.

Except there wouldn't be a honeymoon. Or a wedding.

"I can't believe he just left," she whispered.

The warm hand on her bare shoulder made her jump. "I really am sorry," came Dylan's husky voice.

Claire couldn't help a derisive snort. "No, you're not."

"Yes, I am."

"Bullshit." For the first time since Dylan arrived to drop his bomb, hot tears stung her eyes. "You're loving every second of this. You hate me and you probably think I had it coming, huh?"

"That's not what I think at all, Claire." Now he sounded irritated.

"Sure, Dylan, because you were *dying* for me to be your sister-in-law. Well, congrats, you won't ever have to see me again after today, so just do me a favor and stuff your sorries in a sack, okay? All I want from you right now is to help me carry this stupid suitcase and drive me to a hotel." Her lips tightened. "Do you think you can handle that, soldier?"

A muscle in his jaw twitched, his eyes flashing with resentment, but the hard look quickly faded into resignation. With a curt nod, he picked up her suitcase and said, "I can handle that."

Chapter Two

"Mom, I promise you, I'm okay. What? No, I swear, I left of my own free will. I just couldn't face all those people… I know, but…maybe he was right, okay? Maybe getting married would've been a mistake."

Keeping his eyes on the road, Dylan listened to Claire's side of the conversation. Despite himself, he experienced a twinge of admiration that even in the face of Chris's betrayal, she was still protecting him. She had every right to curse Chris until she was blue in the face. Every right to scream and throw things and burn all of his belongings in a ritualistic trashcan fire. But rather than paint Chris as the villain, she was practically defending his decision. Dylan couldn't help but feel grudgingly impressed.

"Please tell Shanna how grateful I am that she dealt with the guests and the club manager, and tell her I'll call her tonight, okay?"

Dylan's shoulders stiffened at the sound of his mother's name. He hadn't given her the heads-up before sneaking Claire out of the mansion, and he knew she'd be furious about his desertion, especially with Chris gone too.

But what else was he supposed to do? His first priority had been to get Claire out of that country club. The woman had been seconds away from a full-blown breakdown.

His mouth went dry as the memory of Claire stripping out of her wedding dress flew into his head, and now a different part of his anatomy was stiffening. No denying it—Claire McKinley was a damn sexy woman. All that tousled auburn hair, those X-rated curves, the fuck-me red lips… the woman was designed to get a man nice and hard. To make matters worse, her big brown eyes gave her that perpetually vulnerable look that triggered a man's hero complex, should he have one. And Dylan, unfortunately, had suffered from a serious case of *hero* his entire life.

He'd never been able to walk away from a damsel in distress—protecting Claire from the embarrassment and questions that awaited her in the ballroom had been instinctual.

"Please don't argue with me about this," Claire was saying. "I really want to be alone for a bit." She paused. "I know you do, but I need some space. I'll call you from the hotel, okay?"

The second she hung up, the iPhone in her hand started to vibrate. And vibrate. And vibrate some more.

"Oh sweet Jesus, I'm getting like a million text messages," she muttered.

Dylan glanced over and saw the frustration glimmering in her eyes. "Your mom and dad?"

"Yep, along with my boss, maid of honor, cousins, coworkers."

"They all have a ton of questions, huh?"

"Duh." She made a sound of exasperation. "I'm turning it off. This is ridiculous."

She swiped her finger over the touch screen, then dropped the phone in the cup holder of Dylan's rental.

"I can't believe this is happening," she mumbled. "My parents are freaking out."

"So's my mom. You're not the only one with a thousand incoming texts." He tapped the front pocket of his trousers, where he'd tucked his cell phone. "My leg is going numb from all the vibrating."

"My mother said the guests are gone and the catering staff packed everything up. She's going to take all the food home with her, since it's already been paid for." Her voice cracked. "Oh, and my dad won't let me pay him back."

Dylan fought a pang of sympathy. He'd never understood why the bride's family was expected to foot the bill for the wedding. Chris's boss may have arranged for the venue, but the McKinleys had taken care of everything else—food, flowers, string quartet. Judging by how tasteful and beautiful the ballroom had looked, Dylan suspected financing the shindig had been pretty costly for Claire's parents. He felt bad for them. They'd seemed like really nice people, and his brother had completely screwed them over by running out on their daughter.

"I guess I should text Chris and let him know which hotel I'll be—what the hell, Dylan? Where are you taking me?"

That she hadn't noticed their destination until now spoke volumes about her state of mind. As the airport became visible in the distance, he felt Claire's amber-colored eyes boring into his cheek.

"Where are we going?" she asked in a tight voice.

"The Coast Guard Air Station." He flicked the turn signal and changed lanes, then sped off the freeway exit ramp.

"Why on earth are we going there?"

"We're catching a ride with a buddy of mine. He's a Coast Guard pilot."

"A ride? A ride to *where*?"

"I'm taking you back to San Diego with me."

Silence descended over the interior of the SUV. He snuck a peek at Claire and found her looking at him like he'd just told her he was a closet Backstreet Boys fan or something. The mixture of confusion and horror on her face was almost comical.

He was pretty confused himself. What the hell was he doing taking Claire home with him? He didn't even like the chick. In fact, for the past year and a half he'd actively been rooting for Chris to come to his senses and dump her.

So really, what he *needed* to do was drop her at a hotel, high-five Chris for seeing the light, and forget Claire McKinley ever existed.

Except…in a complete twist of insanity, his brother had suddenly soared to the top of Dylan's shit list. After the despicable—not to mention dishonorable—way Chris had behaved, Dylan was firmly on Team Claire in this fucked-up situation.

He couldn't believe Chris had run away like that. No, he couldn't *understand* it. As a SEAL, Dylan met challenges head-on, even when those challenges were terrifying or painful or guaranteed to bring some discomfort.

Well, he refused to abandon Claire the way his brother had. He might not be the woman's biggest fan, but she didn't deserve to have everyone pitying her, or whispering about her, or worse, laughing behind her back. Since Chris and Claire had all the same friends, and with her one non-mutual friend out of town, Dylan knew she wouldn't find much of a support system here in the Bay Area.

"I'm not going anywhere with you," she grumbled. "Take me to a hotel."

He stayed on route, driving right past three airport hotels, which solicited a string of curses from the woman beside him.

Dylan raised his eyebrows. "Shit, McKinley, you sound like a character from an HBO show. Where the hell did you learn some of those phrases?"

For a second, humor danced in her eyes. "HBO." The amusement promptly faded. "I'm serious, Dylan, I don't want to go to San Diego."

"I really think you should," he said gently. "At least for a night or two."

"Oh, you think I should, huh? Because you magically know what's best for me, is that it?"

"You said so yourself. You need space." He shrugged. "Well, you ain't gonna get it here, honey. You'll be alone at that hotel for an hour, two hours tops, and then your parents will weasel the location out of you and swoop in with the sympathy parade." When she didn't answer, he shot her a pointed look. "You know I'm right."

"Maybe, but—"

"And I know your best friend is in South America—"

"Sierra Leone—"

"—which means you can't cry on *her* shoulder, so—"

Now she was the one interrupting him. "So you want me to cry on *your* shoulder? No thanks, pal."

As the gate for the Coast Guard station came into view, Dylan abruptly pulled over to the side of the road.

"What now?" Claire demanded angrily. "Are you kicking me out of the car?"

"What the hell are you talking about? Why would I—" He stopped talking and sucked in a calming breath. How did this woman always manage to rile him up?

He exhaled in a measured pace. "Look, you have three options."

"Oh really?"

Her mocking tone brought another rush of irritation, which he forced himself to ignore. Hell, she was allowed to be a bitch today. Getting ditched on her wedding day definitely gave her a free pass.

"Option one," he announced. "You go to a hotel and prepare yourself for the sympathy parade."

Unhappiness washed over Claire's face.

"Option two, you go home and get the confrontation with Chris out of the way."

Her delicate jaw tensed.

"Option three, you hop on the chopper with me, crash at my place for a day or two, and when you feel up to dealing with all this, you come home."

Your place?

The little voice gave him pause. Technically he ought to be consulting his roommate before he—

Roommate? the voice interrupted, sarcastic now.

He fought a spark of aggravation. Okay, fine, Aidan Rhodes was much more than a *roommate*.

As Claire sat there in silence, visibly pondering the choices he'd given her, Dylan fished his cell phone out of his pocket.

He'd planned on shooting a discreet text Aidan's way to let him know they might have some company, but Claire spoke up before he could.

"No. I don't run away from my problems," she said firmly. "Maybe that's yours and Chris's MO, but not mine."

His nostrils flared at the accusation. "I don't know where you're getting your intel, honey, but I don't run from my problems. Never have, never will."

"Either way, I can't just leave town. I'll regroup for a couple of hours at the hotel, and then talk to Chris."

As if on cue, Dylan's phone buzzed in his hand.

Chris's number flashed on the screen.

"Speak of the devil," he told her.

The wounded look in her big brown eyes triggered the urge to pull her into his arms, but he pushed the crazy idea aside. He didn't blame her for looking so hurt, though—Chris should be calling his bride right now, not his brother.

"What are you waiting for?" she muttered. "Answer it."

Dylan raised the phone to his ear, but he didn't greet his brother with even an ounce of warmth. "What do you want?"

There was a pause. "You're angry."

"No fucking kidding."

"Dylan...look, I know you're pissed at me and I'm so sorry I ran away like that. I took the coward's way out and I feel like a total ass, okay?"

"No, *not* okay. Nothing you did today was *okay*, Chris."

A remorseful breath filled the line. "I'm sorry. I really am. And I promise you I'm going to make this right. I'll make it right with Claire, and with Mom, and the partners, and most of all, you. But first, I need you to do one more thing for me."

Incredulity lodged in his throat. "Are you serious? After everything that went down today, you have the nerve to ask for another favor?"

Next to him, Claire made a harsh sound of disdain, and a quick glance at the passenger seat revealed she was eyeing him warily. Actually, no, she was eyeing his *phone*. The way she'd curled her hands into fists and pressed them on her thighs told Dylan she was trying to stop herself from grabbing the cell out of his hand.

And speaking of thighs...he couldn't help but notice that her dress had ridden up, revealing her smooth, pale skin that he couldn't seem to quit staring at...

Disgusted with himself, he yanked his gaze off those firm thighs, hoping she hadn't noticed him checking out her legs.

"I just need you to pass along a message," Chris pleaded in his ear.

"To who?" Dylan said suspiciously.

"Claire."

He almost blurted out that Claire was sitting right next to him, but he swallowed the confession. He got the feeling Chris might panic and hang up if he knew she was there.

"What's the message?" he asked in a curt voice.

"Tell her I'm sorry. I know I owe her an explanation and I promise to give her one. Just...not now. Tell her we'll talk when I get back."

Dylan's spine went rigid. "Get back from where?"

"Aruba. I'm leaving for the airport now."

For the life of him, Dylan couldn't formulate a single response. As shock and disgust pounded into him, he was tempted to whip his phone out the window just so he wouldn't have to hear his brother's voice anymore.

Chris, however, seemed oblivious to the waves of hostility radiating over the line.

"I know it sounds heartless, but the trip's already been paid for and it's nonrefundable. Aruba was first on our itinerary, and I'm definitely heading there, but I don't know yet if I'll do London and Paris like we'd planned." A pause. "Claire's welcome to use her ticket too, I suppose, but I think that would be awkward for the both of us, so I'd recommend she not do that."

The rage bubbling in Dylan's gut was so uncharacteristic it caught him by surprise. He didn't get this angry. Ever. He was usually calm under pressure, cool, collected, in complete fucking control of himself.

But at this very moment, he wanted to murder his own brother.

Straight-up *murder* him.

Releasing a slow breath, he shifted his head so he didn't have to see Claire's dark expression in his peripheral vision. "You're unbelievable," he hissed into the phone. "Right now, in this moment? I can't believe we're even related. I'm so fucking ashamed of you."

"Hey!"

Chris's outraged gasp only pissed Dylan off even more. "Don't worry, I'll pass your message along, big brother," he snapped. "And now I'm going to hang up before I say something I might regret."

Proving he didn't make idle threats, he punched the *end* button and tossed his phone in the cup holder, where it rattled against Claire's discarded iPhone.

The anger refused to abate. His vision was a sea of red, his hands gripping the steering wheel so tight his knuckles had turned white, but the alternative was punching the damn dashboard, and he wasn't in the mood to have an airbag deploy in his face. Jesus fucking Christ. This entire day had been a fucking nightmare, and it just kept getting worse and worse.

"What did he say?"

Claire's cautious voice broke through the haze of fury. For a second he was tempted to lie, but he couldn't bring himself to cover for his brother. Chris didn't deserve any clemency, not after everything he'd done.

"He said he's sorry and he'll talk to you when he gets back," Dylan reported through gritted teeth.

She went quiet. Her confused expression soon gave way to horror as understanding dawned. "He's going on our honeymoon?"

Dylan nodded.

"*He's going on our fucking honeymoon?*"

Her chest heaved from her labored breathing, drawing his gaze to her cleavage. And proving that he had zero decorum, his inner manwhore refused to let him overlook the fact that this woman had great tits. No, *remarkable* tits.

"Oh my God. Who *does* that? I can't believe I was going to marry such an insensitive ass!"

Dylan shifted in discomfort when he noticed the tears filling her eyes. Fortunately, the moisture clinging to her long lashes didn't spill over. If she started crying, he knew he'd have no choice but to take her in his arms, and he was determined to avoid that. Just because he was helping her out didn't mean they were best buds or anything.

"Well, on the bright side, your apartment is free," he said feebly.

She gave a vicious shake of the head. "I can't go back there. If I see anything that reminds me of Chris right now…"

She didn't finish that sentence, but Dylan could fill in the blanks. "So what do you want to do?" he asked her.

Two teardrops broke free from those thick eyelashes and streamed down her flawless ivory cheeks. "Number three," she mumbled. "I choose option three."

Chapter Three

A COUPLE HOURS LATER, CLAIRE TURNED TO DYLAN IN CONFUSION AS their taxi came to a stop in front of a modern high-rise with an endless amount of windows sparkling in the afternoon sunlight.

"Where are we?" she asked suspiciously. "I thought we were going to your place."

He leaned forward and handed the driver some cash, then reached for the door handle. "This is my place."

"Since when?" Claire wrinkled her brow. The last time she and Chris came to visit, Dylan had been living in a house in Coronado with his teammate Seth, a scruffy badass SEAL with a chip on his shoulder.

"Since about a month ago," he answered.

They got out of the cab and Dylan rounded the vehicle to grab their bags from the trunk. It was just past three o'clock, and the sun was so bright Claire squinted to avoid being blinded and wished she hadn't shoved her sunglasses into her carry-on. She couldn't believe how warm it was, especially for December. On the plus side, she happened to be wearing a sundress so thin she may as well be naked.

On the minus side, the barely-there dress had resulted in an hour-and-a-half-long helicopter ride in which Dylan's eyes had been glued to her breasts.

Which was perplexing, because…he was gay, right? She still couldn't figure it out, but the memory of Dylan's tongue in another man's mouth was completely incongruous to the way he'd been ogling her on the chopper.

And speaking of perplexing, what the *hell* had compelled her to come back to San Diego with this man?

Clearly she'd suffered a mental breakdown after hearing that Chris was leaving town, but by the time common sense decided to make a return, they'd already been landing on the helipad at San Diego's Coast Guard base.

After the taxi sped off, Dylan lugged their bags toward the glass doors at the building's entrance. He didn't turn around to see if she was following, but he did call out a mocking, "You coming?"

She trailed after him, still mystified by their surroundings. How on earth could Dylan afford to live here? The building was way too luxurious for a SEAL's salary. They stepped into a beautiful lobby with dark oak furniture, cream-colored carpeting, and tasteful artwork on the walls, and were immediately greeted by the uniformed security guard sitting behind a spacious counter.

Dylan smiled and nodded at the bulky African-American man, then introduced Claire as his houseguest. The fact that the guard wrote down her name told Claire that security was taken seriously in this building.

Her flip-flops snapped against the lush carpet as she and Dylan headed toward a corridor to their left. She winced at each *snap snap*, feeling way too underdressed. It didn't help that Dylan still wore the crisp black suit he'd donned for the wedding, which made her skimpy dress and plastic shoes look even more out of place.

"This place is so fancy," she whispered. "How can you afford to live here alone?"

"Always so concerned with finances, aren't you?"

The contempt in his voice raised her hackles. "What's that supposed to mean?"

Dylan pressed the elevator button. "Nothing at all," he said vaguely. "And to answer your question, I don't live alone."

Ding. The elevator opened with a chime and he strode into it without elaborating.

Claire hurried in after him. "You're still living with Seth then?"

"Nope."

His response was casual, but the shuttered look on his handsome face answered her next question. He lived with the dark-haired man. The man he'd been kissing that night.

Heat flooded her cheeks, and, to her extreme embarrassment, she experienced a spark of arousal. Damn it! She wasn't allowed to get turned on by it anymore. She'd been trying so hard to stifle that reaction these last couple of months.

But now that the proverbial door had more or less been opened, she found herself walking right through it.

"So. Um." She swallowed. "Are we ever going to talk about what happened back in September?"

Dylan shrugged. "There's nothing to talk about. You walked in on a private moment between me and Aidan. No biggie."

"Aidan? Is that his name?"

"Yep."

The elevator continued its ascent, the numbers on the electronic panel rapidly flashing before stopping on the number *15*.

The doors dinged open.

"Listen," Dylan said as they stepped into a wide hallway, "I really do appreciate that you didn't say anything to Chris or my mom about what you saw that night."

She arched a brow. "And yet you insist the whole thing was *no biggie*."

"It's not. To me, anyway." His eyes went somber. "But it would be a big deal for them. Chris, especially. My brother is very…conservative."

"I know. My best friend is a lesbian, and, well, Chris has never been openly negative but I don't think he likes her very much."

"Yeah, he's a bit of a homophobe," Dylan admitted in a pained voice. "There's a whole thing behind it, but I don't want to get into that. Just know I'm grateful that you kept quiet."

They lingered in the middle of the hall, eyeing each other carefully. Claire realized this was the first time in a year and a half that she and Dylan had had a conversation that lacked any hostile undertones.

Might be pushing her luck, but she figured she should capitalize on the cease-fire. "So you and Aidan…you're…together?" she asked curiously.

He sighed. "It's complicated."

She could only imagine. Dylan didn't just have his family's prejudice to worry about—he was also a navy officer, and no matter how progressive the military claimed to be these days, Claire knew his sexual orientation would probably never be fully accepted. And who knew what circumstances the dark-haired stranger—Aidan, she amended—had to contend with.

Sympathy tugged at her heart, an emotion she didn't normally feel in Dylan's presence. Usually she couldn't look past his arrogant, selfish exterior, but she had to admit, he'd been pretty sweet today. Whisking her out of the country club, bringing her home with him so she could lick her wounds in peace. She hadn't asked him to do any of that, and she still couldn't figure out why he hadn't sided with his brother in all this.

"Anyway, my mom and Chris know that Aidan is my roommate, but not that—"

"—you share a room," she finished wryly.

Dylan shrugged again. "Actually, we don't."

She furrowed her brows. "Why not?"

"Like I said, it's complicated."

A hundred more questions bit at her tongue, but he didn't give her the chance to voice them. He was walking off again, leaving her to stare at his retreating back—and his butt. Because really, she couldn't *not* stare at his butt, so taut and delicious in those snug trousers. And his body was so damn big he made her feel miniature in comparison. Broad shoulders, arms that rippled with power, long legs, a lean yet muscular torso, and of course, that amazing butt.

No doubt about it, Dylan Wade was sexy. And he banked on that sexiness, using it to get whatever he wanted—well, at least according to Chris.

Then again, Chris's credibility was on shaky ground considering he was on his way to Aruba to cash in on the honeymoon *her parents* had paid for.

Choking down the bitterness coating her throat, Claire followed Dylan to a door at the very end of the hall, then waited as he pulled out a set of keys and stuck one in the lock.

A moment later, they walked into the apartment, Claire feeling slightly apprehensive as she examined the surprisingly large front hall. Actually, nothing surprising about it. *Of course* the apartments in this fancy-pants building would be huge.

Since Dylan kicked off his shoes, she did too, and beautiful dark hardwood spanned beneath her bare feet as they ventured deeper into the apartment. The front hall widened and spilled into an enormous open-concept space with floor-to-ceiling windows that provided a view of the city skyline.

"Wow," she blurted out. "This place is incredible."

"Yeah, it's pretty sweet." Dylan dropped her suitcases and his small black duffel on the floor, then swept an arm out and gave her a quick verbal tour. "Living room, dining room. Kitchen's over there, and the bedrooms are down that hall."

Claire's gaze took everything in—the masculine furnishings in the living room and heavy-duty entertainment system, the sleek electric fireplace, the French doors leading out to a sprawling stone terrace. She shifted her gaze and studied the low wall that separated the living and dining area from a big, modern kitchen with gleaming stainless-steel appliances and a black granite counter.

And just like Dylan's old place, this one was also neat as a pin, which only supported her belief that military men were the cleanest on the planet.

She opened her mouth to rave about the apartment a bit more, but the sound of footsteps interrupted. Claire turned her head in time to see Dylan's roommate step out of the corridor.

A pair of unbelievably sexy dimples appeared in his cheeks as he swept his dark eyes over the new arrivals. "Fastest wedding ever, huh?"

Claire was at a loss for words over his sheer hotness, and far too fascinated by the man walking toward them. She'd only caught shadowy glimpses of him back in September, and now she was kind of grateful for that, because if she'd known what this man looked like? He would have haunted her fantasies.

He was as handsome as Dylan, but in a darker, more sensual way. He had olive skin and short dark hair, a pair of intense chocolate-brown eyes, and a bare chest that made her mouth water. Yep, bare. He wasn't wearing a shirt, so her gaze got to experience every sculpted muscle and the tight ridges of his six-pack. Not to mention the tantalizing glimpses of his hip bones, which were revealed by black sweatpants that rode low and told her he was definitely going commando.

The lust that slammed into her was insane. Absolutely insane. Her nipples went rock-hard and her thighs clenched as X-rated images flashed through her mind. She wanted to put her mouth all over this man. She wanted to lick his collarbone and his pecs and his abs, and then she wanted to sink to her knees, pull out his cock and lick that too.

As their eyes locked, something hot and primal rippled through her. She got the feeling he knew exactly what she'd been envisioning, and the notion made her blush and break the eye contact.

"Seriously, what happened?" Dylan's roommate asked. "Your text told me nothing."

Dylan raked a hand through his blond hair, looking frustrated. "Yeah, I didn't want to get into it via text. This is Claire McKinley, by the way. Claire, my roommate, Aidan Rhodes."

Aidan's dark eyes flickered with intrigue. "The bride. Interesting. But no groom."

Claire met his gaze again. "The groom decided he didn't want to marry me so he left without telling me."

He looked startled. "What do you mean, without telling you?"

"Oh, don't worry, he recruited his brother to dump me. I suppose that's better than nothing." The bitterness in her tone belied the smile she'd attempted.

Those magnetic eyes softened with sympathy. "I'm sorry. That must have been tough for you." He turned to Dylan. "You didn't need to stay with your mother?"

"I wanted to get Claire outta there. I'll call my mom in a bit."

Claire's heart skipped a beat at the knowledge that Dylan had put her first, but her response was so infuriating it resulted in making her crabby again. "I'm sure you have more questions," she told Aidan, "but can one of you direct me to the bathroom first? And maybe a room where I can get changed?"

The latter request directed both men's eyes to the dress clinging to her body like plastic wrap. When those hot male gazes rested on her chest, Claire experienced another baffling moment of were-they-or-weren't-they. Gay, that was. Because from the hungry way they were staring at her breasts, she would bet on *were not*.

"You can stay in my room," Dylan finally said.

"I can't take your room," she protested. "Where will you sleep?"

She regretted the question the second it exited her mouth. Her cheeks scorched again, burning hotter when she spotted the smirk on Aidan's mouth.

"I'll sleep in the office." Dylan picked up her bags. "Come on, I'll show you to your room."

She took a step after him, then paused awkwardly and looked at Aidan. "It's really nice to meet you."

"Pleasure's all mine." He still wore that secretive little smirk, but after a beat it faded into a frown. "I really am sorry about your wedding."

"Thanks," she murmured before trailing after Dylan.

He led her into a bedroom with dark-blue walls, a neatly made double bed, and modern, black-painted furniture. Other than a stack of books and magazines on the bedside table and the bulletin board on the closet door, the room lacked any personal touches. It smelled like Dylan, though, that woodsy, masculine scent that had filled her nostrils during the entire helicopter ride.

"Do you mind giving me some time alone?" she asked after he deposited her suitcase and carry-on near the foot of the bed. "I want to shower and call my parents, and maybe lie down for a little while."

"No problem." He headed for the doorway, then lingered there. "Are you hungry? Do you want me to whip up something for you to eat?"

She blinked in surprise. "You cook?"

Annoyance flickered in his eyes. "Yes, I cook."

"Oh. I didn't know that."

"There's a lot you don't know about me."

She felt like he was making a jab in there somewhere, but his tone was light and his expression veiled, so she decided not to push it. "Anyway, I'm not hungry. My appetite left me around the same time Chris did."

Dylan let out a breath. "I'm sorry you've had such a shitty day, Claire."

"Yeah, me too."

They both went quiet for a moment, and then he cleared his throat. "Okay, well, let me know if you need anything. I'm gonna fill Aidan in on what happened and then deal with my mom."

"Thank you for everything you did today," she said, shifting uneasily.

"No prob," he said before sliding out the door.

Once she was alone, Claire sat on the edge of the mattress and ran her fingers over the soft, navy-blue comforter. She felt uncomfortable being here, in Dylan's space, in Dylan's home, yet somehow it felt oddly appropriate. This entire day had been a nightmare, so why not finish it out in the company of a man she hated?

Dislike, a voice corrected.

Yeah, *hate* might be too strong a word, Claire had to concede. She still didn't approve of his behavior or the way he'd abandoned his family, but she couldn't deny that he'd been decent today.

Sighing, she reached into her purse and found her phone. A moment later, she had a tally that made her gawk—forty-two text messages, twenty-one voice mail messages, twenty-four missed calls. Didn't bode well for her email, which was her preferred method of communication.

She only bothered responding to the messages from her parents and her boss, reminding the former that she'd requested space, and thanking the latter for the reassurance that Claire still had the next three weeks off, honeymoon or no honeymoon.

After she pressed send, she checked the world clock app on her phone and nearly wept with joy when she realized she could now call Natasha and actually receive an answer. Long-distance charges be damned, she dialed Nat's number and prayed her friend was still awake.

When Natasha's voice blared over the line, the tears Claire had been holding back all day erupted like a volcanic explosion.

"Oh my God, I *knew* you'd get cold feet!" her best friend exclaimed before Claire even had a chance to say hello. "Don't worry, I wrote up a little speech just in case. Hold on, hon, let me go find it."

Claire laughed through her tears. "Don't bother. It's already done."

"What's already done? The ceremony?"

"The relationship."

"Wait. What?"

A breath shuddered out. "Chris and I didn't get married. He called it off."

"Are you shitting me?"

"Nope," she said glumly.

There was a long pause, and then a heavy sigh reverberated over the extension. "Start from the beginning."

It took ten minutes to tell Natasha everything, and she finished by reluctantly admitting that Dylan had been a good friend to her today, a confession that elicited a laugh from her friend.

"So the asshole brother ended up being the good guy, and the good guy ended up being the asshole," Natasha mused.

"Oh, like you're surprised. You've never liked Chris."

"Not really, no," Natasha said frankly. "But that doesn't mean I didn't support your decision to marry him. As long as you were happy, I was happy. You know that."

"Yeah, I know." She sniffled. "I feel like such a loser, Nat. Like one of those chicks from a bad rom com who gets left at the altar."

"I knew the dude was a pompous jerk, but disappearing like that? That's fucking bullshit."

"I know." She hesitated. "But…"

Natasha's tone sharpened. "But what? And don't tell me you're thinking of forgiving the asshole!"

"No, it's not that. I'm furious with him, I really am, but there was this moment earlier… It was right after Dylan told me that Chris was gone. I was shocked and hurt and embarrassed, but a part of me also felt…*relief.* God, Nat, I was actually kind of relieved I didn't have to marry him."

"That's because he wasn't right for you. I tried to tell you when you first started dating him, remember?"

"He was different then," she protested.

"Uh-uh, no way. The man was a phony, Claire. I knew it from the moment I met him. He was too slick, and his stories about helping others and wanting to make a difference were pure BS."

"What does that say about me then? For not seeing it?"

"It says you're a good person with a big heart," Natasha said quietly. "I think Chris told you everything you wanted to hear, and you believed it because you always try to see the best in people."

"Maybe," she murmured.

"But the fact that you felt relief today says it all, hon. Deep down you must have known it wasn't right."

"I guess. I just wish it didn't have to end in such a humiliating way." She sighed. "Shit, I'm really not looking forward to seeing him and listening to his excuses. I'm pretty sure it'll take all my willpower not to slap him."

"Don't fight the urge. The bastard deserves a good slapping. I can't believe he went to Aruba! Who *does* that?"

"I know, right?"

"Selfish dick."

The outrage in her friend's voice made Claire laugh, and the giddy sound was only confirmation that she would be lost without Natasha. They'd known each other since they were five years old, attended the same schools all the way through to high school graduation, and although their paths had branched off when Natasha enrolled in med school and Claire went for her MBA, the two of them had remained close.

Claire still remembered the day Natasha had come out to her as a lesbian, back when they were seventeen years old. Natasha had been so worried things would change between them, that Claire would freak out and pull away, but the confession only strengthened their bond. Claire had wanted so desperately for Chris to love Nat as much as she did, but he'd never warmed up to her best friend, and now she had to wonder if that had been a warning sign all along.

"Seriously, though, how are you doing?"

"I'm fine," she said truthfully. "But…I'm so embarrassed. I'm dreading having to explain to everyone why we cancelled the wedding."

"You don't have to explain a damn thing. You and Chris broke up. End of story."

She laughed again. "My parents will want more details than that."

"Fine, you can give Nora and Ron the deets. But nobody else needs an in-depth explanation. They can mind their own business." Natasha paused. "I really wish I could fly home and be there for you, do something to cheer you up."

"You've already done a lot."

"Well, I want to do more. I promise you, the second the plane touches down on the runway a couple of months from now, I'm picking you up, bringing you to my place and giving you an epic cheer-up session. We can get really tipsy, sing some awful karaoke and dye our hair blonde just like we did after Sandy dumped me. Deal?"

Claire grinned. "Deal."

They spoke for a few more minutes, but it was nearly midnight in Sierra Leone, and when Natasha confessed she'd been up for the past thirty-eight hours working at the clinic, Claire felt so guilty she practically forced her friend to hang up.

Dropping the phone on the bed, she went over to her suitcase and unzipped it. Her plan was to take off this flimsy honeymoon dress, put on some comfy clothes, and reflect on this day from hell, but when she heard a clinking sound in her bag, the plan promptly changed.

She reached between the stacks of clothes and pulled out the bottle of Lagavulin single-malt scotch, which sold for three hundred bucks a pop. She didn't normally buy such expensive liquor, but she'd wanted to surprise Chris on their honeymoon and toast to their marriage with his favorite brand.

As she traced the edges of the bottle's label, she thought about the plan of action Natasha had just outlined. Getting tipsy sounded pretty damn appealing…but who said she had to wait until March? At the moment, she couldn't think of anything better than getting a little wonky in the head and not thinking about this disastrous day for a little while.

With a decisive nod, she started to untwist the bottle cap, then froze when she heard muted footsteps coming from the hallway. She expected a knock on the door, but it didn't come. Instead, another door opened and closed, and then there was nothing but silence.

Her face grew hot as she pictured Dylan and Aidan alone in a bedroom together. Embracing. Or maybe doing more than embracing…

She quickly banished the wicked thought before it put down roots and sprouted a whole bunch of dirty images in her head.

But as she opened the Lagavulin bottle and brought it to her lips, she couldn't help but wonder what was going on in the other room.

Chapter Four

AIDAN FOLLOWED DYLAN INTO THE MASTER BEDROOM, NOTING THE rigid set of his roommate's shoulders—and was that guilt in those deep green eyes? Clearly it was, because the second the door closed, Dylan lobbed an apology in his direction.

"I'm sorry, man."

Aidan wrinkled his forehead. "For what?"

"For bringing Claire here without warning."

Dylan dragged both hands through his dirty-blond hair before shrugging out of his black suit jacket. He tossed it on the king-sized bed, then loosened his slate-gray tie, yanked it off and threw that aside too.

Aidan's gaze tracked the movement of Dylan's long, callused fingers as they unbuttoned the top two buttons of his white dress shirt. Then the SEAL let out a weary groan and stretched his arms over his head, causing the muscles on that broad chest to flex in the hottest possible way.

The sudden, all-consuming arousal that seized Aidan's body no longer startled him. He'd been attracted to both sexes for as long as he could remember, but his attraction to Dylan surpassed anything he'd ever experienced. He was addicted to the man, craved him on a whole other level, and no matter how many times he fed the addiction, no matter how many mind-blowing releases they gave each other, he constantly wanted more.

Snapping out of it, he leaned against the tall dresser and watched as Dylan flopped down on the bed. "You don't have to be sorry. You did the right thing getting her out of town." He hesitated. "Did Chris seriously just bail without telling her the wedding was off?"

"Yup."

"Wow." Aidan searched his vocabulary for an adjective with some tact, but in the end, he couldn't control what came out. "Your brother's a fucking asshole, man."

"No kidding." Dylan shook his head a few times. "He just *left*. I get that he was panicking—"

"No excuse."

"—and that he didn't want to hurt her—"

"No excuse."

"—but that's no excuse," Dylan said, rolling his eyes.

Aidan offered a sheepish smile. "Sorry, I should've let you finish. But yeah, your brother needed to man up and talk to Claire. He planned on *marrying* the girl, for fuck's sake. He owed it to her to tell her what was on his mind instead of dumping her via messenger and running away."

"I know, but I couldn't stop him. He pretended he was going to see her, and then he took off and left me holding the bag. And the messed-up thing? I think he made the right call. Not the running away part, but canceling the wedding. He and Claire are all wrong for each other."

"Still, she doesn't deserve that kind of treatment."

"Of course not." Dylan's gaze darkened with displeasure. "But that doesn't mean I want to spend the next few days holding her hand and wiping her tears and telling her everything's gonna be okay."

"You don't want to, but you will."

The SEAL's eyebrows lifted in challenge. "Oh, I will, huh?"

"Yup. Because unlike your brother, *you* are not an asshole. You're a good guy, and we both know you have a major hero complex. So no matter how much you dislike the woman—who, by the way, is smoking hot, bro—you're going to be there for her, just like you were this morning." Crossing his arms, Aidan slanted his head to the side. "Am I wrong?"

After a moment, a defeated sigh rumbled out of Dylan's chest. "No, you're not wrong. Claire can stay for as long as she likes." He faltered. "That is, if it's okay with you."

"How many times do I have to tell you? This is your place too. You can invite whoever you want over."

"But this is much more than me inviting a chick over for an evening of dinner and fucking. She'd be a houseguest. A snooty, bitchy, annoying houseguest."

"She doesn't seem that bad."

"Trust me, she is. She's a snob."

Aidan furrowed his brows, slightly perplexed by the note of scorn in Dylan's voice. He'd known the man for a couple of years, had been living with him for more than a month, and this was the first time he'd heard Dylan speak about someone else with such distaste.

It made absolutely no sense. Dylan loved *everyone*. And everyone loved him right back. Men, women, children, pets—every living creature that came into contact with Dylan Wade adored him within minutes. Aidan had never met anyone more charming or likable, not to mention genuine, so to hear Mr. Congeniality throw insults Claire's way was more than a little bewildering.

Dylan must have picked up on the cloud of doubt in the air, because his tone grew defensive. "You don't know her the way I do. She's obsessed with money, for one. Every time I've seen her she's taken bitchy cheap shots about how I'm not rolling in the dough, or she's gone on and on about Chris and his corporate job. Oh, and she has zero respect for my mother."

Aidan frowned. "What makes you say that?"

"She made some shitty comments last year about how housewife doesn't count as a real job. We argued about it."

"I see."

"Why are you looking at me like that?"

"I'm just wondering…are you sure your animosity toward her doesn't stem from the fact that she caught us making out?"

"What? Of course not."

The look of surprise on Dylan's face made him laugh. "I'm not judging you, man. I know you don't want your family to know about us, so Claire knowing makes her somewhat of a threat."

"Trust me, she's not a threat. And it's not that I don't want my family to know," Dylan said in a tired voice. "I'd just like to figure out what this is before I attempt to explain it to someone else."

Aidan totally seconded that. He had no idea what "this" was, either. Yeah, Dylan turned him on like nobody's business, but they were also friends. Best friends. And that's what troubled him the most. Sex always complicated shit, and the last thing he wanted was to lose Dylan's friendship. He valued it way too much to give it up.

At the same time, he couldn't bring himself to give up the sexual nature of their relationship, even when the practical side of him knew they couldn't have a future. A real one, anyway, with the whole happily-ever-after part.

As much as it sucked, they weren't enough for each other and they both knew it.

But that didn't mean he couldn't take advantage of the time they had left.

"I missed you," he said gruffly, moving away from the dresser.

"I was only gone a day." The teasing look gave way to a sheepish smile. "But I missed you too."

Dylan got to his feet at Aidan's approach, and a second later their mouths found each other. It was a fleeting kiss, a feather-light brush of their lips—or at least it was before Dylan angled his head and deepened the contact.

The moment that hot, wet tongue slid into Aidan's mouth, he was a goner. No stopping this kiss, no controlling the way his dick turned to granite and tried to poke right out of his sweats.

"Fuck, I totally missed you," Dylan muttered.

Their tongues tangled, breaths mingled, and it wasn't long before Aidan clapped his hands on Dylan's hips and jerked the man's lower body to his. At the feel of a telltale erection pressing into his thigh, he let out a hoarse moan, then slid one hand to cup the tantalizing bulge.

"Mmmm, probably not a good idea," Dylan said ruefully, but the way he thrust into Aidan's palm told a different story.

"*Great* idea," Aidan murmured back.

He stroked the hard outline of that long, thick cock, chuckling when the SEAL's head lolled to the side in pleasure. Applying more pressure, he palmed the stiff erection, then brought his mouth to the other man's neck and sucked on his hot flesh.

Dylan jerked in surprise before groaning with approval. His hips continued to move, seeking contact, but Aidan abruptly dropped his hand.

"Seriously?" Dylan choked out. "You initiate a handjob and don't follow through? Cocktease."

"Oh, come on, we both know you want a lot more than my hand."

With a mocking smile, he pushed the man toward the bed. When the back of Dylan's knees hit the edge of the mattress, Aidan gave him a shove and forced him into a sitting position.

A second later, he dropped to his knees.

"What are you doing?"

"You really need to ask?" He reached for Dylan's waistband, and then the metallic sound of a zipper opening echoed in the room.

"What if Claire knocks on the door?"

"Then we tell her we'll be right out, you tuck your cock back in your pants, and we finish this later."

With that said, he yanked on Dylan's trousers and boxer-briefs, and grinned at the erection that eagerly sprang up to greet him.

"You know, you don't have to give me a BJ to cheer me up," Dylan rasped. "I wasn't the one who got left at the altar."

The bead of precome glistening on the mushroom head of Dylan's cock made Aidan lick his lips, but he didn't make a move to claim his prize just yet. "You want me to stop?" he challenged.

"God, no."

"Okay then."

With a grin, he wrapped his fingers around the root of that hard shaft and gave it a leisurely pump.

A shudder rocked Dylan's body. "More," he ordered. "Give me your mouth."

The husky demand sent a dark thrill up Aidan's spine. Same way he didn't understand every other aspect of their relationship, he also didn't get their sexual dynamic. With other guys he'd slept with, he was the one making the demands, the one taking control of the encounter. With Dylan, they both took the role of aggressor, a fact that confused the shit out of him. He didn't like letting anyone else call the shots in the bedroom, yet for some reason he allowed Dylan the privilege.

Of course, he got to call the shots right back, which meant that Dylan's commands often went unanswered.

"You'll get my mouth when I decide to give it to you," Aidan replied.

To punctuate that, he continued to jack Dylan off in languid, borderline-bored strokes that soon had the other man swearing in frustration.

When he tipped his head back and saw the sheer agony reflecting in Dylan's eyes, he decided to have some mercy. Keeping their gazes locked, he leaned in and wrapped his lips around the engorged head.

"Oh Jesus," Dylan croaked. "Oh, that's good."

Good was a fucking understatement. *Good* didn't even do justice to the way Aidan felt when he was sucking this man's dick. He loved every second of the act. Loved feeling that thick cock pulsing in his mouth. Loved the way Dylan's hands tangled in his hair. The way Dylan moaned right before he came all over his tongue.

"I need it hard and fast. Let me fuck your mouth, Aid."

"Not yet," he said with a chuckle, and then he licked the salty drop pooling at the tip.

He flicked his tongue over the little slit for a few seconds, then licked his way down the length of the rock-hard shaft, eliciting a harsh curse from the man he was in the process of teasing.

Sure enough, Dylan had caught on to what Aidan was doing. "Fucking tease," the SEAL grumbled.

He rolled his eyes. "Right, like you don't do the same damn thing to me every time you suck me off."

"I don't tease. I just take my time," Dylan protested. "Can you blame me for being thorough?"

The man raised a valid point. Aidan had a great appreciation for Dylan's thoroughness in the bedroom, that was for sure.

As lust seized his groin, he ignored his painfully hard erection and refocused on the task at hand. This time he didn't torment. Didn't go slow, didn't build up to anything.

He simply took Dylan's cock into his mouth and sucked hard.

"Fuck. Fuck, just like that, man. Faster."

Aidan quickened the tempo, moving his mouth up and down, tightening the suction with each upstroke.

"Goddammit, *more*."

His soft laughter vibrated against Dylan's dick. He brought his hand into play, using his fist and his mouth to pump and suck, while the fingers of his free hand found the man's tight sac and squeezed it hard.

A sharp pain jolted through him as Dylan fisted his hair and brought his head closer, thrusting so hard and so deep Aidan suddenly had a cock prodding at the back of his throat. He relaxed his jaw and went into deep-throat mode, loving the taste and feel of this man's dick consuming his mouth. His own erection ached inside his sweatpants, pleading for relief, craving release.

"Yeah, that's it. Like that." Dylan rocked his hips, fingers tangled in Aidan's hair, tugging much harder than usual.

It was rare to see the man lose his cool like this, the hair-pulling and the desperate noises and the frantic thrust of his hips. Aidan knew today's wedding fiasco must have upset him much more than he'd let on, and so he ceded control and let Dylan fuck his mouth, giving the man what he wanted, what he needed.

"Play with my ass," Dylan moaned. "Now, Aid."

Without hesitation he dipped his finger into the saliva dripping down the shaft and pushed it into Dylan's ass. The second his finger breached the tight ring of muscle, Dylan let out a strangled cry and went still.

"Fuck. *Fuck.*"

The first jets of come spurted in the back of Aidan's throat. A tidal wave of lust, combined with a hefty dose of male satisfaction, coursed through his blood. He swallowed heartily as Dylan shuddered in climax, while his own cock throbbed with pent-up need and angrily demanded attention.

Twenty seconds and several ragged breaths later, Dylan pulled out of Aidan's mouth and fell back on his elbows. "Damn," he mumbled. "I needed that."

Aidan wiped his mouth with the back of his hand before getting to his feet. "I know you did."

A pair of green eyes suddenly focused on his crotch. "You haven't asked me to return the favor."

He shrugged. "Because this wasn't for me. It was for you. And now I'm going to stop you before that hero complex of yours kicks in and tries to rescue me from a case of blue balls, because I really think we should check on our guest."

The reminder immediately killed the mood, bringing a gloomy expression to his roommate's face. "Crap, I totally forgot she was here."

"I didn't." Aidan hesitated. "I mentioned that she's smoking hot, right?"

Dylan's jaw tensed. "Yeah, you did, but you can forget about it, man.

She won't be the filling in a Dylan-and-Aidan sandwich, so get that idea out of your head."

He masked his disappointment. Dylan's outright refusal was definitely not the response he'd been looking for. Today was the first time Aidan had met Claire McKinley, and when he'd walked into the living room and finally laid eyes on the woman Dylan had been bitching about for months, he'd been floored by how gorgeous she was. With her smooth flawless skin, rosy cheeks and enormous brown eyes, she looked like a porcelain doll. But below the neck, she was a different kind of doll. The kind you found at a sex shop, all tits and ass and endless curves.

"Aw, shit, I know that look," Dylan grumbled. "I mean it, Aid, banish the thought. Forget the fact that I don't like her, okay? She almost married my *brother* this morning. Think of how fucking incestuous that would feel if I took her to bed."

Aidan snorted. "And you having slept with Cash's girl isn't incestuous? Plus, if you think about all the other chicks you and Cash, or you and Seth, tag-teamed in the past, that's a lot of bed bunnies to have in common with other men."

"Don't care. We're not fucking her."

"We, huh?"

Dylan looked uncertain for a second. "Well, shit, *me*, I guess. You can do whatever the hell you want."

"I'd never sleep with someone unless I had your blessing," Aidan said gruffly. "That was our agreement, remember? Besides…"

He trailed off, but Dylan didn't let it slide. "Besides what?"

After a moment, he gave a little shrug, feeling embarrassed. "I prefer it when you're there. It makes the sex better, for some messed-up reason."

"I know what you mean." Dylan sounded uneasy. "Why is that? And why…" Now he was the one stalling.

"Why what?" Aidan prompted.

"Why can't we stick to the whole one-on-one thing, just you and me?"

He had no answer for that, but it was the same question that had been plaguing him for months. Although Dylan had moved in last month after his lease with Seth Masterson elapsed in mid-November, he and Aidan had been sleeping together since the beginning of September. More than three months now, yet they couldn't seem to last more than a week having sex with only each other. They both loved women too damn much, and eventually they ended up going out, meeting a beautiful, willing girl, and bringing her home.

"I don't know," he finally responded. "And I'm not sure tonight is the night to try to figure it out."

"You're probably right."

"I think Notre Dame is playing this afternoon. Wanna catch a bit of the game?" Aidan said lightly.

"Yup."

Just like that, the tension in the air dissolved like a teaspoon of sugar in water. At least on the surface. Inside, Aidan was still troubled, still thinking about all the times he and Dylan had had a warm female body nestled between them.

It was during those moments, when he was running his fingers over a woman's sweet curves and listening to her throaty moans of pleasure, that Aidan was reminded of how much he needed a woman in his life.

But…he needed Dylan too.

He just had no idea how to reconcile those two conflicting needs.

Chapter Five

Claire emerged from the bedroom later that evening and realized she was a lot tipsier than she'd thought. Like swaying-on-her-feet tipsy. AKA completely bombed.

Weird. She hadn't felt drunk when she'd been sprawled on Dylan's bed, nursing the Lagavulin bottle.

Everything was spinning as she made her way down the hall, so the first thing she did when she entered the living room was collapse in the black recliner before the floor gave way under her feet.

It wasn't until she heard someone clear his throat that she noticed Dylan and Aidan sitting together on one of the L-shaped leather couches. Both guys were staring at her. Aidan with amusement. Dylan, disapproval.

"Are you drunk?" the latter demanded.

"No," she said belligerently. Her gaze moved to the enormous flat screen, which was turned to a football game with the volume down. "Oooh, is Tom Brady playing? I wouldn't mind me some eye candy."

"Oh, for fuck's sake," Dylan grumbled. "You're totally drunk."

"I am not."

"And FYI, this is a college game," Aidan piped up. "No Brady, I'm afraid."

She pouted, but football didn't stay on her mind for long. She was suddenly far more interested in the two men on the couch. Aidan, unfortunately, had put on a shirt, but on the bright side, it was a sleeveless basketball jersey that revealed his muscular arms. Dylan had changed out of his suit and into sweats and a white wifebeater, which also showcased his arms.

"You guys have *great* arms," she declared.

Aidan grinned.

Dylan scowled. "Where did you even get the booze? Don't tell me you packed some in your suitcase."

"Actually, I did. It was a surprise for Chris. His favorite scotch so we could toast to our happiness."

Her response softened some of the hard edges in his expression. "Shit. Sorry. I guess you're entitled to get wasted after what happened today."

"Gee, Dylan, thanks so much for giving me permission. I felt so wrong drinking without your blessing. *Thank* you."

"You're welcome," he said graciously. "By the way, you can go ahead and be as sarcastic as you want. You get a free pass tonight."

"Really?" She feigned delight. "So I can verbally abuse you without repercussions?"

"Yup."

"Sweet! How wonderful!"

Aidan snickered, then reached for the remote and flicked off the television. When Dylan uttered a protest, the dark-haired man shrugged and said, "You two are way more entertaining than this football game. So please, keep going, this is a lot of fu—um, probably not a good idea to sit like that, sweetheart."

It took Claire a second to grasp that he was talking to her. She'd just drawn her legs up so she could sit cross-legged, and when she glanced down, Aidan's warning suddenly made sense. In her skimpy beach dress, and with her legs positioned the way they were, both men had a perfect view of her lacy white panties.

"Oh," she blurted out. "I forgot to change into comfy clothes." She paused in thought. "No, wait. I did take off my bra."

"I can see that." The heat that filled Aidan's dark eyes was almost hypnotic. He was staring at her chest like he wanted to devour her whole.

Her nipples instantly responded to his hungry appraisal, hardening and poking against the fabric of her dress.

He wanted her.

A thrill shot through her. Maybe the alcohol was messing with her head, but a man didn't look at a woman the way Aidan was looking at her unless he wanted her, right?

She could have sworn she heard Dylan murmur, "Don't even think about it", but she was too busy maintaining the heated eye contact with

Dylan's roommate, whose mouth now donned a tiny smirk.

"So let's get to it," Aidan told her.

A jolt of desire streaked through her, and she felt her already flushed face turning redder. Was he suggesting what she thought he was suggesting?

"I want to hear you abuse Dylan for a while," he clarified.

The disappointment that flooded her belly was laughable. Okay, she really *was* drunk. Of course Aidan wasn't propositioning her, a woman he'd met mere hours ago. And she was probably misinterpreting his lustful expression too.

"Or we can feed the lady," Dylan spoke up, his tone wry. "Because I'm pretty sure she just downed a shit-ton of liquor on an empty stomach."

"I did," Claire confirmed with a broad smile.

To her surprise, Dylan actually laughed. "Not something to be proud of, honey. Trust me, you'll regret it in the morning." He sighed. "I'll fix you up something small. Maybe a sandwich?"

When he started to get up, she waved for him to stay put. "I'll eat in a bit, and don't worry, I'll feed myself. I feel bad making you wait on me."

"Like I said, you've got a free pass. My brother was a total dick to you today."

Stretching her legs out, Claire stared at her red-polished toes and wiggled them around. "Hey," she said absently, "I'm not seeing double anymore. I have ten toes again."

She shifted her head and met Dylan's eyes. He had the most gorgeous eyes, she decided. They were the palest shade of green she'd ever seen, so vivid they looked photoshopped. Chris's eyes were also green, but darker, and definitely not as pretty.

"You think your brother was right to end it, don't you?" she said slowly. "You don't think it would have worked out between us."

Dylan went quiet for a moment. "Yes," he finally replied. "I don't think it would've worked."

"You might be right about that." She paused. "My friend Natasha said the same thing. She thinks that deep down I knew it too."

"Did you?" he asked roughly.

She hesitated again. "Maybe. I don't know. I mean, I'm upset, but... not as upset as I thought I'd be."

Before he could question the response, she staggered to her feet. "I think I want that sandwich now."

"Poor girl," Aidan murmured as they watched Claire's face disappear behind the refrigerator door. "I still can't believe Chris recruited you to cancel his wedding."

Dylan frowned. "It definitely wasn't his finest moment."

"It was a dick move."

There was no arguing that. Hell, even Dylan's mother agreed that Chris had done a horrible thing today. When Dylan called her earlier to apologize, Shanna had still been mortified by her eldest son's behavior, but fortunately she hadn't been angry at her youngest for taking off too. She insisted Dylan had done the right thing by getting Claire out of town—apparently everyone they knew was whispering about the wedding and stirring up a gossip storm of massive proportions.

A loud thump sounded from the kitchen, followed by a cheerful yell from Claire. "No worries! Just dropped the mayo. It's plastic so it didn't break!"

The glum tone she'd used only moments ago was gone, the delight in her voice unmistakable.

Dylan tried very hard not to grin. He had to admit, drunk Claire was a lot more fun than sober Claire.

Next to him, Aidan didn't bother hiding *his* grin, which ignited the cycle of irritation all over again.

Aidan was attracted to Claire.

Dylan could see it plain as day, and he didn't like it one damn bit. It had nothing to do with jealousy—he and Aidan brought women home all the time. Watching his roommate fuck someone else wasn't anything new or scandalous.

No, it was Aidan's attraction to *this* woman that bugged him. He didn't want Claire fooling Aidan the way she'd fooled Chris, making him believe she was someone sweet and wonderful, when in reality she was a materialistic snob who liked to belittle women who weren't as career-oriented as she was.

Chillax, buddy.

Realizing his chest had tightened with resentment, he inhaled deeply in an attempt to calm himself, then glanced over at his roommate.

Okay, enough with the roommate bullshit, he told himself.

His lover.

Aidan Rhodes was his *lover*.

The memory of Aidan's lips stretched wide around his cock sent a bolt of lust straight to Dylan's groin. Christ, he'd really needed that. He'd left for San Francisco yesterday morning and was back in San Diego less than forty-eight hours later, but he felt like he'd been gone for months. Sitting through that rehearsal dinner last night, getting all gussied up this morning, informing the bride her groom was gone…shit like that took its toll on a man.

Needless to say, he was happy to be home, and to him, home was San Diego. He may have been born and raised in Marin County, but he'd always felt so out of place there. The people in his neighborhood were uber-conservative, the kids from his high school preppy as hell, and that kind of stifling, judgmental environment was definitely not ideal for a guy who loved cock as much as he loved pussy.

"Aw, he's still mad at me."

Claire's voice jerked Dylan out of a train of thought that'd been going nowhere fast.

"I'm not mad," he muttered. "I'm mostly annoyed, and kinda tired. It's been a long day."

"No kidding." She plopped down in the recliner and balanced her plate on her thighs, then picked up her sandwich and took a big bite.

His gaze instantly gravitated to her mouth, rosy red and shaped like a cupid's bow. Each time he looked at her pouty lips, he imagined them wrapped around a dick. Those were definitely blowjob lips, all right.

As usual, Dylan found himself checking out the rest of her, and as usual, his cock liked the view. Claire McKinley was so fucking hot it was actually kind of infuriating. She'd removed all the little white flowers from her hair and now those reddish-brown waves cascaded over one shoulder, glinting like burnished copper in the light spilling down from the ceiling fixture. And that dress. Christ, couldn't she put something else on? The material was so thin he could see every curve and indentation of her body, and her braless state pretty much ensured that he and Aidan wouldn't be tearing their gazes from her puckered nipples anytime soon.

With her smoking-hot body and the alcohol-induced blush on her cheeks, she made such a tempting picture that Dylan's mouth actually watered. He hastily had to remind himself of all the reasons why he shouldn't be thinking about screwing her.

One—she was his brother's ex-fiancée.

Two—he didn't like her.

Three…okay, well, he couldn't think of a third off the top of his head, but the first two reasons were more than enough.

"I'm tired too," Claire said between mouthfuls. "But at least I have the next three weeks off. I can't remember the last time I had *one* week off, let alone three."

The sofa cushions dipped as Aidan leaned forward to grab his Coke can from the glass coffee table. He took a sip, watching Claire in curiosity. "What is it you do for a living?"

She chewed and swallowed before answering, and Dylan suddenly noticed the kind of sandwich she'd prepared. "No jam?" he asked warily.

"Nope. I don't like jam."

"Neither do I."

They looked at each other for a few seconds, neither one speaking. Then Claire turned to address Aidan. "Anyway, I work at a consulting firm."

"Cool. What does that mean exactly? What do you do there?"

A huge grin filled her face. "Consult."

She looked so proud with her answer Dylan couldn't help but laugh. So did Aidan, who said, "Care to elaborate?"

She shoved the last piece of bread into her mouth, then set her plate on the table and got comfortable again. "My firm helps organizations operate more efficiently, in terms of overhead or management or certain protocols. Basically I visit a company and conduct an analysis of their internal workings, and then I tell them how they can do better."

"Sounds interesting." Aidan looked impressed.

"Sometimes it is. But sometimes it's boring."

Aidan laughed and glanced over at Dylan. "Hey, look at that, you two have another thing in common."

"Yeah, what's that?" he asked suspiciously.

"You're both capable of holding serious, articulate conversations even when you're drunk as skunks."

"Hey," Claire protested, "I'm not drunk as skunks. I mean, as *a* skunk." Her dainty eyebrows knitted together. "Do skunks get drunk? Why is that even a phrase?"

"Because it rhymes?" Aidan suggested.

She pursed her lips in thought. "Yes, that makes sense."

Another burst of involuntary laughter flew out of Dylan's mouth.

Shit. He really shouldn't be getting any enjoyment out of this conversation. He wasn't supposed to like this woman, damn it.

Deciding he needed a reminder about who he was dealing with, he looked at Claire and said, "So why did you get into consulting? I bet it was for the money, right?"

"Nope. I got into it because I like ordering people around. Can you believe it? I found the one job that pays me to be a know-it-all." With another beaming smile, she hopped off the chair like an energetic little kid. "I'm thirsty."

Aidan chuckled as she darted toward the kitchen. When Dylan saw the familiar glint in the other man's eyes, he stifled a groan and issued another low warning. "Come on, man, not her. This morning she nearly became my sister-in-law." He checked to make sure Claire was out of earshot, then added, "And I don't like her."

"Too bad," Aidan murmured. "'Cause I like her a lot, bro."

Their hushed conversation died when Claire strode back into the room with a tall glass of water. She sat, took a tiny ladylike sip, and watched them both with a thoughtful expression, for so long that Dylan shifted in discomfort.

"Stop staring," he grumbled. "It's rude."

"But I just can't figure it out," she complained.

"Figure what out?"

"Are you two gay or what?"

The question came out of left field, but it didn't raise his guard or provoke any indignation. If anything, he was surprised she hadn't voiced it sooner, especially after the scene she'd witnessed a couple of months ago.

On the other end of the couch, Aidan was laughing again. "I don't know. Hey, Dylan, are we gay?"

For a moment he was too distracted by that husky laughter to respond. Aidan had laughed more today in Claire's presence than in the entire month Dylan had been living with him. Not that the guy was Grumpy McGrumps or anything, but the one thing Dylan had learned since moving in? Aidan Rhodes was intense. And haunted. Something was definitely haunting him, but Dylan had yet to decipher the shadows he often glimpsed in those chocolate-brown eyes.

He knew Aidan was hiding a lot of pain behind his seductive, laid-back exterior, but getting the man to talk about his emotions was like trying to train a goldfish—futile and exasperating.

"Are you making fun of me?" Claire sounded hurt as she looked from one man to the other.

Aidan grinned. "Nah, just teasing."

"You still haven't answered the question." Her big eyes focused on Dylan. "Are you gay?"

He shook his head.

"Bisexual?"

"Yeah, I guess," he answered with a shrug.

She glanced at Aidan. "Are you bi, too?"

"Yup," he confirmed.

"Huh." Propping her elbow on the arm of the recliner, she rested her chin in her palm and continued to study them. "Okay, so you both like women."

Dylan rolled his eyes. "Yes."

"But you also like men." She chewed on her bottom lip. "And you have sex with each other."

All right, *now* he was starting to feel rattled. The way Claire was staring made him feel like a specimen under a microscope.

"Where are you going with this?" he said irritably.

"I don't know. I just have so many questions and they keep popping out of my mouth." She straightened up and clasped both hands in her lap. "Which one of you is the bottom?"

He choked on the breath he'd just drawn into his lungs, then burst into a fit of coughing. Next to him, Aidan barked out another laugh.

When the coughs subsided, Dylan cast a frazzled look at the curious redhead. "Neither of us is the bottom," he sputtered.

"So you're both the top?"

"We switch off," Aidan said helpfully.

Dylan turned to glare at his buddy. "Don't encourage her."

"Why not? This is highly entertaining."

Claire hurled out another question before he could inform Aidan that his definition of *entertainment* was all sorts of fucked up.

"So if you had to choose, which would it be, men or women?"

"It's not that simple," Aidan said in a gruff voice.

"Sure it is. Just pick one, desert-island style. You can only bring one person with you, and that's the only person you can sleep with for the rest of your life. 'Kay, you ready? On the count of three, pick a person. One. Two. Th—"

"I think it's time for you to go to bed," Dylan interrupted, bolting to his feet.

"But it's still early!" Her gaze moved to the red numerals on the Blu-ray player. "It's, um…" She squinted. "Well, it's blurry, but I think that says eight o'clock."

"Well, like you said, you're very tired."

As he reached for Claire's hand and hauled her to her feet, he sensed Aidan's dark eyes watching in disapproval. Fine, so maybe he was trying to get rid of her, but he refused to spend the rest of the night being interrogated about his sexual preferences. He'd performed his good-guy duty today by whisking her out of the country club, and that was as far as he was willing to go.

To his surprise, Claire didn't launch any protests as he practically dragged her to the corridor on the other side of the apartment. She just kept chatting away—about the same topic he'd been trying to squash.

"Chris told me you're kind of a slut. He said you sleep with a ton of women. So I'm guessing if you had to choose, you'd pick the va-jay-jay over the cock."

Dylan burst out laughing again, and regretted it instantly.

Goddammit. He *really* needed to stop doing that.

"How is it you can say the word *cock*, but you use a euphemism for pussy?" he said with a sigh.

Her cheeks turned bright crimson. "I don't know. I just don't say that word." Her tone grew haughty. "I grew up in a strict household where you weren't allowed to talk about sex or be crude. So sue me. Anyway, what was I saying?"

"Nothing. You were saying nothing."

"Oh, right, how I think you'd choose women." She paused. "Actually, no, I changed my mind. Maybe you'd pick men. You live with a man, so…"

Ten more steps and they'd reach his bedroom. Just ten more steps.

Sadly, they were a measly three steps in when Claire decided to come to a full stop in the middle of the hall.

"What now?" he demanded.

She was staring at him again, except now there was an indecipherable gleam in her eyes that gave him a really bad feeling.

"Unless you were lying to Chris," she said slowly.

She was clearly vocalizing a conversation she'd been having in her own head, because Dylan had no fucking idea what she was talking about.

Her expression turned shrewd. "Did you make up the whole manwhore reputation so Chris wouldn't know you were really into dudes?"

Aggravation clamped around his throat, making it difficult to get out his next words. "No, I did not make anything up. I'm sorry to inform you, but I really *am* a manwhore. I've slept with a lot of women, okay? So now let's get you nice and settled in your room, and I can go back to enjoying the football ga—"

He didn't get to finish that sentence, because the next thing he knew, Claire was grabbing him by the front of his wifebeater and forcing his head down for a kiss.

Jesus Christ, she was kissing him.

And not a peck, either. This was a *kiss*. A hot, deep kiss with a helluva lot of tongue. And the second her mouth latched onto his, the manwhore they'd just been speaking of flew onto the scene like a bull bursting out of a chute.

He immediately took control of the kiss, hands sliding down to cup the firmest ass he'd ever had the pleasure of squeezing, mouth devouring hers like a man starved. Didn't matter that he'd had an explosive orgasm a few hours ago—his dick was rock-hard and raring to go again, and it wasted no time in rubbing up against Claire's pelvis and showing her exactly how much he loved women.

She whimpered, clung to the back of his neck. Her mouth tasted like peanut butter and alcohol, and her hair smelled like lavender, the sweet scent teasing his senses.

Dylan knew he had to stop this stupidity, yet he couldn't seem to wrench his mouth away. Claire's lips were so soft, so warm. Her tongue eagerly explored his mouth, eliciting shockwaves of desire in his body. When she hooked one leg around his hip and he felt the heat of her pussy against his thigh, he groaned with pleasure and started backing her into the wall behind her.

Their mouths were still locked, tongues tangling, and his hands moved from her ass to her waist, sliding down the sexy curve of her hips toward the hem of her dress, which he bunched between his fingers.

He was two seconds from ripping the dress right off her when a gust of reality swooped in and he suddenly realized what he was doing.

And who he was doing it with.

Stumbling back, he muttered a curse and tried to ignore the frenzied beating of his heart. He was still as hard as a concrete block, so hard he was surprised the heaviness of his cock didn't tip him right over.

Claire looked as turned on as he felt. Porcelain cheeks sporting a pink blush, lips moist and swollen from the kiss, tits heaving as she caught her breath.

"What the fuck?" he said with a scowl. "Why did you do that?"

She looked flustered. "I...I wanted to see if you were seriously into women."

"Are you fucking kidding me?"

"I was curious," she said defensively.

Dylan set his jaw and took a step toward her. "Has your curiosity been sated?" He lowered his hand to the painful bulge in his sweatpants and cupped his aching dick. "Is this a clear enough answer for you, Claire?"

A pair of wide brown eyes dipped to his crotch, flickering with heat that made his cock twitch. As she nodded in response, he could see her pulse hammering in the center of her throat.

Silence descended, broken only by the occasional muffled voices coming from the television in the living room. Aidan was still watching the game, Dylan noted. Thank fucking God. He would've had a tough time explaining all this if he'd turned around and found Aidan standing there, especially after he'd ordered the other man to keep his hands off Claire.

"Any other experiment you want to try out on me?" he asked, unable to keep the sarcasm out of his tone.

"Um, no. I think I'm good." Uncertainty washed over her face. "Why did you…why did you kiss me back?"

Million-dollar question right there. He was supposed to hate this woman, not lust over her.

Then again, who said one had anything to do with the other?

"Because I'm a guy," he finally said. "When a woman sticks her tongue in my mouth, I react on instinct."

"Oh. Okay. Right." She tucked a few strands of dark-red hair behind her ear, then proceeded to spit out a string of rapid sentences that were nearly impossible to keep up with. "Anyway, you were right and I'm crazy exhausted so I'm gonna turn in now but thanks again for everything you did today and I'm sorry for what I did just now but I'm sure I won't remember it in the morning so do me a favor and don't remind me of it, okay?"

His head was spinning so fast he felt like he'd just gotten off a Tilt-A-Whirl. "I…yeah, sure, okay. G'night, Claire."

"'Night, Dylan."

She dashed off and disappeared into the bedroom, leaving him alone to run both hands through his hair in frustration.

There were many women he had no business making out with. Close relatives, of course. His buddies' wives, no duh. That Black Widow broad who'd axe-murdered all her husbands, nope, not touching that one. Last but not least, Claire McKinley. Yup, his brother's ex-fiancée-as-of-*this-morning* was definitely not someone he should be locking lips with.

Disgusted and annoyed at his lack of willpower, he ordered his erection to retreat, then stalked back to the living room so he could spend the evening with the person he *wanted* to be making out with.

Chapter Six

"Show of hands—who thinks Dylan's brother is a grade-A douchebag?" Seth Masterson promptly raised his own hand, and was joined by Cash McCoy, Jackson Ramsey and Ryan Evans, who all wore identical looks of disapproval.

"See, it's settled," Seth announced before taking a deep drag of his cigarette.

No sooner did he exhale a cloud of smoke into the late-morning air than a pretty blonde burst onto the patio like a tornado.

"Uh-uh, no way," Shelby Garrett said in a stern voice. "No smoking!"

Dylan grinned as Seth's gray eyes flashed with indignation. Their resident badass had been warned several times to not even *think* about lighting up in Shelby's place of business *or else*, and the woman clearly hadn't been bluffing—she swiped the cigarette out of Seth's fingers and proceeded to drop it directly into his coffee mug.

"Aw, that's cruel, Shel," Seth grumbled. "Now what am I going to drink?"

"Oh, is there something wrong with your coffee?" she asked sweetly. "Go ahead and drink it right along with that nasty butt, seeing as you were determined to put those toxins in your body anyway."

As the other men laughed, Shelby settled in the chair next to Ryan's and glanced at Dylan. "Okay, finish your story. I just had to show my new part-timer how to handle a cake order."

For the tenth time that morning, Dylan had to wonder what Shelby was even doing here. Not that he was complaining or anything. The wife of a former SEAL, Shelby was not only gorgeous, but so easy to talk to, and she was a California girl to the core. The moment she'd learned that the guys were incorporating surfing into their Sunday workout, she'd invited herself along and had been joining them bright and early on the beach every week.

Not much surfing to be done today, though. The water had been too calm, not a decent wave in sight, so eventually Shelby went for a walk while the men finished their workout, and then the six of them had headed over to the Coronado bakery/café Shelby owned.

Dylan had been in the process of telling everyone about yesterday's wedding fiasco, and now he quickly wrapped up the tale. Omitting, of course, the unexpected kiss Claire had planted on him—that was one can of worms he had zero intention of opening.

"So she's staying with you and Aidan now?" Shelby raised her coffee to her lips, her blue eyes watching him over the rim of her mug.

"Yeah, for a few days."

"That was cool of you, rescuing her like that," Cash told him. The dark-haired SEAL reached for the plate of banana muffins Shelby had brought out, grabbed one, and proceeded to shove the whole thing into his mouth.

"Such manners," Jackson remarked in that southern drawl of his. "Jen must be so proud of you."

"Trust me, Jen has no complaints about the way I eat." Cash's blue eyes twinkled. "Food, of course. The way I eat *food*."

"What I want to know," Seth said, "is whether you and Aidan have— cover your ears, Shelby—fucked her yet."

The blonde rolled her eyes. "God, you are such a sleaze."

Seth blinked innocently. "Hey, I was just voicing what everyone else was thinking."

"Uh, I wasn't thinking that at all," Ryan spoke up.

"Me neither," Cash said.

"Didn't even cross my mind," Jackson confessed.

"Oh, come on, you totally were. I mean, you all met her when she came to visit, right? She's a stone-cold fox."

"Claire and my brother were just here for a night," Dylan reminded his former roommate. "You were the only one who met her."

"Ah, right. Well, shit, you guys missed out." Seth offered the other men his trademark scoundrel smirk. "She's sexy as hell—great tits, curves in all the right places. Oh, and she's a redhead. Every redhead I've ever—cover your ears, Shelby—fucked has been phenomenal in bed."

This time the eye-roll came from Ryan. "Dude, do you kiss your wife with that mouth?"

"Yup, and she *loves* it."

Dylan didn't doubt that. Miranda Breslin—well, Masterson now—seemed to have no problem with her new husband's rough edges.

It was still hard to believe Seth was married. Much to everyone's surprise, he and Miranda had eloped to Vegas last month, and Seth had recently confided in Dylan that he was going through the process to adopt Miranda's six-year-old twins. After a shaky start with Miranda and a tenuous relationship with her kids, Seth now worshipped the ground all three of them walked on.

Seeing his buddy so happy never failed to bring a rush of longing to Dylan's heart. In fact, as he looked around the table, he realized that he and Jackson were the only single ones there. Shelby was happily married and raising a three-year-old daughter. Seth and Miranda had tied the knot and were doing the whole family thing too. Ryan and his girlfriend, Annabelle, had recently gotten engaged, Cash and Jen would surely follow suit.

And then there was Dylan. Living with Aidan, yet he hadn't told any of his buddies about the sexual part of that arrangement. The only person who knew was Jen Scott, Cash's girlfriend and Dylan's closest female friend. He'd asked Jen not to say anything to Cash, but it wasn't shame or fear that was stopping him from telling other people. Like he'd told Aidan, he had no clue how to classify what they had, and until he could make sense of it himself, he didn't want to deal with all the questions he knew he'd receive.

"Anyway, speaking of Miranda," Seth was saying, "she wanted to know if you're all planning on coming to our place for Christmas Eve dinner. My mom's flying in from Vegas on the twenty-fifth, so we're doing Christmas Day with her."

"Annabelle and I will be in San Francisco that week," Ryan said. "Seven whole days with the snooty Holmes clan. Can't fucking wait."

Shelby glanced over in sympathy. "They still haven't warmed up to you? Even after, what? Three years?"

"Nah, they've gotten a lot better. Her dad has stopped trying to bribe me into dumping her, so that's progress. And I think he was secretly happy and impressed when I flew up there to ask for his blessing to marry her."

"And he gave it to you," Shelby pointed out, "so I guess that *is* progress."

On the other side of the table, Seth reached over the muffin plate and nonchalantly stole Dylan's coffee from right under his nose.

Scratch that—not nonchalantly at all.

"Seriously?" Dylan said. "You're that lazy? Stealing my coffee instead of walking ten feet to the counter and getting a fresh cup?"

"*That* lazy," Seth confirmed. "Anyway. So Ryan's out. Texas?"

Jackson nodded. "I'll be there."

"John and I won't," Shelby chimed in, sounding apologetic. "We'll be at my parents' place that night, and his family's the next night."

"McCoy? You and the Scotts?"

"Yeah, we're all coming," Cash answered.

"So that leaves the D-Man. You coming or what, bro? Oh, and Miranda says Aidan's welcome too."

Dylan raised his eyebrows. "The D-Man?"

"New nickname I'm trying out." Seth paused. "Is it not working?"

"No," everyone answered in unison.

"Fine. I'll think of something else."

Dylan snorted. "Please don't. You're terrible at giving people nicknames."

"Fuck you. I rock at it," Seth retorted. "Who gave Texas *his* nickname, huh?"

"Yeah, because it's *so* original," Cash said with a laugh. "Calling a man from Texas *Texas*. Pure gold, man."

"Ugh, you guys all have major ADD," Shelby declared. "I want to know more about Dylan's brother fleeing the country on his wedding day."

"That's pretty much the grand summation of it," he said wryly. "Chris left without a word and is now lying on a beach in Aruba."

"Douchebag," Seth muttered.

Shelby's blue eyes shone with compassion. "How is Claire handling it?"

"Well, she got rip-roaring drunk last night, so…" Dylan let the others reach their own conclusions.

"And you and Aidan didn't take advantage of that and—cover your ears, Shelby—double-team her? Prudes." Seth shook his head in mock disgust.

"Why do you bother telling me to cover my ears?" Shelby demanded.

"You don't even give me time to do it! And besides, since when do you care about offending my delicate sensibilities?"

"I live with kids now," the scruffy-haired SEAL replied. "I'm pretty sure I ask Sophie and Jason to cover their ears at least twenty times a day."

Everyone snickered, including Shelby, but the blonde didn't waste any time in steering the conversation back to what she perceived as juicy gossip.

"Is double-teaming actually something you're considering?" she asked Dylan. Then she gasped. "Have you secretly been lusting over your brother's girl this whole time and now you're finally going to make your move?"

He flashed her a dark look. "No, I have not been lusting over her."

The disappointment on her face made all the men laugh.

"Motherhood and wifehood have gotten boring, huh?" Cash teased. "Is that why you're trying to turn the D-Man's life into a soap opera?"

Seth cursed. "You're right. The name doesn't work. Stop using it to spite me."

"I'm not bored at all," Shelby said. "But you've got to admit, the whole situation is very soap-opera-esque."

Dylan rolled his eyes. "Yeah, only if I had a thing for Claire. Which I don't."

"Fine," she said glumly. "Maybe she and Aidan will hook up then. The poor woman got dumped on her wedding day. She deserves some sexytimes with a sexy guy, and Aidan totally fits that bill."

Yep, Aidan certainly had *sexy guy* down to a T. But Shelby's suggestion only succeeded in making Dylan feel edgy as hell. Didn't escape him that Aidan was back at the condo with Claire at this very moment, just the two of them, alone together…

Swallowing a sigh, he claimed the last banana muffin and said a silent prayer that his lover would remember to keep his dick in his pants.

SON OF A BITCH. SHE'D KISSED DYLAN LAST NIGHT.

Claire couldn't erase the memory from her mind, no matter how hard she tried. It was the last thing she'd thought of before falling asleep last night, and the first thing she'd thought of when she'd opened her eyes this morning. And each time the image of Dylan's heavy-lidded green eyes and sexy mouth popped into her head, she was overcome with equal doses of lust and shame.

It had been a good kiss.

Oh, who was she kidding? It had been the hottest kiss of her entire life. Which didn't make any sense, because she didn't even like the guy! Not only that, but he was Chris's brother. Chris, the man she'd almost married. What kind of woman made out with her ex-fiancé's brother?

"You slept late."

She jumped as the husky male voice sounded from the other side of the kitchen. Her water glass nearly fell from her grip. She managed to hold on to it, then turned to give Aidan a tentative smile.

"*Too* late," she answered. "I crashed at eight and woke up at noon. That's a good sixteen hours of my life I'll never get back."

He chuckled. "You needed it. Yesterday was stressful for you."

"Can't argue with that."

The kitchen offered an eat-in counter, so Claire slid onto one of the tall stools and watched Aidan rummage around in the enormous double-door fridge.

"You want something to eat?" he asked without turning around.

As if on cue, her belly grumbled, but she didn't quite trust that part of her anatomy at the moment. Even though she hadn't woken up with a hangover or an upset stomach, she'd consumed nearly half a scotch bottle last night, and she knew from past experience her stomach was going to be sensitive.

"Depends what," she told him. "It's gotta be something light that I can keep down."

He tossed her a sympathetic look over one broad shoulder. "You feeling queasy?"

"No, but I don't want to push my luck."

"Good plan. Okay, well, I'm all about the bacon and eggs after a night of drinking, but maybe you should stick to some toast?"

"Aw, but bacon and eggs sounds so yummy," she said in a glum voice.

He flashed a dimpled grin, and her heart promptly did a happy flip. Gosh, this man was so freaking adorable. Not to mention so incredibly sexy. How was that combination even possible?

Aidan's dark eyes narrowed. "What's the secretive little smile all about?"

"I was trying to figure out if it's possible for a man to be sexy and adorable at the same time."

He let out a surprised laugh. "Ah, okay." His grin widened. "Do you always blurt out whatever's on your mind like that?"

"Usually." She took another sip of water. "I try not to be so forthcoming at work, but in general I'm pretty opinionated and not afraid to be honest."

"Honesty's a great quality to have."

"I'm glad you think so. But not everyone appreciates it."

As he started pulling ingredients out of the fridge and setting them on the counter, Claire got up and tried to help, but he led her back to the stool and forced her to sit.

"You're the guest, and I'm cooking you breakfast. Deal with it." His commanding tone brooked no argument, and for some reason it turned her on like crazy.

"Yes, sir," she said with a little salute.

"So, did we decide whether you're having toast or taking a risk?" Aidan flipped open a carton of eggs.

Claire sighed. "I'm taking the risk. I'm a sucker for bacon."

"Good call. And look, if you end up puking it all up, I'm willing to be a gentleman and hold your hair back."

"Aw, thanks, that's so sweet."

Laughing, she rested her elbows on the smooth black granite and admired the ease with which he moved around the kitchen. He got the bacon going, then leaned against the opposite counter and whisked the eggs in a glass bowl, all the while watching her with curious eyes.

"What's the final answer then?" Aidan slanted his head. "Can men be simultaneously sexy and adorable?"

She replied with no hesitation. "Yes. They totally can."

A heated look passed between them, identical to the one they'd shared yesterday within seconds of meeting. And unlike yesterday's Dylan-provoked desire, her attraction to *this* man made sense.

Actually…nope, still didn't make sense, seeing as she was attracted to Aidan in a confusing, primitive way she'd never experienced. Everything about him teased her senses—his rumpled dark hair, the perfect chest beneath his faded Chicago Bears T-shirt, those dimples. And he smelled so darn good; his lemony-scented aftershave mingled with the aroma of sizzling bacon in the air, and she honestly couldn't decide which scent was more intoxicating.

Last night she'd been convinced this man wanted her. This afternoon was no different. Her striped off-the-shoulder tee and black yoga pants were by no means indecent, yet Aidan's gaze was so seductive, so intense and appreciative, she felt like she was buck-naked.

A crackling sound interrupted the moment of awareness. When Aidan turned to tend to the bacon, she took a deep breath and ordered herself to stop drooling over the guy.

"So who didn't appreciate your honesty?" he asked curiously.

"Chris, for one. He hated how blunt I was, especially if I said something he didn't want to hear."

"Like what?" Aidan lowered the heat on the burner and moved on to the task of scrambling the eggs, but he glanced over his shoulder every few seconds, encouraging her to go on.

"Well, I wasn't exactly shy about voicing my opinion when it came to his country-club friends. Those people are such jerks—you should have seen the way one of the partners' wives treated our waiter one time. And the racism in that club was unbelievable. It made me sick, but Chris didn't seem to give a shit. He just shrugged and said that deep down everyone's a little racist. Can you believe that?"

"Chris doesn't sound like the nicest guy."

Sadness washed over her. "I thought he was. I thought he was amazing, actually. When we first met, he was so passionate about the law and making a difference. He was excited to work in the prosecutor's office and clean up the streets and all that jazz. But instead, he took the job that Lowenstein offered, and suddenly his whole personality changed." She bit her lip in dismay. "He got all prissy and pretentious, and started acting, I don't know, *entitled*, I guess."

"From what Dylan has told me, Chris was always a bit on the conservative side, and I'm pretty sure Dylan mentioned that Chris intended to work for a big defense firm from the start."

Claire frowned. "Yeah, I don't know how much I really trust Dylan's word."

"You should," Aidan said frankly. "He's probably the most honest man I've ever met. And the most honorable."

"Honorable?" Bitterness rose in her throat. "I haven't seen any indication of that, and trust me, he's had many opportunities to prove me wrong."

"What exactly has Dylan done to give you such a skewed view of him?" Aidan's tone was more curious than angry.

"Maybe *your* view is the skewed one."

"Trust me," he mimicked, "I know everything there is to know about Dylan Wade. The guy's got a heart of gold. It's fucking exasperating at times."

She opened her mouth to argue that clearly Dylan's fabled heart of gold didn't extend to his mother, then thought better of it. She wasn't prone to gossiping, and she knew Shanna would be humiliated if she found out Claire was blabbing about her private business with a stranger. Besides, nothing she said would change Aidan's mind about the man he obviously cared very deeply about.

The man Claire had practically sexually assaulted last night…

Crap. Did Aidan know about the kiss? It suddenly occurred to her that he might, and her cheeks grew hot.

"Is there a reason your face just turned redder than a fire engine?" he teased.

Argh. Her stupid redhead skin made it impossible to hide a blush. "I was just wondering if…uh, did Dylan tell you what happened last night?"

"Hmmm, no? Why don't you fill me in?"

Aidan walked to the counter and set a plate in front of her. The aroma of bacon and eggs floated into her nose, and when her stomach didn't churn with sickness, she realized she'd miraculously managed to avoid a hangover.

She accepted the fork he handed her and speared into some eggs, avoiding his eyes. "It wasn't a big deal. I just kissed him."

He didn't answer.

In fact, he stayed quiet for so long that Claire had no choice but to lift her head so she could study his expression. What she saw wasn't betrayal or outrage, but genuine interest.

Aidan dragged one of the stools around the counter so they were sitting across from each other. "Yeah… he failed to mention that to me."

She sighed. "Don't be mad at him. I'm sure he was just too horrified and disgusted to want to talk about it."

Popping a strip of bacon into his mouth, Aidan chewed for a few seconds, then said, "I didn't get us any drinks. You want OJ, water or coffee?"

"Coffee." Confused by his unfazed reaction, she watched him make his way over to the coffeemaker. "So, wait, you're not mad? You don't care that your boyfriend kissed someone else?"

"Boyfriend probably isn't the right word," Aidan admitted as he returned to the counter with two cups of coffee. "We're…friends."

"With benefits," she pointed out. "I mean, you sleep together."

"Yeah." He shot her that dimpled grin of his. "We don't share a room, though. That son of a bitch is a major blanket hog."

His words instantly produced the image of the two men sleeping in the same bed, which succeeded in getting her all hot and achy. They must have tried that particular sleeping arrangement at least once in order for Aidan to know that Dylan stole the blanket, and her pulse sped up at the thought of their tanned, muscular bodies entwined together between the sheets.

"You're doing it again."

"Doing what?"

"Blushing."

"You seem to have that effect on me, I guess." Casting her gaze downward, she focused on eating her breakfast. Well, brunch, seeing as it was past noon.

"So how was it? Did you like kissing him?"

His mocking inquiry sent a shiver rolling through her. "It was okay," she lied.

He responded with a deep laugh. "Bullshit. Dylan's a damn good kisser. I bet you were turned on like nobody's business."

The memory of Dylan's rock-hard erection grinding against her flashed through Claire's head. Her core clenched. Nipples tingled, hardened and poked into her sports bra. Ah crap. Why had she chosen to wear a cotton sports bra? There was no way Aidan would be able to miss the outline of her nipples through her shirt.

From the way his gaze burned with desire, she knew he'd noticed, all right.

"I was drunk," she said. "Everything feels good when you're drunk. But believe me when I say it won't happen again."

"I'm still not sure why it happened in the first place."

"I, uh, wanted to see if you guys are really attracted to women."

There was a beat. Then he burst out laughing. "You needed empirical evidence, huh? Couldn't just take our word for it."

"Like I said, I don't think much of Dylan's word."

They both fell silent as they finished their food, but it was a comfortable silence, free of tension and long enough for Claire's embarrassment to slowly fade away. Aidan didn't seem to care that she'd kissed Dylan, so maybe she didn't need to make a big deal about it, either. So what if she'd made out with Chris's brother? It had been a drunken, foolish error in judgment, never to be repeated.

Across from her, Aidan raised his cup to his lips and sipped his coffee, drawing her gaze to his mouth. God, he had such a sensual mouth, so very sexy, but there were no laugh lines around it. It was odd—she got the feeling he didn't laugh very often, and yet the sound of his laughter had already echoed in the kitchen several times today.

"I need to ask you a question," he said suddenly.

She wrinkled her forehead. "Um, shoot?"

"How do you feel about football?"

The random query sparked a laugh. "I love it," she confessed. "Football is about all my dad and I have in common. When I was growing up, we would watch the games together every Sunday. My mom would bake cookies for us and stay out of our way." She smiled at him. "Is that the right answer?"

His answering smile caused those cute dimples to pop out. "Definitely the right answer. But tell me this, who do you root for?"

"The Niners. Duh."

His expression turned grave. "Uh-oh. Now *that* was the wrong answer. There's only one team worth rooting for, and that's the Bears."

"No self-respecting San Franciscan would cheer for any team other than the Niners, and *especially* not an east-coast team. Jeez, Aidan."

"You know, Dylan is a Niners fan too," he told her, arching his eyebrows. "So maybe you two have more in common than you think."

"I doubt it."

"So stubborn, aren't you, sweetheart? Must be a redhead trait." Still grinning, he slid off the stool and picked up his empty plate. "Hurry up and finish your breakfast. We've got games to watch. And believe me when I say I'm going to thoroughly enjoy watching your team get their asses kicked."

Chapter Seven

Dylan did an honest-to-God double take when he walked into the living room later that afternoon. Followed by a triple take, because the last thing he expected to find was Aidan and Claire on the couch watching football together.

Almost instantly, a strand of irritation wrapped around his spine. "Hey," he said curtly. A glance at the flat screen only added to his bad mood—San Fran was losing 17-3.

Aidan nodded hello. "How were the waves?"

"Nonexistent." He marched over and dropped a green Tupperware container on the glass coffee table, right in front of Claire. "Here, this is for you."

She looked confused. "What is it?"

"Cupcakes. Our buddy's wife, Shelby, owns a bakery in Coronado, and she insisted I bring something back for you."

"For me?" Claire's confusion deepened. "Why?"

"Call it a getting-dumped-at-the-altar present." His tone was harsher than he'd intended, but he wasn't in the mood to apologize.

He'd been looking forward to coming home and shooting the shit with Aidan, not spending time with his brother's ex. But it was clear that Claire wasn't going anywhere. She was curled up on the couch with her knees tucked up, and either he was imagining it, or her socked feet were pressed up against the side of Aidan's thigh.

Nope, not imagining it.

Didn't they look cozy.

"Oh, that was nice of her, I guess," Claire said. "Tell her I said thank you."

"Will do."

"Grab a beer and join us," Aidan told him. "Your team is playing like garbage, but on the bright side, mine isn't."

"Yeah, because I'm *so* invested in your big, bad Bears."

Rolling his eyes, Dylan strode to the kitchen. He returned a moment later with a cold bottle of Bud in his hand, but he didn't sit on the same couch as Aidan and Claire. Rather, he flopped down on the second sofa, twisted off the bottle cap and took a long slug of beer.

"How are the boys?" Aidan asked.

"Same old. Seth and Miranda are having people over for dinner on Christmas Eve. They want us to come." Dylan glanced over. "Do you know if you're heading back to Chicago for the holidays?"

"I haven't talked to my dad yet, but I'm guessing going home won't pan out. He's not big on the holidays."

Since Aidan rarely spoke about his father, Dylan was tempted to push for more details, but he knew the other man would just clam up if he did. And with Claire sitting there, the chances of Aidan opening up were even slimmer.

Or so he thought.

"Are you and your dad close?" Claire spoke up.

Aidan shrugged. "More or less."

"What about your mom?"

Dylan tensed. There was an unspoken rule in the condo when it came to Aidan's mother—don't talk about her. Ever.

And so it came as a genuine surprise when Aidan actually answered the question.

"She died when I was six."

"Oh, I'm sorry. Was she sick?"

"No. She…she got run down by a drunk driver when she was picking me up from school one day." His voice thickened with pain. "She pushed me out of the car's path but didn't manage to get herself out of the way in time."

Shock smashed into Dylan's chest with the force of a jackhammer. Jesus Christ. This was the first he'd heard of it, and he had no idea how to respond.

Claire gasped. "Oh my God. That's the saddest thing I've ever heard. I'm so sorry, Aidan."

There was a flash of movement in Dylan's peripheral vision. When he looked over, he saw that Claire was gripping Aidan's hand and stroking his knuckles.

Dylan locked gazes with his roommate, unsure of what to say to the confession. "You never told me that before," was what came out.

Aidan shrugged again. "I've never told anyone."

And yet he'd opened up to Claire.

The jealousy or resentment Dylan expected to feel did not come. Instead, he was overcome by a strange rush of gratitude. He didn't know why Aidan felt comfortable enough around Claire to share such a private snippet of information, but the revelation offered the insight Dylan had been seeking for months. It allowed some of the puzzle pieces to slide into place and explained the shadows in Aidan's eyes.

"Anyway, the holidays were my mom's favorite time of year, so it makes sense that they bum my dad out." Aidan's voice took on that careless note that hinted he was about to change the subject. Which was exactly what he did. "By the way, Claire roots for the Niners too. So you two can console each other after your loss."

Claire was wise enough to drop the subject, sparking Dylan's grudging approval. "You don't need to win games to be awesome," she said in a haughty tone. "Our guys can go oh-and-sixteen and would still be better than your Bears."

Dylan raised his beer in a mock toast. "Can't argue with that."

The leather cushions squeaked as Claire leaned forward to pick up the plastic container he'd left on the table. She snapped open the lid, peered inside and made a delighted sound. "Oooh, these look so good."

It took about three seconds for Dylan to wish he'd never brought those cupcakes into the apartment. Because if he'd known the way Claire ate cupcakes? He would have thrown them right into the trash.

He hated that he was incapable of tearing his gaze from her mouth. But damn, she looked so fucking sexy nibbling on the chocolate cupcake.

"Wow, your friend Shelby really knows how to bake," she said with a little moan. "These are to die for."

When her tongue darted out to lick the pink icing, Dylan's dick hardened and pressed against the zipper of his khaki shorts. Fortunately, his T-shirt was long enough that it covered his crotch. But there was no concealing the lust in his eyes, and when he shifted his gaze to Aidan, he saw that same rush of heat reflected back at him. That same flicker of interest that Dylan had seen so many times before, usually right before Aidan suggested to a chick that they all go back to his place.

The eye contact caused an unspoken conversation to pass between them.

"I want her naked, Dylan."

"Not gonna happen, bro."

"Jesus, but look how sexy she is."

"Tough shit."

"Um, what's with the death-match stare down?"

Claire's voice interrupted the silent debate, and Dylan declared himself the winner when he saw the resignation settle over Aidan's face.

"Just a football rivalry look we like to flash each other every few minutes," Dylan lied. He took a swig of beer and pretended that everything was A-okay.

Clearing his throat, Aidan turned to Claire. "So you and your dad watched football together, huh?"

"Every Sunday," she confirmed. "It was his only vice."

"Watching sports is a vice?"

"Dad disapproves of the way organized sports go hand-in-hand with gambling."

"Is he very religious?" There was no judgment in Aidan's question, just interest.

"Not at all, if you can believe that." She sighed. "He's a strange man, my dad. Very by the book, and all about right and wrong. His moral code is impossible to live up to, and he has the most archaic ideas about gender roles and how people ought to behave."

Dylan had been trying to focus on the game, but he unwittingly found himself shifting his attention to their conversation.

"Sounds like an oppressive environment to grow up in," Aidan remarked.

"It was, at times. I always had to maintain this good-girl image around him, but if I'm being honest, I think he knew I was a lot wilder than I let on." She laughed. "When I was in high school I used to sneak out all the time to meet my boyfriend, and even though my dad never said a word about it, I'm pretty sure he knew. Oh, and I'm convinced he grew wise to the fact that I was stealing his vodka and watering down what was left in the bottle."

Aidan laughed. Dylan couldn't help but join in. He got the feeling stealing your folks' booze and replacing it with a liquid of the same color was a rite of passage.

"Well, if he never called you out on any of that, he must not be as strict as you claim," Aidan teased.

"Oh, trust me, he's strict. I think he let it slide, though, because as wild as I could get, I was also the most focused kid on the planet. I knew I wanted to go to business school, and I worked my ass off to get the grades for it." She shrugged. "This probably sounds ridiculously arrogant, but I'm one of those people who can drink herself stupid or stay out all night partying and still manage to ace every test."

"So I'm guessing your father is really upset about what happened yesterday."

"He is, but not because the wedding didn't happen. He's furious with Chris for breaking my heart, and he didn't believe me when I told him that canceling the wedding might have been for the best."

"What about your mother? Did you speak to her about it today?" Dylan instantly kicked himself for joining the conversation so readily, especially when he glimpsed Aidan's pleased look.

"Yeah, I did. I told her how a part of me is relieved we didn't go through with it, and then I recruited her to convince my dad of it. The last thing I want is my father tracking down Chris and giving him a talking to." She rolled her eyes. "That's Dad's equivalent of a beating. He just talks to you in a very low voice for several hours."

Aidan looked incredibly amused. "Sounds fun."

"Oh, sure, *tons* of fun."

An uneasy feeling filled Dylan's stomach as he listened to the two of them chatting and laughing together. As much as he hated to admit it, he was beginning to understand what his older brother had seen in this woman. She was smart, funny, beautiful, charming. On the surface, she was the complete package.

However, he'd endured too many of her snooty remarks and judgmental opinions to buy her Miss-Cute-and-Lovable act.

"What did he say to you?"

Dylan frowned when he realized Claire was talking to him. "What did who say to me?"

"Chris." Her voice was soft now, lacking humor. "When he told you he didn't want to marry me, what was his reason?"

"I already told you. He said you weren't right for each other."

"I'm sure he said more than that."

Dylan hesitated, taking a moment to decide how much loyalty he owed to his brother at this point, if any. He and Chris had been close when they were kids, but over the years they'd drifted apart. These days, his brother felt like a complete stranger to him. Hell, Chris hadn't even contacted him since he'd taken off to Aruba, except to send a quick text letting Dylan know he'd landed safely.

"He didn't think you were a good match for him," he finally revealed.

"And?" she pressed.

"And he mentioned something about you sharing personal details with some of the country-club women."

A groove dug into her forehead. "Personal details? What kind of—" She gasped, and then her brown eyes darkened with disgust. "Oh my God. Did he dump me because I told a few rich girls about my *vibrator*?"

The outburst startled both him and Aidan, and damned if Dylan didn't immediately envision Claire lying naked on a bed holding a sex toy between her legs.

The arousal hit him hard and fast, like an injection of heroin right into the vein. He gulped, trying to banish the dirty images wreaking havoc on his brain, but it was too late. They were branded in there forever.

"Is that it?" Claire demanded, practically glaring at him.

"He didn't give me specifics," Dylan said awkwardly.

"Wow. Your brother is really something else. I mean, *wow*. He asked me to get rid of it, by the way. The vibrator."

Aidan choked out a laugh. "For real?"

"He said only single women needed them. And you know what? Those women at the club? They all have secret sex toys hidden away too. Apparently their conservative defense-lawyer husbands share Chris's view on mechanical interference in the bedroom. But I guarantee you none of them owned up to it when they were gossiping about me to their husbands." Her lips tightened in a thin line. "What else did he say?"

Dylan stifled a sigh. But hell, he was already in this deep. Might as well get it all out in the open. "He may have implied that you were unfaithful."

Claire's cheeks hollowed as if she was grinding her teeth together. "He actually said I cheated on him?"

"Not quite. He used the word indiscretion. But again, he didn't offer any details." He studied her face. "You don't seem shocked by that."

"That's because I know exactly what he's referring to." She must have noticed the way Dylan's shoulders tensed, because she hurried on. "I surprised him at the office one day for lunch and I had a run-in with one of his colleagues. This guy named Pres Maxwell, a total slimebag."

Maxwell… Dylan recognized the name. That was the same man who'd warned Chris that Claire wasn't a "good prospect". He kept that tidbit to himself, though, mostly because he didn't want to add more fuel to the fire burning in Claire's eyes.

"Chris had to finish up with a client, so I went to wait for him in the associates' lounge. Maxwell showed up and started pawing at me." Scorn dripped from her every word. "I told him to get lost, but he was very persistent. He tried to convince me that all the associates slept with each other's wives."

Aidan snorted. "Nice guy."

"I told Chris about it at lunch, but he brushed it off and insisted Maxwell must have been joking around. But that creep was *not* joking— he definitely wanted to get in my pants."

"Are you sure you didn't lead him on in any way?" Dylan regretted the question the moment it slipped out of his mouth, but it was too late to take it back.

In a nanosecond, Claire's expression went from annoyed to enraged. "Are you serious?"

He quickly tried to backpedal. "I'm just saying, maybe the guy thought you were sending some kind of signal and—"

"Oh, because I said hello?" she interrupted sarcastically. "Because I asked him how he liked working at the firm? Is that what you consider a signal? That bastard cornered me against the wall and tried to shove his hand up my skirt, and I didn't do a damn thing to invite it! I can't believe you'd even think I would."

The bite to her tone raised his hackles. "I don't know you, honey, and I've never seen the way you behave around other men. Maybe you're throwing off come-hither signals left and right to every man in San Francisco."

Her jaw fell open. Then snapped shut.

After a beat, she rose from the couch and pinned him down with a fierce look. "When I make a commitment to someone, I don't throw off *signals* to other men. I was committed to your brother. I loved him, and I was planning on marrying him. I don't give a shit what you think about me, but let it be known that I've never cheated on anyone in my entire life, and if for some reason I transmit *come-hither* signals then it's definitely not done intentionally. Now, if you'll excuse me, I need to boot up my laptop so I can book myself a flight home."

"Claire—" Aidan started.

"No, I don't want to hear it," she cut in. "A moment of weakness drove me to come here, but I have no desire to stay where I'm not wanted and with people who think I'm some kind of horrible human being."

With that, she marched out of the living room in a huff, her red hair whipping behind her like an angry cloud.

Several seconds ticked by. Dylan had no idea what to say, and the longer the silence between him and Aidan dragged on, the more irritated he got. To make matters worse, Aidan was just sitting there, his dark eyes shuttered, his body language tense.

"Spit it out, Aid," he ordered.

"Fine. You were a real dick to her just now, is that what you want to hear?"

"I'm a dick, huh? Why, because I asked a harmless question?"

"Harmless, my ass. You felt like antagonizing her, so you did." Aidan stood up. "And for what it's worth, I think the two of you have the most fucked-up perceptions of each other. Neither of you is the villain the other one thinks, and if you had one fucking conversation without sniping at each other, I think you'd really get along."

Bitterness trickled through him. "You just want me to get along with her so you can get her into bed."

Aidan responded with a harsh laugh. "Right, like you don't want the same damn thing. You've been sporting a semi since the second she got here. You undress her with your eyes whenever she's in the room. Oh, and you *kissed* her—thanks for mentioning that to me, by the way."

"She kissed me," he grumbled. "And I didn't mention it because it wasn't a big deal, nor was it ever going to happen again."

"Can you at least admit that you want her?"

"Jesus. Fine. I want her. You happy now? But guess what, man, I want a lot of things. Wanting something doesn't automatically mean it's a good idea to go out and get it. So yeah, I think she's hot, and yeah, she gets me hard, but I'm not going to act on it." He let out a frustrated breath. "If you want to sleep with her, go ahead. You have my blessing, okay? But me, I have no intention of ever sleeping with the woman, so for fuck's sake, leave me out of it."

Aidan didn't know whether to curse or laugh as he left Dylan in the living room to cool off. Last time he'd seen Dylan this worked up over being attracted to someone, it had been toward Aidan himself. Dylan had been freaked out about desiring a man out of the context of a threesome, and it had taken him a while to realize that sometimes you couldn't help who you felt an attraction for.

And now Dylan was fighting the way he felt about Claire. A blind person could see how much he wanted her, and Aidan didn't blame him one damn bit. He'd known Claire for only two days and he could honestly say he'd never been more drawn to a woman.

Not only that, but he found her presence strangely soothing. He was still reeling over the fact that he'd told her and Dylan about his mother's death—that was something he never spoke of, yet when Claire asked about his parents, the confession slipped out without warning. Afterwards, he hadn't felt exposed or embarrassed, the way he usually did when he revealed personal details about himself.

Why did he feel so comfortable opening up to Claire when he'd been denying Dylan the same privilege for months now? He had no answer for that, but there was one thing he did know—he didn't want Claire to go yet.

Which was why he wasted no time in heading for Dylan's bedroom so he could hopefully convince one very pissed-off redhead not to skip town.

He rapped his knuckles on the door. "Hey, it's Aidan. Can I come in?"

A gloomy "Sure" came from the other side of the door.

He stepped into the bedroom and found her on the bed with her MacBook in her lap. Her striped shirt had fallen off one shoulder, revealing smooth skin and making his fingers tingle with the urge to stroke all that softness.

"Did you book a flight yet?" he asked.

"No." She met his eyes. "You here to talk me out of it?"

"Yes."

"Don't bother. I'm not staying."

He smiled. "We both know you don't want to go, sweetheart."

"Oh, really? Now you're an expert on what I want?"

Ignoring her squeaky protest, he swiped the computer from her lap and walked over to set it on the dresser. He strode back to the bed and sat beside her. There was a foot of space between them, but he could feel the heat radiating from her body, smell her addictive lavender scent and see her pulse throbbing in her throat.

"I know you don't want to be in San Francisco right now," he said with a shrug. "Your parents will drive you nuts by fussing over you, you'll be sleeping in the apartment you shared with Chris—who at the moment is enjoying your honeymoon without you. And you've got three weeks off, so you're just going to sit around bored and stuck in your own head."

Claire scowled at him. "At least that's better than being accused of inviting a sexual assault."

"He didn't mean that and you know it. Dylan's just in a shitty mood and he decided to take it out on you."

"And that makes it right?" she challenged.

"Not at all. Look, I'm not going to make excuses for him or apologize on his behalf, but you need to know that you're wrong about him." Aidan's heart squeezed. "He's a good guy, Claire. And he cares about people, sometimes a helluva lot more than he should. For some reason, you just rub him the wrong way."

"Well, the feeling is mutual."

"What about me?" he asked impulsively.

Her forehead creased. "What do you mean?"

"Do I rub you the wrong way?"

Surprise flickered in her eyes. "Of course not."

Smiling again, he angled his body so they were face-to-face instead of side by side. "You've enjoyed hanging out with me today, right?"

That appealing blush rose in her cheeks. "Yes. I've had fun."

"Then keep having fun with me. Stay."

She bit her plump bottom lip, and for a second he experienced a pang of envy that Dylan had had the pleasure of feeling those sexy lips pressed against his. Shit, he wanted this woman bad. Like trembling-hands-and-dry-mouth kind of bad.

"So, what, I stick around for a few more days and just hang out with you? Don't you have to work?" She paused. "Come to think of it, I don't even know what you do. Are you in the navy too?"

"Yep, but I deal in naval intelligence. I work a boring eight-to-four out of the base, but I've got a bunch of personal days saved up that I can use if we want to take any day trips."

"Day trips?" She laughed, and the sweet sound tickled his heart. "What kind of stuff are you planning to drag me into?"

"Anything you want. Might as well treat this like a vacation, no? We can check out the sights, drive up the coast, hit Malibu, Catalina, spend a day in LA if you want. So yeah, sightseeing, exploring. I'm even willing to let you drag me to every department store in the state if it means you'll stay."

"Why?"

"Why what?"

"Why do you want me to stay so badly? You don't even know me."

She was doing that cute nibbling thing to her lip again, and he couldn't stop himself—he reached out, grasped her chin, and swept his thumb over that pouty lower lip.

Claire's breath caught. Her brown eyes widened before going heavy-lidded with desire.

Oh yeah, she wanted him. He hadn't missed the way her gaze had gobbled him up when they'd first met, and today he'd seen her checking him out more than once when she thought he wasn't looking.

"I want you to stay because you fascinate me." His voice was so hoarse he had to clear his throat before continuing. "I want to get to know you."

He traced her cupid's-bow mouth with his finger, enjoying the way her breathing quickened.

"Why do I fascinate you?" she murmured, making no move to wiggle out of his touch.

"I don't know. You just do," he said simply. "I guess it's because…well, truthfully, I don't spend time with many women like you."

"Women like me?"

He smiled sheepishly and dropped his hand from her face. "You know, the non-airhead type. The women I've dated, or the ones Dylan and I bring home, they're usually all about living in the moment, having a good time for a night and then moving on. That's not to say they're ditzy or dumb, but they certainly aren't serious, you know what I mean?"

"And you think I'm serious?"

"I think you're…pretty fucking amazing, actually. You're smart, ambitious, funny, sexy—"

"You think I'm sexy?" Her face took on a pinkish hue again.

"So sexy." He met her eyes. "And look, I ain't gonna lie—I'm attracted to you. But I also know you're in a vulnerable place right now and I promise I won't take advantage of that. I really just want to spend more time with you. I can't remember the last time I had this much fun with a woman."

Her throat bobbed as she swallowed. "What about Dylan?"

"What about him? He's the one who asked you to come here in the first place, and I just spoke to him and he said he doesn't mind if you stay."

Fine, so maybe Dylan's exact words had been *leave me out of it* but Aidan was going to take that as the green light for Claire to stick around.

When she shifted in visible reluctance, he gave her the impish grin he'd perfected over the years. "Come on, you know you want to."

She scowled again, but her lips were twitching with amusement. "Jeez, I bet those dimples got you everything you wanted when you were growing up."

"Yep, and they still do." The grin widened. "So what do you say? Will you stay?"

Her indecision hung in the air between them. He could see her brain working, feel her resolve crumbling.

"Okay, you win," she grumbled. "I'll stay. But just for another day or two."

Triumph coursed through him, though he knew it would take more than a day or two to get Claire where he wanted her—naked, moaning and sandwiched between him and Dylan while they drove her to new heights of arousal.

Of course, he would need to work on Dylan too, but that wouldn't be difficult, considering the hunger on the guy's face whenever Claire was in the room.

But it was going to take more than his dimples to make this happen. He'd definitely have to up his game, but fortunately, he'd always been very, very good at games. And this was one he had every intention of winning.

Chapter Eight

It took three days for Aidan to reach a conclusion: he was living with the two most stubborn people on the planet. Although Claire had stuck around, getting her and Dylan in the same room proved to be impossible. They went out of their way not to spend more than five minutes together, and Aidan was growing frustrated with their childish antics.

To make matters worse, Dylan was going to bed early and waking up before dawn because his SEAL team was running training missions all week. He'd been crashing on the pullout couch in the office so he wouldn't disturb Aidan with his comings and goings, and the grueling demos left him beaten and exhausted when he got home. Even if they had been sharing a bed, Aidan knew sex wouldn't be on the table.

As a result, he was so sexually frustrated he felt like a teenager with blue balls after his girlfriend refused to do more than neck. Being around Claire was pure torture. Not being with Dylan was even worse.

Needless to say, it was time to shake things up.

"Hey, guys? Can you come in here for a sec?" he called from the master bedroom.

Since Claire was right across the hall, she popped her head in the doorway within seconds, looking cute as hell in denim shorts and a red tank top, with her hair tied in a low, side ponytail. The two of them had spent the morning at the pier having lunch at a bistro that overlooked the water, then gotten ice cream at Aidan's favorite place in San Diego. Cash McCoy's girlfriend had turned him on to the place, and Claire had absolutely loved it, demanding a taste of every unique flavor in the store.

The more time he spent with her, the more Aidan liked her.

And the more he wanted to get her naked.

Soon, he assured himself.

Claire stepped into the room. "What's up?"

"Hold on. Dylan, I'm serious, get in here," he called. "I've got something to show you guys."

Dylan had been napping on the living room couch, having gotten home an hour ago in an exhaustion coma, so it took a few more seconds before his footsteps finally sounded in the hall.

"This better be good." Dylan strode into the bedroom, covering his mouth as a yawn overtook him. "What is it?"

Aidan stalked toward the walk-in closet as if he was going to get something, then stopped. "Oh shit, I forgot, I left it in the office. Give me a sec."

Nonchalant, he slid out the door, making sure to close it behind him. The second he was in the hall, he sprang into action. He might ride a desk at the base, but he'd gone through basic training the same way Dylan had, and he was quicker than most people gave him credit for.

In no time, he'd grabbed the dining-room chair he'd stashed in the office and had the sturdy wooden back pressed up beneath the doorknob of his bedroom. The second the chair locked into place, he heard a muffled curse.

"What the hell, bro?" Dylan shouted. "Did you just barricade us in here?"

"Yessir," he replied.

"Oh, for fuck's sake, open the goddamn door."

"Seriously, Aidan." Claire's voice, laced with annoyance. "Let us out."

"No can do, sweetheart. I'm tired as fuck of watching you two tiptoe around each other, or listening to you argue like a pair of preteens. It's time you straightened your shit out."

"*We're* the preteens?" Dylan said incredulously. "You're the one who locked us in here!"

He fought a grin. "It's for your own good. And I suggest you use the time allotted to sit down and have a real talk, instead of bitching at one another the way you're so fucking good at."

Another muted curse, this one feminine and so vulgar his eyebrows shot up.

"Ah, sweetheart, such language," he chided. "You're better than that."

"Fuck you, Aidan."

"Yeah, fuck you, Aidan," Dylan echoed.

Chuckling, he reached for the other item he'd liberated from the office, the cardboard box he'd set down on the hardwood.

As he opened the box, he heard Dylan murmur something to Claire, and not even the barrier between them could disguise the determination in the SEAL's voice. But even without that telltale tone of voice, Aidan had known exactly what Dylan's next move would be.

"Hey, man, if you're thinking of kicking in the door, I wouldn't recommend it," he advised.

"Yeah, and why's that? Because you know I'm perfectly capable of smashing this door down."

"Yep, but just know that if you do, your mother's Christmas present will smash right along with it."

Still laughing, Aidan removed the fragile glass angel nestled in the protective Styrofoam. He gently placed the angel on the chair and stepped back to admire his handiwork. Nice. Any damage Dylan inflicted on the door would cause the chair—and the angel—to crash right to the floor.

"How much was that angel again?" he went on, feeling a lot more cheerful than he probably should. "Six hundred bucks? And didn't you get it commissioned by that famous glassblower dude from Sweden? It's one of a kind, right?"

There was a brief silence, then a very quiet, very calm, "You're the fucking devil, Aidan."

"Straighten your shit out," he repeated. "I'll be back in a couple hours. Oh, and I left a box of provisions under the bed, just in case the forced confinement inspires some kind of fucked-up *Alive* situation."

Without letting either one of them respond, he walked away with a spring to his step.

Fine, so maybe he shouldn't be so damn proud about his sneakiness, but enough was enough. He had no idea why Claire believed that Dylan, the nicest guy on the planet, was a selfish asshole. Or why Dylan thought that Claire was a materialistic bitch, when these past few days had shown her to be the most easygoing, fun-loving chick Aidan had ever met.

Whatever the reason for their false perceptions, it was time for them to work out their issues.

"I can't believe he locked us in here." Claire sounded livid as she stared at the door, so intently it was like she was trying to use telekinesis to open the damn thing.

Dylan shook his head, amazed that Aidan had resorted to such juvenile bullshit. He was *so* not in the mood for this, not after spending the past twelve hours crawling around in a forest on a mock hostage extraction with his team. All he'd wanted to do when he got home was pass the fuck out, but thanks to Aidan, he was wide awake and spitting mad.

"He'll let us out in a few minutes, right?" Claire turned around with a desperate look. "He won't really be gone for hours, will he?"

"Yes, he will," Dylan said grimly. "Aidan doesn't mess around."

Her features creased with dismay. "This is so ridiculous. I can't be trapped in here with you."

Offense prickled his skin. He rubbed his tired eyes, then dragged a hand through his sleep-tousled hair and examined the room for anything he might be able to use to dismantle the doorknob. Then he realized it was absolutely futile, because no way would Aidan leave any escape devices lying around. And since they were on the fifteenth floor, going out through the bedroom's small balcony was out.

That left two options—kick down the door and say goodbye to his mother's Christmas present, which he'd taken painstaking effort to secure, or spend the next few hours locked in a room with Claire McKinley.

When he felt her knowing gaze on him, he shot her a scowl. "What?"

"You're considering ruining Shanna's present, aren't you?" she accused. "The idea of being alone with me is *that* bad?"

"Don't give me that wide-eyed indignation. You're not thrilled to be here with me, either."

"No, but I'd suck it up if it meant Shanna gets her angel." Claire paused. "I actually bought her a small crystal one for her birthday."

"You did?"

"Yeah, for her collection. She loves those angels."

"Yeah, she really does."

They both went quiet. After a beat, Dylan sighed and lowered his tired body onto the bed. As he stretched out on his back, he saw Claire watching him with suspicious brown eyes.

"What are you doing?"

"Getting comfortable," he answered. "That angel was a bitch to get my hands on. I'm not going to destroy it just so I don't have to spend a few hours with you."

"Gee, thanks. Nice to know you're willing to make such a big sacrifice."

His nostrils flared. "Does the sarcasm ever stop?"

"Does the good-guy act?"

"It's not an act," he retorted. "Whether you believe it or not, I actually am a good guy."

"Whatever helps you sleep better at night."

Her bitter tone was the last straw. The last few days had been taxing, both mentally and physically, and he had no desire to undergo a character assassination, especially when he'd done nothing to deserve it.

"You know what?" He abruptly moved into a sitting position and rested his curled fists on his thighs. "Maybe Aidan's right. Maybe it's time we let each other know *exactly* what we think of each other."

"Fine," she snapped back. "I've kept my mouth shut for more than a year out of respect for your mother and because Chris asked me not to interfere, but I'm not biting my tongue anymore."

"Good. Let's start then." He set his jaw. "I'll go first. I think you're a snob."

"Yeah? Well, I think you're selfish." Claire's entire body was stiffer than a board as she sat at the foot of the bed and angled herself so they could glare at each other more easily.

"I think you're disrespectful," he told her.

"I think you're a bad brother and a bad son."

"I think you loved Chris's money more than you loved him."

"Oh, that's rich, you bringing up money." Her eyes blazed. "Because as far as I know, you haven't sent a dime home this past year."

"First of all, what's it to you? And second, if you must know, I offered to help my mom out after she left her job, but she said she was doing okay for cash."

"Left her job?" Claire shook her head in disbelief. "For fuck's sake, you don't have to pretend with me. I was going to marry your brother—I know why Shanna got fired."

Surprise spiraled through him. "What did you say?"

"I said I know why she got—"

"Fired," Dylan finished. A sick feeling rose in his chest. "What do you mean, she got fired?"

"Why are you playing dumb?"

"I'm not playing dumb. I'm honestly confused. I don't know what Chris told you, but my mom quit her teller job at the bank. She said she was tired of all the politics there."

When Claire didn't respond, Dylan's stomach churned some more, knots of worry twisting around his insides. Jesus. Was Claire actually telling the truth? Had his brother and mom been lying to him all these months?

"Tell me everything you know," he ordered. "I mean it, Claire. Everything."

"You don't know what happened at the bank?"

He battled another rush of queasiness. "No."

"Shanna got fired, Dylan."

"You mean, laid off?"

"No, fired." Claire's tone grew pained. "She wasn't showing up for work, and when she did, she'd be hours late."

"Are you fucking with me here? Who told you that? Chris?"

"Yes. But I also spoke to your mom about it." She hesitated. "I'm the one who got her in contact with the lady from—" She stopped without warning and averted her gaze.

"The lady from where?" he demanded.

Claire's voice was barely above a whisper. "Gamblers Anonymous."

Dylan felt like someone had dropped a cartoon anvil on his head. He literally got the wind knocked out of him, and all he could do was stare at Claire in wordless disbelief.

Her brown eyes widened at his stunned expression. "You really didn't know?"

It took a few seconds to find his voice, which came out so hoarse it sounded like he was talking through a mouthful of gravel. "My mom has a *gambling* problem?"

Claire nodded.

"Since when?"

"I think it started a few months before Chris and I met. I guess she went to the casino with a few women from her gardening club and she caught the bug. She went back the next weekend on her own, and then the weekend after, and the one after that. Eventually she was going several times a week, which was when she started skipping out on work."

Dylan couldn't believe what he was hearing, but apparently Claire wasn't finished dropping bombs on him.

"She lost all her savings, but even then she couldn't stop gambling, and when her paychecks weren't enough to support the habit, she took out a second mortgage on the house. Except she couldn't afford the mortgage payments either, and the bank started foreclosure proceedings, so that's when she confided in Chris."

He sucked in a breath. "So my brother knew this whole time and didn't say a word about it to me?"

Claire rubbed the bridge of her nose as if warding off a headache. "He told me you knew, but that it wasn't your responsibility to do anything about it. He was the man of the house since your father died, so it was his problem. That's why he took the job with Lowenstein and Tate instead of the assistant prosecutor position."

There were so many unsettling details being thrown around he didn't know which one to focus on.

"What are you talking about? Chris was always going to work for a defense firm. It was the only reason he went to law school, so he could practice criminal law."

She frowned. "No, he didn't. He was committed to the city job. When we first met it was all he could talk about."

"I know he got an offer, but trust me, he never intended to accept. It's always been his dream to be a big-shot defense lawyer."

Her teeth clamped over her bottom lip. Another silence fell over the room as each of them absorbed what had been said.

"Were you—"

"Are you—"

They both laughed awkwardly. "You first," he said.

"Were you really in the dark about all this?"

"Yes." He gave her a grim look. "If I'd known, I would have been doing everything in my power to help my mom out. Why the hell didn't she tell me?"

Even as he voiced the thought, he already knew the answer. Because he was her favorite. Her baby. His mom had tried to shield him from heartache his entire life, painting the world to him as a place full of sunshine and rainbows and cuddly kittens. He was always the last one to find out when something bad happened, and there'd been times when he wouldn't be told at all, only to discover the truth years later.

"Maybe she was trying to protect you."

Claire's soft assessment was spot-on, and though he concurred, that didn't make the situation any less insulting.

"So Chris has been making the mortgage payments this last year?" Dylan asked, still trying to make sense of it all.

Claire nodded.

"What about my mom and the gambling? Has she stopped? Like really stopped?"

"She claims she has, and I haven't seen any signs that she's relapsed. She's also been looking for a new job."

He rubbed the stubble coating his chin, momentarily distracted by the three days' worth of beard growth beneath the pads of his fingers. He wasn't used to his face feeling so damn prickly.

"I can't believe you didn't know." Claire's eyes shone with remorse. "And all this time, I…" She trailed off.

He swallowed. "You what?"

"I blamed you for the changes I saw in Chris. I thought he took that job because it paid more and he needed to support your mom, and then as time passed, he went from this fun, passionate man looking to change the world, to a stiff, pretentious jackass who only wanted to golf and smoke cigars with his colleagues."

Dylan sighed. "He's always been stiff and pretentious. I have no idea how that happened, considering both my parents were so easygoing. I guess I took after them, but Chris, well, I don't know how he got to be so serious and conservative. But he's also incredibly shrewd."

"What does that mean?" she asked warily.

"It means he's a smooth operator when it comes to women. He'll tell you whatever you want to hear, do whatever it takes to impress you. I'm guessing he sensed you were passionate about certain issues, so he spun you a tale about working for the city and fighting for the little guy. And you said you like to get wild sometimes, right? Well, I bet at first, he took you to all sorts of fun places—dinner, dancing, weekend getaways. Am I right?"

There was sadness in her eyes as she nodded.

"Chris is not a party dude, honey. He hates clubs or crowds or going anywhere that doesn't serve twelve-year-old scotch."

"How come I never saw it?"

"Like I said, he's smooth. Always has been."

Dylan experienced a pang of sympathy when he noticed how upset she looked. He was pretty upset himself. Still reeling from the shock of discovering his mother had gambled away her life savings and nearly lost her house. *Their* house, the one Dylan had grown up in, the one filled with so many great memories of his dad.

But his heart went out to Claire too. Chris had totally played her, and knowing that spurred another realization.

"So wait, all those times you and Chris visited here or when I came to San Francisco, all those barbed remarks you made about money and my mom needing to get a job..." He let out a heavy breath. "You're not a greedy bitch at all, are you? And you don't care that my mom was a housewife for most of her life, do you?"

A startled laugh flew out of her mouth. "Um, no. I won't deny I was bitchy to you whenever I saw you, but that was because I was watching my fiancé work his ass off while his selfish younger brother was man-whoring it up in San Diego."

He rolled his eyes. "I'm a SEAL first, manwhore second. I work my ass off, Claire."

She had the decency to look sheepish. "I know. It was just easier to hate you when I focused on your partying."

He couldn't help but chuckle. "Well, since we're making confessions, I guess I have another one."

"I can't wait to hear it." She smiled the first genuine smile she'd ever given him, and damned if it didn't light up her face and transform her from beautiful to exquisite.

"Even when I believed you were a snooty bitch, I still thought you were the hottest woman I'd ever laid eyes." He shrugged, a touch embarrassed. "I think I clung to that feeling of dislike because it made it easier not to lust after you. I mean, we could have hashed this out months ago, but I never took the time to dig under the surface with you. I guess I was using not liking you as my excuse to not pant over my brother's girl."

"Wow. Aidan was right. You really are the most honest man on the planet."

"It's my fatal flaw."

"Honesty is a strength, not a flaw." She paused for a moment. "You thought I was hot?"

The pink flush on her cheeks made him grin. "Not *thought*. I still think it."

"You do?"

"Fuck, Claire, you're gorgeous. You know that, right?"

"I don't give much thought to my appearance, if I'm being honest."

"Well, you should. You're the sexiest woman I've ever met, and I'm sure Aidan would agree with me. Neither of us can take our eyes off you."

She sighed at the mention of Aidan. "Damn him. He was right to lock us in here, wasn't he? If he hadn't, neither of us would know the truth about…well, about everything."

"Yeah, he has this annoying habit of always being right. Drives me bat-shit crazy."

She laughed again, then she slid off the mattress in the blink of an eye.

Dylan raised his eyebrows as he watched her kneel on the floor next to the bed. "What are you doing?"

"I just remembered what Aidan said about provisions. I want to see what that jerk deemed necessary for our survival."

She stuck her arm underneath the bed and felt around for the mysterious box, which caused her ass to jut out in the most delectable way. Dylan's gaze homed in on her firm butt cheeks, hugged by tiny denim shorts. Lord, she had the sexiest body he'd ever seen. He suddenly had the most overpowering urge to strip her clothes off and find out if she looked as spectacular naked as he suspected she did.

A moment later she was back on the bed, dropping a cardboard box on the mattress. She opened the flaps and peered inside with the curiosity of a kid unwrapping a present on Christmas morning.

She pulled out two sandwiches in clear plastic wrap. "Okay, we've got some sandwiches." Next came a bottle of water, followed by the container of Shelby's cupcakes.

Dylan watched with amusement as she continued her inventory.

"Oooh, a crossword book. And…a first-aid kit. Why would we need a first-aid kit?"

"Maybe he thought we'd beat the shit out of each other and one of us would need stitches."

"Maybe." She reached into the box again, coming up with a paperback copy of *War and Peace*. A quizzical expression crossed her face. "Um, okay."

Dylan groaned. "Bastard. He likes to make fun of me because I've never been able to get past the first ten pages."

With another laugh, she went to grab the next item.

Her face went tomato-red when her hand emerged with a box of condoms.

"Magnums," Dylan remarked with a pleased nod. "I'll take that as a compliment."

"Oh my God. I can't believe he left us condoms."

"I can, and it was damn thoughtful of him too." He couldn't control the seductive note that crept into his voice. "So what do you say, honey, should we tear one open and put it to good use?"

Chapter Nine

THE WORST THING ABOUT BEING A REDHEAD WITH FAIR SKIN? IT WAS impossible to disguise a blush. Claire's cheeks had been a thorn in her side her whole life, and as her face heated under Dylan's smoldering gaze, she knew she was transmitting everything she was feeling loud and clear.

Surprise.

Embarrassment.

Arousal.

since they'd kissed, she'd been trying to squash the desire she felt for Dylan, but now that her misconceptions about the man had been exposed, she was having a tough time controlling her hormones. It was one thing to ignore the attraction when she'd thought he was a selfish ass who didn't give a shit about his mother's troubles, another one altogether when she knew he was actually a decent guy.

"Ah, relax. I'm just teasing you." His gorgeous green eyes twinkled. "I was kidding."

She slanted her head in challenge. "Are you? Because you look pretty darn serious."

After a second, he broke out in a grin. "Fine, so I was only half-kidding."

"So half of you wants us to have sex?"

"Actually, about three-quarters of me wants it. One-quarter knows it's probably a bad idea."

"Probably?" She choked out a laugh. "I almost married your brother, Dylan."

"And yet somehow that doesn't seem to bother me anymore."

"Right. Somehow." She snorted. "It's easy to overlook the reasons you shouldn't do something when you want it badly enough."

"And you don't?"

"I don't what?"

"Want it." His lips quirked. "Because you've been giving off come-hither signals since the second you saw that box of condoms."

"Again with the come-hither signals? You really like saying the words *come-hither*, huh?"

"And you're deflecting. Answer the question. Do you want to have sex with me?"

His frankness was oddly thrilling. So was the way he slid closer, eliminating the distance between them. He moved the box of provisions out of the way, then scooted even closer, and Claire's heart began to race. Their thighs were touching, his covered by sweatpants, hers bare thanks to her short-shorts, and the heat of his body sizzled her flesh, eliciting a rush of excitement that rippled through her blood.

"Yes, no, maybe?" he prompted.

It was in that moment Claire realized how honesty might be considered a weakness rather than a strength, because the word "Yes" slipped out of her mouth before she could stop it.

But damn it, she *did* want this. Dylan had set her entire body on fire from that one measly kiss—she could only imagine what he was capable of doing to her if they were naked.

Maybe it made her a mega slut and a terrible person, but she really, *really* wanted to find out.

As his mouth curved in a satisfied smile, Dylan brought his hand to her face and stroked her cheek with his thumb.

"You're always blushing." He cocked his head pensively. "Is that blush limited to your cheeks, though? Or do other parts of you get nice and rosy too? Maybe here, you think?"

He glided his fingers along the curve of her neck and down to her collarbone.

As if on cue, heat suffused her chest.

"Oh, that's nice." His eyes were focused intently on the flush rising just above the neckline of her tank top.

The pads of his fingers were rough, callused, creating a gentle scrape over her skin as he caressed the upper swell of her breasts.

"This is crazy," she murmured.

"Probably."

"Definitely."

He withdrew his hand. "I'll stop then."

Disappointment spiraled through her, and God help her, but her lips formed a squeaky protest. Yes, this was crazy. Yes, sleeping with Chris's brother would be highly inappropriate. But she wanted it to happen. She *needed* it to happen.

"Claire?" His expression was expectant.

"You know the night I caught you kissing Aidan?" she heard herself blurting out.

"How can I forget?" he said dryly.

"That night…what I saw…" She tried to articulate her jumbled thoughts. "The two of you were completely wrapped up in each other, oblivious to the world around you. It was so intense and it made me kind of sad because I'd never experienced anything that even came close to that." She swallowed. "And I was so turned on afterwards."

He looked incredibly intrigued. "Yeah?"

"Yeah."

His voice lowered to a husky pitch. "Did you make yourself come when you went back to your room?"

"Yes."

A groan rumbled out of his chest. "Aw, fuck, Claire, that's hot. You were fingering yourself while I was in the living room twenty feet away?"

"Yes."

She should have been mortified confessing all this to him, but it was impossible to feel embarrassed when Dylan was looking at her with such unadulterated lust. When her gaze lowered to his groin, she made out the unmistakable ridge of his erection, and a resulting rush of moisture soaked her panties.

"Did you come hard?" he rasped. "Was it good?"

She met his sultry gaze. "It was the best orgasm I've ever had."

"Hmmm. Challenge accepted."

"Of course you'd see that as a challenge," she said with shaky laugh. "But yeah…watching the two of you like that…it showed me what I was lacking in my own life."

"Where are you going with this?"

She inhaled a deep breath. "I guess what I'm saying is that I want to experience…well, passion." A wry note entered her voice. "And since we're trapped in here for the next couple of hours, I guess having sex wouldn't be a *totally* preposterous idea."

"Are you trying to convince me, or yourself? Because I was on board from the second you pulled out those condoms."

The grin he flashed her was contagious. "That's because you're a man. Women need some time to rationalize before they jump into things."

"So are you done rationalizing?"

She pondered that. "I think so."

"Good. Then come here and kiss me."

"Come wher—" She yelped in delight as he hauled her onto his lap.

She grabbed his shoulders and clutched the sleeves of his T-shirt, moaning when he tugged on her ponytail to yank her head down. The second their lips met, heat unraveled inside her and danced along her flesh. He kissed her like a man possessed, his tongue sliding inside her mouth with a greedy thrust, robbing her of breath.

Passion. There it was. Surrounding her. Consuming her. She'd never been kissed like this before. Except…wait, that wasn't true, because she'd experienced this very same thrill the other night when she'd kissed him. This time, however, there was no doubt in her mind that he was attracted to women—the hard cock pressing against her ass was all the evidence she needed.

Dylan continued to drive her wild with his mouth, his tongue, his teeth as he nibbled on her bottom lip before sucking on it. His hands traveled down the bumps of her spine, callused fingers snaking beneath the hem of her shirt.

She shivered as he began sliding the material up, those strong hands caressing her stomach, moving closer and closer to the undersides of her breasts.

When his exploration came to an abrupt halt, she voiced her disapproval in the form of a groan.

"Don't worry," he said with a chuckle. "I have every intention of playing with these gorgeous tits, but first I want to enjoy the view. Up you go."

In the blink of an eye, he was helping her to her feet.

"What are you doing?"

A smile lifted the corners of his mouth. "Me? Well, I'm going to lie here like this—" he fell back on his elbows, looking mighty pleased with himself, "—and watch while you undress."

Her eyebrows flew up. "You want me to do a striptease? Am I supposed to dance or something?"

"Naah, no dancing required. And you don't even have to go slow. Rip those clothes off if you want."

"Do it for me." Her brazen order came out of nowhere, surprising them both.

"Nope. Like I said, I'm just gonna enjoy the view."

"Seriously?"

"Seriously." He licked his lips. "Come on, honey, show me some skin."

Although the two of them had worked everything out, a part of her still felt slightly wary, wondering if he was playing a cruel joke on her. Like she would take off her clothes, let him see her naked, and then he'd jump up and say, "Gotcha! I still hate you!"

Dylan must have read her mind, because he let out a breath and stood. "How about this? I'll go first."

"What—"

She didn't get to finish her sentence, because the next thing she knew, he yanked his T-shirt over his head and tossed it aside, then shoved his sweatpants down his legs.

Claire gaped at him, heart pounding even harder. Her gaze darted around like a pinball, unable to land on one particular spot. Every inch of him was pure perfection, from his smooth, tanned skin to his tight six-pack, from the muscular thighs dusted with golden hair to the unmistakable erection beneath his black boxer briefs.

Somehow she managed to find her voice. "The undies stay on, huh? I guess putting yourself on display isn't as liberating as you thought, is it?"

"I'm keeping these on for your sake, not mine." He smirked. "Because the second you see my cock, you'll get all weak-kneed and distracted. Probably applaud for a couple of minutes, too—that's a common response I get from the ladies."

She burst out laughing. "Someone thinks highly of himself."

"Oh, I think very highly of my dick, honey," he said solemnly. "And with good reason. Fuck Helen of Troy—bigger wars have been fought over my cock."

As Claire rolled her eyes, Dylan settled back on the bed and got comfortable. "Now, where were we? Oh, right, you were about to get naked."

With Dylan lying there half-naked, she no longer felt as self-conscious, but her hands did tremble as she reached for the hem of her top. After a beat of uncertainty, she ordered herself to quit being a wuss and swiftly took off her shirt. Her shorts were next, which left her in a black bikini-style bra and matching panties.

She hesitated, fingers poised over the front clasp of her bra.

Dylan's nostrils flared. "Lose the underwear, Claire. I want to see you naked."

A shiver skated through her. Taking a breath, she flicked the clasp and let the bra fall to the floor. Then she wiggled out of her panties and stood in front him naked, just like he'd requested.

No man had ever looked at her the way Dylan was looking at her now. His gaze traveled over her body as if he owned it, leaving little pinpricks of desire in its wake. She felt exposed standing there, and yet at the same time, bold and feminine and so very sexy.

Dylan didn't say a word as he got his fill. He stayed quiet for so long she shifted her feet awkwardly. "Now what?" she murmured.

"Now you come closer."

Her heart thudded as she did what he asked, but just before she reached the side of the bed, he shook his head and said, "Stay right there."

She stayed put, wondering what he was planning to do. Anticipating it.

God, why wasn't he touching her?

He chuckled when he saw the impatience in her eyes. He hopped off the bed and rose to his full height, the sheer size of him sending her pulse into another tailspin. He was so much taller than her, his big body dwarfing her petite one, making her feel both vulnerable and… safe. Because no matter how much bigger he was, no matter how much stronger, she knew this man wouldn't hurt her.

When he lightly rested one hand on her hip, she shivered again. She tipped her head back, expecting him to pull her close and kiss her, but he didn't do either of those things.

What he did was get on his knees and press his mouth directly on her pussy.

"Oh *God*." Nearly keeling over with pleasure, Claire's hands once again grabbed hold of his shoulders so she could steady herself.

"Now, this isn't fair," he said in a raspy voice, peering up to look at her.

She blinked. "What isn't?"

"You're totally bare." His finger traveled along the length of her slit. "How will I know if you're a natural redhead?"

A laugh lodged in her throat. "I guess you'll have to take my word for it."

"Guess so." His breath tickled her sensitive flesh, unleashing a new flurry of shivers.

He leaned in and planted an open-mouthed kiss on her inner thigh, then dragged his tongue across the top of her mound so he could kiss her other thigh. "You've got the softest skin," he muttered.

When he moved his head away again, she glanced down and almost stopped breathing when she noticed his hot gaze focused on her most intimate place.

"Fuck, you've got the prettiest pussy." He ran his finger over her folds again, all the way down to the wetness pooling at her entrance.

They both groaned when he pushed just the tip of his finger into her opening.

"You're so fucking wet," he hissed out. "Fuck, Claire, I wanna shove my tongue inside your pussy and taste you."

Oh. My. God.

She hadn't expected the dirty talk. At all. And it turned her on so much her clit began to throb. Painfully. She was so aroused it actually *hurt*.

She was unsure whether he was waiting for permission to follow through on the wicked picture he'd painted, but when he didn't make a move, she parted her legs wider in invitation.

His eyes burned with approval. "That's it, honey, open yourself up to me."

And yet he still didn't do a damn thing.

"Please. Do something." An unsteady breath flew out of her mouth.

"What do you want me to do?" he asked innocently.

"Don't you dare tease me, Dylan. *Do* something."

"If you insist."

His tongue touched her clit and Claire promptly saw stars.

The warmth of his mouth surrounded that swollen bud as he suckled on it, sending shockwaves of pleasure through her system. It felt so good she almost fell over again, but Dylan gripped her hips to keep her in place.

He made little sounds of happiness as he devoured her. The stubble dotting his chiseled face abraded her sensitized skin, only adding to the mounting pleasure. His tongue moved with a skill that should have annoyed her—because jeez, he must have gone down on hundreds of women in order to get this damn good at it. But the thought only sparked gratitude for all the women who'd—no pun intended—come before her because, well, because he was *this damn good at it.*

"Yes, just like that," she whimpered when he flattened his tongue and started licking her as if she were a tasty lollipop.

The tension began to build, gathering in her core, a tight knot just ready to burst apart, but Dylan had apparently mastered the ability to control the female orgasm, because each time she got close to toppling over the edge, he abruptly yanked her back from it.

"No coming," he chided after he'd stolen an orgasm from her for the third time. "I'm not done yet."

He punctuated that by spearing his tongue into her and fucking her with it until she was close to exploding once more.

"Not yet," he growled, and then that tongue disappeared and stopped doing all the wonderful things it had been doing.

"Are you always this bossy?" she wheezed out.

"Yes. Are you complaining?"

Was she? Hell fucking no. If anything, his dominance was…liberating. So was his confidence—he didn't peek up every few seconds to gauge if she was enjoying it, didn't stop to ask her if he was "doing it okay". He just licked and sucked and teased and *dared* her not to like it.

It was a whole new experience, and the incredible sensations he produced inside her were ones she'd never felt with any of her previous lovers, Chris included.

Do not *think about Chris right now.*

Her brain's sharp command didn't go unheeded. Banishing all thoughts of Chris, she brought one hand to Dylan's head and threaded her fingers through his short blond hair. "Does it look like I'm complaining?" she said in a breathy voice.

His expression turned smug. "Didn't think so. Now be a good girl and come for me."

"But you just said—"

He latched his mouth onto her clit and shoved two fingers deep inside her, and she exploded like a firecracker. The orgasm swept her away in a flash flood of ecstasy, seizing every muscle in her body and pulsing through her nerve endings. She'd never come standing up before, and her knees buckled involuntarily, rocking her equilibrium.

Dylan's grip on her waist tightened, holding her in place as she rode out the release and trembled against his hungry tongue. The second she'd recovered he was on his feet and kissing her, his tongue filling her mouth the same way it had filled her pussy.

She tasted herself on his lips and there was something so deliciously dirty about that. Moaning, she tugged on the waistband of his boxer briefs, but her fingers were shaking so hard she couldn't seem to rid him of the pesky garment. She cursed in frustration. Damn it, she needed him *naked*.

Chuckling, Dylan pushed her hands out of the way and took over. His underwear hit the floor, and she got her wish—he was naked.

And he was incredible.

Her mouth watered as she stared at the long erection that rose up and slapped his navel, prompting him to arch a dark-blond eyebrow. "Enjoying the view?"

"Oh my God. Yes."

She reached out and touched his chest, ran her palm over that hard male flesh, traced the occasional scar she discovered beneath her fingertips. The scars were a reminder of what he did for a living, the danger he faced and the risks he took, but that only heightened her excitement. This man was a warrior. Was there anything sexier?

Her hand continued its southward journey, fingers skimming the defined ridges of his abs before moving even lower. The line of hair arrowing down to his groin fascinated her. She followed the path of those wiry hairs until her hand finally reached his erection.

"Wrap your fist around my cock." His eyes glittered as he voiced the command.

She circled the wide shaft with her fingers and gave it a gentle squeeze.

Dylan hissed out a breath. "I want you to suck me off, Claire. I want your hot mouth on my dick."

Liquid desire pooled between her legs, her body completely forgetting that it had reached climax mere minutes ago. Her heartbeat accelerated as she gazed at the hard cock in her hand. Oh yeah, she wanted to taste him. She wanted to feel the thick length of him lodged inside her mouth.

But before she could experience either of those things, Dylan scooped her up in his powerful arms and deposited her on the bed. She landed on the mattress with a not-so-graceful thump, her jaw dropping.

"What the hell?" she grumbled. "What'd you do that for?"

The predatory gleam in his eyes said it all. He loomed over the bed, gloriously naked, his body so hard and chiseled it may as well have been carved out of marble. A second later, he ripped open the condom box, tore one of the plastic squares off the strip, and rolled the latex onto his erection.

"I thought you wanted my mouth," she teased.

"Couldn't do it," he muttered as he climbed onto the bed. "I would have shot my load in two seconds flat. Almost did the second you put your hand on me."

"And that's bad because…?"

"Because I want to feel your pussy squeezing my cock when I come," he said in a strangled voice.

He covered her body with his, the weight of him sending a jolt of exhilaration through her, and then his mouth captured hers in a punishing kiss that left her gasping for air. His heavy erection rested between her legs, but he didn't thrust it inside her. He just kept kissing her, propping himself up with one arm while his free hand drifted to her chest.

She moaned when he squeezed one breast. "You lied before. You said you would play with my tits."

"I didn't lie. I just got distracted by that tasty cunt of yours."

Oh sweet Jesus.

A knowing gleam filled his eyes. "You like the dirty talk, huh?"

"*So* much."

"Good. Because I like talking dirty." Flashing a roguish grin, he slid a few inches lower and closed his mouth around her nipple.

A wave of pleasure rocked into her. Her breasts weren't particularly sensitive, but Dylan's talented tongue coaxed an unprecedented response out of her. Her nipples grew stiffer than they'd ever been, tingling in a way she'd never felt. They ached, pulsed, and each time Dylan took another deep pull, she felt it right between her legs, until every square inch of her body cried out with impatience.

Whimpering, she shoved her hand in his hair and tugged on those silky strands. "Please, I need you in me."

He slid back up with a smug smile. "You know, only an hour ago you were cursing about being stuck here with me, and now you're begging me to put my dick inside you. Who would've thought?"

She gritted her teeth. "Can we laugh at the irony of this later? Like maybe after I come again?"

"Are you always this bossy?" he mimicked.

She threw his own words back at him. "Yes. Are you complaining?"

"Not one damn bit. Now brace yourself, honey, because I'm about to fuck your brains out."

"Bring it on, *honey*."

Boy, did he bring it.

Claire wasn't prepared for his first thrust. It was so fast and so deep she gasped in startled delight as her body stretched to accommodate him.

"Holy shit, you're tight," he mumbled.

His features tensed, as if he were trying desperately not to lose control. He eased out a few inches, then slammed right back in, and sure enough, his face took on a tortured expression.

"Sorry, honey, but there's no way I'm going to last. You can blame the kung-fu grip of your pussy for that."

She shuddered with laughter, which only intensified the agony burning in his eyes.

"Don't. Move." He choked out the words, gripping her hips to keep her still. "And please, please tell me you're close to coming again."

"No, but I could be." With an amused look, she brought her hand between their bodies and started stroking herself.

Dylan groaned, but he didn't move a muscle. She stared up at him as she rubbed her clit. The tendons of his neck were straining, twitching, as if he could barely hold it together. She could see his pulse throbbing in his throat, and she marveled over his restraint, the willpower he exuded as he allowed her to stoke the fire, to build up to climax.

She moved her fingers in little circles over her clit, getting closer and closer and closer, until a little moan finally slipped out, followed by, "Oh gosh, now. Fuck me *now*."

He pulled out, then plunged in with a hard stroke that hit a spot deep inside and sent her soaring. As she got swept away, Dylan grabbed one of her legs and lifted it up to his hip so he could drive deeper. A moment later he let out a hoarse groan and started to come, the heat of his release warming her core right through the latex.

She'd never had sex like this before. Never come that hard, never felt this sated, and as they both took a few minutes to catch their breath, Claire knew her entire world had just changed.

IF ANYONE HAD TOLD HIM WHEN HE'D WOKEN UP AT DAWN THAT HE'D be ending the day naked and cuddling with Claire McKinley, Dylan would have accused them of smoking too much crack. But here he was, lying in bed with Claire's warm body nestled beside him.

On sheets that smelled like Aidan.

Fuck.

As he breathed in that familiar citrus scent, he battled a spark of guilt, then ordered himself to snuff it out. He refused to feel guilty. Aidan had known exactly what would happen when he'd barricaded the two of them in this bedroom. He'd even left them protection, for chrissake.

But although the guilt faded, it was replaced by a tremor of distress and a pang of longing. Aidan should be here too, damn it. His absence brought an ache to Dylan's heart.

"You don't still think I'm a gold-digger who hates homemakers, do you?" Claire's quiet voice broke the silence.

He had to smile. "No. Do you still think I'm a selfish manwhore who couldn't be bothered to help his mother through her gambling addiction?"

"No," she said softly.

"Good."

He stroked her bare shoulder for a second, then reached up to rub his forehead. Just saying those words—*gambling addiction*—had reignited his anger and confusion. He couldn't believe Chris and their mom had been keeping such a monumental secret from him. They'd almost lost their family home, for fuck's sake. Why the hell wasn't he told?

"I should call her," he said absently. Then he thought better of it. "No, I should fly home and talk to her in person."

"Your mom?"

"Yeah. I want to hear all this from her. I want her to explain to me why she and Chris felt compelled to lie to me for more than a year."

"I really do think she was trying to protect you. You're her favorite, and I bet she was scared of disappointing you. I mean, you should hear the way Shanna talks about you. She's insanely proud of every little thing you do, and she acts like the sun rises and sets for you. That woman adores you."

He swallowed the lump in his throat. "I know, but that's no excuse for lying to me about something so important."

"I'm sure everything will make more sense once you sit down and talk to her," Claire assured him. "Just don't go in ready to attack. Coming clean about the addiction was difficult for her."

She should have come clean to me.

He bit back the juvenile response. Claire was right. His mom had tried to shield him from the darkness, the way she always did.

"Okay, I'll reserve judgment until I hear what she has to say."

"Well, that was easy," Claire said with a laugh. "Are you always so quick to see reason?"

"Hey, I'm a reasonable guy. Aidan's the pigheaded one who needs a lot of convincing."

The thought of Aidan evoked another rush of distress. He drew in a deep breath, only to inhale a lungful of Claire's lavender scent. Damn, she smelled good. Felt good too, pressed up against him like this.

But it was wrong.

This was wrong.

"You okay?" she murmured. "You tensed up all of a sudden."

Misery crawled up his spine. "Shit. Claire. I think this was a mistake."

It was her turn to tense up. "What are you talking about?"

"Us sleeping together. It was a mistake."

The sheets rustled as she sat up. Her ponytail was a mess, most of her hair falling out of it, and she yanked the elastic off as she stared at him with hurt in her eyes. "I thought you wanted it."

"I did. I wanted it badly." He paused. "But we can't do it again."

Her mouth tightened. "I see."

He sat up too, a weary sigh slipping out. "What happened between us just now…it was amazing. No, more than amazing. Probably some of the best sex of my life. But I can't let it happen again."

"Why? Because of Chris?" She ran a frazzled hand through her tousled auburn hair in an attempt to smooth it out.

"No, because of Aidan."

She was quiet for a moment. "Because he wants me too," she finally said.

Dylan wasn't surprised she'd picked up on that—Aidan didn't exactly take a subtle approach when he was attracted to someone.

"Yeah, he does."

"Are you worried he'll be upset that you and I hooked up? You don't want me to be stuck in the middle between you two?"

A laugh burst out of his chest. "The exact opposite, actually."

Her eyebrows furrowed. "What does that mean?"

"It means I *want* you to be in the middle."

Several seconds ticked by before understanding dawned in her eyes, which widened in a flash. "You mean…you want me…and you…and…"

"Aidan," he supplied.

"You want me to sleep with both of you? At the same time?"

Her red cheeks revealed her embarrassment, but Dylan also didn't miss the brief flash of interest in her eyes.

Shit, she was intrigued by it. She was honest-to-God intrigued.

Unfortunately, Claire's next words stuck a pin in the balloon of hope floating around in his chest.

"That's insane," she sputtered. "I'm not…I can't…that's not an option, Dylan." She shook her head in dismay. "Do you guys do that often? Have sex with the same woman?"

"Yes."

When she didn't say a word, Dylan took another breath and exhaled in a rush. "Aidan and I are bi, honey. And yeah, we're into the one-on-

one stuff, but we like having a woman in our bed. We *need* a woman in our bed."

Her continued silence spurred his frustration. "I don't know how to explain it in a way you'd understand, but Aidan and I aren't enough for each other. It fucking sucks, okay? But we both know it, and we've accepted it. Eventually one or both of us gets an itch that only a chick can scratch."

"An itch," she echoed dully. "Do you realize how messed-up that sounds?"

"What can I say? It's the truth." He briefly closed his eyes, knowing he was screwing this up but unsure of how to express his muddled emotions. "Look, I care about Aidan. He's…" Dylan gave a helpless shrug. "He's important to me, and, well, he's part of the package."

"The package being you?"

"Yes. Well, no. What I'm trying to say is, he and I are a package deal." He met her baffled gaze, deciding not to pull any punches. "You either sleep with both of us, or you sleep with neither of us."

Chapter Ten

CLAIRE SAT THERE IN STUNNED SILENCE. A PACKAGE DEAL? SHE EITHER fucked them both, or she didn't fuck them at all?

Was he for real?

"Are you for real?" she blurted out.

Dylan had the decency to look contrite. "That didn't come out the way I wanted it to."

"I don't care how it came out," she huffed. "The question is, did you mean it?"

He didn't respond for a few seconds.

Then he nodded.

"So you won't sleep with me again unless Aidan is there too?" Disbelief continued to spiral through her.

"Is the idea so unappealing?" he asked quietly.

She faltered. At a complete loss for words.

"Just picture it, Claire. You, me, Aidan. In bed together." His voice lowered to a seductive, almost hypnotic pitch. "Picture our hands on your body…our mouths and our tongues and our cocks…touching you, kissing you, fucking you."

Her pussy clenched so hard it hurt. The naughty images he conjured succeeded in making her even wetter than she'd been before, and the humiliating response had her scrambling off the bed in search of her clothes.

Jesus. What was the *matter* with her? Why didn't the idea disgust her? Horrify her? Insult her? That he could even ask her this was so… disrespectful.

And yet she didn't feel disrespected.

And she didn't feel disgusted. Or horrified. Or insulted.

Her mind was working a million miles a second as she hastily put on her clothes. She might have slept with Dylan just now, but she'd been attracted to Aidan from the second she'd laid eyes on him, and she got the feeling if the situation were reversed and she'd been locked in here with *Aidan*? She would have slept with him too.

What the hell did that say about her? Lusting over two men? Entertaining the idea of having sex with both of them?

"You liked what you saw in September, remember?" Dylan kept talking, kept tormenting her. "Now imagine getting to see that again, but not just a kiss. Picture me and Aidan sucking each other off, fucking each other."

She could barely breathe. Her face felt hot, tight, and her throat had closed up to the point of suffocation.

From arousal.

Because she was aroused.

Oh God, what was *wrong* with her?

"Imagine all the dirty, dirty things we could all do to each other," he said in a raspy voice. "Just imagine it, Claire."

Her pussy damn near convulsed. She couldn't look at Dylan, not when he was still sitting there naked as the day he was born.

"Would you…can you put on some clothes?" she stammered, keeping her gaze on her feet. "Please?"

A regretful sigh echoed in the bedroom.

She heard the mattress squeak, and quickly stepped out of the way so Dylan could pick up his discarded clothes. Only when he was dressed did she find the courage to look at him.

"I…" She took a breath. "I'm not that kind of woman, Dylan."

He raised a brow. "You mean the kind of woman who's looking for passion? The kind of woman who fingers herself after watching two men make out? You said so yourself—you realized you were lacking something in your life." A pause. "Maybe this was it."

Amazed laughter bubbled in her throat. "So I was lacking two cocks filling my various orifices? Is that what I need?"

"Passion," he said again.

"There might be such a thing as too much passion."

"Impossible." He stepped closer, those magnetic green eyes focused so intensely on her face she felt like he was peering into her soul. "Just think about it. Keep an open mind. You know, threesomes are more common than you think."

"Yeah, maybe in your circle. But I told you about the way I was raised. I was lucky to even lose my virginity considering how strict my dad is, and the only friend I have who comes close to being sexually promiscuous is Natasha, at least when she's not working double shifts at the hospital, and even then, she usually only has sex with *one person at a time*!"

"Usually?" Dylan's lips twitched.

Claire let out an exasperated breath. "I know she fooled around with a couple of girls in college, but I don't know if it was an official, quote unquote, *three-way*."

"What exactly is an *official* three-way?"

"You're making fun of me again," she muttered.

"Only because I love seeing your face turn all pink like that." He moved even closer, both his rough-skinned hands coming up to cup her chin. "You don't have to be embarrassed that the idea turns you on. And you don't have to give a definitive answer right this second. Just… think about it."

She gaped at him, feeling like she was in a daze. "Think about it," she echoed.

"Yes. Just promise me you will, okay?"

"I…" She cleared her throat, tried to make sense of this craziness. "I don't know if—"

A knock on the door interrupted her.

"Hello, boys and girls!" Aidan's voice, cheery and smug. "I just got back from my run. Decided to be nice and let you out early."

"Wow, what a prince," Dylan called out.

"Everything okay in there?"

"Everything is just fine. Now open the door, you asshole."

"Sure thing, let me just carry our glass angel to safety first."

As Aidan's footsteps receded, Dylan feathered his thumbs over Claire's cheeks and searched her face. "You okay, honey?"

Swallowing, she nodded.

"Good."

Just as the doorknob began to turn, Dylan gave her one last meaningful look and mouthed the words, "Think about it."

Claire choked down a hysterical laugh.

Right.

Like it was even *remotely* possible for her to think about anything else.

FOR THE TENTH TIME IN LESS THAN A MINUTE, AIDAN CHECKED THE alarm clock on the bedside table and confirmed that, yes, it was *still* 12:21 a.m. Annnnnd wait, the one in the minute column switched to a two, officially making it 12:22.

Son of a bitch.

Apparently he was not destined to fall asleep tonight.

He glanced over at Dylan's sleeping body, unable to stop the grin that sprang to his lips. As usual, Dylan had monopolized the comforter and it was now tangled between his legs. He lay on his side, providing Aidan with a perfect view of his bare ass. The SEAL slept in the nude, a habit that Aidan wholly approved of. Because damn, the man looked pretty fucking spectacular naked.

Aidan's groin stirred as he admired the sleek lines of Dylan's body, the strong sinew of his back, the taut ass you could bounce quarters off.

"I can feel you watching me." Dylan's sleepy voice echoed in the darkness of the bedroom.

Aidan had to laugh. "Man, you SEALs really do have eyes in the back of your head, huh?"

"Yep. So let's hear it."

"Hear what?"

Dylan rolled over, twisting the blanket even further and stealing the remaining square inches that had been covering Aidan's right leg.

"You barely blinked after I told you what happened between me and Claire today," Dylan said. "I'm still waiting for you to yell at me or call me an ass for taking what you wanted."

"What we *both* wanted."

"Yeah, but you wanted her first."

Aidan couldn't argue with that, but he also couldn't fault Dylan for succumbing to the same temptation that had been plaguing him for days. When he'd come home earlier, he'd immediately known that the couple had slept together. Not only had the animosity between them disappeared, but the second he'd looked at Claire, her face had turned into a tomato, a telltale sign something wicked had gone down.

He wasn't going to lie—he *had* experienced a pang of jealousy when he'd learned that Dylan had gotten the taste of her that Aidan had been denied, but he knew the blame was solely on his own shoulders. He'd locked them in a room with a bed and a box of condoms, for Pete's sake. Of course they'd make good use of both once they hashed everything out.

And no matter how he felt about them hooking up, he was happy they'd finally cleared the air and worked through their crap.

Of course, he hadn't been expecting an aching cock as a reward for his efforts.

"She wants you too, you know." Dylan's gruff voice interrupted his thoughts.

"I know." Aidan sat up and ran a hand through his rumpled hair. "But she won't be on board for this, man."

"I think she will," Dylan disagreed.

"She hid in your room all day and night—I'm pretty sure that's a clear sign she's not into it. Besides, you heard the way she described her childhood. It was all about right and wrong, Dyl. In her mind, having sex with two men isn't right."

There was a long beat. "Are you sure you're not pissed at me?"

He rolled his eyes. "I'm not pissed at you."

"Good, because you know I'd never do anything to intentionally hurt you."

The emotion thickening Dylan's voice caught him off-guard, elicited a rush of discomfort. He wasn't into deep, emotional discussions, never had been, never would be. They reminded him too much of the shrink he and his father had seen for a couple of years following his mother's death, after one of Aidan's teachers had notified the school counselor of how withdrawn he was in school.

Fuck, he'd hated talking to that shrink. She was always prying into his head, always asking him how he "felt" about this or how he "felt" about that.

"Aid? You do know that, right?"

Even in the dark, he could see the worry glimmering in Dylan's eyes. "Yeah, I know."

"And I still think Claire will come around. But until then…" The mattress shifted as Dylan bridged the distance between them.

Since Aidan was sitting up, Dylan's head was perfectly level with his crotch, and his cock instantly reacted to the other man's proximity, thickening beneath his cotton boxers. Unlike Dylan, he didn't sleep naked, but it wasn't long before he wound up that way.

With his boxers out of the way, Aidan cupped the back of Dylan's head and guided that sexy male mouth to his cock.

The first lick made him shudder.

Dylan peered up at him with a grin, his straight white teeth shining in the darkness. "Everything okay?"

"Mmm-hmmm."

The second lick made him moan. Closing his eyes, he leaned back on the oak headboard and enjoyed the incredible sensations created by Dylan's tongue gliding along the length of his shaft.

Dylan brought his hand into play, curling it around Aidan's cock and pulling the skin back to expose the head, which he promptly drew into his mouth and sucked gently on.

"Mmmm. I like that," Aidan mumbled. "Keep going slow for a bit."

His fingers tangled in Dylan's short hair, hips rocking restlessly as Dylan's tongue laved his cock with long, teasing strokes. Pressure built in his balls, and he knew he wouldn't last long at all. He'd been hard-up all week, drooling over Claire's sweet curves with no results, and longing for Dylan's hard muscles, also with no results. Now that his dick was finally getting some attention, the big guy was overly eager and ready to blow.

"Fuck, I love sucking your dick, man." Dylan's growl of pleasure vibrated through Aidan's body, sending a jolt of electricity right to the tip of his cock.

"Okay, forget slow." The words squeezed out of his chest. "Fast, I need it fa—"

A cell phone rang.

They both froze, then relaxed when they realized it was Aidan's ring tone and not the one that would signal Dylan to report to the base.

"Hold that thought," he said with a groan.

Licking his lips, Dylan lifted his head and grinned. "I dunno…I might decide I'm too tired to finish the job…"

"Hold that fucking thought."

Ignoring Dylan's mocking laughter, he grabbed his phone and glanced at the display. His stomach went rigid.

"Who is it?" Dylan asked.

"My dad."

"Isn't it like three in the morning in Chicago?"

"Yes." Without giving Dylan a chance to respond, he clicked the *talk* button and raised the phone to his ear.

"What's wrong?" he asked in lieu of greeting.

A tired laugh rippled over the line, easing some of his panic. "Nothing's wrong. I know it's late, but I had something to discuss with you. Did I wake you?"

"No, I was up." He slid off the bed and reached for his boxers. He balanced the phone on his shoulder so he could slip them on, then signaled to Dylan that he'd be right back.

The SEAL rolled onto his back with a resigned look in his eyes.

Aidan knew it bugged his roommate that he took his father's calls in private, but his relationship with his dad was weighed down with so much past sorrow that he preferred to keep that part of his life to himself.

He drifted into the living room and sank onto the couch. "What's going on?" he asked his father.

"I wanted to talk to you about the holidays."

"At three o'clock in the morning?"

"I couldn't sleep. The firm's trying to land the commission to design the new World Bank headquarters. I've been pulling quite a few all-nighters working on the proposal."

"I'm sure they'll love whatever you show them." And he totally meant that—the shadows that surrounded Tim Rhodes had never tainted his professional life. Aidan's father was one of the most prominent architects in the country.

"I hope so." His dad sounded distracted for a moment, and there was a shuffling of papers on the line. "Anyway, I wanted to let you know that I'll be out of town from the twenty-third until January fourth. Ronnie and I decided to fly to Switzerland to do some skiing."

Aidan swallowed his disappointment. How shocking. His dad was bailing on the holidays, the way he did every year.

At the same time, he couldn't bring himself to begrudge his father's decision to run away. Ever since Aidan's mom died, Christmas in the Rhodes household had been a wretched, miserable affair. Besides, it was nice to hear that Dad was still dating the same woman Aidan had met when he'd flown in for a visit in the spring.

"So you're still seeing Veronica, huh? How's that going?"

"It's good," his father admitted. "It's…easy. Comfortable."

"That's the way relationships should be, no?"

"Yes. Yes, they should." Tim cleared his throat. "I'm sorry to do this to you last-minute, son. Do you have friends you can spend the holidays with? Your roommate's family, maybe?"

"Yeah, I've got options," he said vaguely. "Don't worry about it. Just go on your trip and have fun on the slopes."

"I plan to." His father sounded relieved. "You're not upset?"

"No, of course not." The lie slid out smooth as cream, having been perfected over the years.

"All right, good. Well… I'll let you get to sleep. I'll email you from Zurich if I get the chance. Happy holidays, Aidan."

"Happy holidays, Dad."

He hung up and dropped the phone on the cushion beside him, breathing through the overwhelming sadness that clogged his throat.

"Your dad is ditching you for the holidays?"

He jumped at the sound of Claire's voice, swiveling his head in the direction it had come from. Sure enough, she was standing behind the large opening in the wall separating the living room from the kitchen.

"What are you doing up?" he asked, getting to his feet.

"I was hungry."

He headed into the kitchen and spotted the sandwich fixings on the counter. "Well, of course you are," he said pointedly. "You didn't join us for dinner."

Even in the shadows, he could see her blushing. "I wasn't hungry then. I am now." She cleared her throat. "Anyway, I'm sorry for eavesdropping. I didn't do it on purpose. You just came in and started talking before I could announce myself, and then I didn't want to interrupt."

"It's okay." He propped his hip against the counter and watched as she resumed the task of preparing a turkey and ham sandwich.

"So your dad is going skiing?" she prompted. "I heard you say something about the slopes."

"Yeah, he's heading to Switzerland for a couple of weeks, so I'll be spending Christmas here. With who, I have no clue yet."

"My holiday plans are up in the air too," she confessed. "Chris and I were supposed to spend Christmas in Paris—that was the last stop on our honeymoon. And since I was supposed to be gone, my parents booked a twelve-day cruise, and now my mom is freaking out and threatening to cancel their trip. I spoke to her earlier and tried to talk her out of it, but I don't know if I was persuasive enough."

"Would it be so bad if they stayed in town?"

"Honestly? I'm not feeling very festive. I'd rather they enjoy themselves in the Bahamas."

"What about you?"

She shrugged, then sat on a stool and took a bite of her sandwich. "I'll figure something out."

"You could spend the holidays with me." The words popped out before he could stop them.

Claire's gaze flew to his. "Are you serious?"

"Yeah. I mean, you've still got another two weeks off, so it's not like you have to rush back to San Francisco. Dylan and I are doing Christmas Eve with friends, and you can join us for that, and I'm assuming he's heading home right after dinner to see his mom, so you and I can keep each other company on Christmas Day."

"You really want me to stay for another two weeks?" She sounded troubled.

"Why not? You already know I like having you around."

"Yeah, but that was before…" She trailed off, averted her gaze, and focused on eating her sandwich.

"Before what?" When she didn't answer, he chuckled. "Before you had sex with Dylan, you mean?"

She lifted her head. "He told you."

"Yes."

"And you're not upset?"

"No."

"Did he tell you the rest?"

"About his mom's financial troubles? Yeah. Fucking sucks, huh?"

"It does. I'm glad he told you. But…I was referring to the *other* rest."

Aidan raised his eyebrows. "The other rest?"

"You know, what he asked me." She set her sandwich on her plate and reached for the OJ carton on the counter. As she poured herself a glass, she kept her head down, and kept talking. "He told me about how the two of you like to, um, you know, sleep with the same woman."

"We do," he confirmed with a nod.

"And that you guys want…um…you want me, I guess."

"We do," he said again.

She paused, and he didn't push her. From this point on, the situation was delicate. He couldn't bulldoze his way to results the way he'd done earlier by throwing Claire and Dylan together. It was time to proceed with extreme caution.

Which was pretty damn difficult to do when he wanted Claire McKinley more than he wanted his next breath.

She looked so beautiful tonight, the shadows dancing around her face and the light from the stove clock catching in her long hair. She'd left it loose and cascading down her shoulders, those wavy red tresses practically begging his fingers to stroke them. She was wearing the same pajamas she'd worn all week, a pair of plaid pants and a pink tank top that outlined her braless breasts.

"For Pete's sake, you and Dylan have perfected seductive looks to a T." Her weary voice alerted him to the fact that he'd totally been caught ogling her tits.

"I'm sorry?"

"Are you asking or telling?"

"Both?"

A reluctant smile stretched across her face, but it didn't stay there for long. "I've been thinking about Dylan's proposition all night," she started carefully.

A burst of disappointment went off in his chest. That was not the tone of a woman who was about to make him a happy man.

"But you're going to have to pass," he finished.

"I…can't."

He nodded. "All right then."

"You don't understand. I'm…damn it, I'm attracted to you, Aidan."

As she said the words, her eyes focused on his bare chest, and the lustful appreciation glimmering in her expression did wonders for his ego.

Her gaze abruptly moved to his face. "But I'm attracted to Dylan too—obviously, otherwise I wouldn't have slept with him. But two men at once? I can't be that woman. And don't get me started on the sleeping-with-Dylan part. I literally got out of a relationship less than a week ago—with his *brother*. What kind of woman sleeps with her ex-fiancé's brother?"

Her hand shook as she brought her glass to her lips and gulped down some juice.

Hating to see her in distress, Aidan rounded the counter, took the glass from her and placed it on the counter. Then he cupped her chin with both hands and fixed her with a serious look.

"You didn't do anything wrong. You can't help who you're attracted to. Dylan just happens to be Chris's brother. Big deal. You and Chris aren't married—you aren't even together anymore."

"It's still crossing a line."

"Who drew the line?" he countered. "Because it looks to me that the line is exactly where it should be, and you're on the right side of it. Chris, on the other hand? *He* crossed a line by running out on your wedding without having the decency to talk to you, and now that bastard is lying on a beach and enjoying what was supposed to be your honeymoon. If you want to play who's-the-asshole, then he's the clear winner."

Her soft laughter echoed in the kitchen. He loved the way she laughed, and he loved that he had the power to bring a twinkle to her eyes when seconds ago she'd looked beaten.

"Fine, he's the asshole," she relented. "But that doesn't change the fact that I'm not comfortable with…you know, with what you guys want from me."

He traced the seam of her lips with his finger, felt her mouth tremble beneath his touch. "Does it make you uncomfortable, or does it scare you because you're actually tempted to do it?"

She looked flustered. "I…I just can't. Please don't push me on this."

"I would never, ever push you into something you didn't want." He searched her gaze. "Do you believe me?"

She nodded. Without hesitation, which spoke volumes about the trust she had in him. The notion warmed his heart.

"Dylan won't push, either. We're the kind of guys who are fully aware that no means no."

To his surprise, Claire suddenly reached out and touched him. Her fingers stroked his cheek, and he sagged into her touch, oddly comforted by it.

"You are pretty damn amazing, you know that?" she murmured.

He swallowed. "So are you."

Their gazes collided and held. Tension gathered in the air, slowly transforming into awareness the longer they stared at each other. Aidan's chest felt hot, tight with excruciating need. His cock hardened, except this time it was all for Claire.

"I want to kiss you," he said gruffly.

Her eyes widened, hand dropping from his face. "Aidan…"

"One kiss." He let out a ragged breath. "Give me one taste, sweetheart."

"It's not a good idea," she whispered.

"No, but I'm still asking for it."

She got very quiet, but her gaze was still locked with his, and just when the silence dragged on a little too long, just when he thought she would shoot him down, she said, "Okay."

He didn't waste a single second. He lowered his head and took possession of her mouth, kissing her hungrily, desperately, days and days of pent-up need spilling over and turning him into a greedy bastard who wanted to do nothing but take, take, take.

Claire's little moan of pleasure got his blood going, fueled the urgency flowing through his veins. He angled his head and deepened the kiss. Thrust his tongue between her parted lips and explored her mouth, purposefully, thoroughly, needing to remember what she tasted like in case he never got this opportunity again.

He memorized every detail. She tasted like orange juice and toothpaste. Smelled like lavender. Felt like heaven with her full breasts pressed against his bare chest.

The last thing he wanted to do was wrench his mouth from her soft, full lips, but he'd asked for only one kiss, and he was a man of his word.

Breathing hard, he broke the kiss and edged backward.

Claire's breathing was just as labored as his, her big brown eyes glazed and shining with passion. "Aidan…" Her voice quivered. "I wish I could be who you and Dylan want me to be."

He smiled. "You are. You're exactly who you should be, sweetheart."

She blinked in surprise.

"And don't worry," he went on. "Dylan and I will be perfect gentlemen from this point on. Like I said, we won't push."

"No?" she said doubtfully. "Then why am I anticipating a seduction attempt or two?"

"I promise you, we won't try to seduce you." With that said, he headed for the doorway, then paused, unable to resist a few flirtatious parting words. "Unless you ask us to."

Chapter Eleven

"THAT IS THE SADDEST EXCUSE FOR A TREE I'VE EVER SEEN," DYLAN declared in disgust.

Next to him, Aidan voiced his agreement, then turned to Claire. "Come on, McKinley, you can't expect us to buy this tree."

"I can, and you will," she said sternly.

She didn't care that both men were looking at her like she'd grown a mustache. Out of all the trees in the lot, this seven-foot evergreen was the one she'd set her sights on and she wasn't going anywhere until that tree was strapped to the top of Aidan's SUV.

Dylan let out an exaggerated sigh. "This is really the one you want? Really?"

"Yes."

"But it's all patchy—that entire branch over there has no needles!"

"Don't care."

"And it leans to the right. Who wants a Leaning-Tower-of-Pisa tree?"

"I do." She crossed her arms. "Look, you know nobody else is going to buy this tree. Don't you think it deserves a good home?"

"It deserves to be tossed in a wood chipper," Dylan retorted.

"*You* deserve to be tossed in a wood chipper."

He raised his eyebrows. "That's your best comeback?"

"Children, please." Aidan raised his hand to silence them, then glanced over at her again. "I'll make you a deal. We'll buy this tree, but only if Dylan and I get to bail on the Walmart portion of the day. I'll give you my car keys and you can get the decorations and gift wrap by yourself."

She beamed. "Deal."

"I can't believe you're humoring her," Dylan muttered. "Come on, man, this tree is going to look shitty in the condo."

"*You're* going to look shitty in the condo," Claire said sweetly.

"Wow, another solid comeback, McKinley."

"Thank you." She caught the attention of the lone attendant in the lot and waved him over. "We'll take this one," she called.

Dylan grumbled the entire time it took to pay the attendant, haul the tree to the car and secure it on the roof.

Claire, on the other hand, felt triumphant and pretty damn happy. In fact, she couldn't remember the last time she'd had so much fun. These past couple of days with Dylan and Aidan had been a total blast—well, if you ignored the sexual tension that continued to hover over the three of them like a canopy.

But just like Aidan promised, neither man had tried to change her mind about the crazy threesome subject that had been broached.

Funny thing was, she was as disappointed as she was relieved. She knew they both still desired her; their hot gazes followed her all over the condo, and with Dylan doing classroom training at the base all week and coming home with Aidan at four o'clock every day, the three of them had been spending a lot of time together. Having dinner. Watching movies. Kicking ass in *Call of Duty* on the boys' PS3.

All very harmless activities, and yet Claire was liable to self-combust any day now. Memories of her encounter with Dylan continued to haunt her, mingling with the memory of Aidan's kiss. The carnal images even followed her into slumber—she'd had so many dream orgasms she'd lost count.

God, how was it possible to feel such overpowering desire for two men? *Equal* desire, to boot, because she wasn't drawn to one man more than the other, and as troubling as it was, when the three of them were together, she felt like everything…made sense.

Which made no sense, damn it!

"Oh, so now you're a Silent Susie after making us listen to you babble about that tree for the past forty-five minutes?"

Dylan's sarcastic voice brought a much-needed interruption to her crazy thoughts. "Sorry, did you say something?"

"I asked if you were cool with Sal's Diner for lunch. We're in the mood for breakfast food."

"I'm fine with that."

"Good, let's get this show on the road then." He proceeded to prove that his gentlemanly nature didn't extend to seating arrangements by shouting out, "Shotgun!"

Since he beat her to it, Claire grudgingly got into the backseat, while he turned to gloat at her from the passenger seat.

Aidan slid behind the wheel, started the car, and a moment later, the tree lot was nothing but a speck in the rearview mirror. When they came to a stop at a red light, Aidan glanced at the festively decorated storefronts in the plaza to their left, then mumbled something that sounded like "California Christmas".

Claire was perplexed. "Did you just say 'California Christmas'?"

Dylan twisted around to grin at her. "Don't mind him. He's got this idiotic idea that Christmas doesn't count unless it's celebrated in Antarctica."

"Snow," Aidan burst out. "It's not Christmas without *snow*."

She laughed. "Oh, you poor East-Coast baby."

"Have either of you even experienced a snowy Christmas?" he challenged.

"No," she admitted.

"I have." Dylan sounded smug. "A couple of years ago the team went wheels-up two days before Christmas, got sent to frickin' Russia, and I can't emphasize how cold and unpleasant that experience was."

"Well, no duh," Aidan retorted. "You were carrying out an op—of course you didn't get to appreciate the snow. You need to be in the holiday spirit in order to get the full effect."

"Nah, I'd rather just celebrate in the sunshine, open some presents and then hit the beach."

As Claire laughed, Aidan just mumbled a few unintelligible words and sped through the intersection.

Twenty minutes later, they were seated in a red vinyl booth at a family-style diner near the harbor, with Claire and Aidan on one side, Dylan on the other. After a perky blonde waitress took their orders, Claire glanced at Aidan.

"I keep forgetting to ask you, but why did you leave Chicago? Did you get stationed here?"

He shook his head. "No, my dad and I moved here when I was a teenager. He owns an architecture firm in Chicago, but he wanted to open a second branch on the West Coast. After high school, I joined the navy and made San Diego my home. Dad stuck around for five years or so to get the new office off the ground, then left it in the hands of his second-in-command and went back to Chicago."

"So what is it you do on the base? What's your rank?"

"Lieutenant junior grade."

"And the job description part?" she pressed when he didn't expand.

His dark eyes grew shuttered. "Naval intelligence."

"Okay…which means…?"

On the other side of the booth, Dylan rolled his eyes. "Honey, he does a lot of super-secret intelligence stuff that he's not allowed to talk about. I don't even bother to ask anymore because I know I'll just get the same vague non-answer."

She laughed. "Fine, then I won't ask, either. Hear that, Aidan? You can continue your super-secret life in peace."

"Thanks, sweetheart," he said dryly. "I appreciate that."

As they waited for their food, the subject changed to the holidays again. Dylan's expression turned glum. "I've decided not to talk to my mom about the money shit until after the New Year. The holidays are her favorite time of year. I don't want to upset her."

"That's probably a good idea," Claire said.

It still angered her that Chris and Shanna had withheld such important information from him. If she'd known Chris had been lying to her about Dylan having complete knowledge of the situation, she would have rectified that a long time ago. Dylan should have been told that his mother had been spiraling out of control, and now that she knew him better, she had no doubt he would've done everything in his power to help Shanna.

"So you're going to spend Christmas with her then?" she asked.

"Actually, no."

Both she and Aidan looked at him in surprise. "Since when?" Aidan demanded.

"Since she called me this morning and told me she got invited to spend the week in Palm Springs with one of the ladies from her gardening club." Dylan shrugged. "I told her to go. With Chris out of town, it would be just the two of us, and I'd rather she have some fun with her friend, considering what a tough year she's had."

"Here you go, guys." The waitress strolled up to their table juggling three plates in her hands.

She served Claire and Aidan without comment, but when she set Dylan's plate in front of him, her entire demeanor changed. Suddenly she was toying with a strand of her hair and smiling prettily at him.

"Is there anything else I can get you?"

Claire's body stiffened. The waitress might as well have added, "Like me, perhaps?" She was blatantly ogling Dylan like he was a yummy meal and she couldn't wait to dig in.

Hands off, bee-otch.

The streak of possessiveness that shot through Claire's body was unexpected, not to mention unwelcome, and she received a great amount of satisfaction when Dylan barely glanced at the blonde and said, "Nah, I'm good."

Noticeably disappointed, the waitress flounced off.

The moment she was gone, Aidan cast Claire a sidelong look. "I felt that," he murmured.

"Felt what?"

"Yeah, felt what?" Dylan chimed in.

A slow grin curved Aidan's mouth. "Little Miss Claire got all tense when that chick was flirting with you."

Dylan turned to her in extreme fascination. "Really?"

As usual, Claire felt her cheeks flame up. "I did not."

"Yes, you did," Aidan said cheerfully.

"Fine, maybe I did. But that's because she was practically undressing him with her eyes," she grumbled. "It was very rude."

"Yeah, I'm sure your RoboCop shoulders were a direct result of the waitress's bad manners." Grinning, Aidan picked up his knife and fork and sliced off a piece of the vegetable omelet he'd ordered.

"Made you jealous, huh?" Equally amused, Dylan dug into his own meal—a greasy bacon, egg and sausage combo that would probably send him into cardiac arrest on the way home.

Claire gritted her teeth, grabbed the maple syrup container and dumped a generous amount of syrup on her stack of fluffy pancakes.

"That's a lot of syrup," Dylan remarked as he watched her pour.

Aidan nodded in agreement. "Careful, sweetheart, you don't want your fingers to get all sticky."

He said the word *sticky* in the most seductive tone, and a rush of heat traveled straight to her core.

Ignoring them both, she picked up her utensils and started eating.

"Aw, look at that blush, Aid. We're making her mad."

"Or turning her on," Aidan countered.

Her thighs involuntarily squeezed together.

"Probably a little bit of both, I guess."

"Nah, she's not mad. That shade of red means annoyed."

"True," Dylan said. "And you're right, the pink splotches on her neck are a definite sign she's turned on."

Claire's fork clattered onto her plate. "*She* is sitting right here, assholes."

"Is there something wrong with us analyzing your face's various shades of red?" Dylan said silkily.

She turned to glare at Aidan in accusation. "You promised you wouldn't seduce me."

His laugh was downright mocking. "Trust me, this isn't seduction."

"No? So teasing me in public and getting me all hot is, what, normal lunch etiquette?"

"Yep," they said in unison.

She grabbed her fork and speared a piece of her pancake. "I hate you both," she informed them.

Dylan just grinned. "No, you don't."

"No, you don't," Aidan echoed.

For one exasperating moment, she looked from one man to the other, noting their smug expressions, feeling the waves of sensuality rolling off their big, hard bodies. As usual, her body reacted, breasts growing heavy, pussy tingling, heart squeezing with both heat and emotion.

She didn't understand it. The all-consuming lust, the relentless need, the strange rush of tenderness. But damn it, they were right. She didn't hate them at all.

What she hated was the way they made her feel.

When Natasha called later that evening, Claire practically dove off the leather couch to grab her cell phone from the coffee table. It was only ten o'clock, but she'd been looking for an excuse to disappear into her bedroom for hours now. She didn't even care that Aidan was looking at her with that knowing expression. Maybe if he dialed down his potent sexuality, she wouldn't have to seek any escape she could.

The remainder of her day with the guys had only grown more and more intolerable, what with their constant teasing and the way they'd "innocently" kept brushing up against her the entire time they'd put up and decorated the tree. As a result, she'd spent the whole evening so turned on she couldn't walk without her core aching or take a breath without her breasts tingling.

Fortunately, Dylan left around eight o'clock to meet "the boys", as he called them, which left only Aidan to contend with. He'd stayed behind to do some work in his office, then talked her into watching a movie with him under the romantic glow of the Christmas tree lights. Of course, he'd made sure to sit directly beside her when he had a whole other couch and two armchairs to choose from.

For some reason, the men had chosen today to break their no-seduction promise, and Claire got the feeling she was two heated looks and double entendres away from caving.

Unless Natasha could talk her out of it.

"Hi!" she said eagerly. "What's up?"

Natasha's laughter tickled her eardrum. "Wow, you sound ridiculously happy to hear from me. Miss me much?"

"Miss you tons," she confessed.

"Right back atcha, hon. I have some time before I start my shift so I figured I'd call and see how you're holding up."

"What time is it there? Oh, and I'm fine."

"It's just past five in the morning, and you don't sound fine at all. Your voice is doing that weird grumble it does when you're annoyed. I guess you heard from Chris, huh?"

"Actually, I haven't. Not even a text since he went to Aruba. I'm assuming he's on his way to London now for the second leg of our honeymoon."

"Bastard."

"Yup."

"Are you still in San Diego with Chris's brother?"

"Yeah, but I don't think I'll be staying for much longer." She hesitated, sighed, then decided not to beat around the bush. "I had sex with him."

Nothing but silence echoed on the extension.

"Nat? You still there?"

"Still here. You're joking, right?"

"I'm afraid not."

"You…you really had sex with Chris's brother?"

"I really had sex with Chris's brother."

"Wow. I have no idea what to say to that, except maybe…are you fucking *nuts*?"

"I've been asking myself that same question ever since it happened. And before you say anything else, you should probably know that it gets worse."

"Is that even possible? Oh my God, hold on. I want to light a smoke so my brain can calmly absorb all of this."

There was a rustling on the line, followed by the hiss of a lighter, and then Natasha's intake of breath, a familiar sound that had Claire shaking her head in disapproval.

"You're smoking again?" she accused her best friend. "You said you quit."

"Can you lecture me about it another time? Right now I need you to tell me what the hell is going on over there."

"Like I said, I slept with Dylan."

"Mmm-hmmm, we've already got that part down. What else?"

"Well, he has a roommate…Aidan…And I—"

"You slept with his roommate too?" Natasha exclaimed.

"No, no, I didn't. I mean, I kissed him, but—"

"You *kissed* him?"

"Argh, would you let me finish already? I really need your help here, Nat."

"Sorry. Keep going."

It took ten minutes for Claire to describe—in great detail—the insane situation she'd found herself in, and when she finally wrapped up, Natasha sounded utterly stunned.

"Wow. So the two of them want to fuck you together?"

"Yup."

"And you're attracted to both of them?"

She sighed. "Yup."

"What are they like?" her friend asked curiously.

Claire chewed on her bottom lip for a moment. "They're both pretty wonderful. Dylan is the more easygoing of the two. We bicker a lot, but he's so much fun to be around, and he's sweet and sexy and…"

She drifted off, still pondering. "Aidan is more serious, but equally awesome. Something about his intensity makes me feel…protected. Except I feel that way with Dylan too. He's so relaxed on the surface, but I know he could kill a man without batting an eye. They both can." She moaned. "And that turns me on, by the way! Why does that turn me on?"

"Because military men are hot," Natasha said frankly.

"Says the lesbian."

"Hey, just because I'm into chicks doesn't mean I can't find men attractive."

"Fair enough. Besides, you're right. They *are* hot. They're so fucking hot I'm going crazy. I need your advice. Tell me what you think about all this."

"Okay, well, this is a no-brainer. You—"

"Have to say no," she finished.

"—have to say yes."

Claire's jaw dropped. "Wait, what?"

"You have to say yes. Duh."

"How is that *duh*? Are you seriously encouraging me to have a threesome with them?"

"Hells to the yeah! Claire, you have two sexy dudes wanting to make you come every which way, and not only that, but they're into making *each other* come every which way—do you realize how hot that is?"

"I cannot believe you're saying this. You were supposed to talk me out of doing something crazy."

"Why is it crazy? People have threesomes all the time."

"Would you and Gwen want a random woman joining you in the bedroom?" Claire challenged.

"Sure, depending on who she was and if Gwen and I were both attracted to her. But neither of these guys is random. You've been living with them for more than a week. I say go for it. You're entitled to have a little fun."

"You're a traitor," she mumbled.

"Nope, just a woman who doesn't think sex needs to be complicated."

The sound of footsteps captured Claire's attention. A moment later, she heard male voices wafting from the other side of the apartment.

"Great, Dylan's home," she said gloomily. "Now they'll gang up on me again."

Natasha let out a delighted laugh. "Let them."

She heard more footsteps, closer this time, then a low male chuckle that had definitely come from Aidan. She tensed, expecting a knock, but the men walked right past her door. A few seconds later, there was a loud clatter followed by a thump, as if something had been knocked over in the other room.

She frowned. "Nat, I have to go. I just heard a noise and I want to make sure everything's okay."

"No prob. Make sure to text me after the threesome, 'kay?"

"Ha-ha."

"I'm serious. I'm going to want all the deets."

Claire rolled her eyes and said goodbye, then left the bedroom and headed toward Aidan's room. The door was ajar, which meant she had no problem hearing the male groan that rang out from within.

She froze in place. That hadn't sounded like a groan of pain…at least not the kind of pain incurred by an injury.

Her pulse kicked up a gear.

Walk away, her common sense ordered.

Rather than take that very sound advice, she found herself creeping closer. It wouldn't hurt to take a quick peek, would it? Just to make sure the boys really were okay? Because she'd definitely heard a crash. And a thump. And she'd be a bad person if she didn't at least check to make sure that—

Jesus H. Christ.

A sense of déjà vu slammed into her as she encountered a very familiar scene.

Heart thudding, she hovered just out of sight of the doorway, but in a position that allowed her to see inside Aidan's room.

Up against the tall oak dresser, the two men were locked in an embrace that sent a bolt of desire straight to her core. Claire forgot how to breathe as she watched the hottest make-out session ever unfold before her eyes. Groans of pleasure drifted into the hall, then a series of tortured expletives as the men began clawing at each other's clothes.

Pants hit the floor. Shirts were whipped aside. Boxers disappeared.

Her entire body burned as if she'd stepped into a raging inferno.

Naked. Oh God, they were naked now, but she only had a view of Aidan's back. And backside. Holy hell, he had the greatest ass, round and tight and sexy. Dylan must have agreed, because his hands instantly slid down to squeeze those taut buttocks.

They kissed again and the flash of tongue she glimpsed made her swallow a moan. She needed to walk away. Now. Right now.

But her feet stayed rooted to the hardwood.

"Suck my cock." Dylan's low command sent a shiver running through her.

"Ask me nicely," came Aidan's mocking response.

"Get down on your knees, Aid, and suck my goddamn cock."

Every muscle in Claire's body tightened with anticipation. The loud pounding of her heart muffled their voices, so she inched closer, needing to hear what they were saying.

"I fucking love drunk Dylan," Aidan growled. "Always going all alpha on me."

"Good for you, man. Now suck drunk Dylan's cock."

When Aidan dropped to his knees, Claire almost fainted.

Stars danced in front of her eyes, bothersome white dots that made everything look hazy. She blinked rapidly to clear her vision. No way was she missing a second of this. No. Fucking. Way.

She watched Aidan grip the root of Dylan's erection with one hand. Ever so slowly, he leaned in and wrapped his lips around the glistening mushroom tip.

Her mouth fell open as Aidan's head began to move up and down Dylan's cock. He sucked with fervor, using his fist to pump the thick shaft on every upstroke, and each time his mouth enveloped the entire hard length, Dylan groaned with abandon.

"Fuck, yeah. Oh Jesus, keep doing that, man."

Man. Not *baby* or some other endearment, Claire noted, and that hoarse syllable merely underlined what she was witnessing. A man giving another man a blowjob.

Natasha was right. There was nothing freaking hotter.

Dylan began moving his hips in earnest, his hands thrusting into Aidan's dark hair to control the pace.

Claire couldn't look away. Couldn't focus on anything other than the long, glistening cock tunneling in and out of Aidan's accommodating mouth. When Dylan let out a strangled curse, she managed to wrench her gaze up so she could see his expression. The look on his face stole the breath right out of her lungs.

Raw pleasure, pure lust.

Her gazed drifted back to Aidan, whose head was bobbing, whose enthusiasm floored her, whose erection was unmistakable as it slapped his belly with his every move. She wouldn't have expected him to be the submissive one, the one on his knees moaning as Dylan's dirty commands directed his movements.

Ironically, the second she made the observation, it got turned on its head.

"I need you in me," Dylan mumbled.

Claire's breath caught. She thought she might have misheard him, but then he repeated himself, leaving no doubt as to what he wanted.

"God, Aidan, I need you in me. Come up here and fuck me, damn it."

Chapter Twelve

DYLAN WAS AROUSED TO THE POINT OF PAIN, HIS BALLS HARDER THAN bowling balls, every drop of blood in his body pooling and throbbing in his dick. He totally regretted having a few beers with Cash and the boys at their favorite dive bar tonight. Alcohol always turned him into a raging horndog, as all his buddies could confirm, and though he wasn't one for melodrama, he knew that if he didn't come soon, he might actually die.

"You want me in your ass, huh?" Aidan's voice was all gravel as he rose to his full height, putting them at eye level.

Knots of anticipation formed in Dylan's groin. "Yes. I want you in my ass."

His gaze dropped to Aidan's cock, eight inches of rock-hard power. He bit back a moan as he watched that cock grow even fuller, a pearl of moisture seeping from its tip.

"Goddammit, Aid, stop standing there and give it to me."

Amusement flickered in Aidan's chocolate-brown eyes before darkening into sinful promise. "Turn around. Put your hands on the dresser and don't move."

Taking a breath, Dylan did as ordered. He braced both palms on top of the sleek oak and waited. Listened to the sound of Aidan's footsteps heading for the bed, the creak of a drawer, the ripping of a condom wrapper and the plastic snap of a tube opening.

When warm hands caressed his back, he sucked his breath in. Continued to wait with patience he certainly didn't feel. He wanted to bring one hand to his cock and jack off, but Aidan had told him not to move, and there was something wickedly hot about being at the other man's mercy, letting Aidan control when and how he came.

Aidan's breath tickled the nape of his neck as the man moved closer. The feel of an erection pressing against his ass cheeks made him shudder.

"Stop being a cocktease. Give me what I want."

There was a husky chuckle. "How bad do you want it?"

Warm hands slowly traveled down to Dylan's ass, giving it a light squeeze. He groaned. "So goddamn bad."

When slick fingers slid between his ass cheeks and probed his entrance, his head fell forward, the anticipation growing, surging in his veins.

Aidan took his time getting him ready, using a generous amount of lubrication, teasing Dylan by pushing just the tip of one finger inside.

"I love this tight ass," Aidan muttered. "Feels so good clamped around my cock."

He groaned with impatience, ready to burst, ready to beg, but before he could voice his frustration, Aidan slipped two fingers inside and started fucking him with them.

"Oh *fuck*," he moaned. The slight burning sensation gave way to ripples of pleasure that pulsated in his ass and cock.

"Christ, I wanna fuck you." Aidan added a third finger, and Dylan's body stretched to accommodate it. "I wanna shove my dick in your ass and fuck you hard."

"Do it," he begged. "*Please*."

The desperation in his voice roused another chuckle from the man who was determined to torment him. Aidan continued to push his fingers in and out in a leisurely rhythm that caused sweat to break out on Dylan's brow.

He bore down on those long fingers and pleasure jolted through him, but he knew this didn't feel half as good as the sensation of being filled by this man.

"I swear to God, man, if you don't shove your dick inside me right now I'm gonna kick your—"

Aidan plunged in with one fluid stroke.

The threat died on Dylan's lips and his head damn near exploded from the deep, erotic intrusion. Aidan's cock was buried in his ass, and it felt so criminally good he almost blacked out.

And that was before the man began to move—once Aidan started ramming into him with hard, fast strokes, Dylan's surroundings faded away, his entire world reduced to a haze of pleasure and the sound of flesh slapping flesh.

"Love fucking you," Aidan mumbled, digging his fingers into Dylan's hips.

He buckled back, meeting him thrust for thrust, growling when Aidan drove even deeper and faster. The dresser shook and smacked against the wall. Their ragged breathing heated the air.

"You wanna come, don't you?" Aidan reached around and gripped Dylan's erection in his fist. "You're close, aren't you?"

A groan choked out. "*Yes.*"

"Good, because I wanna feel your hot come on my hand when I blow my load inside you. Do it now, man."

That was all it took, the harsh command, the rough pump of Aidan's hand on his dick. The climax boiled in his balls, but just before it could spill over, a flash of movement crossed Dylan's peripheral vision.

He turned his head and that's when he saw her. Standing there watching. Rosy-red lips parted, cheeks flushed, breasts rising and falling with each shallow breath.

Their eyes locked and Dylan exploded like a Fourth of July fireworks display, the pleasure searing his balls before shooting out in all directions, seizing every muscle in his body. Hot jets sprayed into Aidan's hand, which instantly made the other man lose control.

"Oh fuck, coming. Coming inside your ass, man." Breathing hard, Aidan rested his forehead on Dylan's shoulder and trembled in release, his cock throbbing in Dylan's tight channel.

Dylan's gaze never left Claire's. Her brown eyes blazed with molten heat as they stared at each other.

Maybe he should have felt embarrassed that she'd witnessed him being dominated this way, but he didn't. He only felt exhilarated and sated.

He tilted his head slightly, offering her an unspoken invitation.

Join us.

A second passed. Two. Three.

And then she broke the eye contact and stumbled off.

He didn't feel an ounce of disappointment as Claire disappeared in the shadows, because even though she'd fled just now, there was no doubt in his mind she'd be back.

He'd seen the hunger in her eyes. He'd *felt* it. Claire McKinley was going to be theirs, all right.

Hell, she already was.

She just didn't know it yet.

When Claire entered the kitchen early the next morning, she made a conscious and diligent effort not to meet the eyes of the two men sipping their coffees at the kitchen counter.

Nope, wasn't going to look at them. As long as she avoided all visual contact, she would be just fine and fully capable of acting like she hadn't seen anything out of the ordinary last night.

"Morning," Aidan said lightly.

"Morning."

"Morning," Dylan piped up.

"Morning," she murmured again.

There. She'd managed to greet them both without making eye contact.

She opened the fridge, taking an extra long time rummaging through it even though the carton of milk she wanted was right there on the middle shelf. The frigid air was a relief, blasting her scorching cheeks and cooling her down. God, she didn't think she'd stopped blushing since the moment she'd crept up to Aidan's door and seen—

Nothing. You saw nothing.

She snatched the milk carton, then walked over to the cabinets above the counter to find a bowl. Except the cupboard was a good five inches out of reach, forcing her to get on her tiptoes and stick her arm up in a strained effort to connect with the handle.

Out of nowhere, Aidan came up behind her, his lips dangerously close to her ear. "Let me help you with that."

His lemon-scented aftershave teased her senses, made her feel lightheaded. Why did he have to smell so good?

He opened the cupboard, pulled out a ceramic bowl and held it out.

She accepted the bowl with a soft "thank you".

And without meeting his eyes.

"So what are your plans for the day?" Dylan asked her as she ducked into the pantry for a box of Corn Flakes.

"I wanted to hit the mall to do some Christmas shopping." She prepared a bowl of cereal, then sat at the opposite end of the counter and started to eat. Quickly. Because the faster she ate, the faster she could leave the kitchen and pretend she'd never seen—

Nothing. You saw nothing.

"Want us to drop you off before we head to the base?" Aidan offered.

"It's six-thirty in the morning, Aidan. The stores don't open until nine."

"Right. My bad. You'll be okay taking a cab, then?"

"I'll be just fine." Crap, that sounded snippy. She almost lifted her head to shoot him an apologetic look, then thought better of it.

From the corner of her eye, she saw that Dylan had drained his coffee and was sliding off his stool. He strode toward the dishwasher and opened the door, then bent over to place his empty cup in the tray.

I want you in my ass.

Dylan's desperate plea to Aidan echoed in her mind, and a hot shiver scurried up her spine. Oh God, the way he was bending over like that, his ass hugged by those camo pants… But there'd been nothing covering that ass last night, not unless you counted Aidan's muscular thighs pressed up against Dylan's buttocks as Aidan's cock slammed into—

"You okay there, sweetheart?" Aidan inquired in a gratingly cheerful voice.

"I'm fine," she muttered.

"If you say so."

But she was the furthest thing from *fine*. Now that she'd allowed that one memory in, the rest were buzzing in her head like a swarm of bees.

Aidan on his knees, his lips stretched around Dylan's cock.

Dylan begging to be taken.

Aidan taking him.

Both of them coming.

The whole scene had replayed in her dreams last night, the filthiest, sexiest, raunchiest dreams she'd ever had in her life. She'd woken up between each one, panting, sweating, quivering from what she suspected had been actual orgasms. And each dream had ended the same way—with Dylan's green eyes burning with ecstasy as he held her gaze and orgasmed.

He'd *seen* her. He'd seen her standing there, and yet he hadn't said a word. Hadn't sought her out last night, wasn't mentioning it this morning.

She didn't know whether to be relieved or disappointed.

"All right, we're taking off." Aidan's voice jolted her back to the present. "Call my cell if you need anything, okay?"

"Okay." She kept her gaze firmly on her empty cereal bowl.

As they shuffled toward the doorway, Claire couldn't believe she'd made it through the entire exchange without a single look in their direction. She was about to give herself a mental pat on the back when Dylan's silky voice drifted her way.

"Hey, Claire?"

Her head lifted involuntarily, causing the accidental meeting of their eyes.

"Yeah?" she said warily.

"You were moaning in your sleep last night." Chuckling, Dylan sauntered out of the kitchen.

"Who do you think would win in a fight, Costner's Robin Hood or Crowe's?" Aidan stretched his legs out and absently glanced at the TV, which was playing the Russell Crowe version of the aforementioned film.

Dylan was lying on the other couch, his head propped up by a throw pillow. "That's a trick question," he said immediately. "The real winner would be Cary Elwes from *Men in Tights*."

Aidan burst out laughing. "Why?"

"Duh. Because he speaks with a British accent." In an impressive move, Dylan recited the line *in* a British accent.

"Shit, that's actually a badass British accent, bro."

"I know, right?"

They turned their attention back to the screen, but Aidan wasn't particularly interested in the movie. He was too busy wondering what Claire was doing in Dylan's bedroom. She'd been hiding away all night, same way she'd done last night, and the night before, and the night before that.

He had to give her credit—the woman had successfully managed to avoid them for three days now, a damn near impossible feat considering they were living in the same condo.

Aidan knew all about Claire's initiation into the wonderful world of voyeurism, and damn, he wished he'd gotten to see her face that night. Dylan insisted she'd liked everything she'd seen. Judging by the blush that had graced her cheeks ever since, Aidan suspected his roommate was right.

"She's only got a week and a half of vacation time left."

"I know." Dylan sounded as glum as Aidan felt.

"I don't want her to go." The confession slipped out before he could stop it.

"Me neither."

They fell silent again, watching the movie with mutual disinterest.

When he heard soft footsteps a few minutes later, Aidan's heart did an involuntary flip. He eagerly sat up just as Claire stepped into the living room, but his rising excitement plummeted the moment he saw her face.

"What's wrong?" he said instantly.

Looking pale, she focused her gaze not on Aidan, but Dylan. "If I ask you something, do you promise to give me an honest answer?"

Concern filled Dylan's eyes. "What's going on?"

"Just promise."

"I promise. Now what is it, honey?"

"Did you know Chris was having an affair?"

Aidan had not been expecting *that*. Neither had Dylan, because the man's jaw dropped in shock.

"What?"

Claire walked over to the armchair and sat down with a miserable expression. "Did you know?"

"Of course not." Dylan shook his head, looking flabbergasted. "What do you mean, Chris was having an affair?"

"I don't know for sure, but that's what the evidence suggests."

"What evidence?" Dylan asked sharply.

She sighed. "I was on Facebook messaging a few friends from college, you know, just passing the time, and I was looking at some of their pictures. This one friend—well, more of an acquaintance, really—she's a lawyer and she posted some pics of this charity event that took place a few months ago. Chris attended, but I couldn't go, so he went alone. He's in one of the pictures, looking very cozy with this skinny blonde who has her arm around his waist."

"That doesn't mean they were having an affair," Aidan pointed out.

"I'm not done," she said tersely. "So the blonde in the picture was tagged—her name's Stephanie Lowenstein, and she's a mutual Facebook friend of mine and Lisa's, my lawyer friend. So I clicked on Stephanie's profile."

Aidan's stomach clenched. Shit, he didn't like where this was going.

"Her privacy settings are nonexistent, which means I was able to look at everything on her timeline. Including her pictures."

"Aw, fuck," Dylan swore. "My brother was in some of them?"

"In a lot of them, at least the most recent ones." Claire's mouth set in a tight line. "She's in London with him right now. And she was in Aruba with him last week."

Dead silence crashed over the room.

On the other couch, Dylan's face went from shocked, to stricken, to downright furious.

"Are you serious?" he demanded.

"As a heart attack. And these pictures were *a lot* more cozy than the one from the party."

"That fucking bastard. What the *hell* is my brother thinking?"

"Probably that he's hit the jackpot. This girl is obviously related to Frank Lowenstein, the senior partner at Chris's firm. She's probably his daughter, which means she's not only loaded, but has crazy connections and a membership to that stupid country club, and she probably comes with a million other perks Chris would appreciate."

Claire shoved a strand of hair out of her eyes. "I can't believe him. I mean, I have to assume he was involved with her before the wedding, right? You don't go away with someone unless the two of you have some sort of previous involvement, or at least a flirtation, right?"

Dylan let out a breath. "Yeah, I'd say they were most likely involved."

Biting her lip, she looked down at the hands she'd clasped in her lap. "I don't even know why I'm so upset. It's just…fuck, call me a loser, but it's an ego thing, I guess. I've never been cheated on before, and I hate the idea that someone found another woman more desirable than me. Even if that someone is Chris." Her head lifted abruptly, her gaze seeking out Aidan's, then Dylan's. "You think I'm desirable, right?"

Aidan barked out an incredulous laugh. "Are you kidding me? You're the most desirable woman on the goddamn planet."

"Hands down," Dylan confirmed.

"You're just saying that to make me feel better."

Aidan patted the couch cushion next to him. "C'mere."

She hesitated.

"Claire. Don't make me pick you up and carry you here," he warned.

She must have known he'd totally follow through on that threat, because she got off the armchair and joined him on the couch.

Aidan took her hand and dragged his thumb over her knuckles. "We're not saying what you want to hear in order to make you feel better. And you know what? Forget feeling better—you have absolutely no reason to be upset in the first place. Chris is an ass—" He glanced at Dylan "No offense, man."

"None taken."

"—And he doesn't get the right to put that sad look in your eyes," Aidan finished. "Let him have his Stephanie Lowenstein. I'm sure they deserve each other. You, on the other hand, deserve way better."

Hopping off the couch, Dylan marched over and settled on the other side of her. He reached for her free hand and gave it a gentle squeeze. "You deserve the best," he declared. "You, Claire McKinley, deserve to be worshipped."

She smiled. "You guys are too sweet."

They both shrugged modestly.

"I'm serious," she insisted. "You're the sweetest, kindest, most amazing men I have ever met."

"You don't have to shower us with compliments," Dylan said with a grin. "We're already whipped by you. Case in point—that god-awful tree over there."

"He's right," Aidan agreed. "I mean, for us to even allow such a monstrosity into our home says a lot about—"

She cut him off with a kiss.

Claire's lips were soft, warm, sweeter than honey. She kissed him tenderly, with only the fleeting brush of tongue, and before he could even react, she was gone. Shifting around and bestowing that same loving kiss on Dylan's lips.

"What was that for?" Dylan murmured.

"Just felt like it." Smiling, she got to her feet, her hands toying with the bottom of her bright yellow T-shirt. "So I was thinking…"

Hope erupted in Aidan's chest, but he refused to acknowledge it. Not until Claire made her intentions clear.

And she made those intentions crystal clear by pulling her shirt over her head and then wiggling out of her leggings.

His breath lodged in his throat. Her skimpy white bra barely covered her full breasts, and the matching panties were nothing but a little triangle with two thin straps. She was beautiful. Stunning. Extraordinary. There weren't enough adjectives in the English language to describe the vision of female perfection standing in front of them.

Lord, her bare skin looked so soft to the touch. He wanted to run his fingers over all that silky feminine flesh, but he resisted the urge, awaiting her next move.

"Claire, you don't have to…" Dylan trailed off, his eyes glued to the curves she'd put on display.

Aidan picked up where the other man left off. "You don't have to prove anything," he said gruffly. "You're the most beautiful woman I've ever met. If this is about wanting to feel desirable, then you've already got your answer."

A little smile tugged on the corners of her mouth. "Actually, this is about me wanting to be worshipped."

Aidan exchanged a look with Dylan, who seemed equally anxious. Neither of them wanted her to do something she truly didn't feel comfortable doing.

"You said that's what I deserved, right?" Raising a brow, she glanced at each of them in challenge.

"Yes," Dylan said.

"Then prove it, because if I ever needed to be worshipped, it's right now."

Without waiting for an answer, she began walking away, drawing both their gazes to her perfect ass. She halted when she was halfway to the corridor, reached around to unhook her bra, then tossed the lacy garment in their direction.

Keeping her back to them, she peeked over her shoulder with a coy smile. "You boys coming, or what?"

Chapter Thirteen

CLAIRE'S HEART WAS BEATING PERILOUSLY FAST AS SHE ENTERED AIDAN'S bedroom. Her hands shook with both excitement and nervousness, but she tried not to focus on the latter. Because she wanted this.

She really, *really* wanted this.

It had nothing to do with the discovery that Chris had brought another woman on what should have been their honeymoon. She didn't have feelings for Chris anymore, at least not this latest version of him. Or rather, the man he'd been all along but she'd been too blind to see it. The Chris who wanted to work in the prosecutor's office and who liked taking her dancing didn't exist. The real Chris didn't deserve her, and he'd played no role in her decision to give in to Dylan and Aidan.

She couldn't avoid the truth any longer—she had feelings for them both. She desired them both.

And she wanted both of them to fuck her.

The guys walked into the room without a word. She'd left the light off, and neither man made a move to flick the switch. They just stood there in the darkness, shadows dancing on their respectively handsome faces, making the entire encounter feel so very dirty.

It was Dylan who spoke first. "Get on the bed, Claire."

A dark thrill shot through her. She climbed onto the mattress of the king-sized bed and lay down on her back, resting her head on the mound of pillows leaning on the headboard.

Aidan turned on the light, dimming it to a sexy glow, and then the two men approached with slow, methodical strides. Predatory, almost.

Her pulse raced as they started to undress. Their shirts came off first, exposing bare chests heavy with muscle, gleaming abs, powerful arms.

The pants were next, the material hitting the hardwood floor with a soft rustle.

Dylan wore nothing underneath. His erection rose to full salute, making her mouth water.

Aidan pushed his white boxers down his hips, and Claire got her first view of his cock. Longer than Dylan's, but not as thick. Now her mouth went bone-dry.

Hot male gazes roamed her body, which was stretched out on the bed for them like a sacrificial offering. But rather than take what she was freely giving, they turned to look at each other. And then they kissed.

Claire's panties flooded with moisture. Oh Lord. She would never get used to the sight of them doing that. Their mouths locked together, tongues teasing and exploring. She gasped when Aidan cupped Dylan's ass and yanked the other man closer, grinding his cock against Dylan's.

The kiss lasted for several more seconds, then broke off abruptly, and the next thing she knew, Aidan was sitting next to her on the bed. She squeaked in surprise when he tore her panties off her body. The fabric ripped with a hiss and was tossed aside, leaving her completely exposed to his hungry gaze.

"I've been dreaming about this pussy for more than a week," he said in a serious tone. "Dylan says you taste like heaven."

Still standing by the bed, Dylan nodded earnestly. "She does, man. Makes the sexiest sounds when she comes too."

"Spread your legs wider," Aidan ordered.

She parted her thighs, anticipation coiling inside her like a rattlesnake. She wanted his mouth on her, but he was taking his sweet time giving it to her.

Licking his lips, he brought his hand between her legs and stroked her with the tip of his index finger.

She shuddered, wanting more. Needing more.

That finger skimmed down to her opening and swirled around in the moisture pooled there.

"So wet. Fuck. I need a taste." He promptly lowered his head and lapped her up his with tongue.

Claire's hips shot off the bed. "Oh, that's good."

"Only gonna get better, baby."

He wasn't lying. Once he got going, she turned into a puddle of mindless, quivering lust. His tongue probed her—long, thorough licks that made her moan. Pinpricks of pleasure rose on her skin, and she rocked her hips to meet his greedy tongue, every muscle in her body quivering, tightening, throbbing.

She caught a flicker of movement and realized Dylan was jerking himself off. His green eyes burned, lips slightly parted as he watched Aidan go down on her.

"How does she taste, bro?" he murmured.

Aidan raised his head and licked his lips, which were glossy with her juices. "So fucking sweet." Then he resumed his feasting, shoving a finger into her tight sheath as he sucked on her clit with fervor.

White dots danced in front of her eyes. She was close. Really, really close. But she didn't want to come yet. She wanted these incredible sensations to last forever. Her eyelids fluttered closed, then popped open when a deep groan from Aidan vibrated in her core.

Dylan had moved to the foot of the bed and was kneeling on the hardwood as he enveloped Aidan's cock with his mouth.

Never in her life would she have thought she'd be in this situation. Being devoured by a hot male mouth while another man sucked that man's dick.

Her wide eyes tracked Dylan's every move, the way he took Aidan's shaft all the way to the back of his throat, how he squeezed Aidan's balls with one strong hand, the wet sucking sounds he made as his mouth traveled up and down that hard length.

"Come for me." Aidan's voice was thick with desire. "I want you to come all over my face, Claire."

God, another dirty talker. Why didn't that surprise her?

He lowered his mouth again and fastened it on her clit. As he sucked, he fingered her in a steady rhythm, and it wasn't long before an orgasm seized her body and swept her away to a whole other dimension.

When she crashed back to Earth, she glimpsed the satisfied look glittering in Aidan's eyes. Her gaze moved back to Dylan, who was no longer tending to Aidan, but watching her.

"I love the look on your face when you come," he told her.

She was too blissfully numb to respond, unable to do anything more than lie there and quiver.

Dylan got on the bed and lay on his side next to her. He reached for her hand and brought it to his erection, curling her fingers around that wide shaft. She immediately began to stroke him, then felt her other hand being yanked to Aidan's cock as he settled on her other side.

Oh wow. She couldn't believe this was happening. Aidan's cock was slick from Dylan's saliva, making it easy to move her fist along the length of him.

She thought about spitting in her hand to get Dylan nice and lubed, but she impulsively reached between her legs instead.

Dylan growled when she brought her hand back to his cock and resumed stroking. "God, honey, that was the hottest thing you've ever done. Rub those sweet juices all over my dick."

Although she'd just climaxed, she was nowhere near sated. Continuing to stroke both men, she turned her head and planted a soft kiss on Dylan's lips, then shifted in the other direction to do the same to Aidan.

And it was to Aidan who she murmured, "I want you to fuck me. I want to know what your cock feels like inside me."

He groaned and pushed his erection deeper into her hand. "Christ. Yes." He rolled over to open the top drawer of the end table, and rolled back with a strip of condoms and a tube of lube.

He and Dylan wasted no time covering themselves with condoms, and then Dylan's warm mouth was on her neck, nipping at her feverish flesh before kissing a path up to her earlobe. "So you want Aidan, huh? Not me?"

Her gaze flew to his. Oh shit. Had she offended him? "No, I mean, I just...you and I already...and me and him haven't...and..."

His husky laughter warmed her ear. "I'm just teasing you, honey. I'd love to bury myself inside you, but there's somewhere just as enticing for me to be."

Her breath hitched when she noticed the two men exchange a look. A sizzling, wicked look that ended with Aidan moaning.

"You like the sound of that, huh?" Now Dylan was teasing his other lover. "You want me in your ass while you fuck Claire?"

Her heart stopped as she waited for Aidan's reply, which came swiftly and without hesitation. "God, yes."

Aidan tossed the lube to Dylan. His gaze dropped to Claire's breasts, and a moment later, he leaned in to nuzzle them.

When his tongue darted out and licked her nipple, she jerked in delight. "You two always seem to forget about my boobs," she mumbled.

"Ah, I'm sorry, baby. It's just because your pussy is so damn distracting." He flashed her his dimpled, little-boy grin, then took her nipple in his mouth and sucked so hard it sent a spasm right to her core.

Dylan moved to the foot of the bed to kneel behind Aidan. One strong arm came around and grasped Aidan's cock, causing heat to ripple through Claire's body.

She was on fire again and in desperate need of release. With a groan, she commandeered Aidan's erection from Dylan's hand and guided it to her opening. He slipped inside, one inch at a time, until his shaft was buried to the hilt.

"You're so damn tight, sweetheart. Fucking love it." Aidan withdrew halfway, then drove into her again.

"Feels good to be inside her, doesn't it?" Dylan's arms wrapped around Aidan from behind, his fingers toying with the man's flat brown nipples.

Claire watched in fascination as Dylan's deft fingers pinched those rigid buds, loving the way Aidan's expression glazed over with pleasure.

"Fuck her harder," Dylan ordered. "I wanna hear the sexy sound she makes when you slam all the way in."

Aidan pulled his hips back, then plunged in deep.

When Claire moaned, both men chuckled, looking mighty pleased with themselves.

She opened her mouth, armed with a sassy remark, but then Aidan thrust into her again. And again. And again. Until all she was capable of doing was closing her eyes and holding on for the ride, crying out in pleasure each time he hit her sweet spot.

When he went still and began to pull out, she groaned in disappointment, trying to trap him inside by bearing her inner muscles down on him.

"Just a second, sweetheart," he choked out. "Give me a second to… Oh sweet Jesus. Oh, that feels good."

Claire's eyes flew open as she realized what was happening. Dylan was slowly working his way into Aidan's ass. His face was buried in Aidan's neck, lips planting soft kisses on the man's skin.

"Relax for me," Dylan murmured. "Fuck, that's it. Let me all the way in, man."

Claire studied Aidan's expression, floored by the sheer and utter ecstasy she saw there. "You like it," she whispered.

His voice was gruff. "Yes."

"What does it feel like, having something in…um…"

"In my ass?" he said with a chuckle.

"Aw, honey, are you an anal virgin?" Dylan spoke up, lifting his head to grin at her.

She nodded, her cheeks burning.

Aidan leaned in and brushed his lips over hers. "Don't be embarrassed. From what I hear, the ass play feels better for us, anyway, so I don't know how much you're really missing."

"But we'll definitely try it out if you want," Dylan added in a seductive tone. "Hey, Aid, tell our girl what she can expect."

Aidan suddenly rocked forward, the power of Dylan's thrust pushing his cock into her pussy. All three of them groaned.

"Pressure," Aidan mumbled. "There's pressure at first. And a burn."

Dylan drove deep again.

His features went taut. "A good burn. Feels…good." He stopped. Moaned. "So…good." Then he stopped talking altogether and kissed her.

Dylan set the pace, controlling it with long, even strokes, and as crazy as it sounded, Claire felt like she was being fucked by them both. Each time Dylan slammed into Aidan, it was like he was slamming into her too. And each time Aidan groaned against her lips, she groaned too, because she knew he was feeling the same explosive rush of pleasure she was.

Time stood still as the three of them moved together. The pressure between her legs grew unbearable. Aidan's erection was lodged inside her, but she needed him to move faster, needed him to find the rhythm that would send her soaring.

"More," she begged. "Please, Dylan, give us more."

He laughed huskily. "Greedy little thing, aren't you?"

"*Please.*"

"All right, but only because you asked nicely."

The moment he quickened his tempo, Aidan's hips moved the way she wanted them to and his cock drove as fast and as deep as it needed to in order to detonate that knot of pressure.

Claire convulsed, losing herself in an orgasm that started between her legs, then soared up to her throat and down to her toes. It was a full-body orgasm, the most intense thing she'd ever experienced in her life, and each time she thought it was over, another wave of pleasure shuddered through her.

"Love your ass," Dylan choked out. "Feels so good squeezing my cock like that. Fuck…oh fuck, I'm gonna come."

The moment Dylan grunted in climax, Aidan followed suit, his cock jerking inside her as he came with a strangled groan.

It took a while for Claire's heart to beat normally again. She lay there trying to catch her breath as Aidan pulled out of her throbbing pussy and Dylan handled the task of ditching their condoms. And then the three of them were lying together, Aidan on his back with Claire's head on his chest, Dylan spooning her from behind, one limp arm thrown over her waist and resting on Aidan's abdomen.

"I'm so sleepy," she murmured.

Aidan's laugh vibrated beneath her ear, and the steady beating of his heart only succeeded in making her drowsier. "We wore you out, huh?"

"Mmm-hmmm."

She sighed when she felt Dylan's lips brush over her shoulder. "You okay? No regrets?"

"No regrets," she whispered, and then she fell asleep sandwiched between them, kept warm by the heat of their bodies.

Chapter Fourteen

Christmas Eve

"Okay, we need to decide one thing before we go in," Claire announced after Aidan pulled up to the curb in front of Seth Masterson's house.

She was in the backseat again, so both men had to twist around to look at her. "What are you talking about?" Dylan asked.

"Well, the two of you have this habit of, how do I put it nicely? *Pawing* at me every chance you get."

They shot her sheepish grins, because they both knew she was right. For the past few days, they hadn't been able to keep their hands off her. If Claire was in the room, at least one of them was right there beside her, touching some part of her body. Stroking her shoulder while she read the newspaper. Fondling her ass when she loaded the dishwasher. Kissing her neck as she flipped pancakes on the stove.

Not that she was complaining. She loved the endless affection, same way she loved the deliciously naughty things they did to her in the bedroom every night. There was no doubt about it—she was addicted to these men. She craved them every second of the day, eagerly awaiting their return from the base each afternoon so the three of them could lose their clothes and drive each other wild.

But that was in the privacy of the condo. Tonight they would be in public, surrounded by Dylan and Aidan's friends, and she was feeling panicky about people knowing she was sleeping with two men.

"You can't do that in there." She gestured to the townhouse across the street. "I don't want your friends to think I'm some kind of skank."

"They would never think that," Dylan assured her.

"Maybe not, but I still don't feel comfortable with them knowing about us. The three of us, I mean. So maybe tonight, just one of you can be my date?"

She felt bad asking it, but neither Dylan nor Aidan seemed insulted by the request. They simply glanced at one another, and then Aidan said, "Rock, paper, scissors you for it?"

Dylan shook his head. "Nah. The choice is obvious. You'll be her date."

Aidan's dark eyebrows furrowed. "Why is that obvious?"

"Yeah," Claire said warily. "Why is that obvious?"

Dylan spoke in a gentle tone. "Because they all know you were going to marry my brother. It might seem, I don't know, *weird* if you're suddenly involved with me. It makes more sense that you'd be seeing Aidan."

She couldn't argue with that, but his reasoning still made her feel ill at ease. She had to wonder if they'd be having these types of conversations often. Because really, how was it going to work when they were out in public? One day she'd be Aidan's girl, the next day Dylan's? Aidan would be her boyfriend when they went out for ice cream, Dylan when they were at the beach?

Her head started spinning, so she forcibly shoved the silly thoughts aside. What was the point in worrying about any of this? In less than a week, she'd be going back to San Francisco. Back to her job. Back to real life.

And real life didn't include having wild, passionate sex every night with two navy officers.

A pang of sorrow squeezed her heart at the idea of saying goodbye to them, and she had to banish that thought too. It was Christmas Eve. It was supposed to be a happy night, not a time for feeling sad.

"Okay, I'm seeing Aidan, then," she agreed.

They got out of the car and crossed the street, heading for the house where Dylan had lived up until a couple months ago. The moment they walked through the door, two dark-haired cyclones burst into the hall and attacked Dylan.

"Dylan!" Their high-pitched shrieks nearly shattered Claire's eardrums, but she was smiling as she watched Dylan scoop the kids into his arms, which only made them squeal louder.

Sophie and Jason Breslin looked exactly the way she remembered them. When she'd been here in September, she and Dylan had accompanied Seth and the kids to a carnival, where they ended up getting quite a scare after Sophie took off without telling anyone. Luckily, the little girl had been found, and she looked happy as a clam as she chattered away in Dylan's arms, telling him all about her visit to Santa yesterday.

"And he said I was gonna get a doll!" Sophie's dark ponytail swung around, her brown eyes shining with excitement. "And a yellow dress and—"

"—a new baseball glove and an X-Box!" Sophie's twin brother Jason was talking equally fast, waving his hand in front of Dylan's face in an attempt to claim all the attention.

"Whoa, one at a time, squirts," Dylan interrupted with a laugh. "You're making my head spin."

Holding the two six-year-olds as if they weighed no more than a feather, he strode into the corridor.

Claire and Aidan exchanged an amused look, then trailed after Dylan and the kids. The most delicious smells permeated the house, making Claire's stomach rumble. She'd had a light breakfast because she'd wanted to save herself for this evening's turkey dinner, and the aromas in the air made her ravenous for some food.

When they entered the living room, they encountered nearly a dozen people. The only one Claire recognized was Seth, Dylan's former roommate, and the tall scruffy SEAL wasted no time introducing her to his brand-new bride, Miranda.

Claire had barely finished saying hello to the pretty brunette when she was being introduced to someone else. Cash McCoy, a dark-haired hottie with piercing blue eyes, who quickly called a stunning blonde over and introduced her as his girlfriend, Jen.

Next was Carson Scott, a fair-haired man with a chiseled GQ face, and his wife Holly, a petite pixie of a woman with bright green eyes, apparently Jen's brother and sister-in-law.

Matt O'Connor was the one with the shaved head, and his girlfriend Savannah had ash-blond hair and laughing gray eyes.

Jackson Ramsey rounded out the group, a lanky man with dark hair, whiskey-brown eyes and a Texas drawl that made Claire melt.

"Nice to meet you, sugar," he said with a smile, sticking out his hand.

Smiling back, she shook his big, callused hand. He held on a little too long, and the appreciation flaring in his eyes was hard to miss.

Dylan and Aidan didn't miss it, either, because suddenly she was being ushered toward the couch and told to sit down and take a load off.

She hid a grin, kind of enjoying the possessive way they'd dragged her away from the sexy Texan.

Other than Aidan, every man in the room was a SEAL, and every woman was outgoing and talkative. For the next hour, Claire found herself in a million different conversations that were impossible to keep up with, and through it all, Miranda's twins bounced around the room from person to person, or ran around the eight-foot Douglas fir in delight.

"Sorry about them." Miranda leaned in from the other couch and shot Claire an apologetic smile. "They're super excited because this is the first year we've had such an enormous tree. Well, that and because they get to spend Christmas with Seth this year."

Claire smiled. "You don't have to apologize. Your kids are adorable."

"I think so too." Miranda stood up and searched the room for her husband. "Seth, help me with the turkey?" she called out.

Seth didn't even hesitate. With a beer in hand, he abandoned his conversation with Dylan and Cash, and dashed into the kitchen with his wife.

"Oh, he's so whipped," Jen said with a laugh. "I absolutely love it."

Claire glanced back at the blonde, who was sitting right beside her. Aidan was on Claire's other side; he wasn't touching her, but the heat of his thigh and scent of his aftershave were comforting. There were so many people here, all of them strangers to her, and a part of her felt like an interloper.

At least until Jen grabbed her hand and squeezed it tightly. "Look, I promised Cash I wouldn't bring this up—" She rolled her eyes. "He thinks it's inappropriate holiday subject matter. But I just want you to know that Dylan's brother is a total douchebag."

Claire choked out a giggle. "Wow. Well. That's honest."

"I'm serious. Everything I know about the guy, I absolutely hate."

"Me too," Holly chimed in from the other end of the sofa. "I met him right after Dylan joined the team, and all he did was drone on and on about cigars. Do I *look* like a cigar aficionado? Why did he pick me, of all people, to have that conversation with?"

"At least you didn't get the golf talk," Jen told her sister-in-law. "When I met him, he went on for a good half hour about the new putter he bought."

Claire sighed. "Yeah, Chris is really obsessed with that putter."

"I'm so sorry he walked out on you on your wedding day." Jen's voice was laced with genuine sympathy. "That's unforgivable and you deserve a whole lot better."

"Thanks. But if I'm being honest, I was relieved he didn't want to go through with it. I think I knew marrying him would be a mistake, but I just couldn't admit it to myself."

"It still doesn't excuse his taking off," Jen declared. "I can't believe someone like that is actually related to Dylan. Dylan's like the sweetest guy on the planet."

"He's been pretty wonderful these past couple of weeks," she confessed.

"Hey, sis, come settle an argument between me and McCoy." Carson's booming voice sounded from across the room.

Jen rolled her eyes again. "I love how I've become their referee. Every time they bicker, I'm the one they both look at, thinking I'll back them up."

"I'll go with you," Jen's sister-in-law offered with a laugh. "That way you can take Cash's side and I'll take Carson's, and everyone's happy."

Claire grinned as the two women excused themselves. That left an empty spot beside her, which Jackson quickly took advantage of.

Dylan, who'd been chatting with Matt and Savannah, immediately swiveled his head, tensing up when he spotted Claire's new couch mate. He didn't march over like a caveman, but he did keep an eye on them, which made her want to laugh.

"So, sugar, how much longer are you in town for?" Jackson asked.

"Just another week."

She felt Aidan stiffen, but he didn't say a word.

"Did you get a chance to do some exploring? Please tell me those boys have been showin' you a good time."

Oh, he didn't know the half of it…

"Yeah, we did a few things," she said vaguely. "It's been fun."

Aidan chuckled softly.

"Well, if you need another tour guide, I'd be happy to show you a few places." Jackson flashed a devilish smile that succeeded in making her heart skip a beat.

Lord, did the SEAL program only recruit heartthrobs or was it simply a coincidence that all of Dylan's teammates were drop-dead gorgeous and oozed charm?

She thought she'd managed to mask her reaction to Jackson's killer grin, but clearly she hadn't, because suddenly Aidan's arm came around her, his hand resting possessively on her shoulder.

Jackson immediately got the hint, his eyebrows rising. "Ah, Rhodes has already staked his claim, I see."

As usual, Claire's cheeks turned bright red. She didn't quite like the idea that she was something to be "claimed", but Jackson's blatant appreciation combined with Aidan's obvious jealousy and Dylan's watchful gaze did wonders for her ego.

How many other woman could say they had three very attractive men interested in them?

"Dinner's ready! Get your asses in here, boys and girls." Seth's mocking voice wafted out of the kitchen, prompting Jackson to shoot her one last grin before he wandered off.

Claire was about to get up when Aidan tugged on her hand. He pulled her toward him and kissed her before she could protest. Brushed those firm lips over hers, slipped her a little tongue and then broke it off.

"What was that for?" she asked.

He pointed at the ceiling.

Her gaze followed his finger to note the sprig of mistletoe hanging above them.

She laughed. "I didn't even notice that."

Heat flared in his eyes. "Why do you think I told you to sit here?"

"So it was your evil plan all along."

"Yup." His endearing dimples popped out. "C'mon, let's eat."

She'd just gotten to her feet when she spotted Matt and Savannah lingering near the doorway. From the distrustful way the couple was looking at her, she realized they must have witnessed her and Aidan's kiss.

Wariness circled her insides, growing stronger when Matt clapped a hand on Aidan's shoulder and casually fell in step with him.

Leaving Claire alone with Savannah.

"Hey," she said tentatively.

A pair of gray eyes pinned her with a hard look. "So your rebound is Aidan?" the blonde asked coolly. "I assumed it would be Dylan, if anyone."

Discomfort tightened her belly. "I'm…Aidan is…" She cleared her throat. "It's not a rebound. Aidan and I are just enjoying each other's company. Just having a little harmless fun."

Savannah pursed her lips. "A little harmless fun."

The suspicion in the woman's tone irked her. "Look, no offense or anything, but what's it to you? You were introduced to me as Matt's fiancée. Why do you care who Aidan spends time with?"

"Aidan is a good friend of ours. Matt and I care about him."

"Yeah? Well, so do I." Claire knew she sounded haughty, but she didn't care.

"Good, then that means you don't want to see him get hurt." Savannah paused ominously. "So you're not going to hurt him, are you, Claire?"

Needles of indignation pricked her skin. "No, I'm not going to hurt him." She cocked her head. "Will you beat me up if I do?"

"Damn right I will."

They eyed each other for a moment, like two animals vying for territory, and then Savannah broke out in a smile and said, "Let's go eat. That turkey smells delicious."

"I really liked your friends," Claire remarked during the car ride back to the condo. "For the most part, anyway."

Confused, Dylan glanced over from the passenger seat. "What do you mean, for the most part?"

"Well, there's that one teeny tiny issue of Savannah threatening me."

In the driver's seat, Aidan swiveled his head to stare at her. "She fucking did what?"

"Oh, you know, threatened to kick my ass if I ever hurt you."

Aidan's jaw dropped. "Son of a bitch. Great. Now I'm gonna have to kick *her* ass."

Claire waved a careless hand. "Oh, don't worry, she was just looking out for you. She and Matt are very protective of you, by the way."

"That's because he used to fuck them," Dylan piped up. He found this entire conversation highly amusing, and he had to wonder if Savannah would issue the same threat to him when she learned he was sleeping with Aidan too.

"Excuse me?"

Claire sounded so displeased that Dylan couldn't help but turn around again. Sure enough, he noted her shoulders had gone rigid.

Chuckling, he repeated himself, slower this time. "He used to fuck them."

The unmistakable jealousy burning in her big brown eyes told him that had Matt and Savannah been in the SUV with them right now, Claire would've clawed both their eyes out.

"It was just an occasional thing," Aidan said sheepishly.

"Besides, doesn't it make you feel better about the whole threesome thing?" Dylan added. "Everyone we know has 'em. It's the norm in our circle."

"Well, I hope you're not planning on paying them a visit anytime soon," she told Aidan, her voice tight with irritation.

"Aw, she's jealous," Dylan teased.

Aidan caught her eye in the rearview mirror and put those dimples of his to good use. "Don't worry, sweetheart, I'm not going anywhere. I'm right where I want to be."

Dylan wholeheartedly agreed. This time with Claire and Aidan had been so amazing he still couldn't believe he wasn't dreaming it. He was so ashamed of his previous attitude toward Claire—she was not at all what he'd thought her to be, and the more he got to know her, the harder he fell.

Claire McKinley was smart, gorgeous, sarcastic, compassionate. And open. So fucking open. She spoke her mind, never tried to hide what she was feeling from him and Aidan, and he loved and appreciated that about her. A lot of women expected a man to be a mind reader, but hell, a little guidance was nice, and Claire was a master of honest communication.

She was also the hottest, most passionate woman he'd ever met. Her sexual appetite was voracious, and Dylan knew he and Aidan appealed to the wild side she'd been forced to hide growing up. They fueled it, fed it, and damned if they weren't having a good time doing it.

Ten minutes later, Aidan pulled into the underground parking of their building and the three of them made their way upstairs. The condo board had a strict rule about keeping the hallways decoration-free, so there was nothing Christmasy about the corridor as they crossed the cream-colored carpet toward their apartment.

Inside was another story. The tree was lit up and the ornaments were twinkling, giving the room a holiday feel that the hallway had lacked.

When Dylan moved to flick on the light, Claire intercepted his hand. "No, don't," she urged. "Look how pretty the room is with just the light of the tree."

He couldn't deny there was something magical about it. The red and silver ornaments shone like little gems, the glow from the strings of light creating a romantic ambience.

"You guys want some coffee?" Aidan asked.

"Fuck, yes," Dylan answered. "I'm drowsy as hell from all that turkey."

"None for me. I don't want to be up all night," Claire said. "But…hey, do you have any hot chocolate?"

With an indulgent smile, Aidan leaned in and brushed a kiss over her cheek. "I'll see what I can do."

As Aidan headed for the kitchen, Dylan led Claire over to the couch and pulled her down beside him. He wrapped his arm around her and planted a kiss atop her head, inhaling the sweet lavender scent of her hair.

"I've been wanting to hold you all night," he said gruffly. "I thought I would explode from not touching you."

She nestled closer, her loose auburn tresses tickling his neck. "Me too."

He ran his fingers up and down her arm, his calluses scraping along the soft wool of her green sweater. "I hope Savannah didn't upset you."

"Nah, like I said, she was just looking out for Aidan. I totally understood. And by the end of the night, I kinda warmed up to her. She's pretty hilarious. And I adored Jen. She's so nice." Claire paused. "And beautiful. I don't think I've ever met anyone that good-looking before."

Dylan shrugged. "She's okay."

Ha. Fine, so he was lying through his teeth—Jen was drop-dead gorgeous. But he was scared that if he acknowledged her beauty, Claire might pick up on the fact that he knew Jen as carnally as Aidan knew

Savannah, and no way did he want to see Claire's look of cloudy displeasure directed at him.

Unfortunately, he underestimated her. He was no mind reader, but clearly *she* was.

"Oh, for the love of God," she groaned. "You too?"

"Me too what?" he asked innocently.

"'She's okay?'" Claire mimicked. "Dylan, that girl is more than *okay*. She's movie-star beautiful. Argh. You totally slept with her, didn't you? And let me guess, Cash was there too."

He sighed. "Yeah."

A note of challenge crept into her voice. "Out of curiosity, who else at that dinner have you slept with?"

"No one but Jen," he assured her. "And Cash. Well, kind of."

"Kind of?" She looked amused.

"I blew him."

After a beat, Claire burst out laughing. "Well, at least you're honest."

"To a fault." He smiled. "But I promise you, I've only been with Jen and Cash. And Aid has only been with Savannah."

"Good."

She placed a possessive hand on his thigh, eliciting a rush of satisfaction. Damn, he loved that Claire was staking her claim.

It really had been pure torture not being able to touch her tonight. Every time he'd looked at her, he'd had to battle the overwhelming urge to pull her into his arms and kiss her senseless, but he hadn't wanted to embarrass her in front of the gang. His friends would never be openly rude or judgmental, or probably even care that Dylan was with her, but he couldn't deny that Claire jumping into bed with her ex-fiancé's brother so soon after the break-up didn't look great.

The funny thing was, the fact that Claire had almost married Chris didn't bother him in the slightest anymore. No, what bothered him was that he *wasn't* bothered by it. Because…why the hell not? His brother had lived with this woman for more than a year, had nearly made her his wife, for fuck's sake. So why didn't he feel like he was betraying Chris? Because his brother was a jerk? Because he'd known from day one that Claire wasn't right for Chris? All of the above?

Aidan returned to the room with a tray of steaming mugs, officially putting an end to Dylan's internal self-examination.

"Hot chocolate for the lady." Aidan handed Claire her mug. "And coffee for the gentleman."

Dylan gratefully accepted the coffee and blew on the hot liquid to cool it. As Aidan settled in the armchair, Claire glanced over at the small stack of gifts beneath the tree.

"So when are we opening presents?" she asked. "My parents and I usually do it on Christmas morning, but I know some people like to do the whole gift thing tonight."

"My dad and I do it tonight," Aidan said in a gruff voice. "When he doesn't bail on the holidays, that is."

"At my house we do both," Dylan told them. "We each open one present on Christmas Eve, and the rest in the morning."

"Oooh, I like that idea," Claire said. "Can we all open one tonight?"

He and Aidan both shrugged as if to say, "Why not?"

Beaming, she hopped off the couch and made a beeline for the tree. "Can I pick which ones you open?"

Aidan smiled at her. "Go for it."

As Claire rummaged through the presents, Dylan had to wonder what the heck she'd bought during her numerous trips to the mall last week. They'd agreed to get each other only one or two things, and stick to a limit of a hundred bucks, and although all the packages she'd come home with were fairly small, there were quite a few of them.

She stalked back to the couch and handed each of them a present. "Now be warned, these are my joke gifts," she said with a grin. "I'm saving the good ones for tomorrow."

He and Aidan glanced at each other. "You first," Aidan said graciously.

Dylan quickly tore the wrapping to reveal a Cliff Notes study guide to the novel *War and Peace.* He laughed in delight. "Best gift ever," he told Claire.

Aidan went next, unwrapping his present to find a narrow cardboard box. He flipped it open and pulled out a black ballpoint pen, then raised his brows and glanced at Claire.

"Oh, it's not just an ordinary pen," she informed him. "It's the kind that has invisible ink. You know, so when you're jotting down your super-secret spy notes, nobody will see what you're writing."

Aidan threw his head back and laughed. "I love it."

Claire was already moving back to the tree. "Okay, which one should I open?"

"The blue one," they answered in unison.

Her soft laughter floated in the dimly lit room. "Is this the joint gift you two were teasing me about?"

"Yup," Dylan confirmed.

She returned to the couch, resting the large rectangular-shaped box on her lap. She stared at the green bow taped to the center of the plain blue box, then gave them a dry smile.

"This is your idea of giftwrapping, huh?"

"Wrapping paper is overrated and unnecessary," Aidan replied. "Sort of like clothes."

Dylan nodded. "Exactly like clothes. Especially *your* clothes, honey. I don't know why you bother wearing any, if I'm being honest. Now open our beautifully wrapped box."

She lifted the lid, and a moment later, she was laughing again. "Of course. Why am I not surprised?"

Dylan and Aidan exchanged grins as Claire held up the sheer, red merrywidow and matching G-string.

"So let me get this straight, this is a present for *me*? Because it seems to me like it's more of a present for you guys."

Aidan's voice lowered to a smoky pitch. "Trust me, you're going to get as much enjoyment from it as we are."

"How do you figure that?"

"You'll really enjoy the way we tear it off you," Dylan said helpfully.

"Hmmm. Let's see if you're right." She tucked the lingerie under her arm and stood up. "Give me a few minutes."

After she hurried away, Aidan joined him on the couch and flashed his dimpled grin. "Good call on the lingerie."

Dylan grinned back. "I thought so."

It felt like an eternity before they heard her footsteps. They were both fidgeting with impatience by that point, Dylan's cock straining against the fly of his khakis. A glance at Aidan's lower body showed him to be in a similar state, sporting a bulge beneath his gray wool trousers.

They both hissed when Claire stepped into view.

Dylan couldn't tear his gaze off her. The lacy red outfit hugged her mouthwatering curves, making her look like she'd just stepped out of a Victoria's Secret catalog. Her full breasts were pushed up and practically pouring out of the built-in bra, and the little black center bow looked so naughty Dylan wanted to rip it off with his teeth.

"C'mere," Aidan growled.

With an impish smile, Claire took her sweet time sauntering over to them. "How do I look?"

Dylan licked his lips. "Good enough to eat."

She did a little spin, showing off the dental-floss-thin strip of lace nestled between her firm ass cheeks.

"Holy fuck, get over here," Aidan burst out.

Dylan laughed as Aidan stuck out his arm and grabbed hold of Claire's hand. He yanked hard and she fell into Dylan's lap, her back colliding into his chest with a thud.

He wrapped his arms around her to keep her in place. She shivered when he nuzzled her neck, then moaned as Aidan swiftly bent down and kissed one rigid nipple through the lace.

Dylan chuckled. "I think she likes that."

"Not half as much as I do," Aidan muttered before tugging on the lacy cups to expose Claire's breasts.

Aidan's mouth closed over a rosy nipple. His throat worked as he suckled her, and Claire made a happy purring sound that brought a smile to Dylan's lips.

Aidan's dark lashes fluttered as he peered up at her. "You okay there, baby?"

"Uh-huh."

Dylan amused himself by playing with her silky red hair, and watched as Aidan feasted on those delectable tits. Damn, there was nothing hotter than the sight of Aidan sucking on those stiff nipples, squeezing those full mounds, kissing the creamy valley between her breasts. His cock strained against Claire's ass, his heart beating dangerously fast as his arousal levels skyrocketed.

"Put your mouth on her pussy," he muttered. "I wanna see you fuck her with your mouth, man."

Claire moaned again.

With a mischievous smile, Aidan slid down her body, grabbed the flimsy waistband of her G-string and ripped the straps. Then he threw the torn panties aside and buried his face between Claire's legs.

Turned on beyond belief, Dylan grasped Claire's chin and forcibly moved her face toward his. When he kissed her, she instantly parted her lips and granted his tongue access, and he plunged it into her mouth, exploring every sweet crevice while Aidan lapped at her pussy.

Claire began to whimper and squirm in his lap, rocking her hips against Aidan's face. All that squirming succeeded in turning his cock into an iron spike. He thrust upward, grinding against Claire's ass, the mind-blowing friction bringing him to a new level of hardness.

When Aidan slipped two fingers inside her, she shuddered and squeaked with delight. "Oh *God*, that's good."

Dylan laughed again and resumed sucking on her neck, angling his head so he could watch Aidan's every move. So fucking sexy, seeing Aidan's tongue slide over that wet pussy.

"You like the way he eats you, honey?" Dylan's tongue skimmed up the curve of her jaw toward her ear. He took the delicate lobe in his mouth and sucked.

"Uh-huh." Her breathing had become labored.

"How much do you like it?"

"Mmmmmm."

"How much, Claire?"

"I…um…oh God. I'm going to come."

And then she did, trembling wildly in his arms and pressing her face into the crook of his neck. When she bit into his flesh, Dylan felt the first tingles of release in his balls.

Fuck. *Fuck.* He tried to stop it, clamped his teeth over his bottom lip to stave off the climax, but it was too late. Not since he was thirteen years old had he come in his pants. But tonight, on Christmas Eve, at the age of twenty-nine, he shot his load like an inexperienced teenager as the soft, warm woman in his lap shook with an orgasm of her own.

When both he and Claire recovered, Aidan rewarded them with a mocking laugh. "All right. Claire? I understand, what with me licking her up. But you, bro? Where's that famous SEAL endurance?"

"Dude, if you were in my position and she was grinding all over your cock like that, you'd shoot your load in your pants too."

"Maybe. But lucky for me, I get to come on her tits." Dark eyes gleaming with purpose, Aidan stood and unzipped his pants.

He positioned himself in front of Claire, widened his stance, and started pumping his cock. His hand moved over his shaft in fast, furious strokes, the fire in his eyes darkening, burning, until finally he let out a hoarse cry and came apart. His come sprayed Claire's breasts, and her moan of pleasure echoed in the living room and vibrated through Dylan's body.

Aidan's chest heaved as he caught his breath. A moment later, he stumbled out of the room, then returned with a wad of paper towels in his hand.

As Dylan kissed her neck and breathed in her addictive scent, Aidan gently wiped Claire's breasts, then dropped a soft kiss on her lips, showed those sexy dimples, and said, "Merry Christmas, sweetheart."

Chapter Fifteen

Three days. She was going back to San Francisco in three days.

Saying goodbye to Dylan and Aidan.

In three days.

Claire couldn't help but feel like she was walking the plank, about to meet an awful, painful fate—in this case, saying goodbye to the two men she'd come to care deeply about.

The two men she was falling for.

Which was insane. The thought of *desiring* two men had shaken her up and made her feel like some sort of deviant, but *falling* for them? For both of them? Was it even possible to be in love with two people at the same time? And was this even love? Could she be mistaking a case of extreme lust for love?

Her head was a jumbled mess of endless questions, so when her phone vibrated, it was a much-needed distraction.

Since it was her boss's number blinking on the display, she wasted no time in answering. "Hey, Barb, Happy New Year's Eve."

Barbara Valentine responded with a throaty laugh. "I'm pretty sure it's New Year's Day that matters, darling. Do you have a moment to talk?"

"Of course. What's up?"

"Are you booked on a flight home yet?"

"No, I was actually just about to do that." Her gaze drifted to the open laptop sitting on Dylan's bed. She'd left him and Aidan in the living room and ducked in here to book the flight, but she'd been procrastinating from the second she'd turned on her computer.

Because she didn't want to go home.

At all.

"Don't," Barb told her.

Claire wrinkled her forehead. "Don't what?"

"Book a flight. I need you to head to Oceanside."

"What for?"

"The firm just got contracted to do an assessment for a software company there. Since you're already down south, I'm going to put you on it. Spend as much time as you need on site, but realistically, the job shouldn't take more than two or three weeks. Can I count on you?"

Excitement sparked in her belly. Two or three weeks. And Oceanside was less than an hour's commute from San Diego. She could stay here at the condo and easily make the drive to the company's headquarters every day, and all her reports could be prepared off site.

Trying not to reveal how elated she was, she put on a professional voice and said, "You can definitely count on me."

"I knew I could." Barb sounded pleased that Claire was being so agreeable. "I'll email you the details and company profile the day after tomorrow. Businesses go back to normal on the second of the month, but you'll be meeting with the CEO on the third. That's Wednesday morning."

"Sounds good."

"*You* sound good. The time off seems to have lifted your spirits," Barb said, her normally commanding voice softening. "I know what a difficult time this must have been for you."

Difficult time?

Oh right. The wedding.

"It was difficult," she admitted. "But I'm doing much better. It was the right decision not to go through with it."

"It's such a shame." Barb made a clucking noise. "Christopher is such a charming man. And quite successful."

And a total bastard.

She bit her tongue, instead saying, "Chris is a great person, but he wasn't the right man for me." Since she felt uncomfortable discussing her personal life with Barb, she quickly changed the subject. "Anyway, I've been enjoying my time here, so if there are any more jobs in Southern California after this contract, I'd love to be considered for them."

Maybe she was being presumptuous, seeing as how she hadn't even spoken to the guys about the future, but she at least wanted to throw the idea out there.

"I'll keep that in mind," Barb replied. "All right, darling, it's time for me to lock up the office and go home to get ready. Do you have big plans for this evening?"

"Not really. Just hanging out with a few friends," she said vaguely.

"Have fun, then. We'll be in touch."

After Claire hung up the phone, she did a happy little fist pump that fortunately nobody else could see, then hurried out of the room.

She found the boys sprawled on their respective couches, sipping beers as they watched the Bears game on the screen. They'd flipped a coin earlier to see which game would be their "primary" one, and since Aidan had won the toss, Dylan and Claire were forced to catch glimpses of the Niners game when the Bears one was on commercial.

"What do you look so happy about?" Aidan teased as she skidded into the living room.

"My boss just called." She paused for dramatic effect.

Rolling their eyes, both men gestured for her to go on.

"She wants me to do an assessment on a company in Oceanside. It'll be a two- to three-week assignment, so that means…"

Wide grins stretched across their faces.

"You get to stay longer?" Dylan said happily.

"Yep, and I can totally commute from San Diego to Oceanside, which means I don't need to book a hotel up there. All I have to do is rent a car and I can drive back here every night." She paused again, this time with uncertainty. "That is, if you guys want me to stick around."

Aidan's dark eyes took on an intense glint. "Come here."

She went to him without delay, squeaking in delight when he pulled her into his lap. "You know how fucking bummed we've been that you were leaving?" he said gruffly. "We don't want you to go."

Dylan spoke up in a low voice. "If it were up to us, you'd *never* leave."

Her heart did a somersault, then took off in a gallop when Aidan leaned in to kiss her. His lips were firm, his tongue insistent as it slid into her mouth. He kissed her until she was breathless, then pulled back and smiled. "So yeah, we want you to stick around."

She smiled back. "Okay."

"Good. So now, what do we want to do for dinner? Anywhere we go will be packed tonight, so I vote for staying here and grilling up some steaks and maybe—"

Dylan's ringing phone cut Aidan off midsentence.

On the other couch, Dylan swiped his cell off the glass table and checked the screen. His chiseled features instantly tensed. "Fuck."

"Who is it?" Claire asked in concern.

"It's a France country code."

Claire's back stiffened, prompting Aidan to run a reassuring hand up and down her spine.

Dylan answered the phone with a curt "Hello". Then he stopped, listened, and sighed in resignation. "It's only three p.m. here, but happy New Year all the same, big brother."

Since she could only hear Dylan's side of the conversation, it was difficult to get the full scope of what was being said, but Claire understood the gist of it.

"Yeah…no, nothing major, just chilling here… Good, because I'll be there too…yeah, I'm flying in to see Mom the day after tomorrow." Dylan paused for several seconds, and then his face twisted in disgust. "No fucking kidding, Chris." A muscle twitched in his jaw. "Right, of course. Uh-huh…yeah, whatever…I'll see you Tuesday."

He hung up and tossed the phone to the other end of the sofa as if it carried the Ebola virus.

Claire met his eyes. "What do you mean, you'll see him Tuesday?"

"I was actually coming to talk to you about that before you raced in here with your good news." His expression conveyed a whole lot of annoyance, but she knew it wasn't directed at her. "I was going to tell you not to book anything commercial. My Coast Guard buddy got back to me and he's agreed to fly me home the day after tomorrow. My Lieutenant Commander approved my leave request, so I have a day pass to see my mom."

Right, because he still hadn't spoken to Shanna, Claire remembered. And now she also recalled that her and Chris's return flight from Paris had been scheduled for New Year's Day, so he would be back in town the day before Dylan flew in.

"What did he say that made you so mad?" she asked quietly. "When you swore at him?"

Dylan's mouth tightened. "He said, and I quote, 'I guess I should give Claire a call when I get home'."

A gust of anger swept through her. "He *guesses?*" She stumbled off Aidan's lap, too pissed to sit still. "You know what? I'm coming with you on Tuesday. It's definitely time for me to have a talk with your brother." Sarcasm filled her tone. "You know, the talk we should have had the day of our wedding."

Rather than argue, Dylan just nodded. "I think that's a good idea. Now stop pacing and c'mere, honey."

She inhaled deeply and willed herself to calm down. Chris might be an ass, but she refused to let him affect her this way. She wasn't normally an angry person, and she hated this awful feeling of rage constricting her chest.

This time she slid into Dylan's lap, exhaling in a slow rush as his arms came around her.

"What should we tell Chris?"

Dylan frowned. "What do you mean?"

"I mean, your mom knows that you brought me back to San Diego, so he's going to find out I stayed here. And I'm a terrible liar, so if he asks me what you and I did, my stupid cheeks will reveal the truth."

Both men laughed. "She's got a point, bro," Aidan said from the other couch.

"I don't plan on telling him that I slept with you," she told Dylan, "but if he suspects something and calls me on it, I don't think I can lie."

"You don't have to lie. If it comes out, it comes out. Chris is a big boy. He might not like that we're dating, but he'll get over it."

She blinked. "We're dating?"

Dylan rolled his eyes. "Of course we are."

Confused, she slowly turned to Aidan. "Are we dating too?"

Those adorable dimples made an appearance. "Of course we are."

"Oh."

She was still trying to wrap her head around that when Dylan grasped her chin and forced her to look at him. "What, did you think you were here as our live-in sex slave?"

"Well, no, but…"

"This is more than sex, Claire." His vivid green eyes shone with sincerity. "Don't you get that?"

Emotion clogged her throat, then damn near suffocated her when she glanced at Aidan and glimpsed the earnest intensity in his eyes.

"It's more than sex," Aidan echoed huskily. "Much, much more."

"You sure you don't want me to stick around?" Dylan opened Claire's door for her, then got into the driver's seat.

"No, this is something I need to do alone," she answered, but her tone lacked any and all enthusiasm.

He pulled out of the rental agency parking lot and merged into traffic. It was just past eleven in the morning, a bright, sunny day that didn't match his cloudy mood. He was anxious about seeing his mom, anxious about Claire seeing Chris. If there'd been a way to avoid either confrontation, Dylan would have jumped on it.

They didn't say much as he navigated the city's never-ending hills and twisty turns. The sun was so bright Dylan popped his shades on, then chuckled when he saw Claire's pink cheeks.

She sighed happily. "You look so damn hot in those Aviators."

"Yeah? Well, you look so damn hot in *anything*." He winked at her. "And in nothing at all."

He thought she looked especially cute today in her faded blue jeans and white V-neck sweater. Her hair was up in a messy twist, there wasn't a drop of makeup on her face, and she wore no jewelry except for the plain silver watch around one delicate wrist. He loved that about her, how she didn't put an obscene amount of time or effort into her appearance. She didn't need to—her understated, fresh-faced look only made her all the more beautiful.

"Hey, I just realized, your ears aren't pierced," he said.

"I know. I always wanted to get it done, but my dad wouldn't let me," she admitted. "And then when I got older, I just forgot about it."

"You still planning on seeing your folks after you talk to Chris?"

"Of course. My mom would murder me if I came to the city and didn't visit them."

Dylan stopped at a red light and reached over to rest his hand on her thigh. She smiled at the physical contact and placed her small palm over his knuckles.

"So then I'll pick you up from their house later?" he asked.

"Sounds like a plan." With her free hand, she grabbed her phone from her green canvas purse and checked the screen. "No more texts from Chris. I assume he's meeting me at the apartment at noon like we arranged yesterday."

Dylan tensed. Rather than calling, Chris had contacted the woman he'd left at the altar via text message last night, asking her to meet. Claire hadn't told his brother she'd spent the last month in San Diego, but Dylan knew that tidbit would come out today when the two of them spoke.

Again, he couldn't muster up much guilt over the situation. He knew Chris wouldn't be happy when he discovered Claire and Dylan were involved, but after everything his brother had done, Dylan didn't have any sympathy for the guy.

"I'm going to pack another bag when I'm there," she went on. "I didn't bring any work clothes with me for the honeymoon." She paused, bit her lip. "I guess I should pack up my other things too, figure out with Chris who gets what when it comes to furniture and dishes and all that stuff."

Dylan wondered if Chris would want to keep the apartment. Probably. He remembered his brother raving about how "prestigious" the location was and how one of the other associates lived in the same building.

For a moment he felt angry on Claire's behalf—because really, *Chris* should be the one moving out—but then he let it go. If Claire kept the apartment, that meant she'd be staying in San Francisco, and that was the last thing Dylan wanted. He was praying this three-week extension they'd gotten would lead to an even longer stay on Claire's part, but he was hesitant to raise the issue. He knew how much Claire loved her job, and he could never ask her to give it up for him and Aidan.

"It'll all work out," he assured her. "Doesn't matter who gets what. Those are just things, and things don't matter."

She smiled dryly. "They do to your brother. Knowing him, he'll want to debate every last item."

The sedan came to a stop in front of a tall, well-maintained building. Dylan put the car in park. "Should I wish you luck?"

"Probably." She sighed. "This is not gonna be fun. I'll cab it to my parents' house when I'm done here, and you can grab me whenever you're done with Shanna. Oh, and tell her I say hi."

"Sounds good, and I will." He leaned over the center console and planted a quick kiss on her lips. "Good luck. And give my brother hell—he fucking deserves it."

Her amber-brown eyes gleamed. "Damn right he does."

FIFTEEN MINUTES LATER, DYLAN WAS DRIVING ACROSS THE GOLDEN GATE Bridge into Marin County. With the radio blasting one of his favorite Nirvana songs, he headed east toward San Rafael. As sunny as it was, the temperature was only in the low sixties, and a cool breeze drifted in from the open window. He breathed in the fresh air, enjoying the solitude. Living with a roommate meant he didn't always have a chance to be alone with his thoughts, and sometimes he craved some Dylan-time.

It wasn't long before he reached his quaint, tree-lined street and stopped in the driveway of the ranch-style house he'd grown up in.

The house is mother had almost lost due to her gambling addiction. Jesus.

Shutting off the engine, he grabbed his mom's Christmas gift from the backseat, which Claire had taken painstaking care to wrap. The red-and-white-striped paper and big red bow made him smile. He couldn't believe he'd ever thought that Claire didn't like and respect his mother.

With the gift in hand, he walked up the cobblestone path toward the front door. He let himself in without knocking, immediately struck by a wave of nostalgia as he stood in the front hall and inhaled the familiar smell of home.

"Mom?" he called.

"In here, sweetheart!"

He followed her voice into the living room, his gaze settling on the beautifully decorated tree in the corner of the room. When she'd called to wish him a merry Christmas, Shanna had told him their neighbors Charlie and Beth had helped her set up and decorate the tree, and he suddenly had the urge to go next door and thank the sweet, retired couple for helping Shanna out. Sometimes he hated the thought of his mom living alone here, with him all the way in San Diego and Chris wrapped up in his own conceited bubble.

"I'm so glad you're home!" With a beaming smile, Shanna hurried over and wrapped her arms around him.

Dylan hugged her back, marveling over how petite she was. Her blonde head barely reached his collarbone.

"Happy holidays, Mom," he said gruffly.

"Happy holidays, sweetheart." She tugged on his hand, her green eyes shining happily. "Come. Sit. Tell me how you spent your holidays."

"First I want to know all about your trip to Palm Springs."

They settled on the oversized, peach-colored couch, and Shanna spent the next few minutes outlining everything she'd done at her friend's ranch. She looked tanned and relaxed, and so happy that he felt like a total ass for the pain he was about to cause her.

But he couldn't pretend everything was okay, and after they'd chatted for nearly thirty minutes, Dylan took a deep breath and finally addressed the giant elephant in the room that Shanna was oblivious to.

"Mom," he started. Then he stopped. Cleared his throat, tried again. "Mom, there's something we need to talk about."

Her pale eyebrows drew together. "What is it? Is everything okay?"

"No, it isn't. I…I know what's been going on around here. Claire told me everything."

Shanna looked stricken for a second. She swallowed, then pasted on a blank look. "What do you mean?"

"Please don't lie to me." He released a shaky exhalation. "You and Chris have been lying to me for more than a year. So please, just stop."

"Dylan—"

"Why didn't you tell me about the gambling?"

Shanna hesitated. Swallowed again. And then her entire face collapsed and her green eyes filled with tears. "Because I was ashamed."

If there was one thing guaranteed to trigger his hero complex, it was a female's tears. *Especially* his mother's.

"Ah, shit. Damn it, Mom, come here." Dylan put his arm around her trembling shoulders and held her close, his heart breaking at the sound of her quiet sobs.

She pressed her face against his chest, her voice coming out muffled.

"I'm so sorry. I wanted to tell you, I really did, but I was so mortified. I never thought something like that could happen to me. You know me, Dylan, I'm careful with money, I don't make impulse purchases or buy extravagant things. I…" The tears continued to fall, soaking the front of his sky-blue polo shirt. "I was embarrassed and ashamed and angry at myself for screwing up so badly."

Sighing, he smoothed a hand over her hair. "What happened? How did it get so out of control like that?"

She lifted her head and wiped her wet eyes with the sleeve of her thin red sweater. "What did Claire tell you?"

"That you went to the casino with friends, caught the gambling bug and everything went downhill from there."

A weak smile flitted over her lips. "Yes, that sounds about right."

"I'd still like to hear it from you."

After a long moment, she nodded, and the whole story spilled out. It was exactly like Claire had said, only much, much worse coming from his mom's lips.

She told him about her increased visits to the casino, how overjoyed she'd felt when she'd won and how desperate she was when she started losing. She told him about the withdrawals she'd made from her savings account, the mutual funds she'd sold, the second mortgage she'd secured. She told him about missing work, lying to her boss, using up all her personal days and then eventually not showing up altogether.

When she got to the part about how she'd finally had to confide in Chris because the bank had sent her a foreclosure notice, Dylan's chest tightened with both sympathy and anger.

"You should have told me," he muttered.

"I couldn't. I didn't want to see the disappointed look on your face, the one you're wearing now. You've always been my biggest supporter, and you gave me so much encouragement when I decided to go back to work after your father died." Tears welled up in her eyes. "Sam would be horrified if he knew what I'd done."

Dylan's throat started to feel tight. "No, he wouldn't. Dad would have recognized that you had a problem, and he would have stood by you. Don't ever doubt that."

"Do you really believe that?"

"I really believe that," he said firmly.

Shanna's breathing was shallow, but when she spoke again, her voice sounded steadier. "I'm so sorry. I should have told you the truth."

"Yes, but I understand why you didn't. You were scared. And between me and Chris, he's definitely the one in a financial position to help." Dylan's tone became stern. "With that said, I need you to tell me exactly how serious this is financially, so I know how much money to start sending you every month."

Her gaze flew to his. "What? No, Dylan. You don't have to do that. I don't *want* you to do that."

"Tough shit."

She raised her eyebrows and shot him that disapproving Mom look he'd been on the receiving end of many times growing up.

"Tough cookies," he amended guiltily. "I'm serious, though. I'm involved in this now, and I'm doing my part whether you like it or not."

Her shoulders sagged in defeat. "All right."

"Good. Now before we get into all the unpleasant money stuff…" He reached for the present he'd left on the weathered pine coffee table and held it out. "Merry Christmas, Mom."

Her radiant smile got him all choked up again, and when he saw her awed expression after she removed the glass angel from its box, he was feeling teary-eyed himself.

"Oh, it's beautiful." Her gaze drifted to the glass cabinet across the room, which held all the other angels she'd been collecting since before Dylan was even born. Then she threw her arms around him and hugged him so tightly he could hardly breathe. "Thank you."

"You're welcome," he said through the lump in his throat.

They both fell silent, until Shanna finally cleared her throat. "Why don't I make us some coffee? You can open some presents, and then… then we can discuss everything else that needs to be discussed."

"Sounds good. I'll keep you company in the kitchen."

They had only taken two steps toward the doorway when his cell phone buzzed in his pocket. He fished it out and saw Claire's number, then turned to his mom. "Sorry, I have to take this. I'll join you in a sec."

He waited until his mom was out of earshot before answering with a soft, "Hey, honey, how did it go with Chris?"

"It didn't," was the curt response.

"What do you mean, it didn't?"

"I mean, he didn't show up." Claire sounded so incensed her voice was trembling.

Battling a rush of disbelief, he lowered his voice. "Are you fucking serious?"

"Yep, he texted five minutes after I got to the apartment, saying he received a last-minute invitation to have lunch with Lowenstein at some cigar bar and he simply *couldn't* pass up the opportunity. But he was considerate enough to speak to me via Bluetooth while he drove there."

Disgust and amazement mingled in Dylan's blood. "So what did he say?"

"The same thing he told you the day at the wedding, how he and I weren't a good match, we were making a mistake, yada yada."

"And what did you say?"

"I agreed with him and told him I'd been having the same doubts."

"Okay, that sounds cordial enough. Was that it?"

Her long pause was all the answer he needed.

"Aw, fuck, tell me what happened, Claire."

A sigh rippled over the line. "Well, we talked about the apartment for a few minutes. He said he'd like to keep living there. I said fine, I didn't care."

"And?"

"He asked how I spent my time off and how my holidays were. I said I was in San Diego with you and that the holidays were great."

"And?"

"And then I told him I knew that he'd brought another woman on what was supposed to be our honeymoon."

Dylan held his breath. "And?"

"And he went ballistic! You should have heard him. He got insanely defensive. He didn't deny it, but he refused to talk about it either. It was so fucking infuriating!" She huffed out another breath. "He felt no remorse over it, and he didn't even apologize or admit it was insensitive to take someone on *our* trip! Oh, and then he accused me of sleeping with you."

The breath he'd been holding slipped out in a ragged burst. "And?"

"And…well, I may have flown into a bit of a rage and said some things I shouldn't have."

He didn't know whether to laugh or curse. "Oh, shit, what'd you do?"

"I yelled for a bit. Called him an ass and a prick and said I was ridiculously glad I didn't marry him. So then he accused me again of sleeping with you, and I was like, hell yeah, I am, and I told him he was *half* the man that you are and…um…" Her voice was barely audible now. "Well, I may or may not have said that you were a million times better in bed. And then I hung up on him."

Laughter won out, tickling his throat before bursting out of his mouth. "Fuck, Claire, I really do love that fiery redhead temper of yours."

"Are you mad at me?"

"Of course not. I mean, I wish you hadn't goaded him like that, but I understand why you lost your cool, all things considered."

"Still. I'm sorry, Dylan. I shouldn't have said what I did. But…but he bailed on me again! He didn't even have the decency to talk to me in person, and I guess I just flipped out." She swore softly. "Whatever. It's over. I'm done with him and I have no desire to talk to him again." She paused. "How did it go with your mom?"

"Good," he admitted. "We're not done talking yet, so I'll tell you about it later. When should I swing by your parents' place?" He knew Claire's folks lived in Fairfax, a small town west of here and only a ten-minute drive.

"I know my mom wants me to stick around for lunch, so maybe in a couple of hours? I'll call you when I have a better idea."

"Cool. And try not to let this latest bullshit with Chris upset you, okay?" His voice lowered seductively. "I'll totally kiss it and make it better when I see you."

She laughed. "I'm holding you to that, sailor."

No sooner had he hung up than the back of his neck tingled. Dylan spun around and found his mother standing in the doorway holding two ceramic mugs.

"So." Her lips puckered in amusement. "Looks like I'm not the only one who's been keeping secrets."

Fuck. Busted. He didn't bother asking how much she'd heard, because that parting line he'd tossed to Claire pretty much said it all.

"Mom—"

"You're involved with Claire?" To his surprise, she sounded more curious than anything.

"Yes," he confessed.

"Does your brother know?"

"He does now."

"I see." With a brisk nod, his mother handed him one of the steaming mugs and strolled back to the couch. "You can open your presents later. First I want you to sit down and tell me everything."

Chapter Sixteen

"I'm serious," Cash insisted. "I could *totally* do it."

"Withstand the power of the ring? Bull-fucking-shit." Seth took a long swig of his beer, then slammed the bottle on the plastic tabletop. "You lack the willpower."

"Fuck you, man. My willpower is rock solid. I'm telling you, I wouldn't even need to keep it on a chain around my neck. I could be wearing the ring on my *finger* and make it all the way to Mordor without letting the evil consume me."

"What the hell are y'all talking about?" Jackson voiced the demand from the middle of the heated pool, where he stood with water up to his waist and a beer in hand, his sunglasses shielding his eyes.

"*Lord of the Rings*," Seth called over his shoulder. "McCoy thinks he can make the entire journey without giving in to the ring's power. Which he can't."

"This discussion ain't interesting." Jackson waded over to the deck surrounding the pool behind Cash's low-rise building. He set his bottle on the concrete, then illustrated his disinterest by diving away and proceeding to swim underwater laps.

Dylan couldn't say he cared much about this dumb debate, either, but he'd been using the time to gather up his courage. He'd planned on telling his buddies about him and Claire today. And about Claire and Aidan. And *maybe* about him and Aidan, depending on how they reacted to the first two bombs.

He figured it was time to be honest with everyone, especially now that his mom knew the truth. Well, only the Claire part, anyway.

And Chris. Yup, Chris knew too, yet in the four days since his and Claire's visit home, Dylan hadn't received a single phone call, text or email from his older brother about the matter.

He supposed he could always make the first move, but the anger he'd harbored ever since the wedding fiasco had been steadily growing like a tumor in his gut. Maybe he was being immature, but he was tired of being the good guy, the fixer, the one who had to extend the olive branch all the time.

He might have screwed up by getting involved with his brother's ex, but Chris had screwed up too. And just once, Dylan wanted his brother to be the one who apologized first.

"There's really only one person here who'd be affected by the ring, and I'm sorry to inform you, but that's you, buddy."

Dylan looked over at Cash, who was pointing an accusatory finger at their resident smartass.

"Me?" Seth was agape. "You think *I* lack the power of will?"

"No, but I think that out of all of us, you have the weakest moral code." Cash smiled smugly. "You're all about fucking and fighting and doing whatever you please. The ring would eat you alive, dude."

Seth flipped Cash the bird. "I'm a married man, asshole. Trust me, if I can endure an entire day at Bed, Bath & Beyond picking out *shower curtains*, then I can definitely trudge through Middle Earth and drop a piece of metal into a fire pit."

Cash immediately objected. "The ring brings out your *darkness*, and you, my friend, are as dark as—"

"Oh sweet baby Jesus, can we please, please, *please* stop talking about this?" Dylan burst out. "I've been listening to this insanity for *twenty* minutes and I can't take it anymore. Why is this even a topic of discussion?"

Cash offered a sheepish look. "Jen and I had a *Lord of the Rings* marathon yesterday."

"Well, that's nine hours of your life down the drain," came Jackson's drawl. Dripping wet, he climbed out of the pool and rejoined the group. As he dried himself off with a striped blue towel, the Texan turned to Dylan with a grateful look. "The world owes you a debt of gratitude for puttin' an end to this nonsense."

He grinned. "My pleasure."

Jackson dragged one of the white lounge chairs closer to the table, then stretched out on it with his hands propped behind his damp head.

"Oh, hey, is that mighty fine redhead still staying at your place? And if so, is she still hooking up with Aidan?"

There it was, an opening so wide he'd be a total chicken-shit if he didn't walk through it.

Taking a breath, Dylan ran one finger over the trail of condensation on his Bud Light bottle, then glanced around the table. "I actually wanted to talk to you guys about that. I'm…uh, kinda seeing Claire now."

Three sets of eyebrows soared.

"You poached her right out of Aidan's arms?" Seth demanded. "That's harsh, man."

"And she almost married your brother," Cash reminded him with a frown. "Doesn't that break not only guy code, but brother code?"

"Believe me, Chris doesn't deserve your sympathy. He lost that privilege when he decided to treat everyone who cares about him like horseshit."

"Still, are you sure getting involved with her is a good idea?"

"I like her," he said gruffly. "I like her a lot."

"Yeah, and what does your roomie think about it? Because he and Claire looked pretty cozy on Christmas Eve," Seth said.

"That's the other thing I wanted to talk about." He chose his next words carefully. "She's still seeing Aidan."

The confusion in the air was palpable, at least on Cash's and Jackson's parts. Seth, on the other hand, watched him with mocking gray eyes, a slow smile curving his mouth.

"Son of a bitch. You two are tag-teaming her."

"Dating her," he corrected.

"So then you don't fuck her at the same time?" Seth challenged.

"Well, yes, but—"

"Tag-teaming." Seth laughed in delight. "Good for you, man."

"It's more than sex. Aidan and I…we *adore* her. I can't believe how wrong I was about her. She's…" Embarrassment heated his cheeks. "She's goddamn amazing."

He was rewarded by a whole lotta silence.

Shifting awkwardly in his chair, Dylan studied his friends' expressions and wished one of them would say something already. But their silence dragged on, the only sounds in the air the melodic chirping of nearby birds and the soft hiss of the afternoon breeze.

It was Cash who spoke first. "You're in love with her."

Dylan responded with a helpless shrug. Was he? His chest *did* feel hot and achy whenever she was around. And when she kissed him, he got this fluttering feeling in his stomach, like…butterflies. *Butterflies*, for chrissake.

Shit, he really was a goner.

"How does Aidan feel about her?" Jackson asked warily.

"Same way I do."

When the three men exchanged worried looks, Dylan experienced a prickle of paranoia. "What?"

"It's just…how the hell is this gonna work?" Seth demanded. "She sleeps in your bed one night and Aidan's the other, or is it a three-way every night? And when you go out in public, she holds both your hands? When you meet new people, she introduces you as her boyfriends, plural?"

"I don't know yet, but I'm sure we'll figure it out," he said stiffly.

"What about marriage, kids?" Cash pressed.

"Like I said, we'll figure it out. For now, we're happy with the arrangement. All three of us." He sighed. "Look, I'm not asking for your approval, because this is what it is and I won't change my mind. I just wanted to be honest with you about what's going on, and I need your promise that you'll treat Claire with the utmost respect when you're around her."

Cash looked startled. "Why wouldn't we?"

"Because she's involved with both of us." He hesitated. "I don't want you to think any less of her."

"The only thing *I* think is that she's wastin' her time with you two losers," Jackson said with a crooked grin. "The lady should've chosen me."

With that, the Texan succeeded in lightening the mood, much to Dylan's relief. "I'm pretty sure she made the right choice staying away from you," he retorted. "Your good ol' boy charm would've annoyed her eventually."

"Never." Hopping off his chair, Jackson headed toward the set of steps in the pool's shallow end. "All righty, time for another dip."

"Yeah, that sounds like a good idea." Seth took a last sip of beer and stood up. "Maybe a few laps will help me process all this." His gray eyes found Dylan's. "I need you to know that I'm not judging the whole sharing-a-girlfriend thing. With that said, I really think this is gonna blow up in your face."

"Noted."

Seth stripped off his T-shirt and dove into the water, leaving Dylan alone with Cash.

Who immediately narrowed his eyes, lowered his voice and murmured, "There's more to this whole arrangement, isn't there?"

He shrugged.

"You and Aidan… You've always been more than roommates, haven't you?"

His hand was a little shaky as he picked up his beer. "Jen said something, huh?"

The surprise in Cash's blue eyes didn't look feigned. "Jen? What does she have to do with this?"

"She really didn't tell you?" He suddenly felt like an ass for doubting Jen, who'd promised him time and again that she knew how to keep a secret, even from Cash.

"Jen knew that you and Aidan…?"

"Yeah."

"Well, she didn't say a word about it to me." Cash hesitated. "So you swing both ways, huh?"

Dylan shot a discreet look at the pool, but Jackson and Seth were too busy racing each other to the deep end to pay him and Cash any attention.

"Yes," he said in a quiet voice.

"Huh." Cash nodded. "Cool."

Cool?

That was it?

Dylan smothered a laugh and had to wonder why he'd bothered stressing about this conversation in the first place. He should've known his buddies would support him no matter what.

"Oh, and BTW, that night when I…" Dylan lowered his voice even further "…sucked you off…I wasn't playing out some secret fantasy I'd been harboring about you. It was definitely a spur-of-the-moment thing, and more for Jen's benefit than mine."

"So, what, you *tolerated* having my dick in your mouth to please my girlfriend? Asshole."

He burst out laughing. "Are you seriously offended that I'm not into you in that way?"

"Well, why aren't you?" Cash raised both eyebrows in defiance. "I'm way hotter than Aidan, I've known you longer. Oh, and I'm a generous lover. What's not to like about that?"

"I honestly don't know if you're fucking with me right now."

Cash broke out in a grin. "Mostly fucking with you."

"Mostly?"

"Hey, you know I have a sensitive ego, bro. It needs stroking every now and then."

"Uh-huh. I'm sure it's your *ego* that needs stroking."

"And look," Cash added, his tone going somber, "I know it's easy to brush off whatever Seth says because he's such a smartass, but I think he's got a point. You need to be careful, really know what you're getting into before you commit to this. You know, dip your toe in the water before diving in. Check under the hood before you buy the car. Lick that little taste spoon at the ice cream parlor before ordering two scoops. Um, read the fine print before—"

"Holy shit, I get the point."

"Hey D-Man, is McCoy bothering you?" Seth called from the pool.

"Yeah, but I can take him," Dylan called back.

"You sure? Because I'd be more than happy to kick his ass for you. My punching bag at home doesn't always let me release all my aggression, so I have no problem bashing his pretty face in."

Cash grinned. "And *that* is why he'd never make it to Mordor."

Dylan strode into the condo an hour later to find Claire and Aidan tangled together on the couch. Claire was on her back with her arms twined around his neck and her mouth glued to his, while a bare-chested Aidan lay on top of her, trim hips moving as he rocked against her.

Dylan watched in amusement for a moment, then cleared his throat.

Both their heads swiveled in his direction, their eyes hazy with passion.

"Am I interrupting something?" he asked politely.

Claire offered a sheepish grin. "We got bored waiting for you."

"I can see that."

"You joining us or what?" Aidan lifted one eyebrow.

"You know what? I think I wanna watch for a bit."

Unzipping his fly, he headed for the armchair and twisted it around so he had a better view of the couch. He yanked his surf shorts down his hips, sat bare-assed on the chair and wasted no time fisting his hardening dick.

He gave his erection a few lazy strokes and waited for Claire and Aidan to resume fooling around, but they were just lying there watching him.

"Where's my show?" he taunted.

"Hear that, baby? We're the entertainment." Aidan dipped his head to kiss her, then glanced back at Dylan with mocking eyes. "Since this is apparently all for you, why don't you tell us what you wanna see?"

He licked his lips. "I want Claire to suck your cock."

"What do you think?" Aidan asked her. "Should we give him what he wants?"

"Yes," she said in a breathy voice. She wiggled out from underneath Aidan's powerful body. "Take your pants off and get on your back, *baby*."

Laughing, Aidan shucked his sweatpants and got comfortable, half-sitting, half-lying down with his head resting on the arm of the couch. His cock jutted out, long and hard and demanding attention.

"Get him nice and wet with your mouth, and then wrap your fingers around the base," Dylan ordered, his gaze finding Claire's. "I want you to jack him off. Slowly."

Her lips parted sexily as she bent down to take Aidan's cock in her mouth. Her head bobbed a few times, summoning a deep groan from Aidan, who gave an upward thrust, trying to stay lodged in the warm recess of her mouth.

But Claire was very good at following instructions. As Aidan grumbled in disappointment, she released him with a wet popping sound and curled her delicate fingers around his saliva-slick shaft.

"That's it, nice and slow." Dylan voiced his encouragement as her small fist began moving up and down that hard cock.

He stroked himself idly, his attention glued to the scene before him. When he realized Claire still had a shirt on, he frowned in disapproval.

"Lose the T-shirt. I wanna see your tits bouncing around while you work him."

Heat sizzled in her eyes, telling him she liked the husky commands he was issuing. Without delay, she took off her shirt and removed her sports bra.

He admired her full, perky breasts, the cherry-red nipples that turned into two puckered buds the moment they were exposed to the air. He loved her tits, the sweet little sounds she made when he suckled them.

Claire reached for Aidan's dick and picked up where she'd left off, jerking him off in a slow rhythm. Aidan lay there at her mercy, moaning softly, hips moving in a desperate attempt to increase the tempo.

"He wants you to go faster, but you're not gonna, okay, honey? He pretends he doesn't like the teasing, but he fucking loves it."

Her lips parted again and her tongue came out to moisten her bottom lip. Her face was flushed. So were her breasts, their rosy hue telling him she was beyond turned on.

He tugged harder on his own dick, loving the way her tits swayed with the movement of her arm, loving the impatient growling sounds escaping from Aidan's throat.

"Give him your mouth now, but just suck the tip. Fuck, yeah, like that. No, don't let him go any deeper."

The sight of Claire's lips stretched around the engorged head sent a bolt of lightning to Dylan's balls. Groaning, he fisted his erection and squeezed, enjoying the little shockwaves that sizzled through his veins.

"Keep sucking, just like that. Just a little bit longer, and…now use your hand again."

Aidan's eyes flew open. "You fucking bastard."

Claire's soft laughter echoed in the room, and Dylan couldn't help a chuckle of his own. "My show, remember?"

As Aidan cursed them both, Claire went back to pumping his cock, until Dylan ordered her to blow him again. This time he let her wrap her fist around the shaft while she tormented Aidan's cockhead with feather-light licks.

"Oh, sweet Jesus," Aidan croaked. "You're killing me."

Dylan decided it was time to take pity on the man, who was clearly nearing the point of pain. "All right, honey, suck him hard and fast now."

Claire eagerly got to work, and Dylan's mouth promptly flooded with saliva. She looked so damn hot, her cheeks hollowing as she sucked Aidan, her red ponytail swishing from the fervent up-and-down motion of her head.

His own cock was ready to burst, bringing on a hoarse expletive. "Put a condom on him and ride his cock, Claire," he ordered.

Her eyelids fluttered open, her arm snapping out with purpose to grab the strip of condoms sitting on the coffee table. She had Aidan covered in no time, and then she was wiggling out of her shorts and panties, and impaling herself on his hard cock.

Three groans of pleasure filled the room the second Claire seated herself fully. Dylan could swear he felt the tight clasp of her pussy clutching his own dick like a vise.

"Uh-uh," he chided when she began to move. "Too fast. Slow it down."

Aidan made a sound of sheer agony. "Goddammit, man. I'm dying here."

With a mocking laugh, Dylan walked over to the couch. "You're complaining too much." He grinned. "Here, maybe this will shut you up."

Without warning, he grabbed Aidan by the hair and pushed his cock into the other man's mouth.

A husky moan vibrated along his shaft, and when he glanced over, he saw Claire's eyes burning with excitement.

His lips curved into a smile. "You love seeing us suck each other off, don't you, honey?"

She nodded wordlessly.

"Good, now keep riding our boy."

The hot suction around his cock combined with Claire's little squeaks of pleasure as she rode Aidan was enough to short-circuit his brain. It wasn't long before the only thought he was capable of producing was *go, go, go*.

Dylan wasn't gentle as he drove his dick all the way to the back of Aidan's throat, fucking him with fast, deep strokes. He gripped the man's hair and pumped his hips, thrusting harder, deeper. When he felt Aidan's teeth scrape the underside of his shaft, he swore loudly and shuddered with pleasure that bordered on pain.

And the entire time, he kept his gaze locked with Claire's, knowing from her glazed expression and strained breathing that she was close.

"She's gonna come soon," he told Aidan. "You're gonna feel her cunt squeezing your cock soon as she milks you dry."

With his mouth otherwise occupied, Aidan could only respond with a muffled groan. His dark eyes peered up at Dylan, blazing with such all-consuming desire it took his breath away.

"C'mon, Claire, I wanna see you lose control." He focused his gaze on the junction of her thighs, on the swollen clit she was rubbing with two fingers as she moved up and down Aidan's erection. "That's it, keep touching yourself. Make yourself come and show us how much you like riding Aidan's big cock—"

Claire released a blissful cry as she climaxed.

The moment he glimpsed the ecstasy surging through her eyes, Dylan let himself go. He exploded inside Aidan's mouth in long, hot pulses that racked his body, groaning as he watched the other man's throat working hard to swallow his seed.

But then the exquisite suction was suddenly gone.

"Coming," Aidan grunted. His long fingers dug into Claire's slender hips as he thrust upward and shuddered.

When Dylan glimpsed the shiny come leaking from the corner of Aidan's mouth, he was hit with another spontaneous orgasm, more hot jets shooting out of his cock and spraying Aidan's muscular chest.

Holy shit. He couldn't breathe. Couldn't talk. Couldn't see anything but the black dots dancing in front of his eyes.

He didn't think he'd ever come that hard in his life.

When Claire began to laugh, the wheezy sounds brought an exhausted grin to Dylan's lips.

"What's so funny?"

"I was just thinking…" she continued to shake with laughter, "…thinking how dumb I was for not wanting to be the kind of woman—" another giggle, "who did stuff like this. Because seriously? I've never had this much fun in my life."

They wound up spending the rest of the afternoon lounging on the couch, which was officially Dylan's new favorite piece of furniture in the condo. He and Aidan were in their boxers, Claire in nothing but Dylan's wifebeater, and they were lying in the position that had become their trademark—Aidan on his back, Claire curled up beside him, and Dylan nestled behind her.

Only this time, Aidan had surprised him by reaching for his hand, and Dylan's gaze kept flitting toward the intertwined fingers resting on Claire's hip.

A strange undercurrent traveled between them as Aidan shifted his head to meet Dylan's eyes.

His breath caught, because Aidan was looking at him in a way he'd never done before. Almost like…fuck, Dylan refused to let his mind even go there. The other man had been holding a part of himself back the entire time they'd been together. It had really bothered him at first, but Dylan had eventually recognized the futility in wishing Aidan would be more vocal about his feelings.

Except now, in this moment, there was no mistaking the tenderness in Aidan's eyes.

As their gazes locked, something hot and unfamiliar coursed between them, but the odd intimacy dissolved when Aidan broke the eye contact to answer Claire, who'd been talking about her latest job for the past ten minutes.

"Sounds like there's a reason this place is losing money," Aidan remarked.

"Yeah, no kidding. They literally have four people doing the job of one person," she said in disbelief. "And don't even get me started on one of their software designers. When I was there yesterday, he spent the entire day tinkering with his fantasy football lineup. He kept minimizing the window whenever I walked by, but one time he wasn't fast enough and I totally recognized the site he was on—it's the same one my dad's fantasy league uses."

Dylan laughed. "Well, at least he's doing something somewhat productive and not just fucking around on solitaire."

"He may as well be," she huffed. "This company is going to run itself into the ground. The management has no idea what the employees are doing, their computer system is archaic, and when I went over their expense reports, I found that one designer is invoicing the company for her salon appointments."

Aidan tweaked the end of her ponytail. "I bet you can't wait to sit down with the CEO and use that haughty voice of yours to tell him everything he's doing wrong."

"Damn right I can't wait. I swear, I don't know how half the businesses in this country haven't gone bankrupt yet."

She babbled on for several more minutes about the software company's inefficient management and internal operations, until Dylan finally cut her off and said, "Wow. You really love what you do, don't you?"

"Yeah, I really do. I just wish…" She halted abruptly.

"You wish what?" he pressed.

"Nothing. Forget it. It's silly."

Aidan tugged on her ponytail again. "Oh, just spit it out, sweetheart."

"Fine. Well, it's just…sometimes I wish I could pick and choose the assignments I take. There are certain organizations that are a pain in the ass to deal with, particularly the huge conglomerates. I prefer working with small businesses because I know the owners actually value the advice I'm giving them. The big corporations pay us a ton of money and then brush off everything we say because they think they know better."

"Have you ever thought about going into business for yourself?" Aidan asked curiously. "Starting your own consulting firm?"

"I have, but it's such a scary idea, you know? Besides, I love working for Barb. She pays me well, values my opinions." Claire shrugged. "Maybe one day I'll try it on my own, but for now I'm happy right where I am."

Dylan snuggled closer to her, then stroked Aidan's knuckles with his thumb. "I'm also happy right where I am."

Comfortable silence settled over them, during which Dylan experienced a feeling of pure tranquility he'd never felt before. Screw Seth's warning about this blowing up in their faces. This felt right. This *was* right.

The second the thought entered his head, there was a knock on the door.

Since the building had strict security measures in place, nobody was allowed up without being buzzed in and approved by the lobby guard, which meant their bad-timing knocker was either a neighbor or a member of the condo board.

"Not it." Aidan and Claire blurted out the same two syllables half a second apart.

"You guys are jerks," Dylan said with a disgruntled groan.

"Not our fault you didn't say it in time," Claire answered cheerfully.

Sighing, he climbed off the couch and strode toward the front hall. Rather than open the door, he peered into the peephole first—and his heart promptly stopped beating. Shit.

Shit, shit, shit.

Just as he was debating whether to pretend nobody was home, another sharp knock sounded on the door.

"Dylan, I know you're in there," Chris called angrily. "Your doorman told me you're home, so open the goddamn door."

Fuck, he didn't even have time to go and throw some clothes on. Judging by the seething look on Chris's face, Dylan was scared that if he didn't answer now, his brother might actually break down the door.

He took a breath. Dragged a hand over his hair, which was messy from both Claire and Aidan running their fingers through it.

And then he opened the door.

Chris took one look at Dylan's attire—or lack thereof—and muscled his way inside. "Where is she?" he demanded.

"Chris—" Dylan stepped into his brother's path.

"Where the hell is she?" Chris gave him a hard shove and bulldozed past him, his expensive wingtips slapping the hardwood as he stormed off.

Racing after his brother, Dylan tried to intercept him before he could reach the living room, but it was too late.

Chris froze in his tracks when he spotted Claire and Aidan on the couch. His green eyes narrowed, absorbed the couple's half-naked state, then traveled from the couch to the doorway, where Dylan stood in resigned silence.

Sucking in an angry breath, Chris swung his head back in Claire's direction. "You whore," he spat out. "You dirty fucking *whore.*"

Chapter Seventeen

CLAIRE FELT LIKE SOMEONE HAD YANKED THE RUG OUT FROM UNDER her. She jumped off the couch like her ass was on fire and scrambled around for her clothes, until she remembered that Aidan had stripped her out of them in the kitchen, where they'd fooled around before moving to the couch.

Her arms dangled at her sides in defeat, but she lifted her chin in defiance as she met her ex-fiancé's horrified eyes. "Hi, Chris," she said coolly. "You look tanned."

His breathing came out in uneven pants as he advanced on her, but he stopped when Aidan took an aggressive step forward and protectively moved Claire out of the way.

"How fucking sweet," Chris said in disgust. "Look at your lover, playing the hero." His furious gaze shifted to Dylan. "I can't believe you did this! You steal my fiancée and bring her back to your perverted lair for some disgusting orgy with your roommate?"

Dylan's voice was cold enough to freeze an ocean. "I didn't steal anything. You walked out on Claire, which means you have no right to pass judgment on what she does or who she does it with."

Chris made a sound that was a cross between a growl and a squawk. "I knew you were a horny fucker, Dylan, but this? *This*? Screwing the woman I was going to marry? Next thing you'll tell me, you're screwing *him* too."

Claire saw Dylan's strong jaw harden, saw his hands tighten into fists, but rather than voice a denial or ignore the accusation, he surprised everyone in the room by saying, "Actually, I am."

Deafening silence.

Claire almost laughed at Chris's expression. Shock mingled with revulsion, mixed in with a splash of horror. His face had gone devoid of color, and his mouth hung open as he stared at his brother.

Dylan crossed his arms over his bare chest and slanted his head. "What, no response? No insightful commentary?"

Chris shook his head, once, twice, half a dozen times, as if he couldn't fathom what he'd just heard. Then his ashen face turned beet red, and he looked like he was about to vomit.

"You sick fuck," he hissed out. "Jesus Christ, Dylan, you're in the *military* and you're telling me you're...that you're...a fucking *faggot*?"

Dylan flinched.

Claire gasped.

The breathy sound seemed to remind Chris of her presence, because he was spinning around again, looking at her with such malevolence she started to feel queasy.

"I am so happy I didn't marry you." His voice was low, ominous and dripping with hatred.

She gave him a tired look. "Right back atcha, Chris. In fact, I'm convinced now more than ever that I dodged a bullet."

Rage erupted in his eyes. "You have the nerve to tell me *I* wasn't good enough for *you*? You stupid little *bitch*—"

In the blink of an eye, Chris was on the floor.

Claire hadn't even seen Dylan strike, he moved so fast, and now he was straddling Chris's torso and jamming his elbow into his brother's windpipe. "Don't you ever talk to her like that," he said in a soft but deadly voice. "Say whatever the hell you want about me, or about Aidan, but you speak to Claire with respect."

Chris sputtered, tried to shove Dylan off, but the SEAL's body was inflexible, a rock-hard wall of muscle that refused to budge.

Wide-eyed and a little bit frightened, Claire watched as Dylan dug his forearm deeper into Chris's throat, nowhere near done raking his brother over the coals.

"And you know what? I've had it up to here with your homophobic bullshit. Jesus Christ, so one of your buddies made a pass at you in high school. Big fucking deal. Get over it already."

The revelation left Claire dumbfounded. Chris had never shared that piece of information with her, but the moment she heard it, so many things clicked into place. Like why Chris had always been so rude to Natasha, or why he'd cringed every time a gay couple passed them on the street.

Unwelcome sympathy washed over her, which only pissed her off even more, because why the hell was she feeling sorry for this man? He wasn't worth the energy it took to pity him.

Dylan must have agreed, because he abruptly released his brother and stood up. In nothing but his boxers, he made a formidable picture, gleaming muscles and sleek sinew and raw power.

The moment Dylan stepped away, Chris bolted to his feet, eyes blazing with indignation. "Don't you *ever* lay a hand on me again, little brother. If Mom ever found out you did that—"

"You really want to have a conversation about Mom right now? Because I'd be fucking happy to do that, man. I'd love to know why you chose to lie to me about her gambling problem and the fact that we almost lost our fucking house!"

Chris didn't even have the decency to apologize. "I'm the man of the house, Dylan. I take care of Mom, not you."

"The only person you take care of is yourself," Dylan retorted. "And now if you don't mind, I'd like you to leave. Maybe one of these days we can sit down and have a mature conversation about all this, but right now, I can't stand the sight of you."

"Believe me, I feel exactly the same way." Chris spared one last look in Claire and Aidan's direction, then spun on his heel and marched out.

A few seconds later, the front door slammed with so much force the living room walls shook.

Aidan, who hadn't uttered a single word during the exchange, gingerly touched Claire's shoulder. "Are you all right?"

Letting out a shaky breath, she met his worried eyes and managed a nod. "Yeah, I think so."

They both turned to Dylan, whose face had a vacant look to it.

"Shit, man, I'm sorry," Aidan said roughly. "That was…brutal."

Dylan didn't respond.

As concern tugged at her heart, Claire hurried over to him and grasped his chin with both hands. His five o'clock shadow scraped her skin, and she rubbed her palms over the bristly dark-blond hairs in a soothing motion.

"Hey, it's okay," she murmured. "You know everything he said was out of anger, right? A knee-jerk reaction to seeing…what he saw."

"I'm not upset about what he said," Dylan muttered. "I'm upset about who he *is*."

The pain in his eyes made her chest ache. "He's not a bad person, Dylan. He's just…ignorant. And selfish. But he *is* capable of love—I know he loves your mom, and I know he loves *you*. He'll come around eventually."

Claire couldn't believe the words coming out of her mouth. After everything that just happened, she shouldn't be defending Chris or rationalizing his behavior. She should be suggesting they throw a party to celebrate his departure, maybe pop open a bottle of champagne and propose a toast.

Still, no matter how hurt and angry she was, Chris was still Dylan's brother. He was family. And if she and Dylan and Aidan were ever to have a real future, she knew they'd have to mend fences with Chris sooner or later.

But it wasn't going to happen overnight, so when Dylan brushed off her words with an unintelligible mumble, she didn't push him. Instead, she wrapped her arms around his waist and held him tight.

And kept holding on until, finally, he lifted his arms and hugged her back.

CLAIRE COULDN'T BELIEVE HOW FAST THE NEXT TWO WEEKS FLEW BY. Terrifyingly fast. Heartbreakingly fast. As she parked her rental in the visitor's parking lot behind the Savvy Tech building in Oceanside, she couldn't help but bite her lip in dismay. The only thought that had been running through her mind all day was, *now what?*

What happened now that the assignment was wrapping up? What happened to her relationship with Dylan and Aidan when she returned to San Francisco?

And it *was* a relationship. She was no longer fooling herself into believing this was nothing more than a brief fling between three people in lust with each other. She cared deeply for both men, and the mere thought of leaving them made her feel like someone was scraping a dull blade inside her chest and slicing her heart to jagged ribbons.

The last two weeks had been the happiest of her life, filled with endless laughter and lively conversation and wild, passionate sex that left her breathless.

Aidan's intensity thrilled her; Dylan's lust for life inspired her.

Aidan's serious, closed-off nature brought out a nurturing, sensitive side she hadn't known she'd possessed, while Dylan's openness and unceasing optimism gave her a sense of soothing comfort she'd never felt before.

How could she ever say goodbye to either one of them?

The sound of a car door slamming jerked her from her thoughts. She glanced over and noticed that a silver Lexus had just parked in the space beside hers. When the driver stepped out, Claire blinked in shock.

She hastily grabbed her laptop case and leather portfolio from the passenger seat and slid out of the car just as her boss approached.

"Barb," she said uneasily. "What are you doing here?"

Barbara Valentine looked as elegant as always in her tailored black pantsuit and dove-gray Louboutin pumps. Her black hair was twisted in a neat bun, and the string of pearls around her slender neck sparkled in the morning sunshine.

"I thought I'd sit in on your meeting with Sanders," Barb answered smoothly.

Although unexpected, Barb's being here was not unusual—Claire's boss often sat in when her consultants presented their findings to a client. Nevertheless, Claire felt apprehensive about Barb showing up out of the blue.

"Are you prepared for the presentation?" the older woman asked, oblivious to Claire's growing agitation.

She managed a smile. "Of course."

"Good. Let's go inside."

They walked into the building and informed the lobby receptionist about their meeting with Bryant Sanders. Five minutes later, the two women were being ushered into the conference room where Claire had spent quite a lot of time over the past few weeks.

She was still unsettled by Barb's presence, but she forced herself to concentrate on her job instead of her nerves, setting up her laptop and loading the PowerPoint presentation she'd slaved over last night.

"Claire, good to see you again." Savvy Tech's CEO strode into the room and greeted her with a warm smile. Sanders was a lanky man with a head of salt-and-pepper hair and a pair of wire-rimmed glasses resting on a thin nose, and he'd been incredibly accommodating throughout Claire's assessment of his company.

They shook hands, and then Sanders turned to Barb. "I'm glad you could join us, Barbara. And I must say, I've been very impressed with Claire's diligent observations and insightful analysis."

"Claire is very good at what she does," Barb agreed with a smile.

The compliment eased some of her nerves, and a few minutes later, the presentation was underway and Claire didn't have time to feel nervous. In a brisk voice, she presented her findings to Sanders, going into detail about every aspect of his company and every flaw she'd discovered during her evaluation. Several times, the CEO interrupted with questions that she answered readily and knowledgably. When she outlined the solutions she'd come up with in order to make the company run more efficiently and increase its profits, Sanders looked more than pleased.

The meeting lasted a little more than an hour, and after it wrapped up, Sanders took the thick report Claire had prepared and thanked her profusely for all her hard work.

And through it all, Barb gazed at Claire in approval, squashing any notion that something was amiss.

At least until the two women were alone again.

The second they were back in the parking lot, Barb's eyes took on that odd light again. The look was impossible to decipher, and the longer Barb stayed quiet, the more uncomfortable Claire became.

"Is everything all right?" she asked her boss.

Barb donned a thoughtful look. "Let's grab a coffee, darling." She took off walking.

Confused, Claire fell into step with the other woman. Five minutes later, they were seated at a corner table in the Starbucks across the street from Savvy Tech.

"You did a fabulous job in there," Barb told her.

She tried to ignore the queasy churning of her stomach. "Thank you."

"I mean it, darling—that was a thorough, well-prepared assessment."

She murmured another *thank you* and brought her cup to her lips. The coffee was way too hot to drink yet, burning her tongue the second she took a sip. Wincing, Claire set down the cup and ran her tongue over the roof of her mouth in an attempt to ease the pain.

Barb continued to watch her. "All right, let's not waste any time. Something has been brought to my attention, and since you know I'm a woman who doesn't like to beat around the bush, I'd like for the two of us to clear this up right here and now."

A sick feeling crawled up her throat. "Okay. What is it?"

"I've been informed that you've spent the last two months involved in a polyamorous relationship."

Claire flinched as if she'd been struck. "W-what?"

Barb rephrased her previous sentence. "A relationship with two men."

But Claire didn't need a fucking clarification. She knew exactly what her boss meant—and she knew exactly who her *informant* was.

That bastard.

The goddamn bastard.

Pure blind rage whipped through her like a loose cable in a storm, and it took every ounce of willpower to keep it from showing on her face.

Chris.

Chris had gone to her *boss*.

He'd told Barb that Claire was sleeping with two guys.

The sheer audacity of his actions left her speechless. Was he *insane*? How could he do something like that? This was her goddamn career he was messing with!

God, and to think, she'd been biting her tongue for the past two weeks, urging Dylan to consider making things right with his brother. She'd assured him all this would blow over, that Chris would eventually calm down and realize as unorthodox as the situation was, the three of them were happy and weren't doing anything wrong. Aidan had concurred, speculating that Chris would come to accept it sooner or later.

But she and Aidan had been wrong.

"I can see from your expression that it's true."

Barb's voice, which had grown considerably cooler, penetrated Claire's incensed thoughts.

Taking a breath, she curled both hands over her coffee cup. Not just because they were shaking, but because she feared she might accidentally mistake Barb for Chris and strangle the life out of her.

"I have been seeing two men, yes," she answered in a careful tone. "However, I don't see how my personal life has any bearing on my professional relationship with you, or my position at this firm."

Barb's cheeks hollowed as she tightly pursed her lips. "But I'm afraid it does. In fact, your personal life directly affects your professional one."

"I disagree. And I have to be honest, Barb, but I don't feel comfortable discussing this with you. Who I date is none of your concern and—"

"Actually, it is my concern," her boss interjected. "I hate to do this, but I must refer you to the contract you signed when I hired you five years ago."

Barb bent over and snapped her briefcase open, then extracted several sheets of paper stapled together. She set the stack on the table and slid it over to Claire, who immediately recognized the standard contract every consultant at Smart Solutions was asked to sign.

"Turn to page five."

Clenching her teeth, she flipped through the contract and found page five.

"Paragraph three," Barb prompted, tapping a red-manicured fingernail on the tabletop.

Claire felt all the blood drain from her face as she read over the morality clause imbedded into the contract. She remembered reading it five years ago, and every subsequent year when her contract had been renewed, but she'd never in a million years dreamed she'd be accused of breaching that clause.

"As you can see, you agreed to conduct yourself in a certain manner, and that any behavior reflecting negatively on the company would be grounds for termination." Barb paused. "I'm afraid that openly living and engaging in a sexual relationship with two men reflects negatively on the company. We have an image to maintain, Claire. The clients who hire us expect qualified, upstanding professionals to assess their business needs."

She felt numb. And nauseous. And her fucking tongue still throbbed from that burning-hot coffee.

Swallowing hard, she met her boss's eyes and spoke in a dull tone. "What exactly are you saying, Barb?"

"What I'm saying, darling, is that I'm going to have to let you go."

WHEN AIDAN GOT HOME FROM THE BASE THAT EVENING AND SAW CLAIRE'S face, he immediately knew something bad had gone down. Even from across the room, he could see the tears clinging to her thick eyelashes.

"What's wrong?" he demanded.

Since Dylan was behind him and had yet to glimpse Claire's expression, the SEAL thought Aidan was talking to him and replied in a bewildered tone. "What are you talking about, man? Everything's fi—" He halted when he spotted Claire, then said, "What's wrong?"

"I just got fired," she said flatly.

They were at her side in an instant, sandwiching her on the couch, bodies angled so they could both see her face.

"What the hell are you talking about?" Dylan asked.

She opened her mouth. Then closed it. Then opened it again and a whole lotta words poured out. Aidan listened in stupefied silence as she told them everything her boss had said. He wasn't prone to violent thoughts, but at that moment he wanted to rip Chris Wade's head right off his shoulders and punt it into a tar pit.

Too far. Dylan's brother had gone too fucking far by speaking to Claire's boss, and Aidan's vision turned into a red mist of fury as he listened to her soft sobs.

"My brother told your boss you were engaged in an inappropriate sexual relationship?" Dylan's voice was harder than steel, eyes glittering with the same rage boiling in Aidan's gut.

She nodded wordlessly.

Raking both hands through his hair, Dylan released a string of curses that finally ended with, "I don't even know who he is anymore. I never dreamed he would stoop this low."

"What am I going to do? I can't believe I lost my job," Claire moaned.

As she buried her face in her hands, Aidan's heart cracked in two. He wasted no time drawing her close, while Dylan stroked Claire's back in reassurance.

"It'll be okay," Dylan murmured. "Everything will be okay."

Aidan's heart splintered a little bit more each time Claire let out another quiet sob. He tightened his grip and held her against his chest, and in the back of his mind he wondered why it was so damn easy to show her physical affection when he kept everyone else at arm's length. Including Dylan. *Especially* Dylan.

Inhaling an unsteady breath, he met the other man's gaze over Claire's head and saw his own concern reflected back at him. But he also discerned a flicker of longing, which only deepened when Dylan's eyes rested on the hand Aidan was using to stroke Claire's hair.

Damn it, he hated seeing that look of yearning on Dylan's face. He knew the other man was unhappy with his inability to vocalize his feelings, to be tender and affectionate outside the bedroom, but every time he opened his mouth to try to tell Dylan how he felt, his throat closed up and he couldn't get the words out.

But now was not the time to dwell on his own inadequacies. Claire needed him. Claire needed *them*.

It was a while before she finally calmed down, and when she lifted her head, Aidan was floored by the intensity blazing in her big brown eyes.

"I'm fine. I'm going to be fine," she said firmly, but he knew she was trying to convince herself more than she was trying to convince them. "I'm smart and ambitious and qualified, and I'll be able to find another job, no problem."

"Or—" Dylan spoke tentatively, "—you could open your own consulting firm."

She faltered. "I…don't know if I'm ready for that."

"Why not?" Aidan said quietly. "You've always wanted to go solo, and now you've got the chance. You have the experience, you have the contacts. Why not give it a shot?"

She bit her lip. "Well, I guess I…I mean, I do have enough money saved up, not just in terms of capital but also to support myself for a couple of years if I'm unemployed…"

Her voice trailed off, and Aidan could see that sharp brain of hers kicking into gear, working over the idea. A spark of pride ignited in his chest. Goddamn, this woman was incredible. It was impossible to knock her down.

Or at least that's what he thought before Claire's phone rang.

She leaned forward and grabbed the phone from the coffee table, then frowned. "It's my dad." In the blink of an eye, her face went a shade paler. "You don't think…he wouldn't have…?"

Without finishing, she answered the phone with a quick, "Hey, Dad. What's up?"

When she gasped, the answer to the questions she hadn't been able to voice became clearer than a Times Square billboard.

Would Chris go to Claire's parents?

Yes, he would. And yes, he had.

Aidan suddenly felt sick. He couldn't hear a word Claire's father was saying, which reminded him of what she'd said about Ron McKinley's tendency to talk in a scarily quiet voice when he was angry.

"Dad—"

Whatever her father cut her off with brought a flash of panic to Claire's eyes.

Her voice trembled as she tried again. "Dad—" She paused, then made a strangled sound. "Fine! Yes, it's true. Is that what you want to hear?"

Aidan's heart dropped to the pit of his stomach. When he glanced over at Dylan, he saw deep distress digging a groove into the man's forehead.

"Can I please talk to her? Please, just put Mom on the phone." Claire listened for a moment before her entire face collapsed. "Can I at least come home so we can talk about it?" Ashen, she awaited a reply. Her eyes welled up with tears. "I can't do that, Daddy…No, don't say that…I—"

She halted, then turned to Aidan in shock. "He hung up on me."

He tried to pull her close again, but this time she rejected his comfort. She jerked up to her feet, two trails of moisture sliding down her porcelain cheeks.

"Chris showed up at their house and told them about us." A splash of bitterness crept into her tone. "I don't know why he decided to wait two weeks to drop the bomb, but apparently this has been a busy day for him."

Dylan stood up slowly. "What did your father say?"

"He said he's disappointed and horrified by my behavior, and that he'll never approve of what I'm doing." She brushed away her tears with her knuckles. "He ordered me to end it. I said I couldn't do that, and that's when he told me that as long as I'm involved with the two of you, I'm not welcome in his house."

Aidan's heart throbbed with agony. Shit.

He took a step toward her, as did Dylan, but she held up one trembling hand to stop them.

"No. I can't do this right now. I know you guys want to help, but…I…" She took a breath. "But I just need to be alone."

She hurried out of the room, leaving him and Dylan standing there helplessly.

HANDS-DOWN, THIS WAS THE DAY FROM HELL. A NEVER-ENDING nightmare. She'd gotten fired, her dad had disowned her—what was going to happen next? Was a meteor going to crash into her rental car? Would the ceiling cave in on her head? Would the dog she didn't own get hit by a car?

Oh, hush. Self-pity doesn't become you.

Claire inhaled a long, deep breath and sat on Dylan's bed. She'd gone into his room rather than Aidan's because she hadn't wanted to see the tangled sheets on the king-sized bed she'd been sharing with her men.

Yep, *her* men, as her father had referred to them.

If you don't end it with your men, you're not welcome in my house, Claire.

Blinking through a new onslaught of tears, she keyed in the password to unlock her phone and quickly brought up her mother's number. Her dad had refused to give her the phone, but Claire prayed her mom would at least answer her cell.

To her overwhelming relief, Nora's voice came on the line. "Claire! What on earth is going on over there? Chris came by and told us the most disturbing things."

"Where's Dad?" she asked. "Why didn't he let you talk to me before?"

"He's upset, sweetie. I didn't want to force the issue when he refused to give me the phone. But he went to take a walk to clear his head, so we have some time." Nora paused. "Your father said you confirmed everything Chris said. Is that true?"

She swallowed. "Yes."

"You're involved with Chris's brother, then? And…and his roommate?"

"Yes."

There was another pause, followed by a heavy sigh. "Oh, sweetie, what are you doing?"

"I…" Her voice cracked. "It's complicated."

"It's wrong, that's what it is. You need to stop this. Put an end to it now."

"I can't."

"Yes, you can. Just come home, Claire. I know the breakup with Chris was difficult, and obviously it had more of an effect on you than we thought. You're confused and you're not thinking clearly."

"I'm not confused," she said softly.

"You need to pack your bags and leave. Your father is very upset about this, but he'll forgive you, as long as you break it off with those men and come home."

"I can't do that. Mom…I think I love them."

Silence. Lasting so long Claire thought her mother had hung up.

"Mom, are you there?"

"Claire, this is crazy. Do you realize how crazy that sounds?"

"I know it's crazy," she burst out. "But it's real, damn it! I have feelings for them, for both of them. Real, strong feelings, and I can't walk away from that."

"Your father will never accept this." Her mom hesitated. "I don't know if *I* can accept it."

Pain jolted through her, but Claire wasn't about to back down. "Mom, I love you and Dad, but this is my life, and I live it for me. You don't have to agree with all my choices, and if you and Dad are willing to cut me out of your lives because of this, then that's on you. I'm sorry you don't approve, but like I said, I'm not walking away from them."

"Even if it means your father will never let you come home again?"

Her throat burned with regret. "Even then." She let out a wobbly breath. "I'll give you some time to digest this and call you in a few days, okay? Just…please try to keep an open mind. At least meet Dylan and Aidan before you write me off forever."

A distressed sob met her ears. "Claire, just come home."

"I can't."

"Claire—"

"Bye, Mom."

She hung up, feeling bruised and beaten and so very tired. Her eyes hurt from all the tears she'd shed, and her face was still damp, prompting her to leave the room and duck into the hall bathroom, where she gasped at her reflection in the mirror.

Her mascara had run like crazy, glaring evidence that the word *waterproof* on the applicator was pure and total bullshit. She looked like a madwoman—streaky black lines on her cheeks, red-rimmed eyes, splotchy skin.

And yet neither Dylan nor Aidan had commented on it. They'd held her and comforted her and whispered reassurances without once pointing out she looked like a rabid raccoon.

As she left the bathroom, there was an unexpected spring to her step, which was damn peculiar considering she'd just lost her job and probably her parents. She was giving up everything for these men—why wasn't she more freaked out about it?

She got her answer the moment she entered the living room and saw both men leap off the couch, their eyes shining with concern.

She belonged here with them. She belonged *to* them.

And they belonged to her.

"Are you leaving?" The gruff inquiry came from Aidan.

With the slight shake of her head, she walked toward them and said, "I'm not going anywhere."

Chapter Eighteen

"So a little birdie told me you and Dylan are both dating Claire."

Aidan rolled his eyes. "And does that little birdie go by the name *Seth*?"

Chuckling, Matt rested his elbows on the iron railing of the second-floor balcony and glanced over. "Actually, it was Cash. He said Dylan told the boys about it the other day when they were chilling by the pool."

Aidan wasn't surprised that McCoy had shared the news with his roommate, but he'd been hoping to be the one to tell Matt. He and O'Connor were tight, had been ever since they'd run into each other on the base several years back, and other than Dylan, Matt was Aidan's closest friend. The two of them had indulged in a shit-ton of threesomes, including some seriously hot nights with Matt's fiancée.

"So it's true, huh? You're both dating the same woman?"

After a beat, Aidan nodded.

"And how's that working out for you?" Matt asked in a careful tone.

"Pretty damn good," he admitted.

"I see." The other man's skepticism was unmistakable.

Aidan didn't blame Matt one bit for being skeptical. He still couldn't wrap his head around it, either. A relationship between three people? He wouldn't have ever dreamed a scenario like that could actually work, and yet it did. At least for them.

"Okay, I *don't* see," Matt blurted out, retracting his previous remark. "I mean, I get it in the sexual sense—you know how much I love a little variety in the bedroom. But romantically? I don't get it."

Aidan moved away from the railing and swiped his beer bottle from the small table before sinking into one of the plastic chairs. Matt flopped down in the other chair, mystified.

"Seriously, dude, you've gotta explain it to me."

"It's just like any other relationship, except there's another person in the mix. I care about Claire, and so does Dylan. And she cares about both of us." He sighed. "I still feel guilty as hell, though."

Matt furrowed his dark eyebrows. "Why?"

"She lost her job because of us, and her parents aren't speaking to her."

His throat clogged at the memory of Claire in tears. That had been three days ago, but just as she'd promised, Claire hadn't gone anywhere. She was as committed to their unconventional arrangement as he and Dylan were, a fact that continued to floor him.

Claire McKinley was so fucking incredible. So smart, and so sweet, and so passionate she blew his mind. He couldn't believe a woman like her actually existed. A woman who was willing to welcome two men into her bed, into her heart. A woman who was willing to accept that those two men also desired each other.

"That's rough," Matt said sympathetically. "Is she looking for a new job in San Diego?"

"She's actually thinking of starting her own business. She's doing some research to see what it'll take, and hopefully that works out for her. She's damn good at what she does. The last thing I want is for her to settle for a job she's not passionate about."

"What about her parents? You think they'll come around?"

"I hope so. It would be a damn shame if they don't."

"So you're really in this for the long haul?" Matt asked.

"Yes," he said quietly. "I know it doesn't make sense to you, but I'm happy, man. This…this *thing* we have, it's exactly what I need."

Matt went silent for a moment, then threw out a curveball that made Aidan's mouth go dry.

"You're screwing Dylan, too, huh?"

His hand froze before he could bring his bottle to his lips. "What makes you say that?"

"Oh, come on, man, I may be from the south but I ain't slow," Matt drawled. "And for someone who works in intelligence, you're mighty transparent sometimes. You and Wade were dancing around each other all summer. Whenever you were in the same room together? *I'd* get a fucking hard-on. I'm serious—major sexual tension, Aid."

He had to laugh. So much for thinking he'd been stealthy about hiding his attraction to Dylan.

"Am I right?"

"Yeah, you're right," he confessed.

"So this is, like, a *true* three-way, huh?" Matt sounded intrigued. "You're dating both of them."

"Yes."

"And it's actually working out? No jealousy or arguments or one of you feeling left out?"

"Nope." Aidan grinned. "Claire and Dylan bicker like children, but I'm there to turn them over my knee if need be."

Matt laughed. "You were always damn good at spanking. Remember that night you got Savannah's ass nice and pink?" His green eyes smoldered. "Fuck, that was hot."

As the SEAL took a long swig of his beer, Aidan noticed the man looking a wee bit flustered. His grin widened as realization dawned.

"You miss me," he said in delight.

Matt set his bottle on the table and ran a hand over his shaved head. "Sometimes."

"Sometimes? Nuh-uh. I think you and Savannah are totally jonesing for some Aidan."

He got a middle finger in response, but then O'Connor let out a breath and flashed a sheepish grin. "Fine, we miss you. That's why my girl got all bitchy when she saw you kissing Claire on Christmas Eve. We were planning on inviting you over that night."

Aidan raised his eyebrows. "What happened to the whole, *We're engaged now—it wouldn't be proper to fuck you anymore?*"

"We realized that being engaged doesn't mean we've gotta turn into a boring married couple who only fucks in the missionary position every night."

"Every night?" He snorted. "Do boring married couples even have sex that often?"

"Ask Carson and Holly. Those two fuck like every five minutes. I'm pretty sure they ducked into the bathroom on Christmas Eve to get it on."

"Oh, they did," came Seth's voice.

Matt and Aidan glanced at the open sliding door, where Seth's big frame had appeared. Beyond Seth's broad shoulders, Aidan glimpsed Cash shrugging out of a brown leather jacket.

"You're back early," Matt remarked. "I thought you were catching the eight o'clock screening."

"Sold out," Seth grumbled. "Everyone and their fucking mother decided to buy tickets for the movie, so we figured we'd come back here and watch *Die Hard*. You guys in?"

"Hell yeah," Aidan said. "I was trying to convince Claire to watch it the other night, but she's all about the shitty rom coms."

Seth flashed a cocky grin. "Miranda hates rom coms. She says they're too unrealistic."

As the three of them headed inside, Seth picked up the previous subject. "Anyway, Carson and Holly totally got it on Christmas Eve." He scowled. "And you want to know the worst part, other than having to picture my LT going to town on his wife? Having to explain to the rugrats why they heard, and I quote, 'farm noises' coming out of the bathroom."

Aidan and Matt burst out laughing.

In the living room, Cash loaded up the movie while everyone got settled on the two couches with their beers. But before McCoy could press *play*, Seth turned those shrewd gray eyes on Aidan and said, "So the relationship ménage is still going strong?"

Aidan met his gaze head on. "Sure is."

"I still don't get it."

He shrugged. "You don't have to get it. Not your life, remember?"

"He's just jealous because his life isn't as interesting," Cash spoke up with a grin. "He's got two kids to raise. You get to have kinky three-way sex every night. No contest."

"Miranda and I have kinky sex," Seth protested.

"Uh-huh," Aidan said indulgently. "So how does that work with the twins constantly running underfoot? Do you get to fuck her on the kitchen counter every morning?"

"After the kids go to school," Seth answered smugly.

"Does she suck your dick in the shower?"

"When the rugrats go to bed."

"Hmmm." Aidan offered a cheeky smile. "Does she moan like crazy when you're fucking her pussy and another cock is buried in her ass?"

Matt choked out a laugh. Cash looked envious.

And Seth just sighed. "Fine, I guess my sex life isn't as kinky as it used to be. Hey, where's the D-Man, by the way? He'd be all over *Die Hard*."

"When I left him, he was involved in a serious COD battle with Jackson," Aidan said. "Claire and I couldn't take it anymore so I dropped her off at Savannah's for girls' night." He turned to Matt with a warning look. "And I swear to God, if Savannah threatens my girl again, I *will* kick her ass."

Matt raised a brow. "You'll have to go through me first."

"Is that supposed to scare me? I could kick your ass any day of the week."

Seth clapped his hands together. "Shit, now *that* I'd love to see." He glanced at Cash. "A death match between O'Connor and Rhodes?"

"I'd fucking pay to see that," Cash retorted. "My money's on Matt."

"Forget that—I'm all about Aidan. Didn't you snag an invite to that heavy-duty boxing camp during your navy training?"

Aidan found himself under Seth's scrutiny again. "Sure did," he confirmed.

Matt rolled his eyes. "I'm a SEAL—there's no way in hell Rhodes is kicking my ass."

Seth and Cash exchanged a look, which led to Aidan and Matt exchanging a look of their own.

"Don't even think about it," Matt warned.

But the two men were already hopping off their respective couches and beginning to drag the coffee table out of the way.

"This is *so* happening," Cash announced. "I've got a hundred bucks on Matt."

Seth grinned. "Get ready to lose some money then."

Despite himself, Aidan had to laugh. "What happened to *Die Hard*?"

"Fuck that. Live action is so much more rewarding." Cash crossed his arms over his broad chest. "So are you two gonna pussy out, or do we have ourselves a fight?"

Aidan glanced at Matt again, who simply shrugged and said, "It has been a while since we sparred…"

With another laugh, Aidan got to his feet and stripped out of his V-neck tee. "All righty. Let's do this shit."

"Wow. When you commit to something, you *really* commit," Annabelle Holmes remarked, amusement dancing in her eyes.

Claire laughed. "I know, right?" She waved a hand when the brunette made a move to refill Claire's wine glass. "No more for me. I'm already tipsy as hell."

Jane Becker wagged her finger in disapproval. "Tipsy is not an unacceptable state to leave girls' night in. Our goal is to get rip-roaring drunk and then go home to have our way with our men."

From their various positions around Savannah's living room, all the other women were nodding and grinning. Claire had to laugh again. She was suddenly so glad she'd taken Jen up on her offer to come here tonight. She hadn't been thrilled the gathering was taking place at Savannah's, but the blonde had been on her best behavior since Claire's arrival, and all the other women were so damn friendly.

For the past two hours, she'd chatted easily with everyone. Holly, Jen, Miranda and Savannah, she already knew. But this was her first time meeting Annabelle, who was engaged to Ryan Evans, and Jane, who was married to the team's Lieutenant Commander. She liked both women immensely, especially Jane, who was as a blunt as Savannah but far more humorous about it.

"So is it a three-way every night then?" Annabelle pressed, looking more than a little curious about Claire's current living arrangement.

She felt her cheeks heat up. "Pretty much. But sometimes it's one-on-one if one of the guys goes out."

Or if *she* wasn't around, but Claire kept that tidbit to herself because she knew Dylan and Aidan didn't want to announce to everyone that they were sexually involved. Dylan had told her Jen was in the loop, though, and from the secretive smile the blue-eyed blonde shot her, Claire knew Jen was thinking the same thing she was.

"What about dates?" Jane asked. "Do the three of you go out?"

She nodded. "Yeah, but we don't go overboard on the PDA or anything. Usually just hand-holding."

Annabelle giggled. "Does everyone's jaw just drop when they see the three of you holding hands?"

"Sometimes." She smiled impishly. "I get a lot of envious looks from other women."

"Well, duh," Savannah said, grinning widely. "You're walking around with two of the sexiest men on the planet. Chicks are probably jealous as hell when they see you." The grin dissolved into a guilty look. "I was jealous too, if I'm being honest."

"Ooooh," Jane teased. "Look at that, Claire, you brought out Savannah's green-eyed monster by stealing Aidan away from her."

Discomfort rose up her spine, but it faded when she saw the sincerity shining on Savannah's face. "I'm not jealous anymore, I promise," the woman assured her. "It just caught me off-guard seeing Aidan kissing you that night. Matt and I have always thought of Aidan as *ours*, know what I mean?"

"I get that," Claire said. "He's pretty damn special. I don't blame you for feeling possessive over him."

"But it's nice to see him looking so happy," Savannah admitted. "He's not the kind of man who wears his emotions on his sleeve, but lately he's always smiling and laughing, and it's all because of you."

Claire was genuinely touched. And she knew exactly what Savannah meant. Aidan had been opening up more and more to both her and Dylan. The other night, he'd even told them about how guilty he'd felt after his mom's death, how living with the knowledge that she'd died to save him had eaten him up inside. Afterwards, Dylan had pulled her aside and thanked her for being there. He claimed that her presence was good for Aidan, and now Savannah was saying the same thing, which only cemented Claire's decision to stay.

Her parents were still avoiding her calls, and she was still unemployed, but when it came to her love life, she'd never been happier. She was holding on to the hope that all the other parts of her life would fall in line too. Preferably sooner rather than later.

The conversation was interrupted by Savannah's phone, which vibrated with an incoming text. She glanced at the screen and laughed. "Matt is requesting we all put our clothes on because he's on his way up. He doesn't want his buddies beating him up for seeing their women naked."

Annabelle looked mystified. "What on earth does he think we do on girls' night?"

"According to his fantasies, we all get naked and have a pillow fight."

Everyone laughed.

"We should do that one time just to fuck with him," Jen suggested.

A few minutes later, the front door of Savannah's loft swung open and Matt strode in.

Sporting a very swollen, very black eye.

His fiancée immediately bolted to her feet. "What the hell, baby? What happened?"

A second later, a very sheepish-looking Aidan entered on Matt's heels, prompting Claire to gasp. His gorgeous eyes were just fine, but his bottom lip was split and caked with dried blood.

She was at his side in a heartbeat, touching the side of his mouth in concern. "What the hell?" she echoed.

"Ah, darlin', it's just a little shiner," Matt told Savannah.

"And just a busted lip," Aidan assured Claire.

The two women glanced at each other, then turned to glare at their men.

"You two got into a fight?" Savannah demanded. "Please tell me the other guys got it worse."

"Um…" Aidan shifted on his feet. "There were no other guys. We, uh…"

"Fought each other," Matt supplied.

A loud snicker came from the living area.

Matt glanced past his fiancée's shoulders and offered a careless wave. "Evening, ladies. Thanks for getting dressed so fast."

"No problem," Jane said with a snort. "You know we don't like anyone walking in on our nude pillow fights."

Claire narrowed her eyes at Aidan. "Why were you fighting each other?"

"Just for fun."

"For fun?" Disbelief fluttered through her as she stared at his swollen lip. "How is beating each other up *fun*?"

Behind them, the other women began gathering up their purses and jackets, chuckling amongst themselves. Miranda was the first to approach, pausing in front of the guys with a suspicious cloud in her hazel eyes.

"Why do I get the feeling my husband played a part in this?"

Aidan's lips twitched. "It may or may not have been his idea."

"Of course." She sighed. "How much money did he lose?"

"None," Matt grumbled in response. "Your asshole husband bet against me, and then he and your asshole boyfriend—" he glanced at a grinning Jen, "—decided that Rhodes was the winner because black eye trumps split lip."

"They have a point," Savannah told him.

Disbelief filled his expression. "You're saying I lost?"

"Sorry, babe, but I think you did." Her lips curved seductively. "Don't worry, you'll still be a winner tonight. Just wait until everyone leaves and then you'll be winning all over the place."

"I'd better be," he muttered.

Another male voice boomed from behind as a man with a dark buzz cut and the body of an action hero strode inside. "Where's Jane?" he demanded. "I've been waiting downstairs for twenty min—oh you've got to be kidding me."

The newcomer stared at Matt's and Aidan's faces and swore. "For the love of Jesus, do you guys require twenty-four-hour supervision? Every time I turn around, one of you gets into a brawl!"

Jane pushed her way through the group and threw her arms around the man's neck. "Oh, relax, Beck. They were doing it for fun tonight. Now say hi to Claire. Claire, this is my husband, Thomas Becker."

Claire eyed the imposing man for a moment, wondering how someone as easygoing and boisterous as Jane had wound up with someone so intense. "It's nice to meet you," she said, extending a hand.

"Claire is Aidan's girlfriend," Jane told her husband.

"Nice to meet you." Becker shook her hand before turning to his wife. "I've been waiting downstairs for a while. I tried to call to let you know I was picking you up early, but you weren't answering your phone."

"Oh, shoot, it must have been on silent. Sorry." Jane leaned up on her tiptoes and kissed his square jaw. "How much longer do we have the sitter for?"

Becker's eyes flickered with heat. "An hour and a half."

The next thing Claire knew, the couple was practically sprinting out the door with the quickest of goodbyes, which made everyone laugh.

The other women stuck around to hug Savannah and thank her for having them over, and a few minutes later the group descended the narrow steps leading to the ground floor of Savannah's building. Outside, the night air was brisk, making Claire wish she'd brought a coat. Goose bumps rose on her bare arms, and she shivered as she followed Aidan to his SUV.

"Call me," Jen told her when they reached the curb. "We'll have lunch this week."

"Sounds good," Claire answered.

She hugged the blonde goodbye, then did the same with Miranda, Holly and Annabelle, who all piled into the Jeep waiting at the curb. Claire didn't recognize the dark-haired man behind the wheel, but from the big kiss Annabelle gave him as she slid into the passenger side, Claire deduced it was Ryan Evans, Annabelle's fiancé.

"I can't believe you and Matt got into a fist fight tonight," Claire grumbled once she and Aidan were alone in the car.

"Well, technically it was more of boxing match."

She glared in the face of his dimpled smile. "I told you you're not allowed to use those dimples to distract me."

"What about my mouth? Can I use that to distract you?"

Before she could blink, he leaned over the center console and kissed her. His tongue slipped through her parted lips, teasing and exploring and successfully making her forget all about his brawling—at least until she tasted blood in her mouth.

She broke the kiss and sighed. "Why are boys so dumb? How is kicking the shit out of each other an enjoyable pastime?"

"Sometimes it feels good to release some aggression," he said with a shrug.

"Well, I'd prefer you release it in a way where there's no possibility of you actually getting hurt."

"I didn't get hurt." He smiled. "But it's nice to know you care."

"Of course I care."

Aidan started the engine and steered away from the curb. "You think Dylan and Jackson are still wrapped up in their video game?"

"God, I hope not." Her hand covered his over the gearshift, and she seductively stroked his knuckles. "But if they are, then it's his loss, because the second we get home, you and I are locking the bedroom door and fucking each other senseless."

He gave a husky laugh. "Sounds like a plan."

"And we should be extra loud so Dylan knows exactly what he's missing."

They came to a stop at a red light, and suddenly the mood in the car shifted from lighthearted to serious as Aidan turned to her with imploring dark eyes. "Are you happy, Claire?"

She wrinkled her brow. "Of course."

"Really, truly happy?" he pressed.

"Really, truly happy," she said softly.

His gaze continued to probe her face, and then a sweet smile tugged on his lips. "So am I."

"Good." She smiled back. "Now let's go home."

Chapter Nineteen

Three months later

"DID NATASHA MAKE HER FLIGHT?"

Claire slid under the covers and nestled next to Aidan, who slung his arm around her and began stroking her hair. The only light in the bedroom came from the red numerals on the alarm clock, which showed that it was nearly one a.m.

"Yeah, I managed to get her to the airport on time," she replied. "Barely."

"I told you going to that late movie was a mistake. You cut it way too close." He grinned. "I was totally expecting to have a hot lesbian in our guest room for another night."

Claire laughed. "Nat wouldn't have minded that at all. She absolutely loved you guys. I really wish she'd gotten to spend more time with Dylan, though."

"Next time," Aidan said lightly. "She already promised she'd be back in June."

"Yeah, but June is *so* far away."

She was so bummed to see her friend go. Natasha's return flight from Sierra Leone had barely landed before she'd gotten on another plane to visit Claire. They'd spent every possible minute together this past week, and Claire had loved every second of it. She'd missed Natasha's wacky personality and outrageous sense of humor, not to mention her unconditional love and support.

And Claire hadn't lied just now—Natasha had adored Aidan and Dylan. She loved them so much, in fact, she'd even joked about "converting" to straight just so she could steal them away from Claire. Natasha's blessing had meant the world to her, especially since her parents continued to deny her their approval.

But in spite of that, Claire didn't regret her decision to stay in San Diego with Aidan and Dylan. Living with them was better than she'd ever dreamed it would be. They took turns cooking and doing chores. They never ran out of things to say. They went out to dinner, watched movies, hung out at the beach. And at least once a week, they were surrounded by friends—swimming at Cash and Matt's place, Super Bowl party at Jen's apartment, dinner at Seth and Miranda's.

She no longer thought of everyone as *Dylan's friend*, or *Aidan's buddy*. They were her friends too now, even Savannah, whose good-humored sarcasm and carpe diem attitude had eventually won Claire over—though the blonde's grudging confession that Claire was good for Aidan hadn't hurt, either.

She still couldn't believe how easily everyone had welcomed her into the fold. She was involved in a committed ménage a trois, for Pete's sake. Yet they were all taking it in stride, as if a relationship between three people was a normal, commonplace occurrence. Even Dylan's mother accepted the arrangement, which was the most surprising thing of all. When Shanna had visited last month, she hadn't batted an eye when she'd witnessed the easy affection that existed between the three of them.

Now, Claire rested her head on Aidan's bare chest and listened to the steady beating of his heart, suddenly overcome with a feeling of tranquility. The only thing missing was Dylan's hard body pressed up behind her, and his absence was a constant source of worry for her.

The SEAL team had been called to action three days ago, and although Aidan assured her the lack of contact was normal, she still hated not knowing where Dylan was or whether he was okay. She had no idea how Jen or Miranda or Savannah handled their men's abrupt departures and subsequent radio silence without falling to pieces. At least Claire had Aidan to distract her—the other wives and girlfriends didn't have a second man they adored holding their hand through such a stressful time.

She wished Dylan would come home already. She knew Aidan longed for the same thing, even though he put on that strong, stoic front of his. Truth was, it just didn't seem right when the three of them weren't together.

"Do you think he's all right?" Her soft question hung in the bedroom.

Aidan squeezed her shoulder. "I'm sure he's fine. Dylan's hardcore, baby. You tend to forget that because he's so relaxed and cheerful all the time, but trust me, our boy can take care of himself and then some."

She smiled. Our boy. She loved it when Aidan said stuff like that.

"I just hate not knowing. It's so frustrating." She sighed. "When Nat and I visited Savannah at her shop yesterday, she said the waiting and worrying isn't so bad after a while, but I can't imagine not freaking out whenever he gets called off on some dangerous mission."

"I know. It sucks," Aidan said simply. "But Savannah's right, you do get used to it. Now, the thing that's *really* going to suck? Is when he gets deployed."

That hadn't even occurred to her. "When does that happen?"

"I'm not sure which stage of the deployment cycle the team's in, but I imagine it'll happen at the end of the year sometime, and then they'll be gone for six months."

"You're right, that *will* suck," she said unhappily.

"Yeah, but you'll still have me." He slid down the mattress and rolled onto his side so they were lying face-to-face, but the second he leaned in to kiss her, the phone on the bedside table rang.

Groaning, Aidan grabbed the cordless. One glance at the caller ID, and a frown marred his lips.

"Who is it?" Claire asked.

"I don't recognize the number, but it's a Chicago area code." He sat up and answered with a brusque hello, then went quiet as he listened. "No, Veronica, of course I remember you. What's going on?"

Claire felt a flicker of distress as she studied Aidan's expression. His dark eyes had filled with concern, and it wasn't long before his face turned paler than the sheet beneath them.

"I'll be on the first flight out," he blurted into the receiver, and then he was no longer on the bed.

Claire was momentarily stunned as she watched him run around the bedroom like a madman, in search of some clothes. Then she snapped out of it and flew off the mattress. She rushed over to him, stilling his frantic movements by clutching his shoulders. "What's going on? What happened?"

"I have to go." He ducked out of her grip and snatched a pair of sweatpants from the easy chair under the window.

"Aidan. Damn it, tell me what's going on."

"My father had a heart attack."

She gasped. "Oh my gosh. Is he okay?"

"No."

The desolation in his voice tore at her insides.

"His girlfriend says they're taking him into surgery tomorrow for a triple bypass, to apparently 'alleviate the obstruction', whatever that means." He continued to dress in a hurry, his panic thickening the air. "He had a heart attack a few years back, but he told me he was doing fine. He never said a goddamn word about…" Aidan swore softly. "I have to check the flights…and call a cab…and I have to…"

He trailed off, his eyes so wild Claire snapped into action.

She marched up to him and grasped his chin this time. "Aidan. Hey. It's going to be fine."

His blank expression was a tad worrying. "What?"

"I'll handle the flight, okay?" She was already grabbing her laptop from the end table. "I'll take care of everything you need, baby."

The endearment slipped out without warning. It was the first time she'd called him that, and it seemed to shake him out of the numb trance he'd fallen into.

"Go make yourself a cup of coffee," she ordered. "You need the caffeine."

Twenty minutes later, Claire found him pacing the kitchen with a mug in his hand.

"All right, your flight leaves in two hours. We have just enough time to get you to the airport before the check-in counter closes." She held up the sheet of paper she'd printed in his office. "This is your confirmation. Come on, let's go."

Aidan blinked, startled. "You're coming with me?"

"Just to the airport." Her lips tightened in displeasure. "There was only one seat left on the plane. I could have booked us on the next flight, but it leaves five hours from now and I know you want to get there as soon as possible."

His gorgeous eyes flickered with an emotion she couldn't make out. "You would have gone all the way to Chicago with me?"

"Of course."

He placed his mug on the counter, and she noticed his hand was shaking. "Why? Why would you do that?"

With purposeful steps, she crossed the kitchen and stroked his stubble-covered jaw. "Haven't you figured it out by now? I'd do anything for you." She smiled. "I love you, silly."

Surprise, pleasure and awe flooded his face, along with a flash of uncertainty that had Claire immediately regretting saying those words. Not because she didn't mean them, but because now wasn't the time. In fact, it was the *worst* time to drop an L-bomb, when his mind was on his father, when his shoulders were rigid with fear.

Not only that, but she didn't want to put him in a position where he was forced to say it back before he was ready.

Which was why she quickly gave him a kiss on the cheek and took a step back. "Come on, time to go, baby. I didn't break nearly enough speeding laws on my first trip to the airport tonight. But the second time's the charm, right?"

It was eleven o'clock the next morning when Aidan finally walked into the hospital. He'd come straight from the airport and wasted no time in stalking up to the nurses' station and demanding to know which room his father was in.

After he got the information he wanted, he took off like a light toward the elevator bank. The nurse had told him his father was in the ICU, and as he rode the elevator, his heart was pounding so fast he feared it might actually stop. Wouldn't that be just fucking ironic. Father and son bonding over heart attacks.

He felt like a total slob in sweatpants, a ratty black hoodie and cross-trainers, but had to chide himself for giving a shit about his appearance when his father was about to go in for triple bypass surgery.

When the elevator dinged open, he hurried down the fluorescent-lit corridor toward yet another nurses' station, where he had to show his ID in order to be taken to his father's room. He hadn't thought the intensive-care unit enforced its "family only" policy so strictly, but apparently it did, and as he and the nurse passed by the waiting area, Aidan was startled to see a familiar face.

"Wait," he said abruptly. "That's my father's wife waiting in there. You have to let her in to see him."

The nurse frowned. "She said she was his girlfriend."

"Yeah, well, she's his wife," Aidan lied. He signaled to Veronica Hanson, who jumped up when she spotted him.

Veronica was a pretty woman in her fifties, with blonde hair streaked with gray and kind blue eyes that were brimming with tears. "Aidan!" she burst out.

The next thing he knew, he was enveloped in a breath-stealing embrace by a woman he'd only met once. Bringing his lips close to her ear, he murmured, "Play along" then pulled back and glanced at the nurse. "Veronica and my dad got married a few months ago. She just hasn't had the chance to go through the whole name-change process yet."

"So much paperwork," Veronica murmured.

The nurse eyed them suspiciously before shrugging in resignation. "Follow me."

She led them through a pair of restricted doors, then down another long hallway until finally coming to a stop in front of his father's room.

"He can only have one visitor at a time," she said briskly. "His cardiologist should be here shortly to discuss the surgery."

After the nurse left, Aidan turned to Veronica. "How is he? Did the doctors at least tell you anything?"

She nodded miserably. "They said he went into cardiac arrest twice in the last four hours. They're worried he might not be stable enough to undergo the surgery."

"What happens if he doesn't have the surgery?" Aidan asked grimly.

Her anguished expression said it all.

Choking on the lump in his throat, he turned to the window of his dad's room, but the blinds were drawn so he couldn't see inside.

"Go," Veronica urged. "You're his son. You should see him first."

He hesitated. Christ, he didn't want to walk into that room. Didn't want to see his father lying there, hooked up to machines. Their encounters were sad enough as it was.

But he had no choice. This was his father, for chrissake.

Taking a breath, Aidan opened the door and walked inside.

Tim Rhodes was lying on a hospital bed in the middle of the private room. His dark hair, still full and free of gray, looked greasy and unkempt. His dark eyes were closed but snapped open at Aidan's entrance.

"Aidan," his dad said gruffly.

As he approached the bed, he grabbed the nearby metal chair and dragged it closer to his dad. Sitting was a damn good idea—his legs were close to buckling from seeing his father so pale and beaten.

"Hey, Dad." He swallowed. "How're you doing?"

"Still alive, so that's something." The attempt at humor fell flat, and neither man smiled at the joke.

"They said you need surgery."

"If my heart is strong enough to allow it."

Aidan's throat was so tight he could barely force out any words, but he managed one wobbly question. "Were you having heart problems again?"

"None that I knew of. I've been taking care of myself ever since the last one five years ago. Eating right, exercising, I even quit smoking last year."

It spoke volumes that Aidan hadn't known that. Conversations in which they shared any part of their lives were few and far between, and his heart constricted painfully as he realized he hardly knew the man lying on the bed. This was his father, damn it, and he knew nothing about him.

"I'm glad you came."

The emotion lining Tim's voice came out of left field, startling Aidan into saying, "You are?"

"Of course I am. You're my son. Is it so shocking that I'd want to see my son before I died?"

Panic erupted in his chest. "Don't fucking say that. You're not going to die, Dad."

"There's a chance my heart will stop on the table. Doctors said so."

"There's also a chance it won't." Aidan battled a spark of resentment. "For once in your life, can't you be positive about something? You're always so damn pessimistic, so wrapped up in the bad things instead of focusing on the good ones."

Rather than look upset by the accusation, Tim's eyes took on a somber light. "You're right. And that's why I'm glad you came, Aidan."

"I don't follow."

"Ever since you were born, I tried so hard to shield you from those bad things you just mentioned. I carried the burden alone, and I know sometimes the frustration and heartache and sadness bled through that strong front I was putting up."

Aidan had no idea where his father was going with this, and a part of him wasn't sure he wanted to know.

"I'm sorry I wasn't always there to talk to you, and I'm sorry I never truly let you in and showed you how I was feeling, but it was too damn hard, and I knew that doing it would lead to a conversation I never wanted to have with you." Tim went quiet for a moment, the steady beeping of his heart monitor the only sound in the room. Then he cleared his throat. "But we need to have that conversation now."

"What are you talking about?"

"In the event that I don't make it through surgery, there are some things you need to know, Aidan."

CLAIRE WAS CLIMBING THE WALLS. SHE HADN'T HEARD FROM AIDAN OR Dylan in two days, and if one of them didn't walk through that door soon, she was going to *freak the fuck out*.

"Honey, I'm hoooooome."

From her perch on the couch, Claire froze, wondering if she'd imagined that familiar singsong voice. Dylan?

No, her mind had conjured it up, cruelly making her believe her prayer had been answered and Dylan had just walked in the door.

"Claire? Aid?"

Her heart nearly jumped right out of her chest when Dylan strode into the living room.

God, she *wasn't* imagining him. He was *here*.

"Oh, thank God!" She lunged off the couch and hurried toward him, throwing herself into his strong arms so hard their chests collided with a violent thump.

"Hey, now," he said with a laugh, his arms coming around her waist. "What's with the dramatic hello?"

Claire hugged him even tighter, breathing in his woodsy scent and sinking into the familiar hardness of his body. She pulled back to run her fingers over his week's worth of beard growth, and searched his playful green eyes for any sign that he'd gotten injured during his mission.

He looked completely fine, an observation that brought a rush of relief. Still, she couldn't help but demand, "Are you okay? Did you get hurt?"

Dylan grinned. "Not a scratch on me."

"Promise?"

"I promise." He glanced around. "Where's Aidan?"

The question sent Claire's spirits plummeting back to freak-out mode. "Chicago," she said bleakly. "His dad had a heart attack."

"Holy shit." A furrow of concern dug into Dylan's forehead. "Is Tim okay? Is *Aidan* okay?"

She bit her lower lip. Hard. "I have no idea. I drove him to the airport two days ago, he called when he landed in Chicago, and that was the last I heard from him. He's not picking up his phone, he's not answering my texts or my emails…" She sucked in a breath. "I'm so worried. I called the hospital to get an update on Aidan's dad but all they would tell me is he made it out of surgery and is still in the ICU."

Dylan looked upset. "Let me try him." He fished his phone out of the pocket of his dusty fatigues. A minute later, he lowered the phone and cursed. "Voicemail. I'll shoot him a text."

That yielded no results either.

"Fuck," Dylan muttered. "It isn't like him to stay out of touch, especially if you've left him messages."

Claire shook her head in aggravation. "So what do we do now? Just sit and hope that he's not lying in a ditch somewhere in Chicago?"

"I'm sure he's not lying in a ditch. If anything, he's sitting at his father's bedside, and too stressed to call back. Or maybe he doesn't even realize how much time has passed—hospitals tend to do that, one hour just morphs into the next hour, and the next thing you know, it's been two days."

His reassurance did the trick, easing some of the pressure weighing on Claire's chest. "You really think he's okay?"

"I really do." He tipped her head up and swept his thumb over her bottom lip. "And I'm sure you and I can come up with a lot of fun ways to distract ourselves while we wait for our radio-silent lover to make contact."

Her lips twitched, then parted to let out a laugh. "How do you always manage to make me laugh even when I'm at my most upset?"

"It's a gift." With a wicked grin, he stepped forward and scooped her up into his arms before she could blink. "Wanna experience some of my other gifts?"

It was just the distraction she'd needed, and she was shrieking with laughter when Dylan started tickling her side as he carried her all the way to the master bedroom. He deposited her on the bed, then began to strip out of his dirty camo gear until he was standing there naked and erect.

"Here's what's gonna happen, honey," he said with an arch of his brow. "I'm gonna hop in the shower quick fast and wash all this grime and dirt off me. You, in the meantime, will remove every stitch of clothing from that scrumptious body of yours and get yourself nice and wet. I want your pussy drenched when I come out."

A thrill shot through her. "I'm not sure you're allowed to be bossy after being gone for an entire week without even a phone call."

"I *always* get to be bossy. And I'm giving you advance warning—there ain't gonna be any foreplay. I've been thinking about your tight cunt all week and I'm gonna shove my dick inside it the second I walk out of that bathroom."

He flashed her a cheerful smile and disappeared.

Although she was still worried about the lack of contact from Aidan, Claire forced herself to put it out of her mind, at least for a little while. Without hesitation, she took off her shirt and bra, peeled off her leggings and panties, and got comfortable on the bed. Truth was, she *loved* Dylan's bossiness. Aidan's too.

Seven months ago, she'd wanted to feel the same passion and intensity she'd witnessed between the two men.

Well, now she had it. In spades.

When Dylan rejoined her five minutes later, she'd done precisely what he'd demanded—gotten herself so hot and so wet she was squirming on the bed like a dog in heat.

"Honey, you're so good at following orders you should be in the military," Dylan drawled.

He brought his hand to his erection and gave it a firm stroke, his green eyes glued to her fingers, which were idly stroking her clit and coated with her juices.

He watched her for several more seconds, then grabbed a condom from the bedside table and rolled it onto his stiff shaft. A moment later, his big glorious body covered hers, his chest colliding with her breasts.

Her nipples hardened and poked against his pecs, and she rubbed them wantonly against his hot male flesh, loving the incredible friction. His chest was completely hairless, all sleek muscle and smooth golden skin. It felt different compared to the feel of Aidan's chest pressed against her, the scrape of Aidan's wiry chest hairs on her nipples. She loved both sensations equally, though.

Same way she loved both men equally.

"I have been *dying* to be inside you since the moment I left." He entered her in one fluid motion, filling her to the hilt.

Claire moaned and lifted her hips to trap him there.

He chuckled. "Don't worry, I'm not going anywhere. Wrap your legs around my waist."

She did as he asked, digging her heels into his tight buttocks as he started to move inside her. She expected him to fuck her hard and fast, but he did the opposite, rocking into her gently, slowly. Long, deep strokes that made shivers dance along her flesh. It felt so good she thought she might pass out.

Her eyes fluttered closed as she lost herself in sweet sensation, then flew open when Dylan released a tortured groan and said, "I love you."

Her breath jammed in her lungs. "What?"

He didn't deny it, didn't backpedal, just looked deep into her eyes and repeated himself in a husky voice. "I love you, Claire."

Claire's heart promptly soared to another dimension, a world where nothing existed but pleasure and Dylan and Aidan and love. God, she was such a mushy sap. But she couldn't help it—those three words were the most wonderful thing she'd ever heard. Only three other words could rival it, the same three words actually, uttered by Aidan.

And just as easily as she'd expressed her feelings to Aidan, she didn't hesitate telling Dylan what he meant to her. "I love you too," she whispered.

The joy that lit his eyes made her smile. He was so quick to show his emotions, so ready to let the people he cared about into his heart.

No more words were spoken as Dylan dipped his head and kissed her. And then his hips were moving again, and Claire was swept away by a wave of pleasure that warmed every square inch of her body and rippled between her legs.

Dylan quickened the pace, his muscular ass flexing as he thrust into her, his chest slick with sweat and his green eyes awash with desire. He found release first, groaning, latching his mouth to hers in a blistering kiss as he came, and it was the feel of his cock pulsing inside her and the hoarse sounds of his pleasure that triggered her orgasm.

Afterwards, they lay there with their legs tangled together and foreheads resting against each other.

"So you love me, huh?" he said, sounding as sated and contented as she felt.

"Mmm-hmmm. And you love me?"

"Damn right."

Claire's lips curved, but the smile faltered after a second. "I told Aidan I loved him too the other day."

Dylan's happy expression didn't change. "I'm glad."

"He didn't say it back."

"That doesn't mean he doesn't feel the same way. Because he does."

"You sound so certain of that."

"I am certain. He loves you, same way I love you. He just needs a little time before he mans up and tells you."

Claire laughed softly. "He better not take *too* long." She hesitated. "What about you?"

"What about me?"

"How do *you* feel about him? Do you…do you love him?"

It was a long time before Dylan answered, and when he did, his voice was laced with pain. "Yes. I love him."

"Have you told him?"

"Of course not."

She frowned. "Why 'of course not'?"

"Because…well, because I haven't."

"Why not?" she pushed. "Why was it easy for you to tell me you love me, but you can't tell him how you feel about him?"

"Because when I said it to you, I knew you'd say it back. I knew you loved me back."

Her heart cracked in two. Sliding closer, she pressed her lips to his in a soft kiss, then murmured, "Of course he loves you back." She couldn't help an impish grin. "He just needs a little time before he mans up and tells you."

"Touché."

They both laughed, but their good humor faded when Claire's phone buzzed. She'd left it on the end table, and now she lunged for it, relief crashing into her when she saw Aidan's number. She picked up immediately.

"Thank God!" she said instead of a greeting. "I've been so worried about you! Why haven't you answered any of my messages?"

After a long pause, Aidan's ravaged voice filled her ear. "Claire…I need you."

Icy fear clogged her throat. "What's wrong?"

Beside her, Dylan sat up in concern.

"I need you," Aidan mumbled. "Can you come to Chicago?"

A terrible thought struck her. "Is your dad…did he…?"

"My father is fine." His tone was flat, lacking all emotion. "Will you come?"

She glanced over at Dylan with a worried look, then tightened her grip on the phone. "I'll be there as soon as humanly possible."

Chapter Twenty

It took Claire nine hours before she was finally standing in front of Aidan's hotel room door. By that point, she was so tired and impatient and worried that she rapped her knuckles on the door in an unceasing series of knocks that didn't stop until the door swung open and her hand met nothing but air.

"Hey." Aidan appeared in the doorway wearing the same sweatpants and hoodie he'd donned three nights ago when he'd left San Diego.

"Hey," she said softly.

She stepped inside and looked around, noted the room's plain furnishings and drawn curtains, then walked into Aidan's waiting embrace.

His arms held on so tight her lungs were burning by the time he released her. Wary, she watched as he headed for the queen-sized bed and flopped down as if his legs could no longer support his weight.

Sighing, Claire sat beside him and reached for his hand. "What happened? Is your dad all right?"

His skin was cold to the touch, his voice even colder. "He made it out of surgery and is resting comfortably."

"That's good to hear." She hesitated. "You said he has an apartment downtown. Why are you staying in a hotel?"

"Because if I see a single goddamn item that belongs to him, I'll be tempted to march back to the hospital and beat him senseless."

Claire's jaw fell open.

"The only reason I'm still in this city," Aidan went on, "is because his girlfriend begged me to stay until the doctors tell us he's completely out of the woods. Once I know he's not going to die, I'm outta here."

Claire ran her fingers over his knuckles. "Tell me what happened."

"He lied to me."

"What did he lie about?" she asked carefully.

His hand tensed beneath her palm. He stayed quiet.

"Aidan, what did he lie about?"

A ragged breath flew out of his mouth. "Do you remember when I told you how my mother died?"

She nodded.

"Well, turns out that was nothing but a fucking lie."

Confusion washed over her. "What do you mean?"

"I mean my dad *lied* to me. My mother didn't push me out of the way that day, she didn't save me from a reckless driver and then get run down herself." Aidan's bitterness was like a thick layer of smog hanging over the room. "She walked right into traffic. She took my hand and *led* me into the path of a speeding car."

Claire was struck speechless. It took her almost a minute to find her voice. "*What?*" she finally gasped.

"My mom didn't push me out of the way, I *jumped* out of the way, or at least that's what the witnesses on the scene told the cops. Apparently I was in shock afterwards. I blocked it all out, and the shrink told my dad not to push me into remembering, to let it come back to me gradually." Aidan angrily shook his head. "But he pulled me out of therapy because eventually he didn't *want* me to remember. He claims he wanted me to remember my mother as a hero."

Unable to believe what she was hearing, Claire squeezed his hand tighter and searched his tormented eyes. "I don't understand. Why would your mother do that?"

"Because she was schizophrenic." He sounded devastated. "Before she was declared unfit to stand trial, she told the doctors that the voices told her to kill herself and her son. So she listened to the voices."

"Oh my God." Horror spiraled through her, then transformed into another rush of confusion as she realized what he'd said. "Wait, so she wasn't killed by that car?"

"Nope, that's just what my dad told me. She was committed to an institution for the criminally insane, about an hour north of here. She was a patient there for fifteen years before she hung herself by turning her bed sheet into a noose."

Claire's eyes widened.

"Fifteen years," he spat out. "She was alive that entire time and he let me believe she was dead. I spent my whole fucking life feeling guilty that my mother had died saving me, feeling sorry for my dad because he was so fucking sad all the time, and she wasn't even dead! Jesus!"

Claire had no idea what to say. Absolutely no idea. Every word that came out of Aidan's mouth added to that initial shock, until all she could do was let him talk and hope her presence was enough.

"Fifteen years." His breathing grew shallow. "She was alive for fifteen more years after the accident. She was alive when I entered middle school, when I was a freshman in high school, when I went to prom, when I graduated, when I attended college. Fifteen years that I could have visited her, or sent her cards and flowers or…" Another harsh breath. "All that lost time…"

Tears pricked Claire's eyes when she saw the moisture in Aidan's. Without a word, she tugged his hand and pulled him into her arms.

He stiffened for a moment, and then his body went limp and he sagged against her. His dark hair tickled her chin, his hot tears soaking the front of her sweater.

"I'm sorry," she murmured. "I'm so sorry."

She didn't know how long they sat there, how long she held him, how long he cried, and when he lifted his head and urgently sought out her lips, she didn't deny him the kiss he craved. She kissed him back with the same desperation she saw in his dark eyes, their tongues meeting and tangling, their hands entering the fray by grabbing at each other's clothes.

Yanking on the waistband of her yoga pants, Aidan pushed her onto her back and crushed her with his strong body. His hands fumbled to shove his own pants down, his erection sprang free, and then he pushed it inside her without warning. But she was ready for him, slick with desire that had erupted out of nowhere and overcome with the need to soothe him, to please him, to bring him any comfort she could, even if it was of the carnal variety.

Aidan's cock plunged into her again and again. His mouth hungrily devoured hers. The intensity of his passion scared her, thrilled her, liberated her. She met him thrust for thrust, her inner muscles squeezing his thick shaft as shockwaves of pleasure rocked her body.

The spasms of her pussy set Aidan off. He came with a loud cry, moaning her name as his cock twitched inside her. She could feel his heart hammering against her breasts, a fast, reckless rhythm that matched her own erratic pulse.

Letting out a deep breath, Aidan cupped her cheeks with his palms and stared at her with heavy-lidded eyes. "I should have said this three days ago, but…I love you too."

Her chest squeezed with emotion. "I know."

He kissed her tenderly, then slid his cock out of her still-throbbing pussy and rolled over.

And it was at that moment they both realized he hadn't worn a condom.

"Shit," he mumbled. "Are you…fuck, are you on the pill?"

She shook her head in regret. They'd been using condoms this whole time, and she hadn't gotten around yet to finding a doctor in San Diego and getting a birth control prescription.

When Aidan swore again, she gently touched his cheek. "It's not the right time in my cycle, so I think we're okay. But if I…if I get pregnant… gosh, what would we do?"

Suddenly she was the one in need of reassurance, and Aidan didn't hesitate to give it to her. "We'd do whatever you wanted to do. Just know that if you chose to keep it, I think the three of us would make pretty kickass parents."

She bit the inside of her cheek. "I still don't know how any of this is going to work."

"Same way it's been working so far. We live together, we love each other."

"And you want to have kids with me? With me and Dylan?"

"Yes," he said simply.

"What about marriage?"

"If you really want that wedding you didn't get to have with Chris, then one of us will give it to you. No matter whose name is on the marriage license, you'll always belong to us both, baby. And we'll belong to you."

She watched him unhappily. "You don't just belong to me, though. You belong to each other."

Aidan looked startled. "I know that."

"Do you? You know Dylan loves you, right? He loves you, but he's too scared to tell you because he thinks you don't feel the same way, or that you won't say it back."

Distress flickered in his dark eyes. "He really thinks that?"

She nodded.

"I…" His Adam's apple bobbed. "I love him, Claire."

"I know you do." She slid closer and placed her hand directly over his heart, which was beating even faster than before. "But I'm not the person you need to be saying it to."

DYLAN HAD NEVER FELT MORE RELIEVED IN HIS LIFE THAN WHEN CLAIRE and Aidan returned to San Diego four days later. *Four* fucking days. Sure, he'd spoken to both of them on the phone several times, had listened in wide-eyed horror as Claire told him about the secret Aidan's dad had kept from his son all these years, but he hadn't felt an ounce of comfort until now. Until he saw the two people he loved most in the world walk through that door.

He soaked in the sight of them—Claire, with her shiny auburn hair and big eyes. Aidan, with those intense dark eyes and powerful body.

"Welcome back," Dylan said quietly.

Claire came to him first, hugging him tightly before standing on her tiptoes and kissing him senseless.

He'd barely had time to breathe when Aidan stepped in and greeted him with a kiss that packed an equal amount of heat and passion.

Dylan raised his eyebrows when they broke apart. "What was that for?"

Aidan shrugged. "Just missed you, is all."

Pleasure floated through him. "I missed you, too, man."

"Ditto," Claire spoke up. She grinned. "With that said, you're going to have to miss me again, because I have some groceries to pick up."

"Now?" Dylan said. "You literally *just* walked in."

"And when I left four days ago, the fridge was completely empty." She raised her eyebrows. "Did you replenish our supplies during that time?"

He gave her a guilty look. "Um…"

"That's what I thought. Ergo, I'm going grocery shopping. Someone has to make sure my big, manly men are well fed." She glanced at Aidan and held out her hand. "Keys?"

With an indulgent smile, he dropped the car keys into her waiting palm. "Don't take too long."

Dylan observed that the other man was strangely upbeat for someone who'd just discovered his mother had tried to kill him, but he bit his tongue to stop from asking why. If Aidan had managed to find some peace about the whole fucked-up situation, who was he to dredge it all up again?

However, Aidan ended up surprising him—the moment Claire left the condo, the other man fixed him with a sad look and said, "So my mom was alive for half my life and I never knew it."

"I know. I'm so sorry, man."

They drifted over to the couch, where Aidan spent the next fifteen minutes telling him everything that had gone down with his father, including their final visit, during which Tim had asked for his son's forgiveness.

"What did you say?" Dylan asked.

"I told him I needed some time." Aidan sighed. "Claire keeps reminding me that time is something we might not have—I mean, he made it through the surgery and he's definitely on the road to recovery, but who knows what the future holds. He could have another heart attack tomorrow, or next week, or next month. She thinks I should forgive him now, while I still have the chance."

"And what do you think?"

"I think she's right, of course. That woman is always fucking right," Aidan grumbled. "I tried to point out that she isn't even speaking to her own parents, and you know what she said? That it's not for lack of trying. Do you realize she calls them every day? They fucking disowned her for the sole crime of falling in love with the two of us, and she still calls them every fucking *day*. They don't pick up, but she insists that one of these days they'll come around and—why the hell are you looking at me like that?"

Dylan shook his head in amazement. "Do you realize you've spoken more in the last ten minutes than in all the time I've known you?"

Aidan bristled. "That's not true. I talk to you all the time."

"Not about important stuff."

Dragging a hand through his hair, Aidan offered a remorseful look.

"Fuck. You're right. I don't. But I'm gonna try to change that. I don't think I'll ever be as open about everything as you are, but I promise you, I'll try not to keep you guessing all the time about how I'm feeling. Starting now." He took a breath. "I love you, Dylan. I really, really love you. Like a lot."

Dylan couldn't even describe the hot rush of emotion that ballooned in his chest. "You do?"

Aidan nodded.

Swallowing the thick lump in his throat, he edged closer and touched Aidan's jaw. The man hadn't shaved in days, which was totally unlike him. But he looked so unbelievably sexy with all that stubble shadowing his face.

Running his fingertips over the bristly hairs, he brushed his lips over Aidan's and said, "I love you too."

Pleasure flared in those dark eyes he loved so fucking much, followed by a flash of heat that came out of nowhere and led to a wild, openmouthed kiss that Dylan didn't see coming.

That one kiss was enough to set the room on fire. Aidan's tongue filled his mouth and robbed him of breath, and then warm male hands were sliding underneath his T-shirt and running over the bare skin of his chest.

Aidan abruptly pulled back. "Bedroom. Now."

He didn't need to ask twice. In a nanosecond, Dylan was on his feet and racing toward the master bedroom.

They rid each other of their clothes and stumbled naked onto the bed, mouths seeking mouths, chests rubbing together, cocks straining as their lower bodies ground against each other. Every inch of Dylan's flesh was scorching as Aidan's lips traveled along the curve of his jaw, as Aidan's hands roamed his body. When a rough-skinned hand cupped his balls, he groaned with abandon, shuddered with anticipation.

Aidan fondled his tight sac, then gripped his erection and gave it a slow pump. His mouth found Dylan's neck, lips latching on and sucking until Dylan was moaning so loudly he was worried the neighbors would hear him.

"Love you," Aidan rasped. "Love you so fucking much."

Dylan grabbed the other man by the hair and yanked his head up, bringing him in for another kiss as he thrust his cock into that strong male fist.

When that fist suddenly disappeared, Dylan growled in displeasure, but Aidan just chuckled and said, "Not going far. Coming right back."

And he kept that promise, climbing back onto the bed a moment later with a condom covering his erection and a tube of KY in his hand.

"I wanna be inside you." Aidan's eyes burned with desire. "I wanna look into your eyes as I fuck your ass and I wanna see how much you love it. How much you love me."

Excitement gathered in his groin as Aidan lubed up two fingers and teased Dylan's asshole with just his fingertips.

"No prep. Don't wanna wait," he choked out. "I need you, Aid."

Aidan made him wait, but only for a second, only so he could slather the warm lube on the condom, and then he lowered his body so they were chest to chest, groin to groin, thigh to thigh. He propped his forearms on either side of Dylan's head and positioned his cock.

When the blunt head pushed through the tight ring of muscle, Dylan's entire body trembled from the sheer pleasure of that stretching sensation. The burn, the heat, the feeling of completion.

"More," he mumbled.

Aidan slid in another inch, then another, and another, until the entire length of him filled Dylan's ass. They both moaned.

"So good," Aidan said hoarsely. "Always feels so fucking good." He began pumping his hips. Nice and slow. Thorough and sweet.

Dylan gazed into the other man's eyes, floored by what he saw. Gulping, he moved his hand between their bodies and wrapped it around his swollen cock. He was going to explode any minute now. Any *second* now if Aidan kept looking at him with those smoldering liquid-brown eyes, with that unmistakable glimmer of love.

"Not gonna last long at all," Aidan murmured ruefully.

"Me neither," he murmured back.

Their gazes stayed lock as Aidan drove his cock in and out of Dylan's tight passage, each stroke hitting a spot deep inside, eliciting a flash of pleasure that soon gathered in intensity and turned into a raging fire that threatened to burn him alive.

"So…good," Aidan muttered.

"Give it to me…faster," Dylan grunted.

Soon their husky words became broken, nonsensical, just guttural commands and pleasure-laced groans and finally, nothing but strangled curses that heated the air between them.

"Fuck. Oh, fuck." Aidan drove into him so hard the headboard smacked the wall.

Dylan jerked off faster, his fist flying over his cock. "Coming... *Fuck*."

He exploded in a boiling rush, hot come splashing his abdomen. His entire body trembled, moans of ecstasy escaping his lips only to be swallowed by Aidan's kiss. Aidan's tongue slid into his mouth at the same time the cock in his ass began to pulse.

"Fucking *love* you," Aidan moaned. Naked pleasure washed over his face, and he was trembling just as hard as he came.

They were still lying there, Aidan's cock lodged deep inside him, when the landline rang, three long rings that indicated a call from the front lobby.

"Claire must have forgotten her key," Dylan said with a sigh.

With a reluctant groan, Aidan pulled out and handled the task of removing his condom, while Dylan reached for the phone and answered with a quick hello.

Sergio, the guard who manned the desk, spoke in a brusque voice. "I have a Ron McKinley asking to be buzzed up. He says he's here to see Claire."

Dylan almost dropped the phone.

Claire's father was here?

Claire's *father* was *here*?

"Oh," he blurted into the receiver. "Uh...one sec, Serge." Covering the mouthpiece, he directed a panicked look at Aidan. "Claire's father is downstairs," he hissed.

Aidan's face paled. "Shit. *Shit*."

"I know, right?" Dylan quickly brought the phone back to his ear. "Um, let him up."

The second he hung up, both men flew off the bed in a manic search for their clothes. Son of a bitch. What the hell was Claire's father doing here?

Aidan vocalized Dylan's thoughts. "What the hell is he doing here?"

"I have no clue, man. No clue."

"Maybe he's here to kill us," Aidan suggested.

Dylan froze. "Do you think I should get my gun?"

"No. That's the *last* thing you should do! Christ!"

They got dressed in a hurry, then eyed each other up and down to confirm they didn't look like two men who'd just fucked each other's brains out.

When they heard the muffled sound of someone knocking on the front door, they exchanged identical looks of terror.

"Here goes," Aidan mumbled.

"This is *not* going to be good," Dylan mumbled back.

They walked to the front hall together. Might as well show some solidarity, Dylan thought. And they did make an imposing picture standing side by side like that. Maybe that would make Claire's father think twice before murdering them.

Taking a breath, Dylan opened the door.

The man on the other side of it scowled at them. "I'm Ron McKinley," he muttered. "Where's my daughter?"

"She went out for groceries," Dylan said politely. "And we met in December, sir." He gulped. "At the wedding. I'm Chris's brother, Dylan."

He stuck out his hand.

Ron McKinley did not shake it.

Masking his disappointment, Dylan gestured for the older man to enter.

Ron's expression conveyed great distrust as he examined his surroundings. He had his daughter's brown eyes, along with that same shrewd glint Claire got whenever she was assessing a situation before passing judgment. His hair was a different color, dark blond rather than red, and though he wasn't as tall as Dylan's six-foot-two frame, he was an inch taller than Aidan's five-eleven.

"I'm Aidan Rhodes. Pleasure to meet you, sir." Aidan didn't bother offering his hand, because they all knew damn well Ron McKinley wouldn't shake that one, either.

"Have a seat," Dylan said when they entered the living room. "Would you like something to drink?"

Ron regarded the leather couches as if they might be covered with ants, then sat down and stiffly crossed his arms over his chest. He wasn't overweight, but he was definitely bulky, boasting one of those barrel chests that radiated power.

"Drink?" he prompted when the older man didn't answer.

"No, thank you."

Dylan and Aidan exchanged a *what now?* look, then settled on opposite ends of the couch Claire's dad *wasn't* sitting on. Because no way was Dylan getting close to the man. He valued his own life way too much to do something so foolish.

"How long is my daughter going to be?" Ron asked curtly.

"She should be back any minute. In fact—" Aidan hastily grabbed his cell from the coffee table, "—why don't I just give her a call and see what her ETA is."

A few seconds later, Aidan spoke in an overly bright voice that made Dylan choke down a laugh.

"Hey, sweetheart, just wondering how much longer you'll be… Oh, you're pulling into the underground? Super."

Dylan's lips twitched uncontrollably. *Super?* Aidan was rattled, all right.

"No, no, everything's fine. We do have a visitor, though…no, not them… Your father's here." Aidan listened for a beat, then hung up and addressed Claire's dad. "She'll be right up."

Chapter Twenty-One

CLAIRE FLEW INTO THE LIVING ROOM, THEN SKIDDED TO A STOP LIKE a cartoon character. She'd desperately hoped the boys were messing with her, only pretending that her father was here, but nope, not messing around. There he was, her father, sitting on the couch with an expression of extreme misery on his face.

"Dad? What are you doing here?"

Her father's gaze shifted toward the men, then back at her. "Can we speak in private?"

Dylan and Aidan were already shooting to their feet.

"No problem," Aidan said hastily.

"Take your time," Dylan chimed in.

And then they were gone.

Claire would've laughed at their eagerness to flee if she weren't so confused by her father's presence. Rather than join him on the couch, she kept a cautious distance by settling in the armchair. "What's going on?" she asked softly.

"Your mother kicked me out."

Her eyes widened. "Are you serious?"

His unhappiness deepened. "She threw me out of my own house—can you believe that?"

"Why would she do that? Did you two get into a fight?"

"All we've been doing for the last three months is fighting," he said darkly.

Claire's heart stopped. "Because of me?"

His silence answered the question, and she experienced a rush of guilt that made her chest hurt. God, her parents were splitting up. Because of *her*. Because of the choice she'd made, the choice that had apparently torn them apart.

"I had nowhere else to go," her father mumbled. "You know I can't sleep in hotels, and your mother and I don't have many friends, especially any that would take me in. So I got in my car, and…somehow I wound up here." He looked defensive now. "You emailed me the address after you moved in. I figured that meant it was okay for me…for me to come."

"Of course it's okay."

With a sigh, she moved to sit beside him. After a second of hesitation, she gave him a hug.

To her surprise, he hugged her back.

"I'm so sorry, Daddy. I didn't mean to come between you and Mom. I'm surprised she even did this. I mean, she's ignored all of my calls and texts and emails. I thought she was on your side when it came to…well, this whole thing."

"She was, at first." Her father's face grew sad. "But she missed you. And she became resentful, angry at me for pushing you away, and then this morning she just had enough. She told me that unless I fix things with you, she was going to divorce me."

Claire gawked at him. That didn't sound *at all* like her mother. Nora McKinley always took her husband's side in every argument. Always put her husband first. Always let him take the lead.

That she would give Claire's dad an ultimatum like this came as a complete and total shock.

"She's not going to divorce you," Claire said firmly. "She's just upset and not thinking clearly at the moment."

Hope filled his eyes. "Do you really believe that, Claire-Bear?"

Her heart squeezed at the familiar endearment. "I really believe it. And if you want my advice, I'd give her a few days to calm down. I'm sure you two will be able to work it out. You love each other and you've been together for more than thirty years, for Pete's sake. Your marriage is strong, Daddy. So strong it can withstand anything, even your daughter's unconventional love life."

Her father hesitated. "Can I stay with you until I…until your mother and I… Can I stay here?"

She met his gaze head on. "I don't live alone, Dad. This is Dylan and Aidan's home too."

He shifted in discomfort. "I know."

"I won't ask either of them to leave while you're here."

"I know," he said again.

She raised her eyebrows. "And you're okay with that?"

Her father let out a tired breath. "I guess I'm going to have to be."

Day One

Aidan strode into the kitchen on Saturday morning, then halted in his tracks when he spotted Claire's father at the counter, drinking coffee and reading the morning paper.

Damn it. He'd been hoping yesterday's surprise visit had been a bad dream, that really, Ron McKinley was back in San Francisco, passing judgment on his daughter's relationships from afar.

But it wasn't a dream.

Claire's father was here.

Claire's father was their houseguest.

Fucking hell.

"Good morning," Aidan said politely, grabbing a mug from the cupboard.

"Good morning," Ron answered in a tone that more than conveyed his disapproval.

"Did you sleep well?"

He damn well better have, considering his presence had completely disrupted their sleeping arrangements. Although Claire refused to apologize for loving two men, she was still that same girl who'd hidden her wild streak growing up, and she claimed she didn't feel right sleeping in the same bed as them when her father was in the condo. So as long as Ron was here, Claire had decreed that Aidan stay in the master bedroom, her father would get Dylan's room, she'd sleep on the pullout couch in the office, and Dylan was relegated to the living room.

It fucking *sucked*. Even more so because Claire had also decided that having sex while under the same roof as her father was, as she put it, *icky*.

And having a threesome was apparently even ickier.

Aidan was praying Claire's mom took some pity on Mr. McKinley and let him come home soon, because he wasn't sure how long he could last living under these restrictive conditions. But for Claire's sake, he was willing to suck it up. At least long enough for her to repair her relationship with her dad.

"I slept very well, thank you," Ron said stiffly.

"Glad to hear it," Aidan replied.

An awkward silence fell between them.

Ron cleared his throat. "Where's the other one?"

Aidan didn't need to ask for clarification. "He works out on the beach every morning."

"Huh."

"He's a SEAL," Aidan felt obligated to add. "He needs to stay in shape for his line of work. You know, saving the world and all."

He could have sworn he glimpsed a flicker of approval in Ron's eyes, but then the man buried his nose in his newspaper and proceeded to pretend Aidan wasn't in the room.

With a sigh, he poured himself a cup of coffee and left the kitchen.

Day Two

"Holy shitballs! Did you see that touchdown pass?" Dylan let out a loud whistle.

"That was a thing of beauty," Aidan agreed.

Neither of them asked the man on the other couch what he'd thought of the pass; Ron McKinley had been ignoring them for the past hour and a half, his face hidden by the Sunday paper. The only indication he was even in the room was the sound of newsprint crinkling every time he flipped the page.

Dylan had never felt so uncomfortable in his life, and he resented the fact that Claire's father was making him feel this way in his own home. This was the place where Dylan was supposed to kick back and relax, but these last two days he'd wanted to be anywhere but here.

For Claire's sake, he was playing nice with her dad, but damn, winning that man over was next to impossible. Dylan doubted there was anything he and Aidan could do to change Ron McKinley's opinion about the two men his daughter had committed herself to.

Claire, who was curled up in the armchair with an afghan drawn over her legs, rolled her eyes. "I still don't get why we're watching old games that you recorded."

"Because it's Sunday," Dylan retorted. "And we watch football on Sundays."

"But the season's over."

"There's no such thing as an off-season when it comes to football," he said gravely. "Jeez, honey, and you call yourself a fan."

A loud snort of amusement cut through the air.

Everyone swiveled their heads in Ron's direction, but he was innocently reading his newspaper again.

Day Three

"So you're really going to do this? Start your own business?"

Claire met her father's serious eyes. "I'm really going to do it."

The two of them were sitting out on the terrace, the remnants of their dinner littering the large glass table. Aidan had dropped off some takeout for them because he and Dylan were having dinner at Cash and Matt's place tonight, and the thoughtful gesture had warmed Claire's heart. Before he'd left, Aidan had dropped a quick kiss on her lips and told her he hadn't wanted her to spend the evening slaving over a stove when she could be spending time with her father.

She knew her dad had overheard that, and she could have sworn she'd seen him nod in approval before his expression grew shuttered.

"Do you have a business plan yet?"

Her father's brisk inquiry interrupted her thoughts. "That's what I've been working on for the last couple of months," she told him. "But I think I'm finally ready to make this happen."

"Why don't the two of us go over the business plan tonight?" Her dad's voice turned gruff. "That is, if you don't have plans with…uh, your men."

She hid her surprise. This was the first time he'd even acknowledged there were two men living here, let alone *her* men.

And this time, when he'd uttered those two words, he'd done it without any scorn.

Day Four

If he didn't have sex with either Claire or Aidan soon, Dylan was going to fucking explode.

Day Five

"I'm serious, Mom, he's been so great this week," Claire said, balancing her phone on her shoulder as she tried to grab a bowl from the top cupboard. "I really think it's time for the two of you to talk this out."

Aidan came up behind her and intercepted her straining hand. He planted a quick kiss on her knuckles before reaching up and getting her a bowl.

With a look of gratitude, she headed to the counter and poured herself some cereal, feeling her father's anxious eyes on her as she continued to talk him up to her mom.

And the bitch of it was? She wasn't even lying. Her father *had* been great this week. She couldn't say he'd *completely* warmed up to the men she loved, but at least he wasn't looking at them like he wanted to skin them alive anymore.

Definitely progress.

Day Six

"I'm dying here, man." Aidan lit up a cigarette, took a deep drag, and exhaled a cloud of smoke into the night air.

Dylan shook his head in disapproval. "What are you doing? You only smoke when you drink."

"Or when I'm so fucking horny I feel like my balls are going to fall off. I jerked off in the shower *three* times this morning. Three!" Aidan said in disgust.

"Me too."

They exchanged a look and grinned.

But both grins faded fast.

"We need to get him out of here," Dylan said grimly. Then he paused. "Though that's not to say I dislike him. If I'm being honest, I kinda like the old grump."

Aidan's reply was grudging. "Me too."

"He's a damn good poker player." His gaze drifted past the terrace door to the dining room, where Claire's father was shuffling a deck of cards like a professional card sharp. Dylan hadn't been kidding, though—Claire's dad really *was* growing on him.

"That's because he's an accountant. I bet he counts the cards."

"You think?"

"You boys buying back in or what?" Ron McKinley's smug voice wafted through the open sliding door and onto the terrace.

Dylan sighed. "Let's go lose some more money."

"Gee, can't wait."

Day Seven

"It was nice of Dylan and Aidan to treat us to dinner tonight."

Claire knew it took a lot out of her father to say that, and a lot more for him to actually say their names instead of "your men".

She had to admit, "her men" might have actually done it. Officially won Ron McKinley over.

Then again, when you made reservations at the best steakhouse in the city for a man who loved steaks more than life itself, you had a solid chance for success.

She picked up her menu and scanned the unending amount of meat options. "What do you think I should order, the eight-ounce peppercorn or the—"

"You really love them, don't you?"

Her head swung up. "What?"

Ron reached for his beer, took a big gulp, then set the glass down on the rustic wood tabletop. The entire restaurant had a cookhouse-type feel to it, masculine to the core, with animal heads mounted to the wall and country music coming out of the speakers.

"You love them," he repeated. "Dylan. And Aidan."

"Yes. I do."

Her father shifted in discomfort. "Those boys adore you."

She smiled. "I know."

He harrumphed. "Still don't get how it's ever going to work, Claire-Bear."

"We'll make it work," she said simply.

"It's not that easy."

"Yes, it is. I know it doesn't make sense to you, but it works, Dad. It really does. And I hope that in time you'll be able to accept it, and them."

Ron paused for a moment, a thoughtful look in his eyes. "Well, they do know their football. It might be nice to get their advice next season about my fantasy lineup."

Claire burst out laughing. "Oh, Dad, I love you."

"I love you too, sweetheart." He sounded choked up as he said the words.

Their heart-to-heart was interrupted by the arrival of their waiter, a burly man with a buzz cut and a goatee. "Excuse me, but the rest of your party has arrived."

Claire glanced over her shoulder in confusion. Her jaw dropped when she spotted Dylan and Aidan advancing on their table.

With her mother sandwiched between them.

Her father looked equally stunned. "Nora?" he exclaimed. "What are you doing here?"

Claire's mother tucked a strand of auburn hair behind her ear, looking hesitant. "Claire's…um, Claire's friends arranged for me to fly in." Nora suddenly smiled. "I flew in a Coast Guard helicopter. It was very exciting."

Claire noticed that Aidan and Dylan were fighting grins. She also noticed that her father looked extremely nervous as he rose from his chair and walked around the table toward her mom.

"You're here," he said gruffly. "What does that mean?"

Nora shrugged. "Well, right now it means we're all going to sit down and have a nice dinner."

"And afterwards?" Ron pressed.

"Afterwards, we go home."

Claire had never seen such an enormous smile overtake her father's face.

From a discreet distance, the waiter cleared his throat, then glanced at Claire's dad. "Will your friends be staying?" he asked expectantly.

"They're not our friends," Ron said curtly.

Claire froze.

But her dad wasn't finished. "This is my wife," he informed the waiter. "And these are my daughter's boyfriends."

"I can't believe you guys did that," Claire declared as the three of them walked into the apartment later that night.

Her parents had already left to make the long drive north, but not before Claire's mom had hugged not only Claire goodbye, but Dylan and Aidan too. And her father had actually shaken their hands. She was still in disbelief over it.

"We figured your dad needed a little push," Dylan said with a grin. "He was taking his sweet-ass time winning your mom back."

She dropped her purse on the couch, then took Dylan's face between her hands and kissed him deeply. A second later, she gave Aidan the same loving reward.

"I love you guys so much," she murmured.

She hadn't thought it was possible to love one man this much, let alone two, and yet her heart was so full it was about to overflow.

"We love you too," Aidan told her.

"So damn much," Dylan added. His green eyes gleamed with sinful promise. "With that said, you have a ten-second head start before we chase you down, strip you naked, and have our way with you."

"Try to make it to the bed in time," Aidan advised. "Because we're going to be fucking you wherever we catch you. Against the wall, on the floor, the kitchen counter…choose wisely, baby."

She coyly fluttered her eyelashes. "But what if I'm not in the mood?"

Their faces took on pained expressions.

"Are you seriously not in the mood?" Dylan demanded.

She shrugged.

They both went quiet for a moment, and then Aidan flashed that dimpled grin she loved oh-so much.

"Then I guess we'll just have to fuck each other until you come to your senses."

Claire threw her head back and laughed. "Well, at least you're honest. But luckily for you, I'm *more* than in the mood. In fact, I'm so in the mood I'm going to come the instant you put your hands on me." She slanted her head. "I have exactly ten seconds before you have your way with me, huh?"

"Yup. Starting now." Dylan narrowed his eyes. "One."

"Two," Aidan warned.

Claire took off running.

Epilogue

Six months later

"What the fuck is he doing in there? Buying the whole damn store?" Dylan grumbled.

Claire shared his impatience. Aidan really *had* been in that flower shop for a while. At least twenty minutes had passed since he'd ducked inside after insisting they stop and buy flowers for Claire's mother.

The three of them had flown into the Bay Area earlier that morning to spend the day with Dylan's mom. It was Shanna's birthday, so they'd taken her to one of the fanciest restaurants in the city for brunch, a two-hour affair that gave new meaning to the word *awkward* because not only had Chris been present, but he'd brought his latest girlfriend along. Stephanie Lowenstein was a thing of the past, having dumped Chris a few weeks after they'd returned from *Claire's* honeymoon—which Ron McKinley had sent Chris the bill for, much to Claire's amusement.

"Oh, and I totally forgot to ask you," Dylan suddenly said. "What did Tanya say when you two went to the bathroom together? You came back to the table looking like you'd won the lottery."

Claire had to grin. "She didn't say anything important. I just remembered something I'd heard about her from one of the country-club wives. Apparently Chris's new love has made the rounds at the club, sleeping her way through all the men she thinks will elevate her social status." A laugh slipped out. "I can't imagine her sticking with Chris for much longer, not once she realizes it'll be years and years before he makes partner."

"So you're saying my brother's in for an imminent dumping?"

"Very imminent, considering the way she was checking out every other man in the restaurant." Claire arched a brow. "Should we warn him?"

Dylan shrugged. "Warn who?"

His lack of sympathy didn't surprise her, but she still wished Dylan would be more open to mending this rift with his older brother. Despite the fact that he'd brought his bimbo to brunch today, Chris had actually made an effort to speak not only with Dylan, but Claire and Aidan, whom he'd completely ignored when they'd visited over the summer.

Claire knew he still didn't approve of their relationship, but frankly, she didn't care what Chris thought. She loved Dylan and Aidan, and had every intention of spending the rest of her life with them. Although no pregnancy had resulted from her night in Chicago with Aidan, and she was now on the pill, she definitely saw children in their future, and she wanted her kids to be surrounded by family.

Whether she liked it or not, Chris was still Dylan's family, and so she was making an effort for Dylan's sake, and would keep doing it until his relationship with his brother returned to a place both he and Chris were comfortable with.

Aidan was in the same boat with his dad; although he'd forgiven Tim for keeping the truth about his mother from him, their relationship was still strained, but Claire was hoping that would change when Tim and Veronica visited them in San Diego next month.

"Claire?"

She froze at the familiar voice. Frowning, Claire turned around and found herself staring at Barbara Valentine, her former boss.

As usual, Barb wore one of her tailored suits paired with expensive high heels, and her expression flickered with wariness as she glanced from Claire to Dylan and then back at Claire.

"Barb," she said coolly. "It's nice to see you."

Not.

"Good to see you too, darling." The older woman paused for a beat. "I heard you're back in the consulting game."

"Yeah, I'm starting up my own firm. It's still getting off the ground, but I've already secured a few clients."

"I'm glad to hear it." Barb's eyes shifted to Dylan, visible appreciation on her face. "Are you going to introduce me to your friend?"

"Boyfriend," Claire corrected. "This is my boyfriend, Dylan."

"It's a pleasure to meet you."

Barb practically purred out the words, and Claire couldn't blame the woman for her blatant ogling. Dylan looked sexy as hell today in cargo pants and a snug green polo shirt that matched his eyes. With his blond hair slightly rumpled and his chiseled good looks, he made a seriously appealing picture.

So did Aidan, who chose that exact moment to stroll out of the shop with a bouquet of daisies in his hand. His eyes narrowed slightly when he spotted the willowy older woman in their midst. "What's going on?" he asked Claire.

"Nothing, just catching up with my old boss," she told him, fighting a smile.

"Hello," Barb greeted him, her focus now on Aidan's dark good looks and muscular body. "And you are?"

"Oh, sorry, I didn't introduce you." Claire shot the woman a saccharine smile. "This is my boyfriend, Aidan."

Barb looked startled. Her gaze moved from Dylan to Aidan to Claire. "Oh. I see."

Her smile widened. "Anyway, it was really good to see you, Barb, but I'm afraid we have to go. My parents are expecting us for dinner."

She fluttered her fingers in a careless little wave. As she and the boys shuffled past Barb, Claire glanced over her shoulder, choked down a laugh at the envious expression on Barb's face, and gave her former boss a wink.

Then she laced her fingers through Dylan's, slid her other hand into Aidan's waiting palm, and the three of them walked away.

About the Author

A *New York Times*, *USA Today* and *Wall Street Journal* bestselling author, Elle Kennedy grew up in the suburbs of Toronto, Ontario, and holds a BA in English from York University. From an early age, she knew she wanted to be a writer and actively began pursuing that dream when she was a teenager. She loves strong heroines and sexy alpha heroes, and just enough heat and danger to keep things interesting!

Elle loves to hear from her readers. Visit her website www.ellekennedy. com, and while you're there sign up for her newsletter to receive updates about upcoming books and exclusive excerpts. You can also find her on Facebook (ElleKennedyAuthor), Twitter (@ElleKennedy), or Instagram (@ElleKennedy33).

Coming soon! Are you ready for Jackson Ramsey? Enjoy this excerpt from the next book in the Out of Uniform series, As Hot As It Gets*...*

MIA WELDRICK COULD THINK OF A HUNDRED BETTER WAYS TO SPEND a Saturday morning. Sleeping in. Eating breakfast at the diner across the street from her apartment. Jogging. Reading one of the gazillion unread books gathering dust on her shelf.

But she wasn't doing any of those things. Nope, because she was too busy trying to find the cell phone she'd accidentally buried in Tom and Sarah Smith's tulip bed yesterday.

"Oh, for the love of Hey-zeus," she grumbled to herself. "Where are you, motherfucker?"

She desperately hoped her little brother Danny hadn't gone back to sleep after she'd roused him and ordered him to start calling her phone in precisely twenty minutes. She was going to flip the fuck out if she lost all her contacts. Unlike smarter and more practical people, she didn't have a backup list of passwords and phone numbers—everything was in her phone, which meant she couldn't afford to lose it.

Stifling a sigh, Mia scooted over a few inches and lowered her head to the yellow tulips. A sweet scent filled her nose, but no sound reached her ears.

Well, except for the loud throat clearing that suddenly echoed from behind her.

She swiveled her head and instantly spotted the source of the noise. He was obviously Tom and Sarah's neighbor, judging by the rolled-up newspaper in his hand and the serious case of bedhead he was sporting.

"Everything okay, sugar?" he called out.

Oh boy. He had a Southern drawl. That upped his hotness factor by a million, though even without the accent the guy was a perfect ten. Messy light-brown hair, whiskey-colored eyes, a chiseled jawline. And his body wasn't a pain to look at either—it was muscular but lean, long legs encased in faded blue denim and defined biceps poking out of a wrinkled white wifebeater.

"Not really," she called back. "Hey, you mind if I borrow your ears, *sugar?*"

He raised his eyebrows. "Beg your pardon?"

"Come over here and help me listen."

His dumbfounded look made her want to laugh. She knew she sounded like a total wacko, but she really could use his help. She had just a little over an hour to find her phone, go home to change, and hightail it over to the sandwich shop where she worked on the weekends.

"Can I ask what we're listening to?" her dark-haired stranger inquired when he reached her.

Mia tilted her head back in order to meet his gaze. "Holy crap," she blurted out. "You're ridiculously *tall*."

Her stranger grinned. "Maybe you're just ridiculously short."

"I'm five-four. That's average height." Her forehead was starting to sweat, so she pulled off her baseball cap and shoved a strand of damp hair off her face. "How tall are you?" she asked curiously.

"Six-five."

"Like I said, ridiculously tall. I'm talking to a giant. Do you play basketball?"

"Nope. Do you?"

"Sure, I shoot hoops every morning before work."

"For real?"

A laugh flew out. "No, not for real. You actually believed me?"

Before he could answer, she gestured to the other side of the flowerbed. "Anyway, go over there. Tell me if you hear anything."

To his credit, he didn't question the command. He simply crossed the freshly mowed grass with long strides and knelt down in front of the flowers. "What am I supposed to be hearing?"

"Well, if my brother is repeatedly dialing my phone like I ordered him to, then you should be hearing the faint strains of A-ha's 'Take On Me'. I'm really into '80s pop," she said in a self-deprecating tone.

Her stranger stared at her for a moment, before understanding dawned in his gorgeous eyes.

"Wait a sec—you buried your phone in the dirt?"

Mia sighed. "Not on *purpose*. It must have slipped out of my pocket when I was planting yesterday. Hazard of the job." She flopped down onto her knees. "Now, hush. I'd like to find my phone sometime this century. I drove all the way back here this morning and I have stuff to do today."

From the corner of her eye, she saw his big body curling as he bent over the dirt. She had to give him credit—he was definitely being a good sport about this insanity.

And gosh, he was *cute*. She couldn't stop taking peeks at him, so many peeks that she finally had to force herself to wrench her gaze away.

"Over here," he called a minute later.

As relief flooded her body, Mia bounded over to him with a spade in hand. She started digging in the spot he indicated, then stuck her hand in the moist soil and felt around for the phone. Her fingers connected with something hard and solid, the vibrations accompanied by her ringtone tickling her palm.

She triumphantly pulled out the iPhone, brushed dirt off the screen protector, and glanced at her savior with utter delight. "Hells yeah! We did it!"

He seemed to be fighting a laugh, but she didn't care how crazy or silly she sounded. He'd just saved her entire day.

The phone was still blaring out her favorite song with her brother's number flashing on the screen, so she quickly answered the call.

"Hey, Danny, it's me. I found it."

Irritation laced her brother's voice. "I'm so happy for you, dum-dum. Can I go back to sleep now?"

"Call me a dum-dum again and I won't bring home any breakfast."

"Don't care. I'm not hungry. I'm tired. You know, because someone *rudely* dragged me out of bed at *eight o'clock* on Saturday morning." He paused. "Are you coming back here before work?"

"Yeah."

"Fine. I guess you can bring me something to eat, then."

She choked back a laugh, not surprised by his complete one-eighty. Tired or not, teenage boys had voracious appetites, and at sixteen Danny ate like a damn horse. Her weekly grocery bill was proof of that.

"A food gesture will totes make me forget about being woken up today," he added. "But I swear, Mia, if you lose your phone one more time, I'm gonna kick your ass."

"Yeah, whatevs, dude. I'd like to see you try."

"I'll try and succeed," he declared.

"Uh-huh. 'Kay. See you soon."

She was smiling as she hung up. "Little brothers are such a pain in the ass," she told her waiting stranger.

"Trust me, I know. I have a younger sister and she used to be a real pest. How old is your brother?"

"Sixteen. He can be a total shit sometimes, but for the most part, he's a good kid."

The man in front of her slid his hands into the pockets of his faded Levis. He filled out those jeans nicely, she noted. She was ridiculously tempted to ask him to do a little spin so she could check out his ass.

He's not a piece of meat, Mia.

A sigh lodged in her throat. Nope, he wasn't a piece of meat. And even if he was, she didn't have time to indulge. Her chaotic life didn't allow room for tall, handsome hotties who looked spectacular in a pair of jeans.

"So you're doing some work for Tom and Sarah?" he asked.

"Yep. But the job's all done, actually," Mia replied. "Sarah didn't want anything fancy, so it didn't take long to finish everything up."

The disappointment on his chiseled face was unmistakable, but his tone remained friendly as he stuck out his hand. "I'm Jackson Ramsey, by the way. I live next door."

"Mia Weldrick. And I'd shake your hand but mine is all covered with dirt."

"I don't mind getting dirty every now and then."

Her breath hitched as he moved closer, a grin tugging on his lips. When he took her hand, heat suffused her cheeks, burning hotter when she registered the naughty undertones of that remark.

"Was that a line?" she demanded.

"Was what a line?"

"You know, the whole 'I like it dirty' thing. Was that supposed to get me all tingly and weak-kneed?"

Because it worked.

Jackson laughed, a deep, sexy sound that rippled between them. "I didn't say I liked it dirty. I said I didn't mind it. And no, it wasn't a line." He was smirking as he met her eyes. "Why, did it get you tingly and weak-kneed?"

"Nope."

She took a step toward her truck, turning her head just in case her expression revealed the dishonesty of her response. She *was* feeling tingly. Her entire body pulsed with a strange rush of heat, all because of this man's proximity. She hadn't experienced a spark of attraction to anyone in months, maybe years, and she'd forgotten what it even felt like. But the symptoms were definitely hitting her hard at the moment.

"Would you like to have dinner with me sometime?"

The request was gruff and came out of nowhere, bringing a pang of agitation to Mia's stomach.

"Oh boy," she said with a sigh.

"'Oh boy'?" He smiled at her again. "Is that how you respond to all your dinner invitations?"

"No. But that's because I don't get a lot of them," she confessed. "I never go out, which means I don't meet a lot of guys. Honestly, I'm unprepared for this."

"Doesn't require much prep, sugar. A yes or no would do the trick."

She murmured another "Oh boy", torn between lying and being brutally honest. In the end, honesty won out.

"Okay, I'm going to lay it all on the line," she told him. "You're wicked hot, and I'm totally digging the height thing. It makes me feel dainty."

He chuckled. "All right…"

"But I don't want to have dinner with you."

CPSIA information can be obtained
at www.ICGtesting.com
Printed in the USA
LVHW020544090621
689685LV00003B/121